D1178681

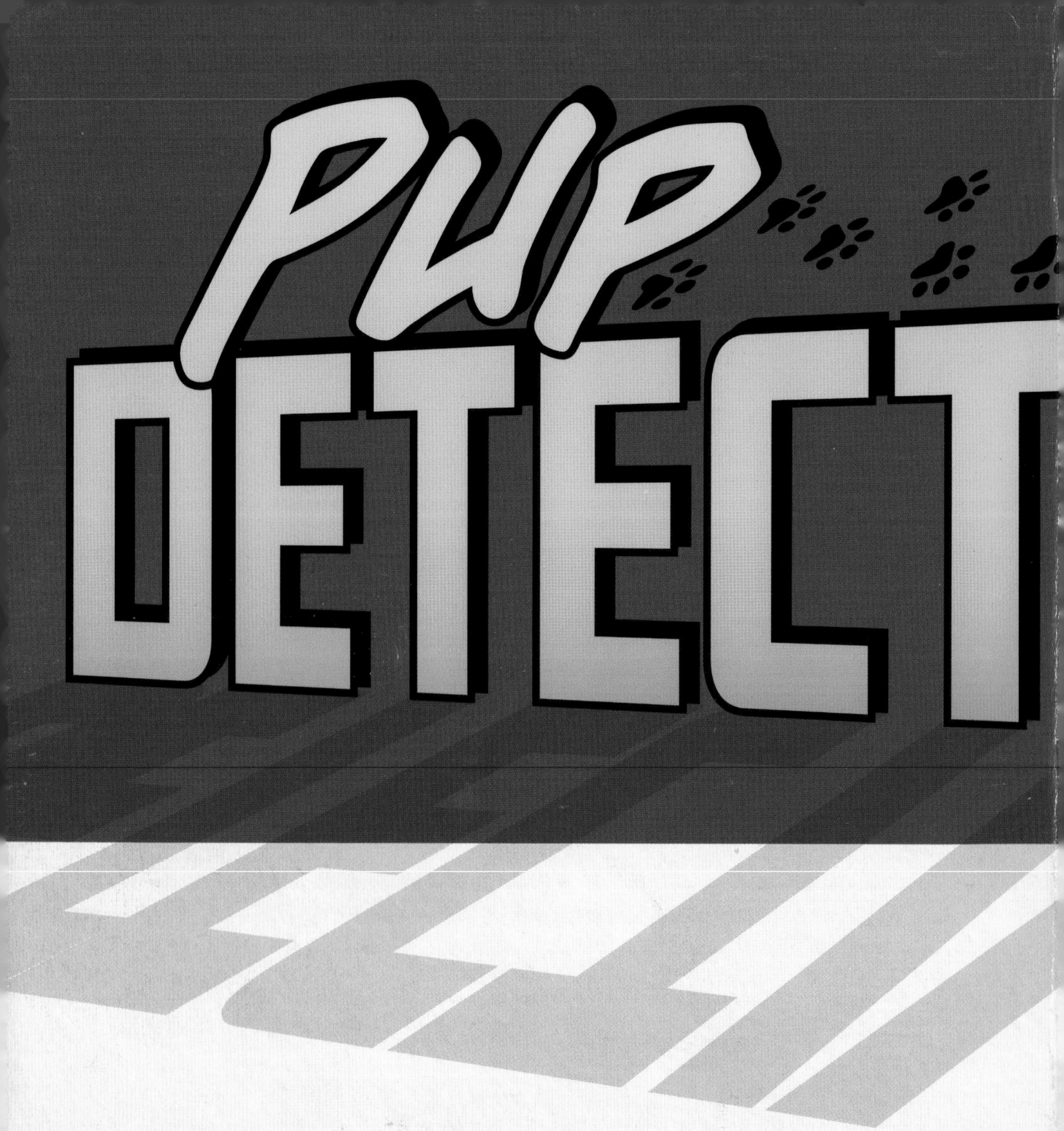
PUP
DETECT

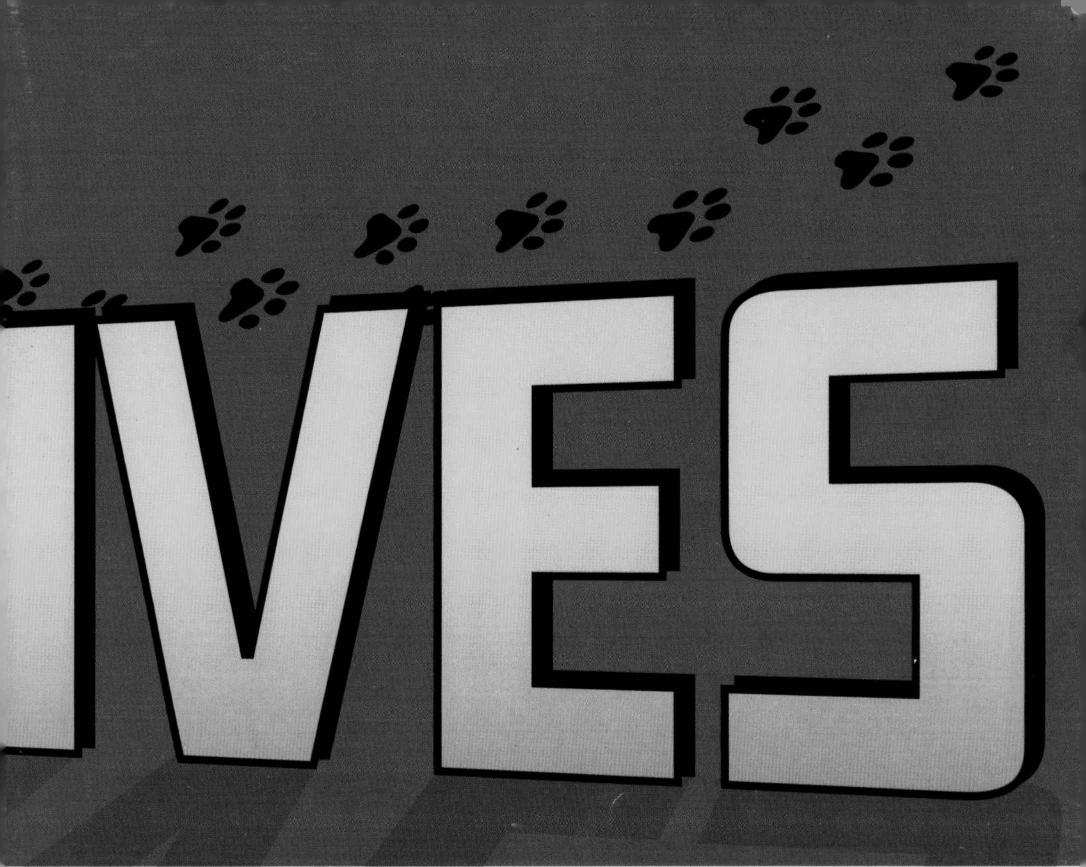
IVES

THE BIG BAD WOOF

Written by FELIX GUMPAW
Illustrated by GLASS HOUSE GRAPHICS

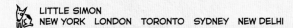

LITTLE SIMON
NEW YORK LONDON TORONTO SYDNEY NEW DELHI

THIS BOOK IS A WORK OF FICTION. ANY REFERENCES TO HISTORICAL EVENTS, REAL PEOPLE, OR REAL PLACES ARE USED FICTITIOUSLY. OTHER NAMES, CHARACTERS, PLACES, AND EVENTS ARE PRODUCTS OF THE AUTHOR'S IMAGINATION, AND ANY RESEMBLANCE TO ACTUAL EVENTS OR PLACES OR PERSONS, LIVING OR DEAD, IS ENTIRELY COINCIDENTAL.

LITTLE SIMON
AN IMPRINT OF SIMON & SCHUSTER CHILDREN'S PUBLISHING DIVISION
1230 AVENUE OF THE AMERICAS, NEW YORK, NEW YORK 10020
FIRST LITTLE SIMON EDITION JUNE 2022
COPYRIGHT © 2022 BY SIMON & SCHUSTER, INC.
ALL RIGHTS RESERVED, INCLUDING THE RIGHT OF REPRODUCTION IN WHOLE OR IN PART IN ANY FORM. LITTLE SIMON IS A REGISTERED TRADEMARK OF SIMON & SCHUSTER, INC., AND ASSOCIATED COLOPHON IS A TRADEMARK OF SIMON & SCHUSTER, INC. FOR INFORMATION ABOUT SPECIAL DISCOUNTS FOR BULK PURCHASES, PLEASE CONTACT SIMON & SCHUSTER SPECIAL SALES AT 1-866-506-1949 OR BUSINESS@SIMONANDSCHUSTER.COM. ART AND COLORS BY GLASS HOUSE GRAPHICS • LETTERING BY MARCOS MASSAO INOUE • SUPERVISION BY MJ MACEDO/STUPLENDO • ART SERVICES BY GLASS HOUSE GRAPHICS • THE SIMON & SCHUSTER SPEAKERS BUREAU CAN BRING AUTHORS TO YOUR LIVE EVENT. FOR MORE INFORMATION OR TO BOOK AN EVENT CONTACT THE SIMON & SCHUSTER SPEAKERS BUREAU AT 1-866-248-3049 OR VISIT OUR WEBSITE AT WWW.SIMONSPEAKERS.COM.
DESIGNED BY NICHOLAS SCIACCA
MANUFACTURED IN CHINA 0322 SCP
10 9 8 7 6 5 4 3 2 1
LIBRARY OF CONGRESS CATALOGING-IN-PUBLICATION DATA
NAMES: GUMPAW, FELIX, AUTHOR. I GLASS HOUSE GRAPHICS, ILLUSTRATOR. TITLE: THE BIG BAD WOOF / BY FELIX GUMPAW ; ILLUSTRATED BY GLASS HOUSE GRAPHICS. DESCRIPTION: FIRST LITTLE SIMON EDITION. I NEW YORK : LITTLE SIMON, 2022. I SERIES: PUP DETECTIVES ; 7 I AUDIENCE: AGES 5-9. I AUDIENCE: GRADES K-1. I SUMMARY: RORA AND THE OTHER PUP DETECTIVES WORK TO STOP AN ART HEIST AND PREVENT RIDER FROM BEING FRAMED FOR THE THEFT. IDENTIFIERS: LCCN 2021049056 (PRINT) I LCCN 2021049057 (EBOOK) I ISBN 9781665912198 (PAPERBACK) I ISBN 9781665912204 (HARDCOVER) I ISBN 9781665912211 (EBOOK). SUBJECTS: CYAC: GRAPHIC NOVELS. I MYSTERY AND DETECTIVE STORIES. I DOGS—FICTION. CLASSIFICATION: LCC PZ7.7.G858 BI 2022 (PRINT) I LCC PZ7.7.G858 (EBOOK) I DDC 741.5/973—DC23
LC RECORD AVAILABLE AT HTTPS://LCCN.LOC.GOV/2021049056
LC EBOOK RECORD AVAILABLE AT HTTPS://LCCN.LOC.GOV/2021049057

CONTENTS

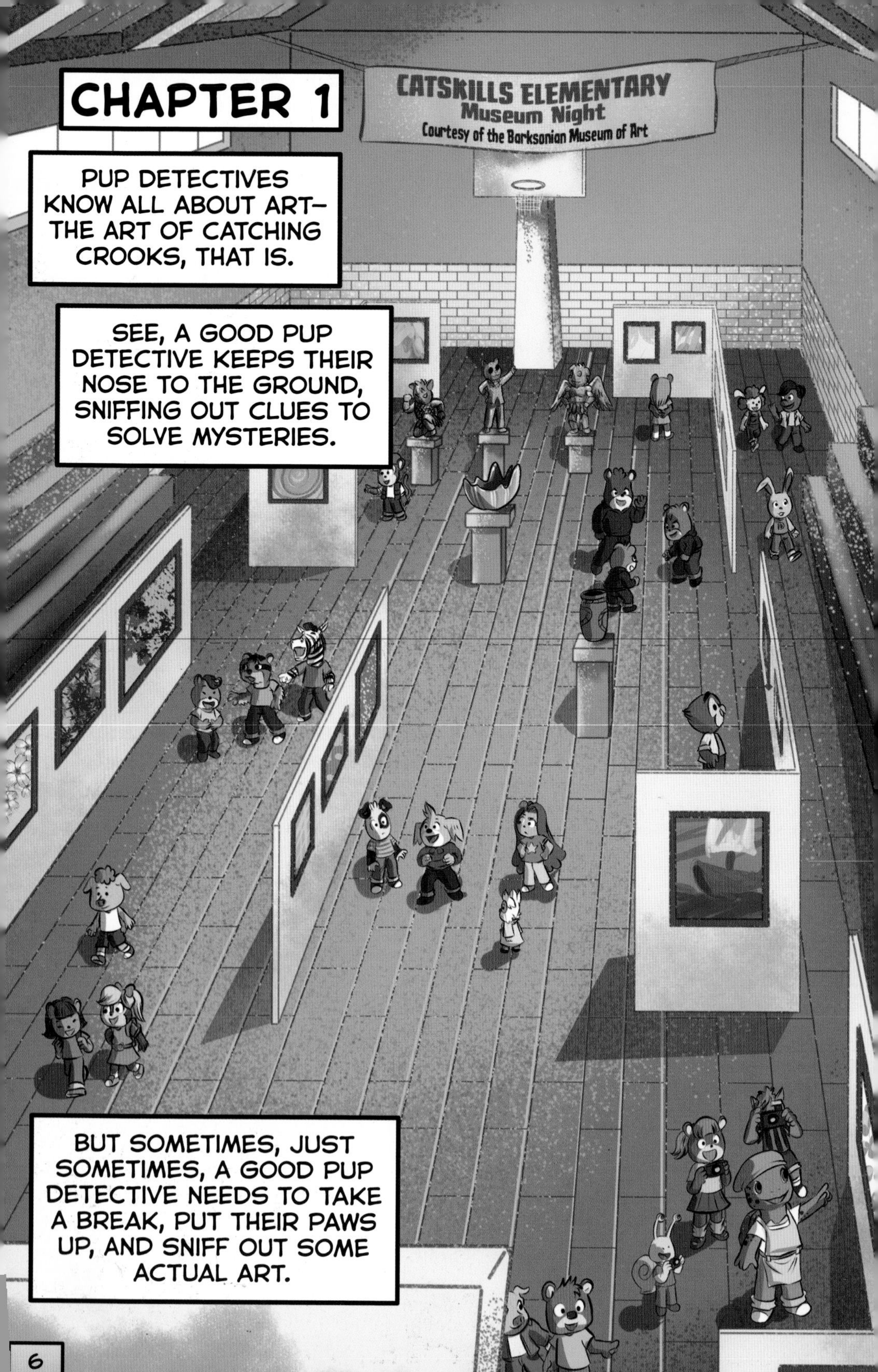
CHAPTER 1
CATSKILLS ELEMENTARY
Museum Night
Courtesy of the Barksonian Museum of Art
PUP DETECTIVES KNOW ALL ABOUT ART–THE ART OF CATCHING CROOKS, THAT IS.
SEE, A GOOD PUP DETECTIVE KEEPS THEIR NOSE TO THE GROUND, SNIFFING OUT CLUES TO SOLVE MYSTERIES.
BUT SOMETIMES, JUST SOMETIMES, A GOOD PUP DETECTIVE NEEDS TO TAKE A BREAK, PUT THEIR PAWS UP, AND SNIFF OUT SOME ACTUAL ART.

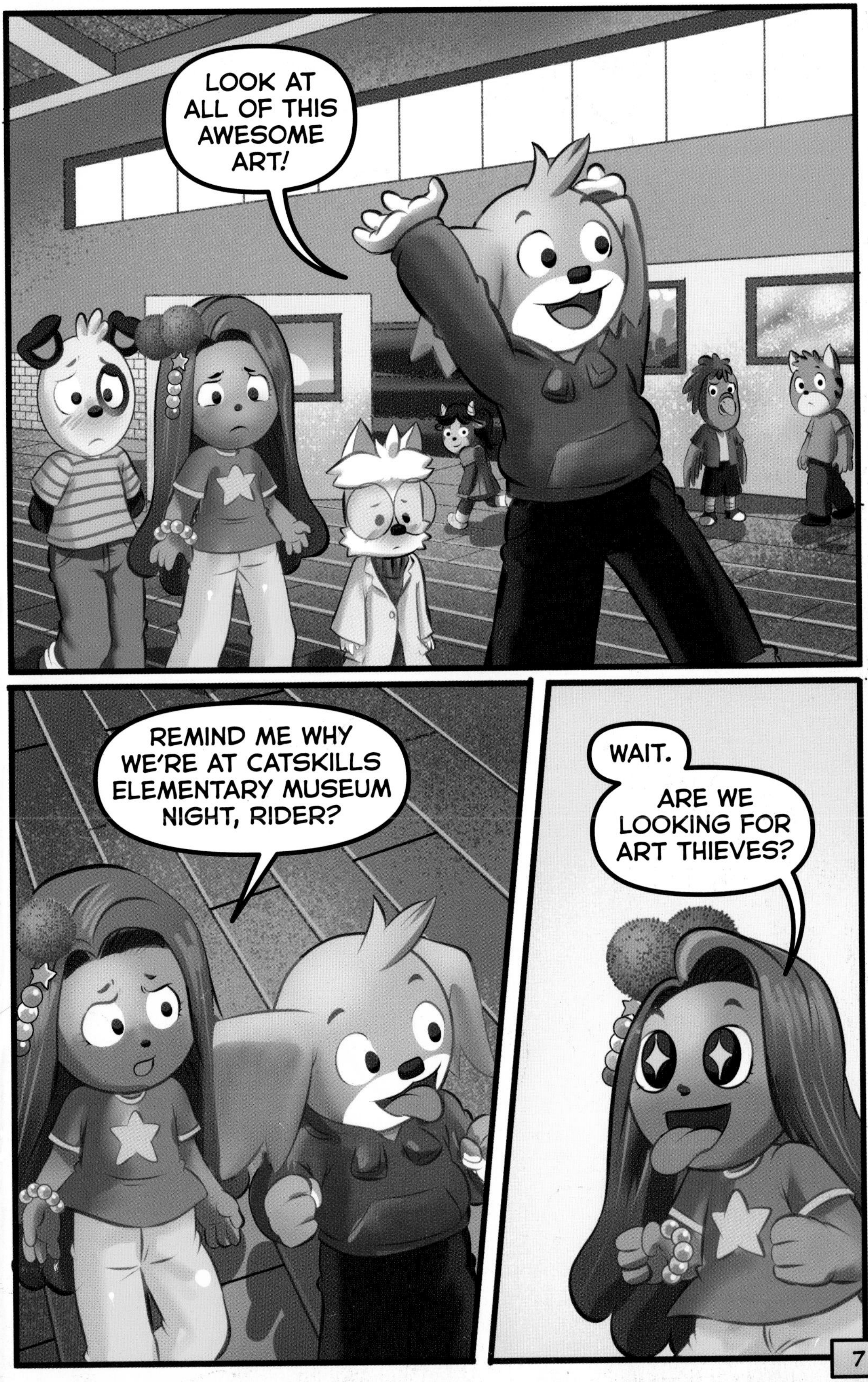
LOOK AT ALL OF THIS AWESOME ART!
REMIND ME WHY WE'RE AT CATSKILLS ELEMENTARY MUSEUM NIGHT, RIDER?
WAIT.
ARE WE LOOKING FOR ART THIEVES?

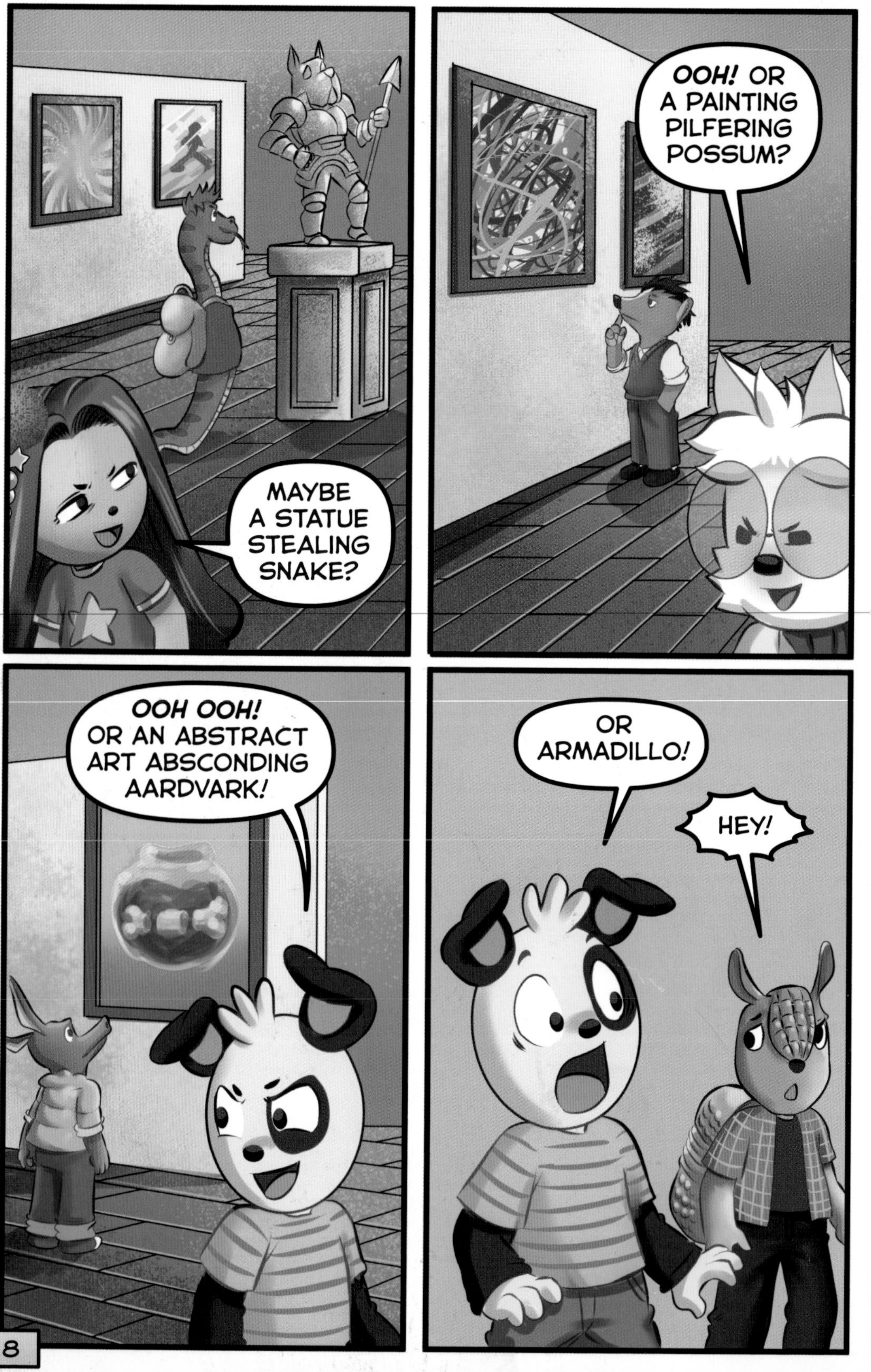
MAYBE A STATUE STEALING SNAKE?
OOH! OR A PAINTING PILFERING POSSUM?
OOH OOH! OR AN ABSTRACT ART ABSCONDING AARDVARK!
OR ARMADILLO!
HEY!

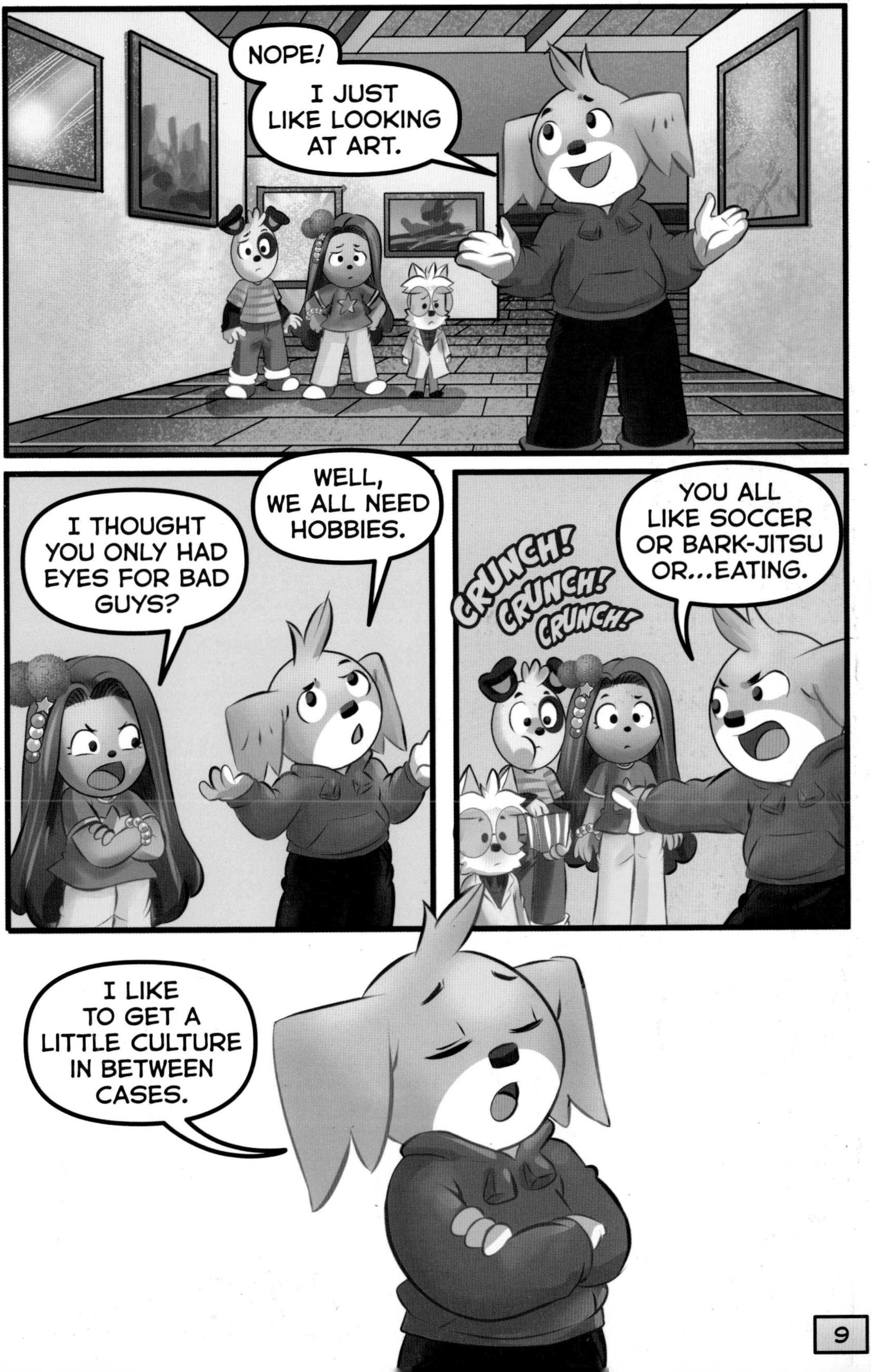
NOPE!
I JUST LIKE LOOKING AT ART.
I THOUGHT YOU ONLY HAD EYES FOR BAD GUYS?
WELL, WE ALL NEED HOBBIES.
YOU ALL LIKE SOCCER OR BARK-JITSU OR...EATING.
CRUNCH! CRUNCH! CRUNCH!
I LIKE TO GET A LITTLE CULTURE IN BETWEEN CASES.

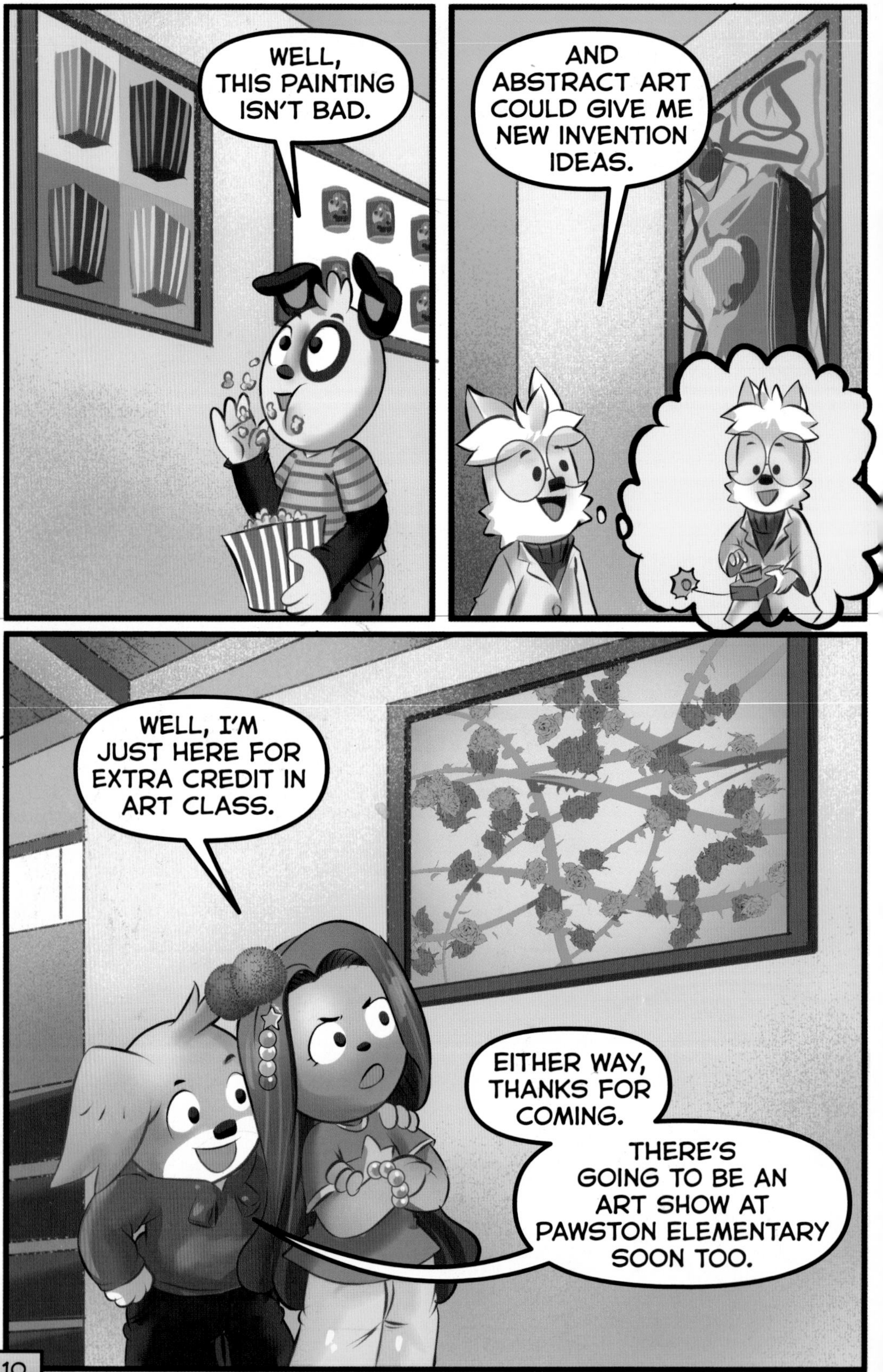
WELL, THIS PAINTING ISN'T BAD.
AND ABSTRACT ART COULD GIVE ME NEW INVENTION IDEAS.
WELL, I'M JUST HERE FOR EXTRA CREDIT IN ART CLASS.
EITHER WAY, THANKS FOR COMING.
THERE'S GOING TO BE AN ART SHOW AT PAWSTON ELEMENTARY SOON TOO.

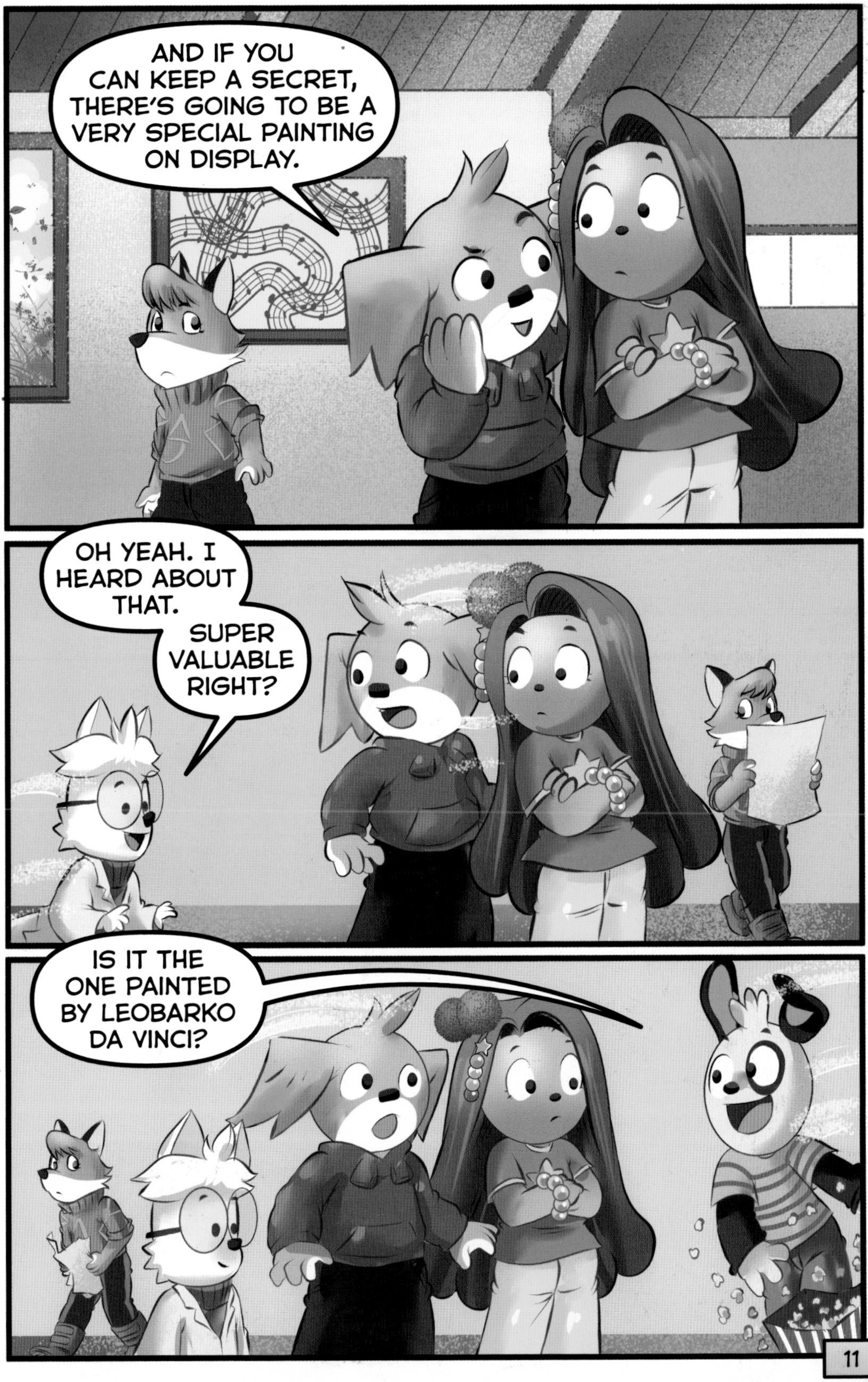
AND IF YOU CAN KEEP A SECRET, THERE'S GOING TO BE A VERY SPECIAL PAINTING ON DISPLAY.
OH YEAH. I HEARD ABOUT THAT.
SUPER VALUABLE RIGHT?
IS IT THE ONE PAINTED BY LEOBARKO DA VINCI?

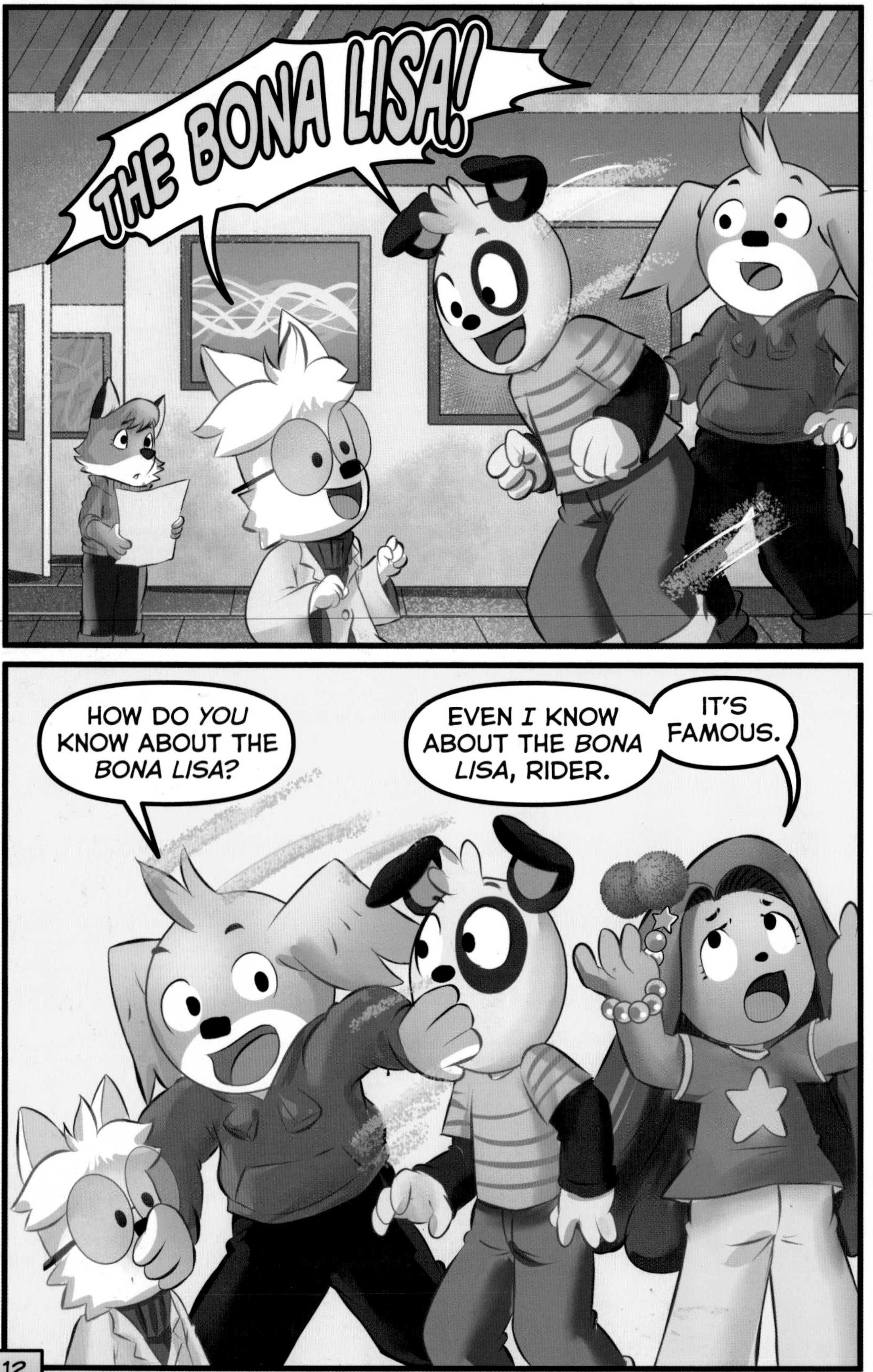
THE BONA LISA!
HOW DO YOU KNOW ABOUT THE BONA LISA?
EVEN I KNOW ABOUT THE BONA LISA, RIDER.
IT'S FAMOUS.

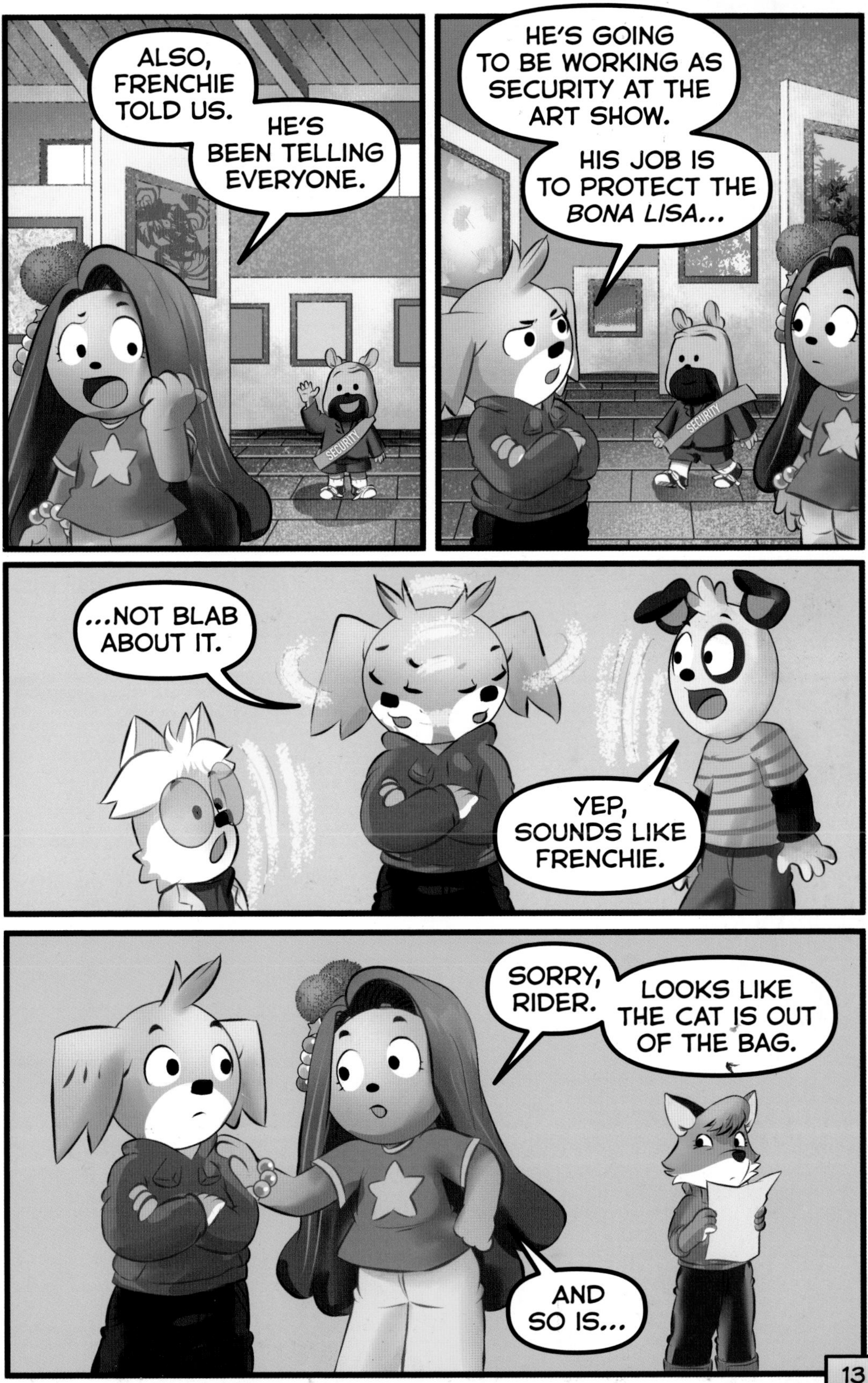
ALSO, FRENCHIE TOLD US.
HE'S BEEN TELLING EVERYONE.
HE'S GOING TO BE WORKING AS SECURITY AT THE ART SHOW.
HIS JOB IS TO PROTECT THE *BONA LISA*...
SECURITY
SECURITY
...NOT BLAB ABOUT IT.
YEP, SOUNDS LIKE FRENCHIE.
SORRY, RIDER.
LOOKS LIKE THE CAT IS OUT OF THE BAG.
AND SO IS...

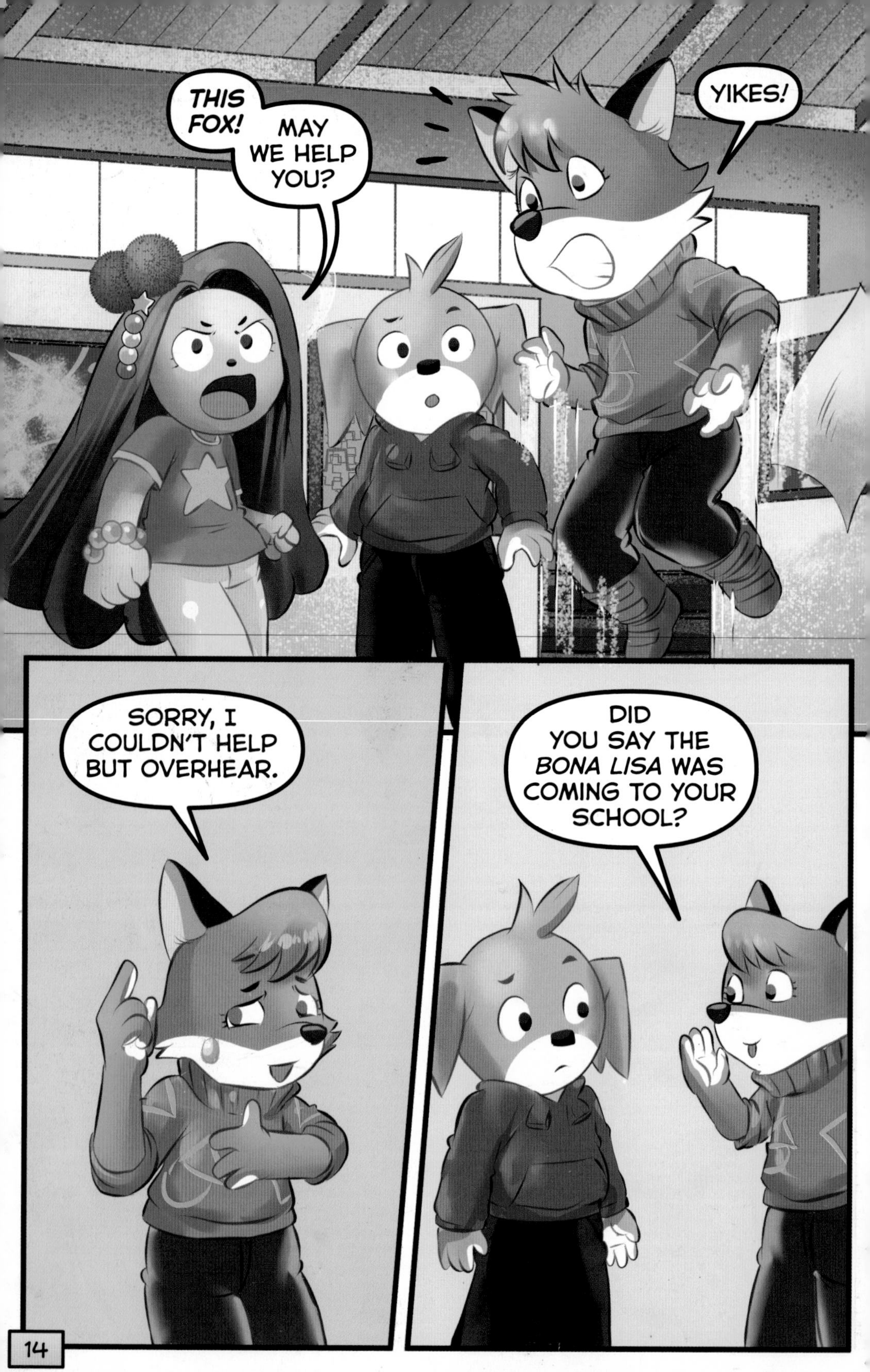

THIS FOX!
MAY WE HELP YOU?
YIKES!
SORRY, I COULDN'T HELP BUT OVERHEAR.
DID YOU SAY THE *BONA LISA* WAS COMING TO YOUR SCHOOL?

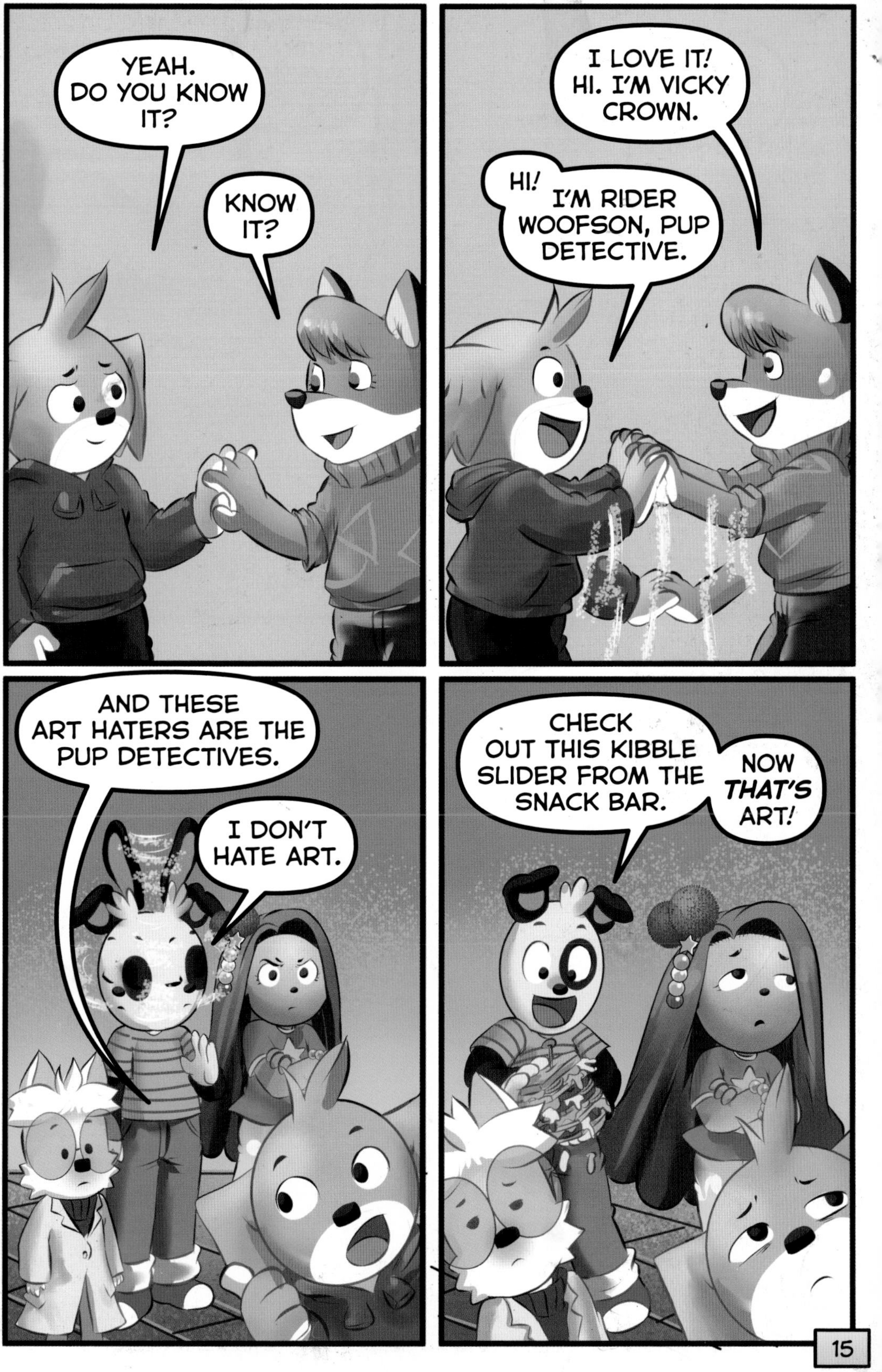
YEAH. DO YOU KNOW IT?
KNOW IT?
I LOVE IT! HI. I'M VICKY CROWN.
HI!
I'M RIDER WOOFSON, PUP DETECTIVE.
AND THESE ART HATERS ARE THE PUP DETECTIVES.
I DON'T HATE ART.
CHECK OUT THIS KIBBLE SLIDER FROM THE SNACK BAR.
NOW *THAT'S* ART!

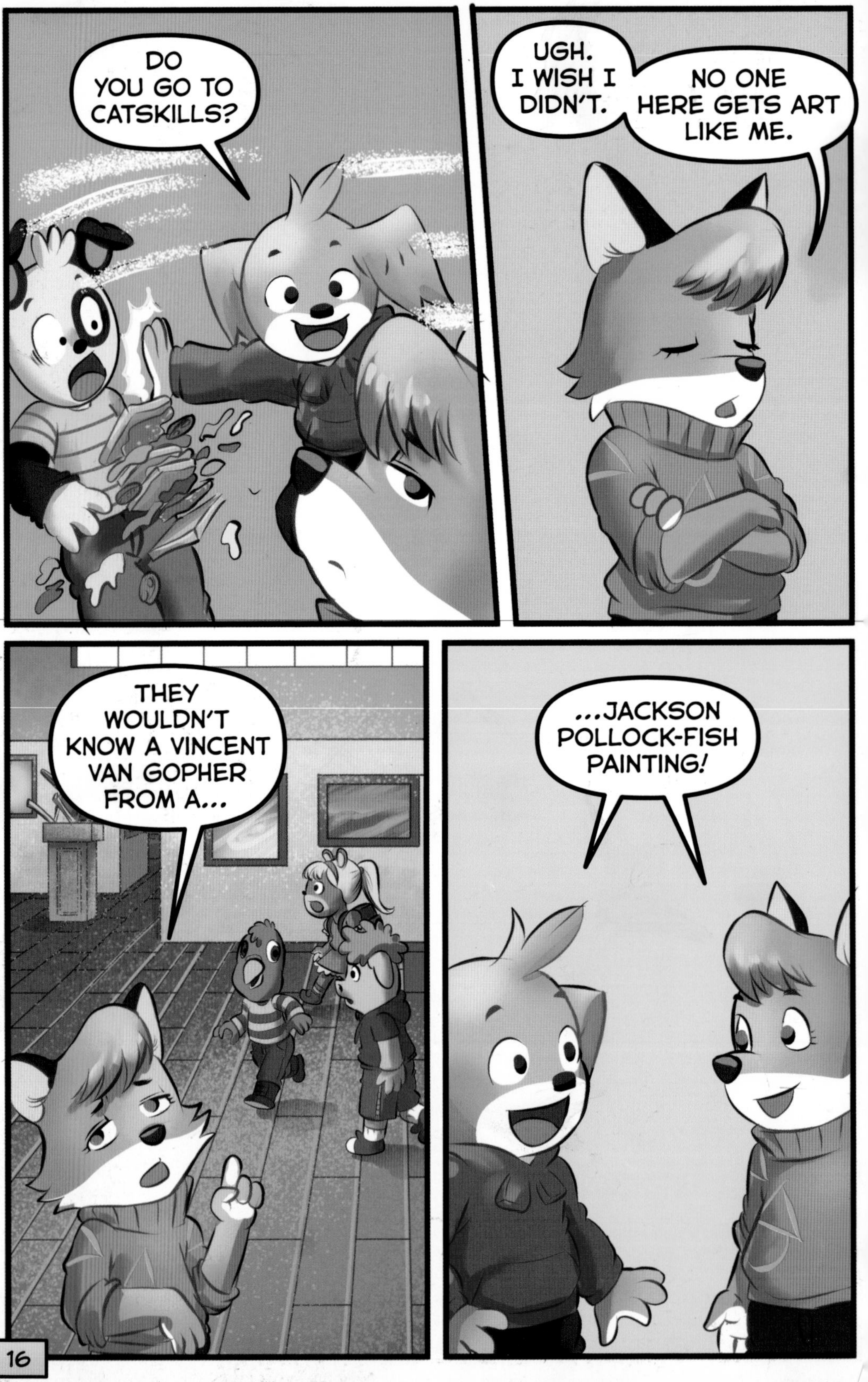
DO YOU GO TO CATSKILLS?
UGH. I WISH I DIDN'T.
NO ONE HERE GETS ART LIKE ME.
THEY WOULDN'T KNOW A VINCENT VAN GOPHER FROM A...
...JACKSON POLLOCK-FISH PAINTING!

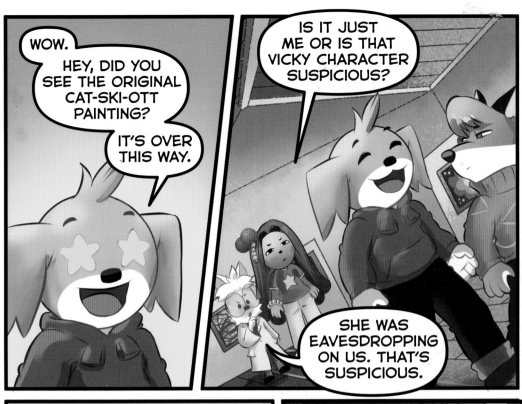

WOW.

HEY, DID YOU SEE THE ORIGINAL CAT-SKI-OTT PAINTING?

IT'S OVER THIS WAY.

IS IT JUST ME OR IS THAT VICKY CHARACTER SUSPICIOUS?

SHE WAS EAVESDROPPING ON US. THAT'S SUSPICIOUS.

AND SHE DIDN'T APPRECIATE MY SANDWICH.

VERY SUSPICIOUS.

KEEP YOUR EYES AND EARS OPEN, PUPS.

DID YOU SEE THIS?

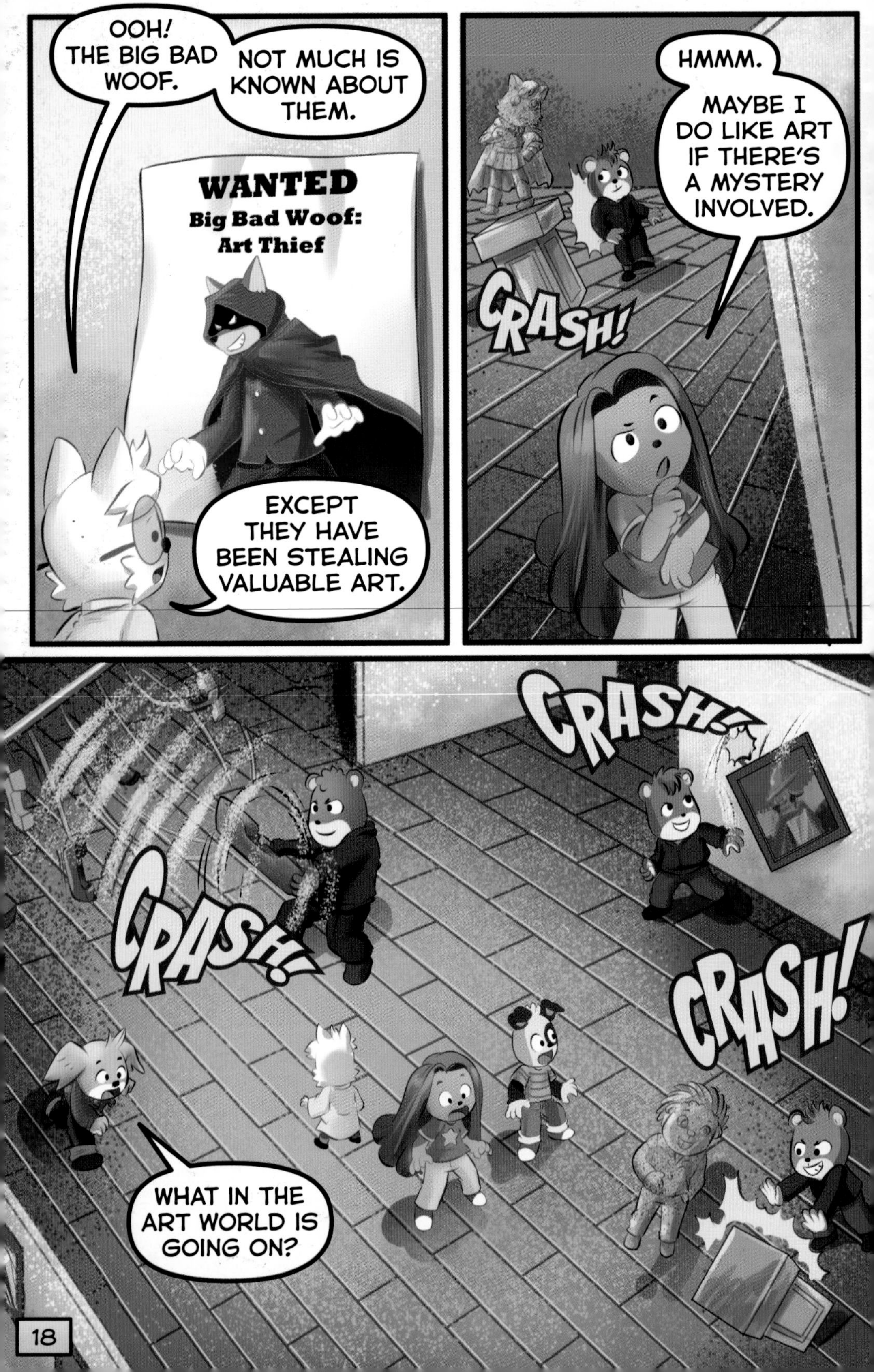

OOH! THE BIG BAD WOOF.
NOT MUCH IS KNOWN ABOUT THEM.
WANTED
Big Bad Woof: Art Thief
EXCEPT THEY HAVE BEEN STEALING VALUABLE ART.
HMMM.
MAYBE I DO LIKE ART IF THERE'S A MYSTERY INVOLVED.
CRASH!
CRASH!
CRASH!
CRASH!
WHAT IN THE ART WORLD IS GOING ON?

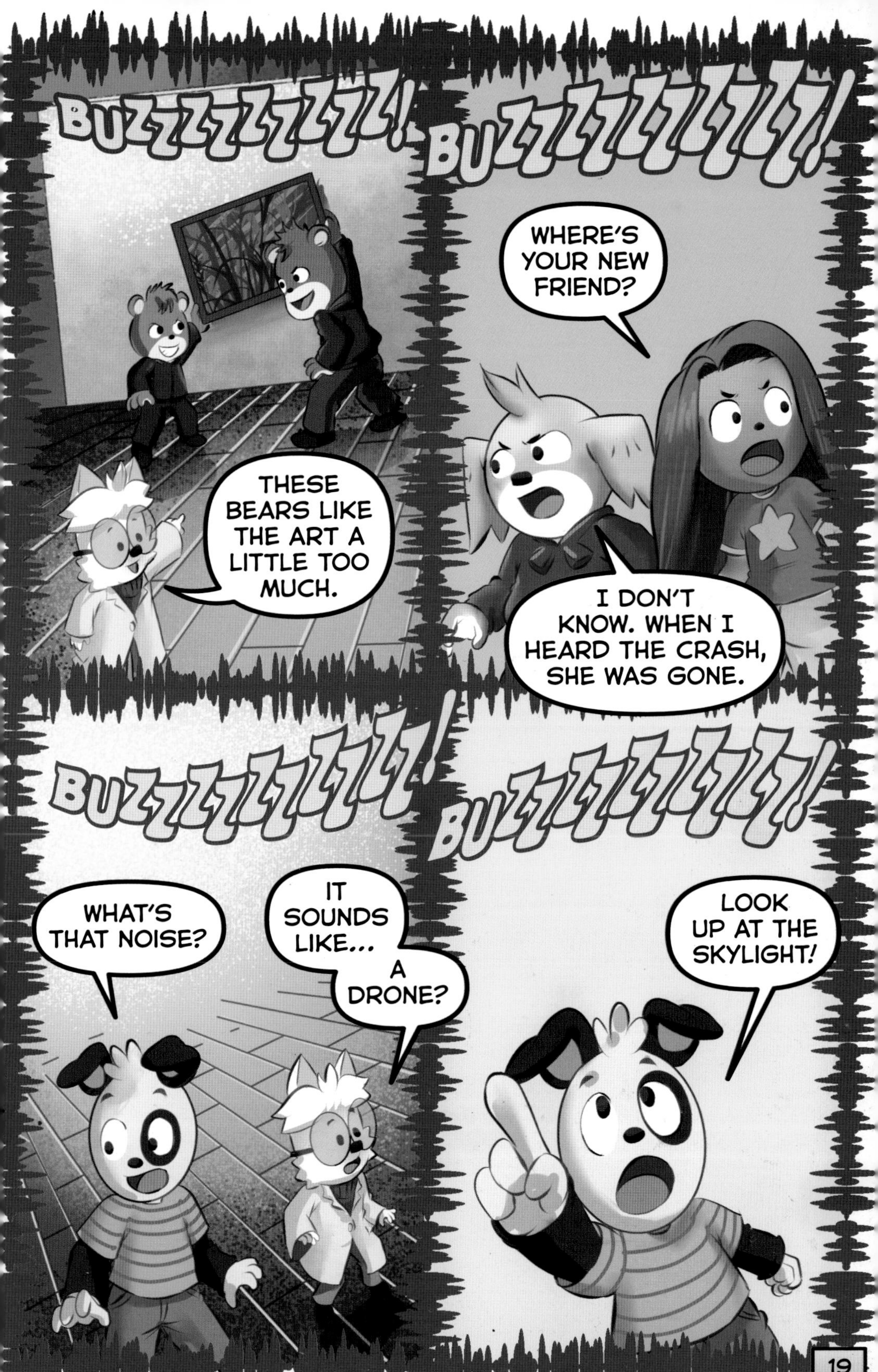
BUZZZZZZZZZ!
THESE BEARS LIKE THE ART A LITTLE TOO MUCH.
BUZZZZZZZZZZ!
WHERE'S YOUR NEW FRIEND?
I DON'T KNOW. WHEN I HEARD THE CRASH, SHE WAS GONE.
BUZZZZZZZZZZ!
WHAT'S THAT NOISE?
IT SOUNDS LIKE...
A DRONE?
BUZZZZZZZZZZ!
LOOK UP AT THE SKYLIGHT!

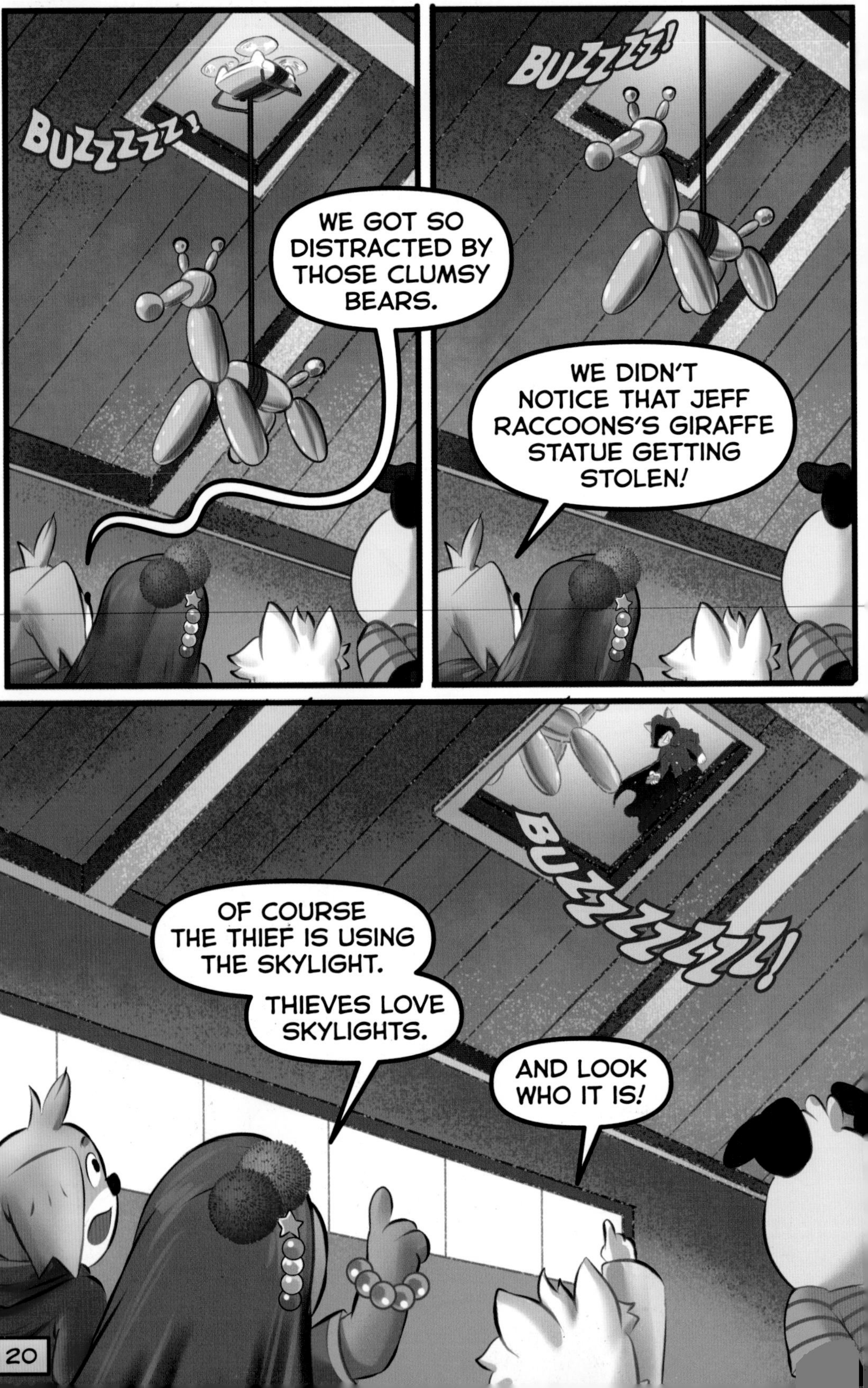
BUZZZZZZ!
WE GOT SO DISTRACTED BY THOSE CLUMSY BEARS.
BUZZZZZ!
WE DIDN'T NOTICE THAT JEFF RACCOONS'S GIRAFFE STATUE GETTING STOLEN!
BUZZZZZZZ!
OF COURSE THE THIEF IS USING THE SKYLIGHT.
THIEVES LOVE SKYLIGHTS.
AND LOOK WHO IT IS!

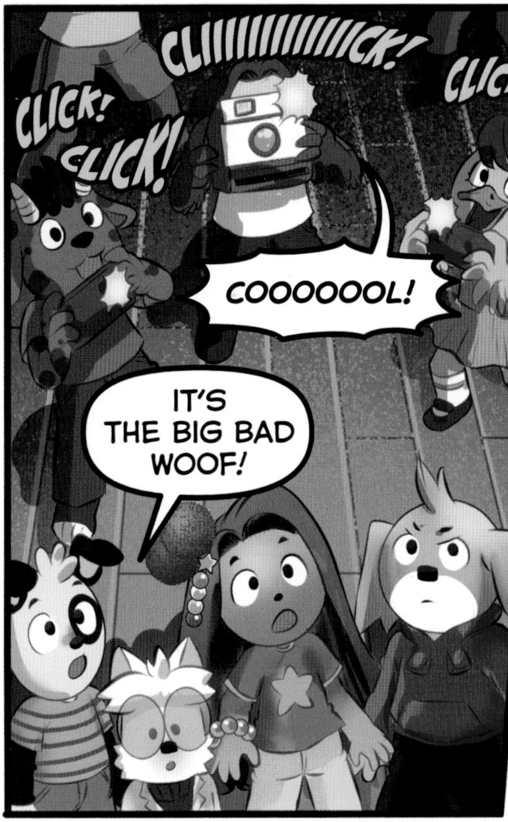
CLIIIIIIIIIIIICK!
CLICK!
CLICK!
CLICK!
COOOOOOL!
IT'S THE BIG BAD WOOF!

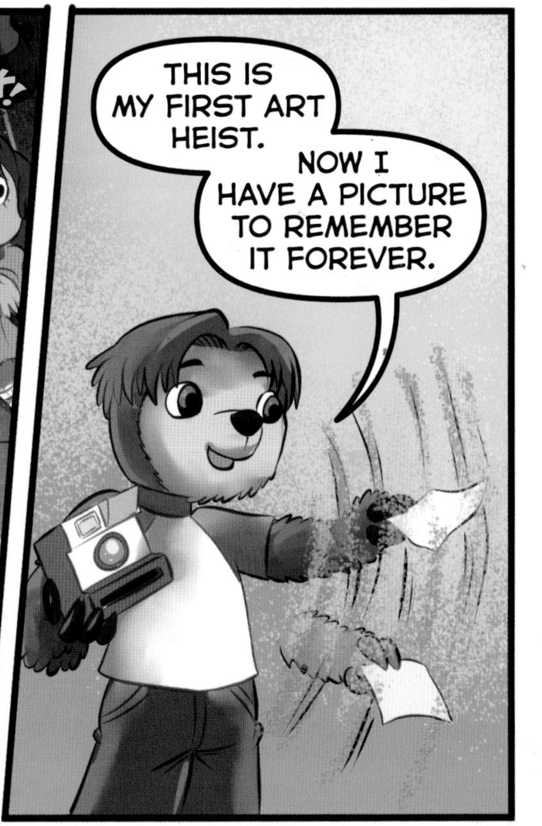
THIS IS MY FIRST ART HEIST.
NOW I HAVE A PICTURE TO REMEMBER IT FOREVER.

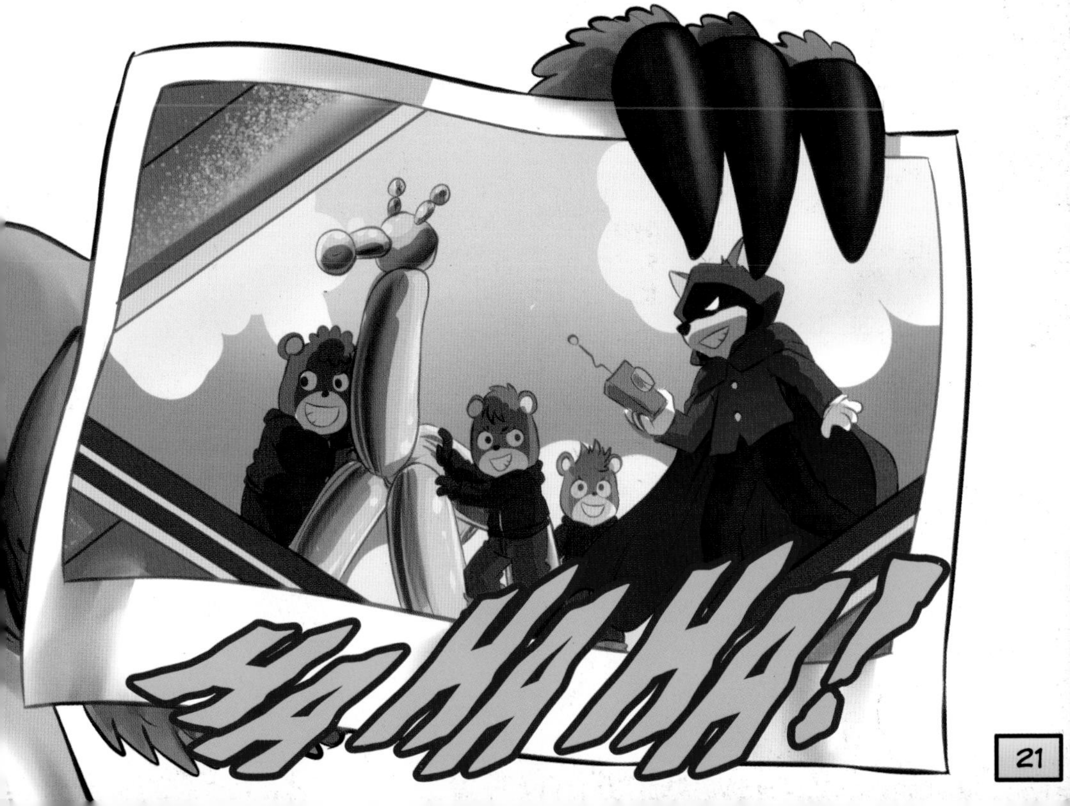
HA HA HA!

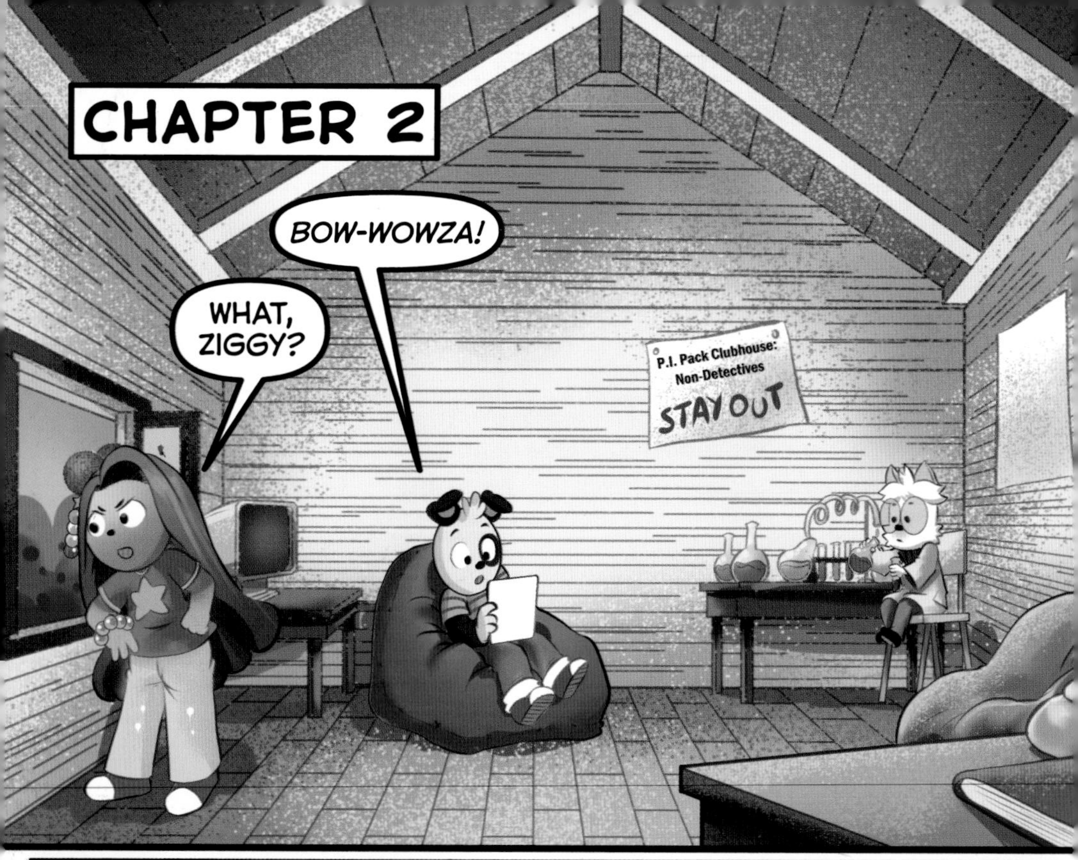
CHAPTER 2
BOW-WOWZA!
WHAT, ZIGGY?
P.I. Pack Clubhouse: Non-Detectives
STAY OUT

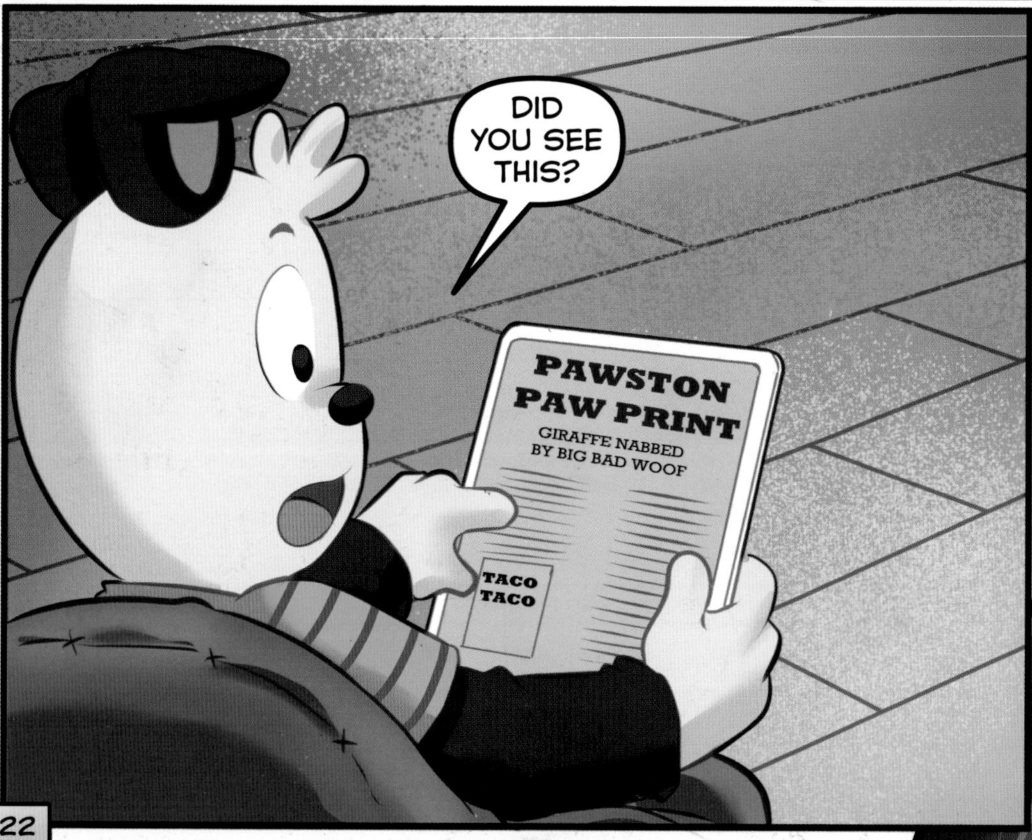
DID YOU SEE THIS?
PAWSTON PAW PRINT
GIRAFFE NABBED BY BIG BAD WOOF
TACO TACO

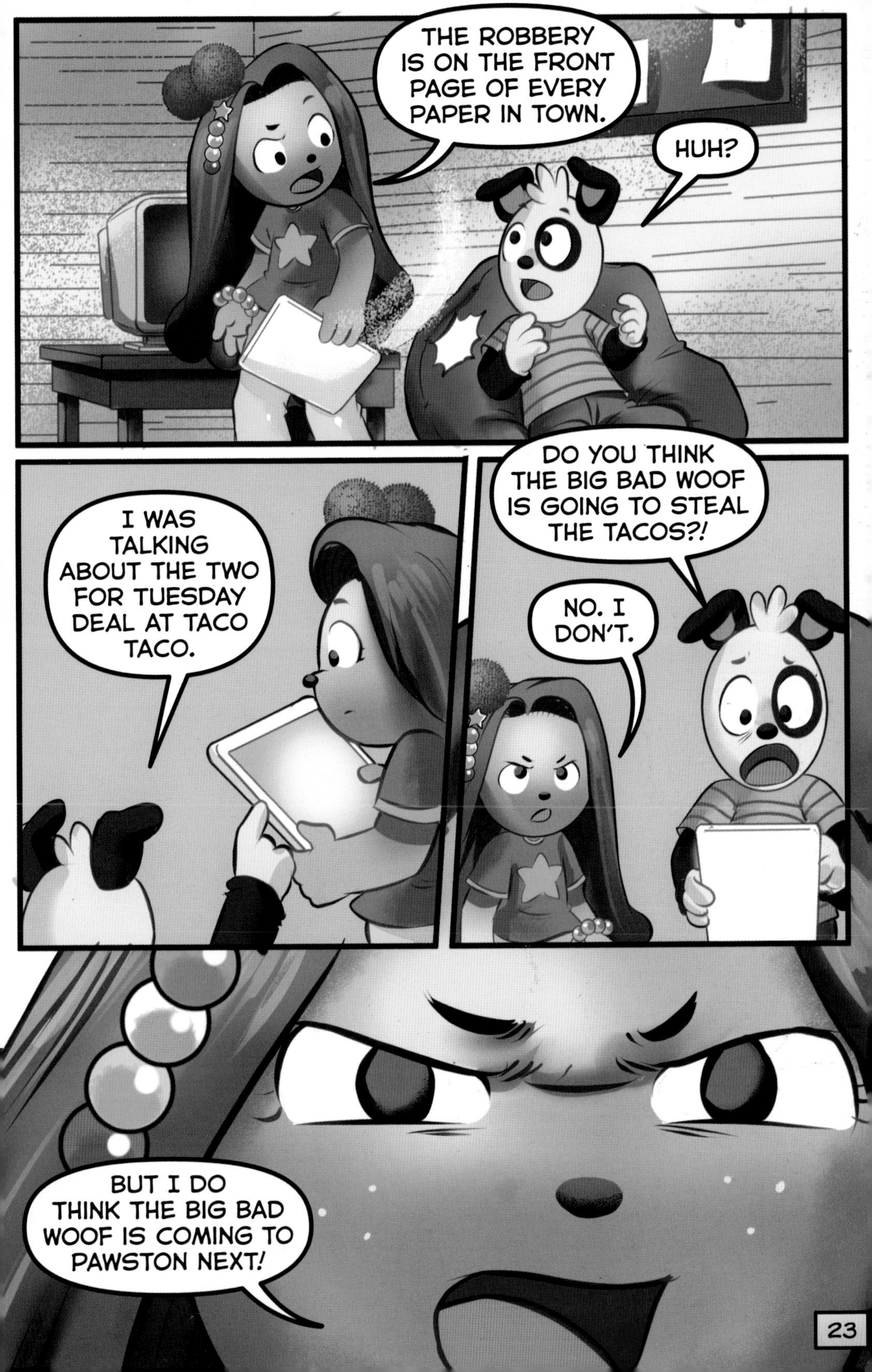
THE ROBBERY IS ON THE FRONT PAGE OF EVERY PAPER IN TOWN.
HUH?
I WAS TALKING ABOUT THE TWO FOR TUESDAY DEAL AT TACO TACO.
DO YOU THINK THE BIG BAD WOOF IS GOING TO STEAL THE TACOS?!
NO. I DON'T.
BUT I DO THINK THE BIG BAD WOOF IS COMING TO PAWSTON NEXT!

OOOOH. WE SHOULD GO BACK TO CATSKILLS TO INVESTIGATE!

WHAT ABOUT RIDER?

HE'S TAKING THE DAY OFF, BELIEVE IT OR NOT.

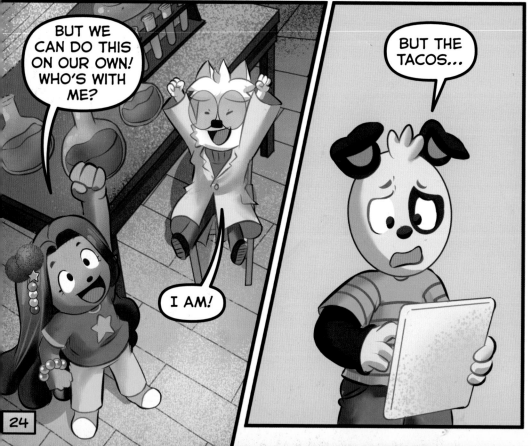

BUT WE CAN DO THIS ON OUR OWN! WHO'S WITH ME?

I AM!

BUT THE TACOS...

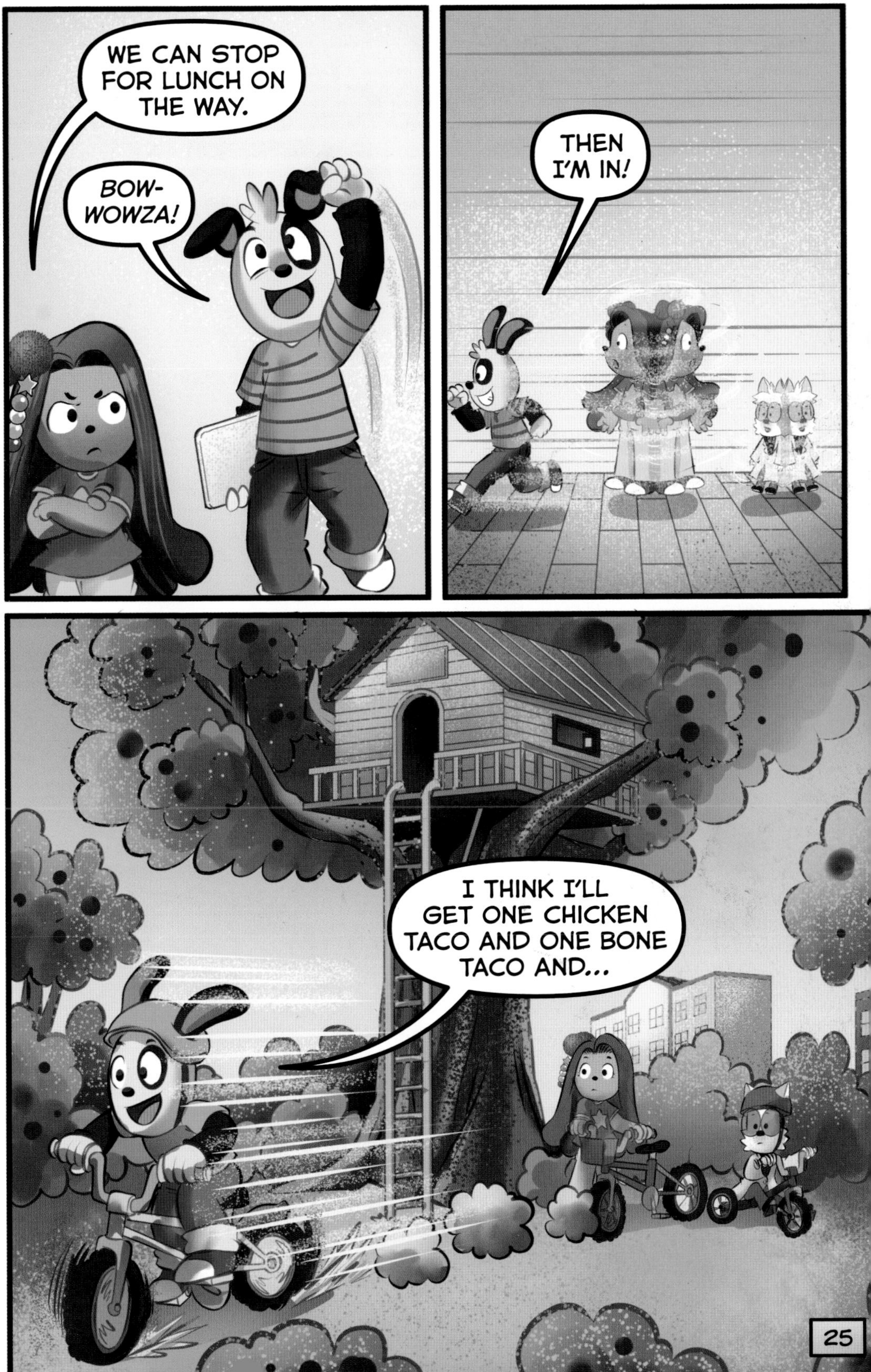
WE CAN STOP FOR LUNCH ON THE WAY.
BOW-WOWZA!
THEN I'M IN!
I THINK I'LL GET ONE CHICKEN TACO AND ONE BONE TACO AND...

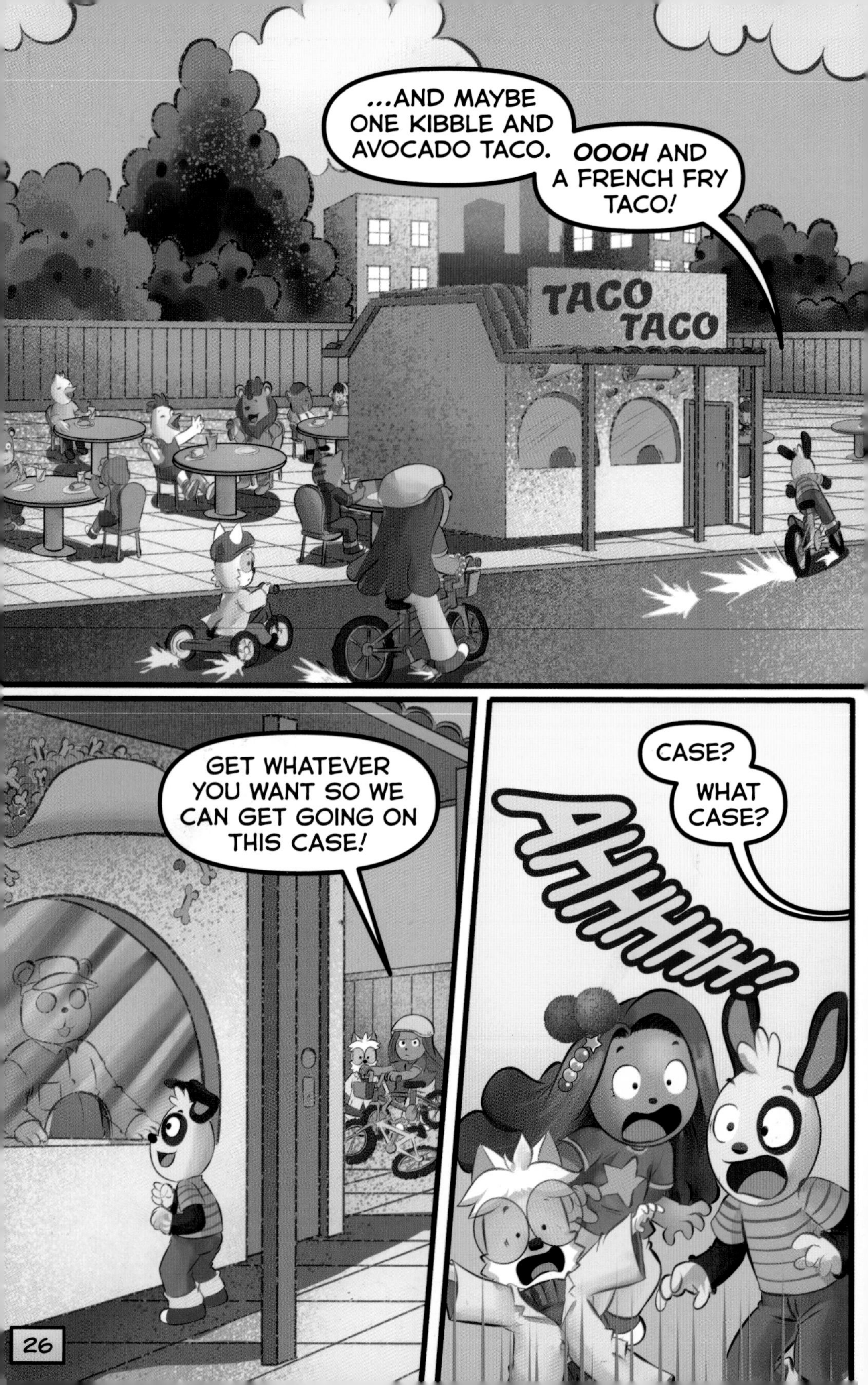
...AND MAYBE ONE KIBBLE AND AVOCADO TACO.
OOOH AND A FRENCH FRY TACO!
TACO TACO
GET WHATEVER YOU WANT SO WE CAN GET GOING ON THIS CASE!
CASE?
WHAT CASE?
AHHHHH!

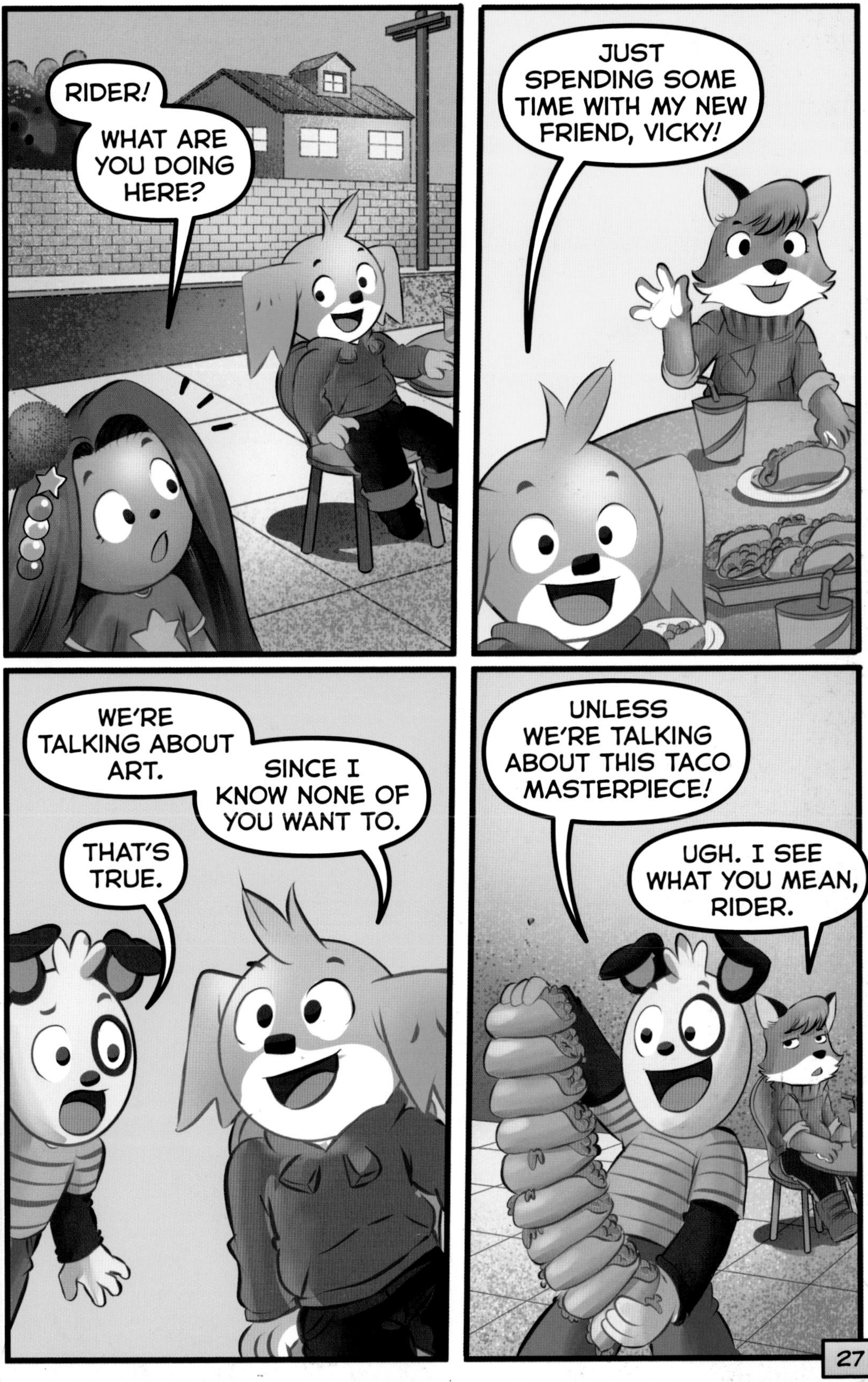
RIDER!
WHAT ARE YOU DOING HERE?
JUST SPENDING SOME TIME WITH MY NEW FRIEND, VICKY!
WE'RE TALKING ABOUT ART.
SINCE I KNOW NONE OF YOU WANT TO.
THAT'S TRUE.
UNLESS WE'RE TALKING ABOUT THIS TACO MASTERPIECE!
UGH. I SEE WHAT YOU MEAN, RIDER.

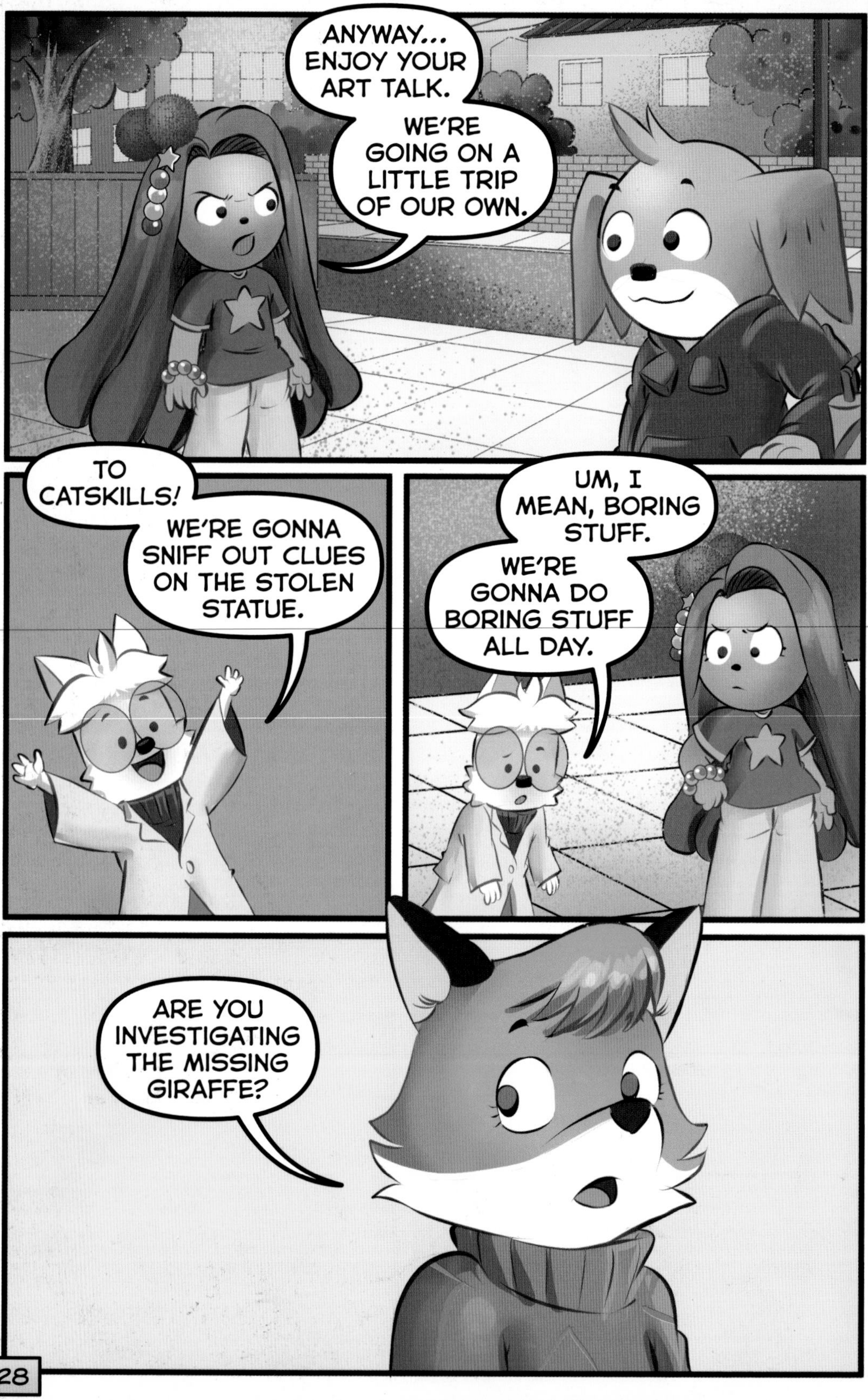
ANYWAY... ENJOY YOUR ART TALK.
WE'RE GOING ON A LITTLE TRIP OF OUR OWN.
TO CATSKILLS!
WE'RE GONNA SNIFF OUT CLUES ON THE STOLEN STATUE.
UM, I MEAN, BORING STUFF.
WE'RE GONNA DO BORING STUFF ALL DAY.
ARE YOU INVESTIGATING THE MISSING GIRAFFE?

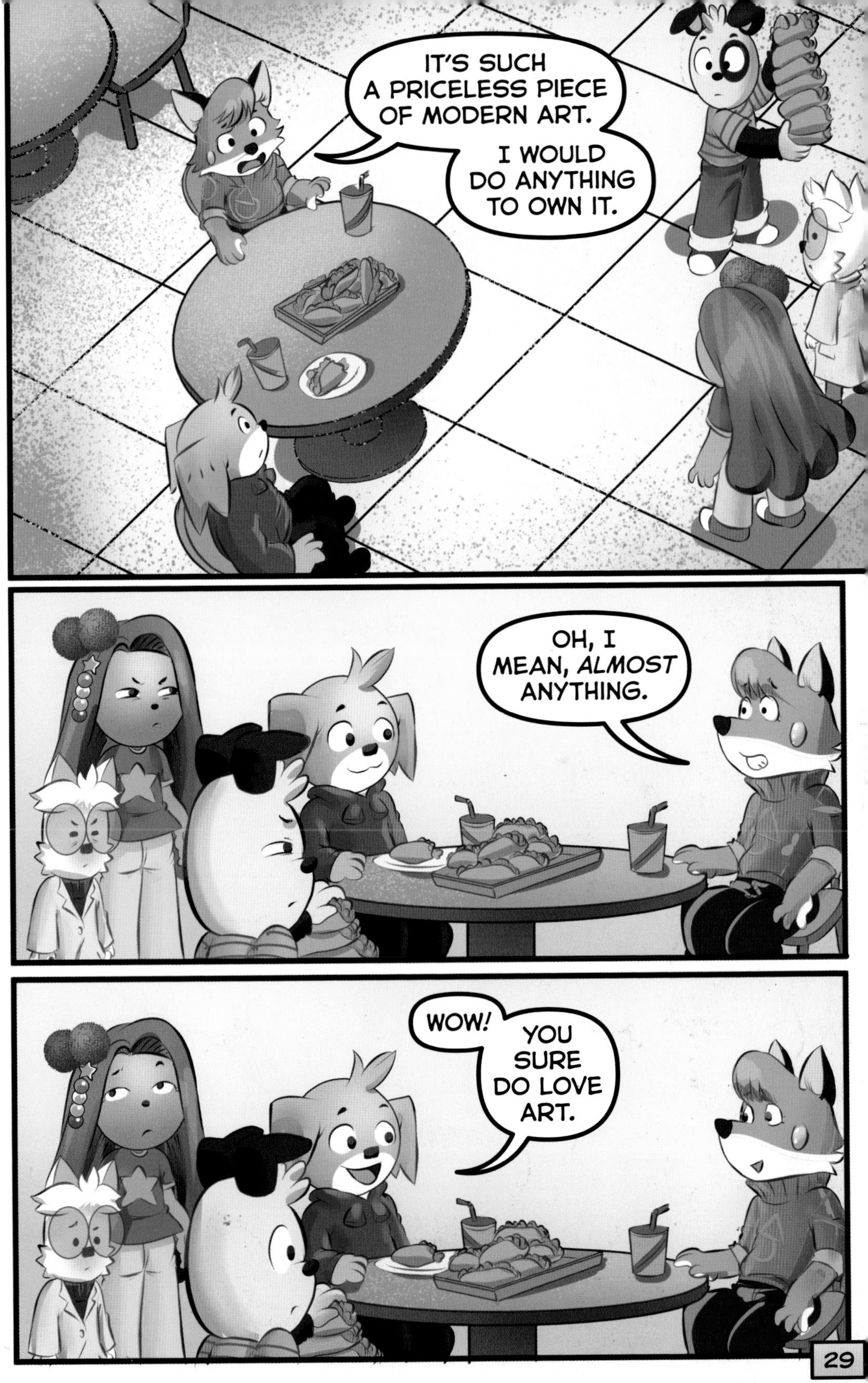
IT'S SUCH A PRICELESS PIECE OF MODERN ART.
I WOULD DO ANYTHING TO OWN IT.
OH, I MEAN, ALMOST ANYTHING.
WOW!
YOU SURE DO LOVE ART.

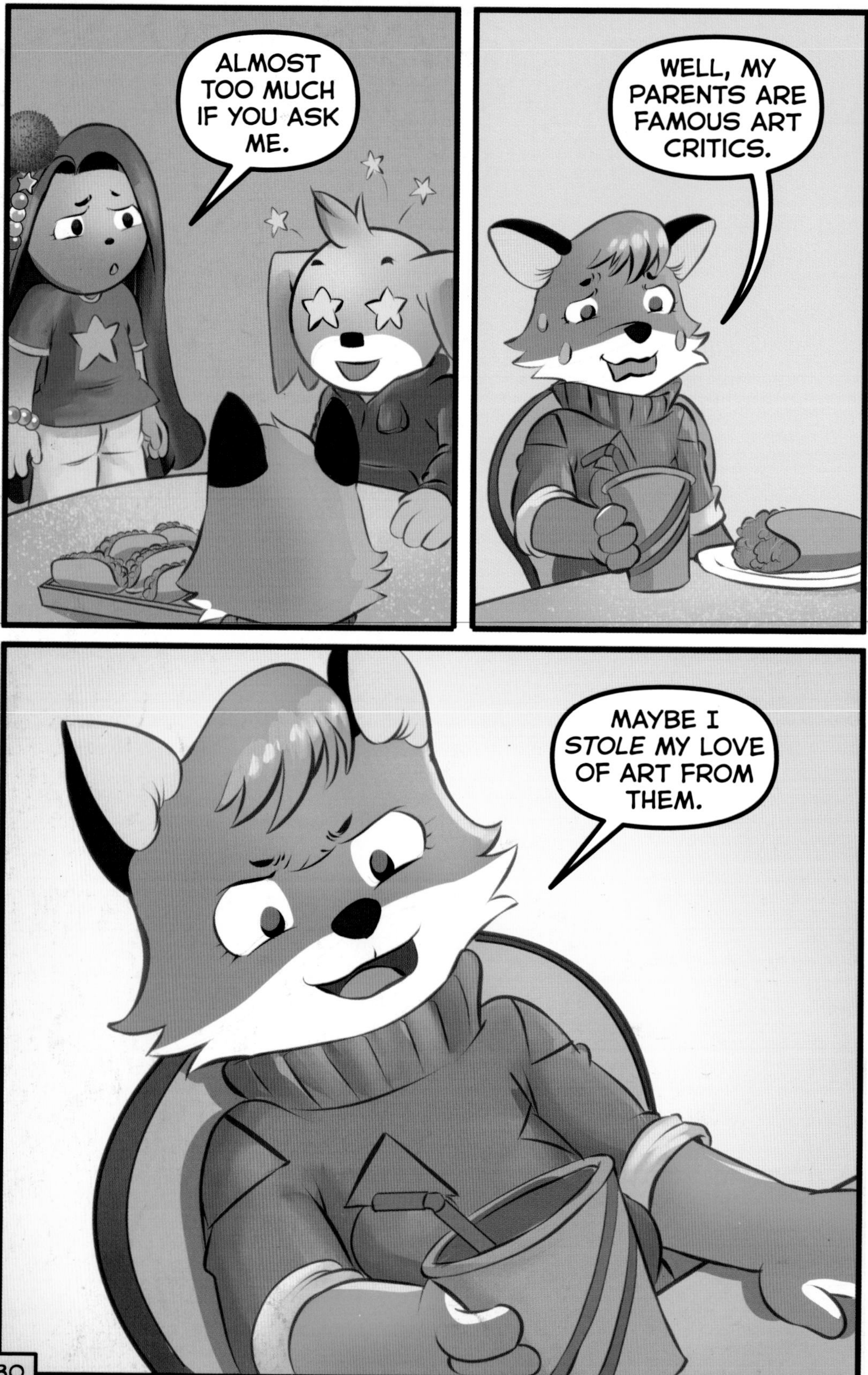
ALMOST TOO MUCH IF YOU ASK ME.
WELL, MY PARENTS ARE FAMOUS ART CRITICS.
MAYBE I *STOLE* MY LOVE OF ART FROM THEM.

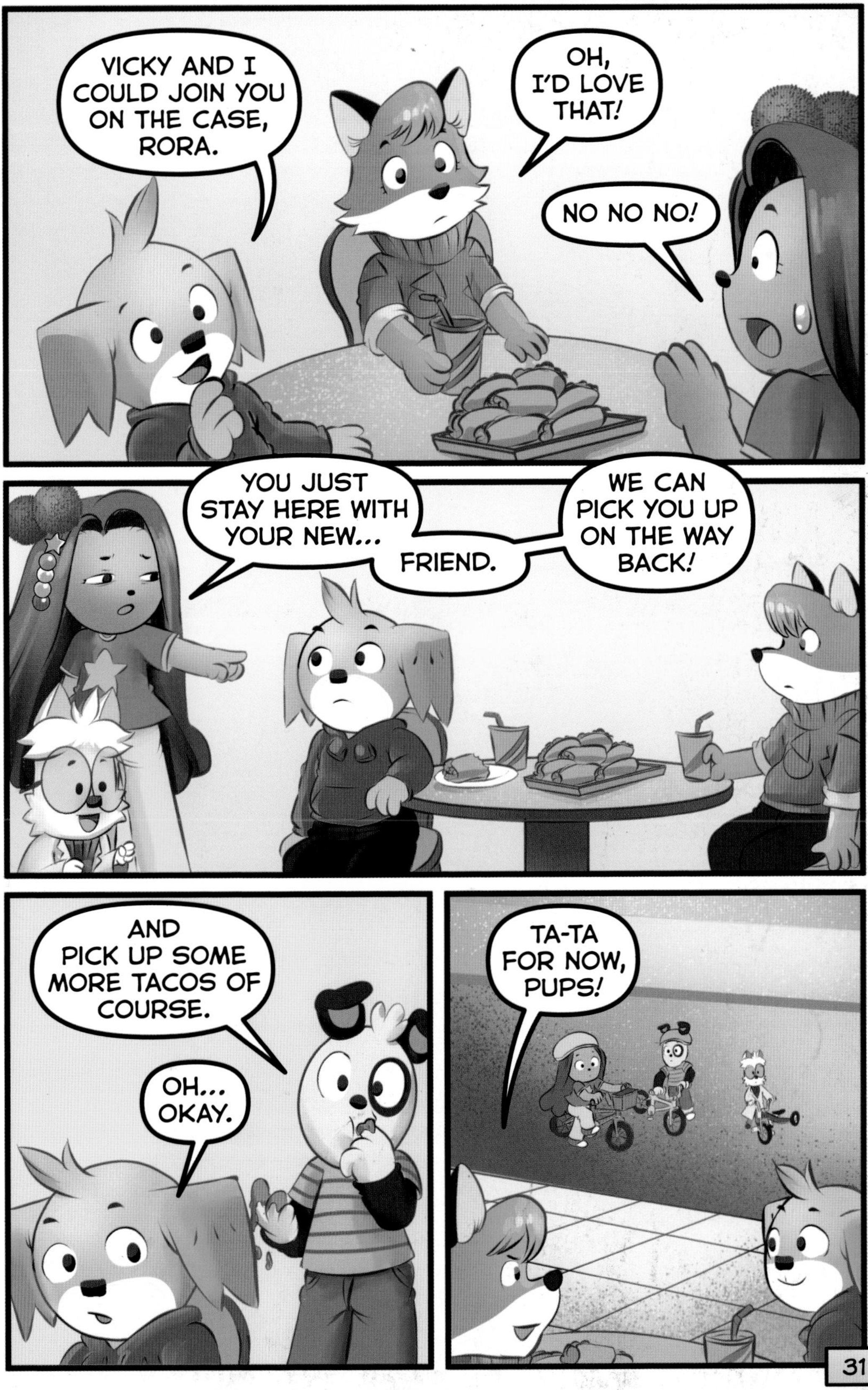
VICKY AND I COULD JOIN YOU ON THE CASE, RORA.
OH, I'D LOVE THAT!
NO NO NO!
YOU JUST STAY HERE WITH YOUR NEW...
FRIEND.
WE CAN PICK YOU UP ON THE WAY BACK!
AND PICK UP SOME MORE TACOS OF COURSE.
OH... OKAY.
TA-TA FOR NOW, PUPS!

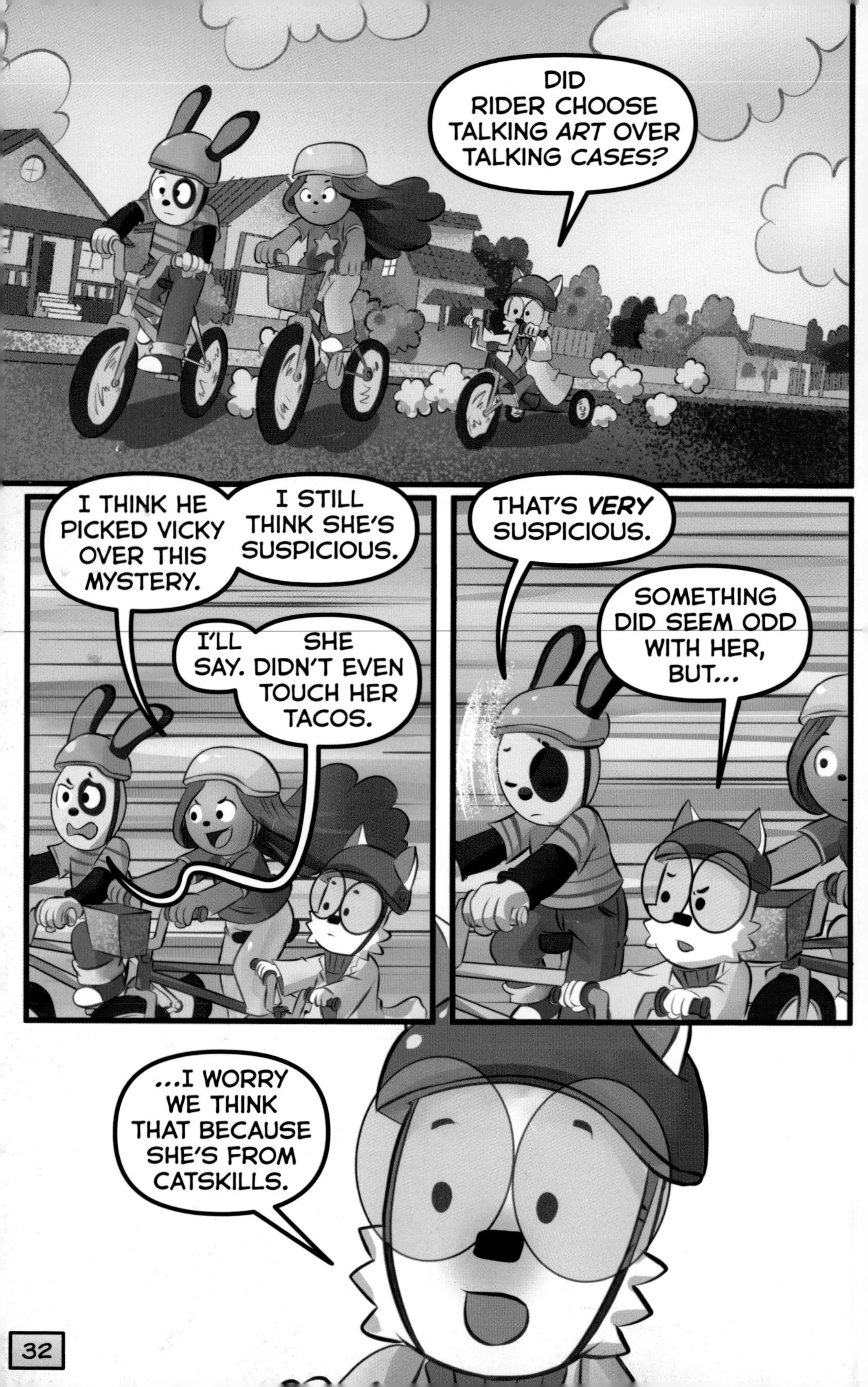
DID RIDER CHOOSE TALKING *ART* OVER TALKING *CASES?*
I THINK HE PICKED VICKY OVER THIS MYSTERY.
I STILL THINK SHE'S SUSPICIOUS.
I'LL SAY.
SHE DIDN'T EVEN TOUCH HER TACOS.
THAT'S *VERY* SUSPICIOUS.
SOMETHING DID SEEM ODD WITH HER, BUT...
...I WORRY WE THINK THAT BECAUSE SHE'S FROM CATSKILLS.

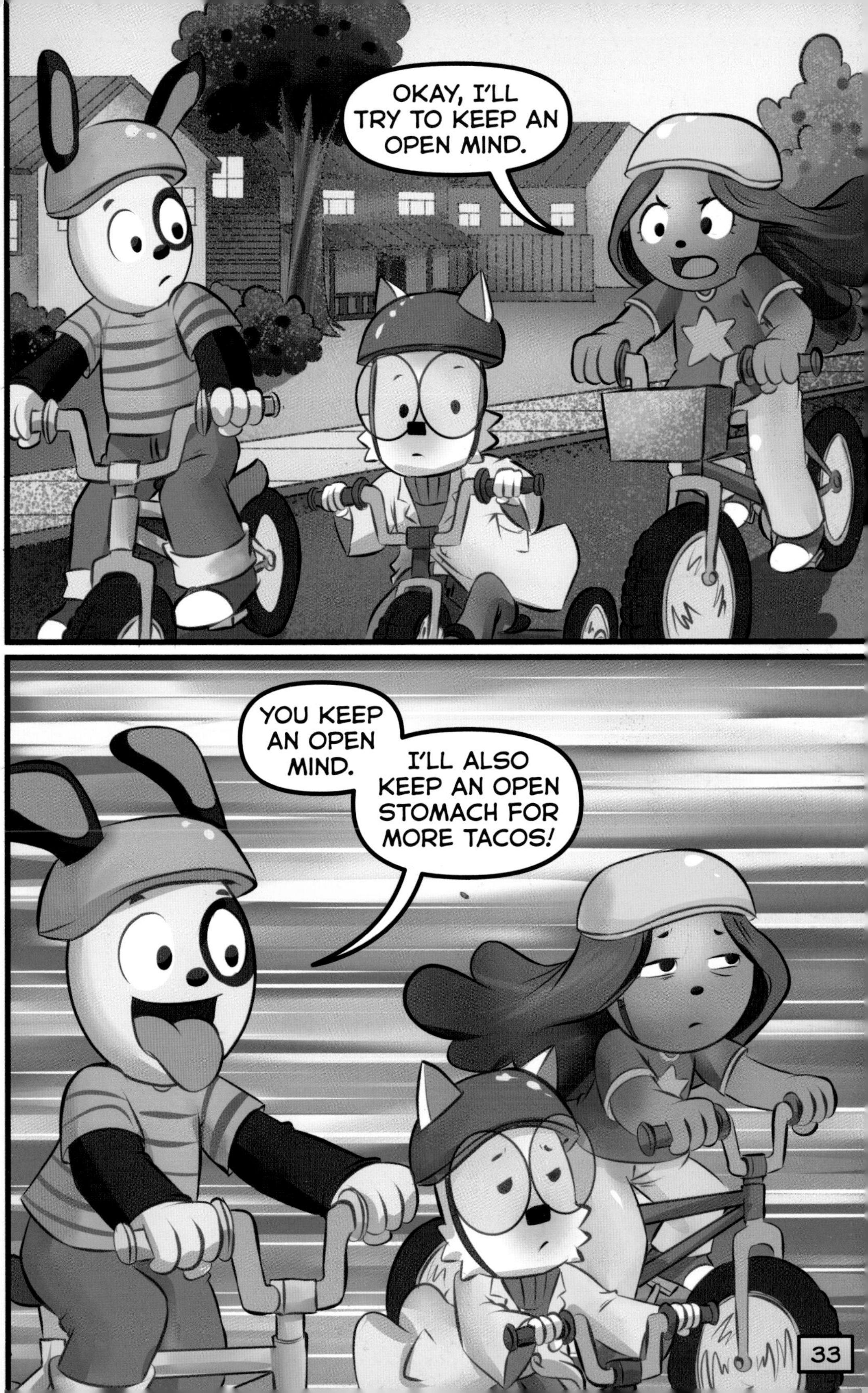
OKAY, I'LL TRY TO KEEP AN OPEN MIND.
YOU KEEP AN OPEN MIND.
I'LL ALSO KEEP AN OPEN STOMACH FOR MORE TACOS!

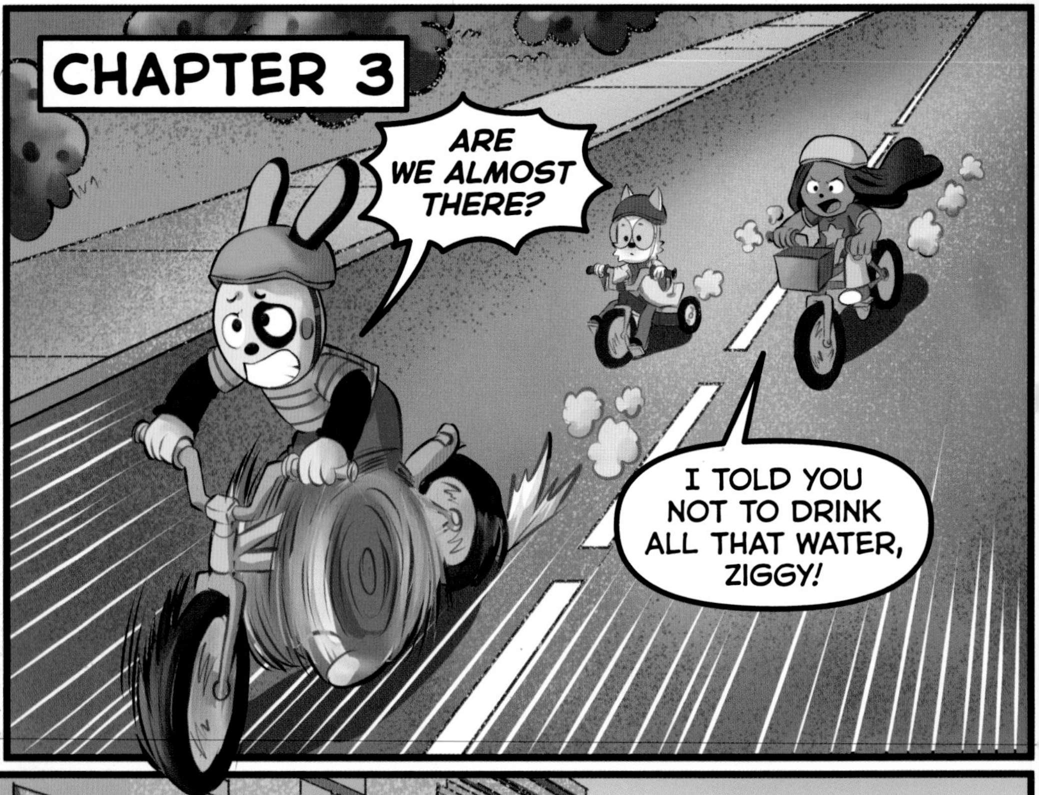
CHAPTER 3
ARE WE ALMOST THERE?
I TOLD YOU NOT TO DRINK ALL THAT WATER, ZIGGY!

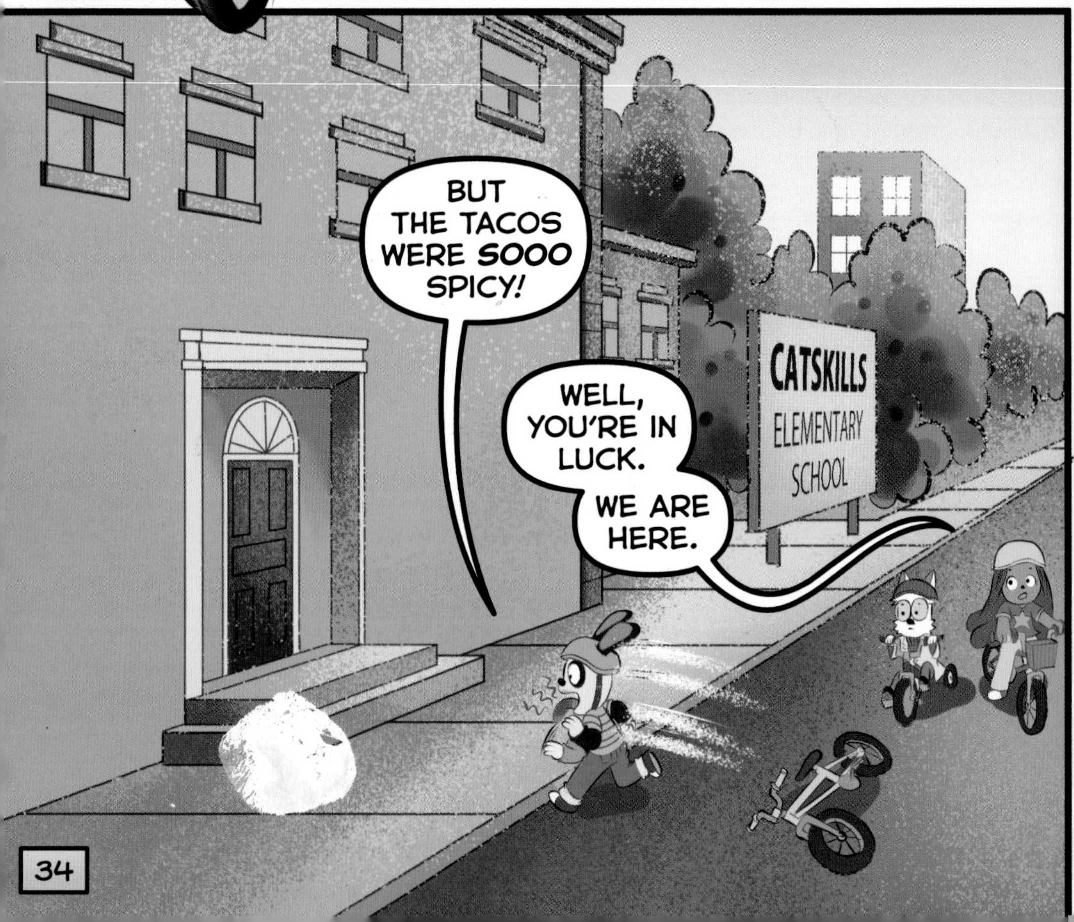
BUT THE TACOS WERE SOOO SPICY!
CATSKILLS ELEMENTARY SCHOOL
WELL, YOU'RE IN LUCK.
WE ARE HERE.

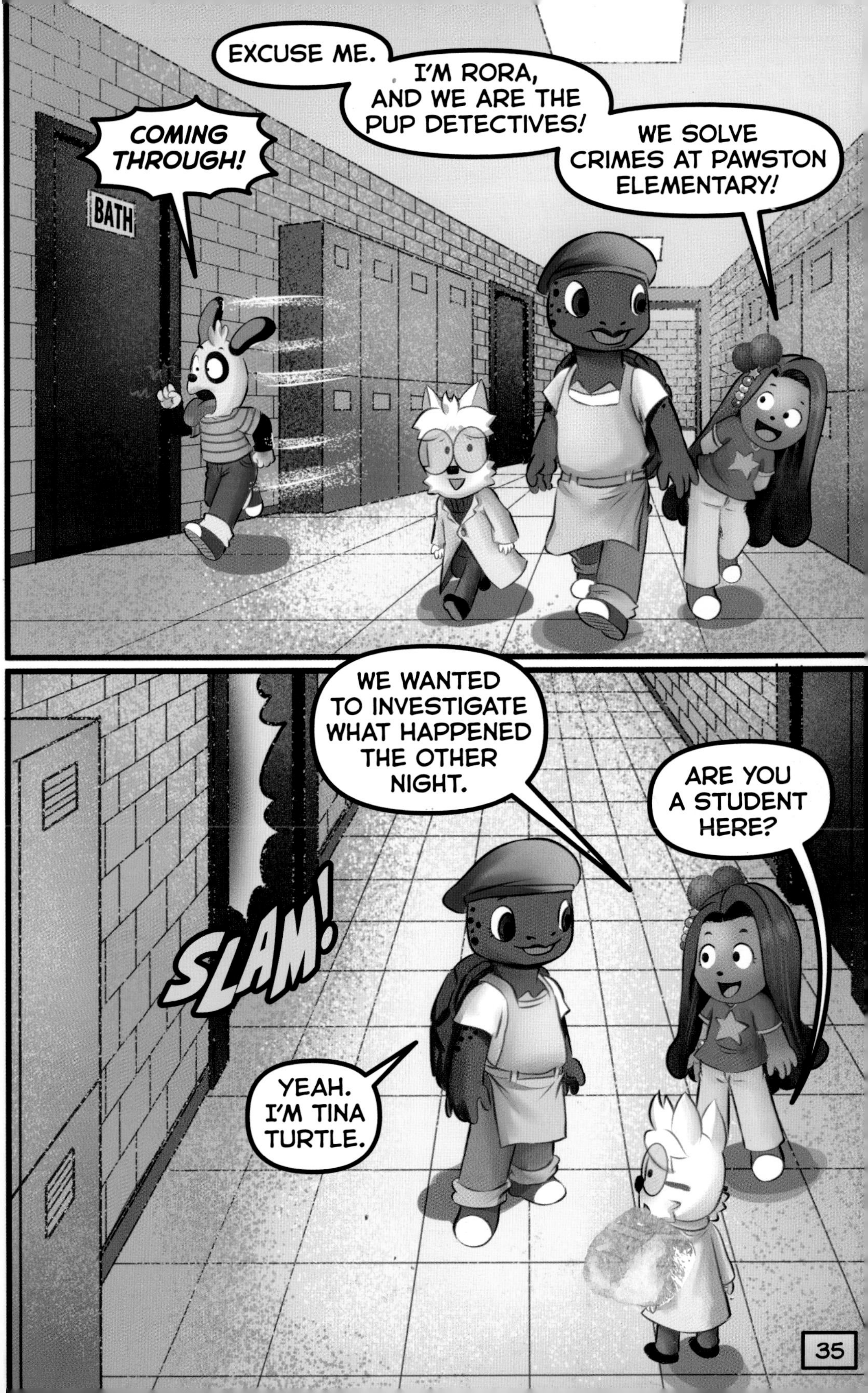
COMING THROUGH!
EXCUSE ME.
I'M RORA, AND WE ARE THE PUP DETECTIVES!
WE SOLVE CRIMES AT PAWSTON ELEMENTARY!
BATH
WE WANTED TO INVESTIGATE WHAT HAPPENED THE OTHER NIGHT.
ARE YOU A STUDENT HERE?
SLAM!
YEAH. I'M TINA TURTLE.

I'M THE HEAD OF THE CATSKILLS ART CLUB!

SO YOU MUST KNOW VICKY CROWN?

HMM, THAT NAME DOESN'T RING A BELL.

INTERESTING. TINA, DID ANYTHING ODD STAND OUT TO YOU ON MUSEUM NIGHT?

ANYTHING ODD?

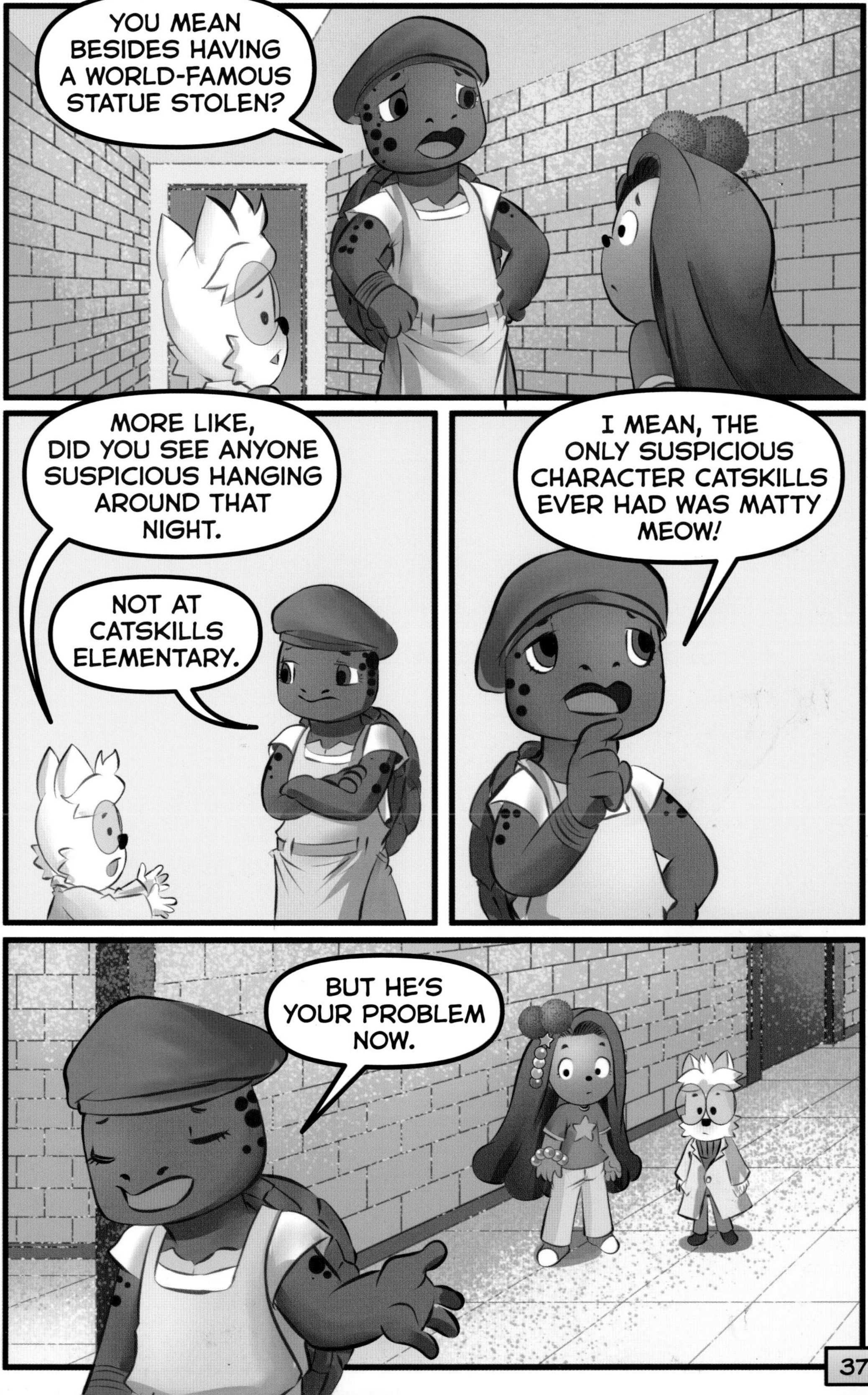
YOU MEAN BESIDES HAVING A WORLD-FAMOUS STATUE STOLEN?
MORE LIKE, DID YOU SEE ANYONE SUSPICIOUS HANGING AROUND THAT NIGHT.
NOT AT CATSKILLS ELEMENTARY.
I MEAN, THE ONLY SUSPICIOUS CHARACTER CATSKILLS EVER HAD WAS MATTY MEOW!
BUT HE'S YOUR PROBLEM NOW.

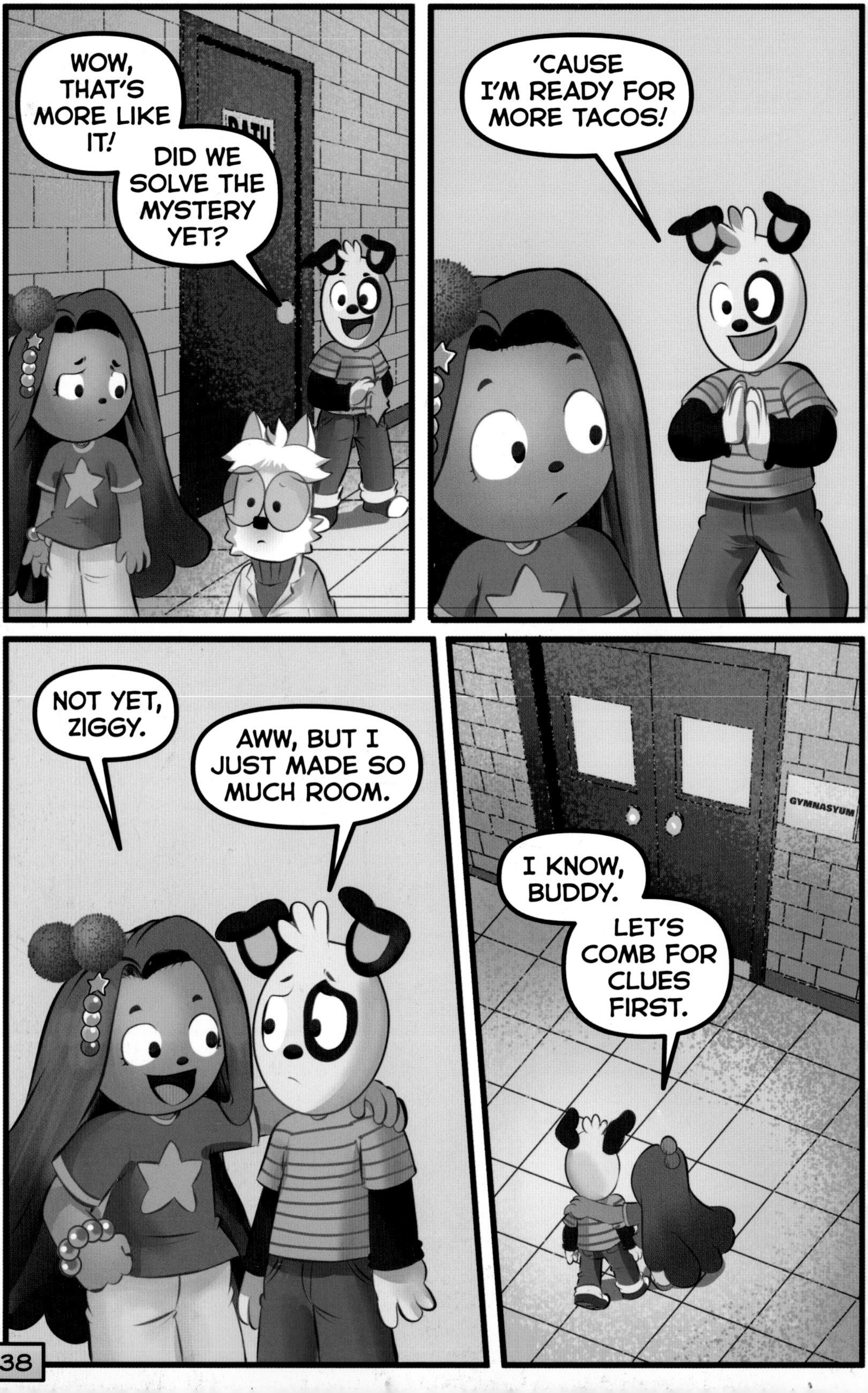
WOW, THAT'S MORE LIKE IT!
DID WE SOLVE THE MYSTERY YET?
'CAUSE I'M READY FOR MORE TACOS!
NOT YET, ZIGGY.
AWW, BUT I JUST MADE SO MUCH ROOM.
GYMNASYUM
I KNOW, BUDDY.
LET'S COMB FOR CLUES FIRST.

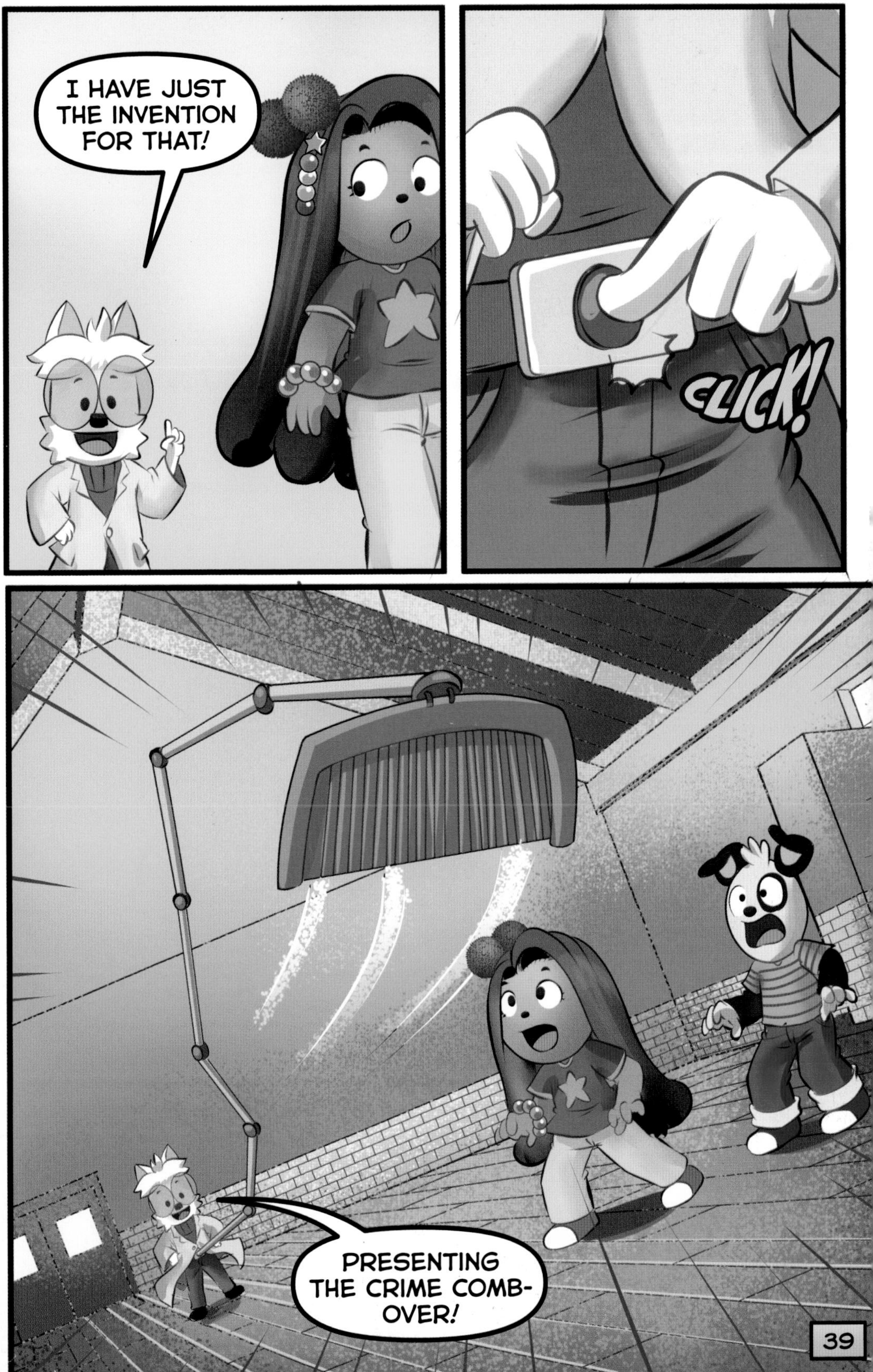
I HAVE JUST THE INVENTION FOR THAT!
CLICK!
PRESENTING THE CRIME COMB-OVER!

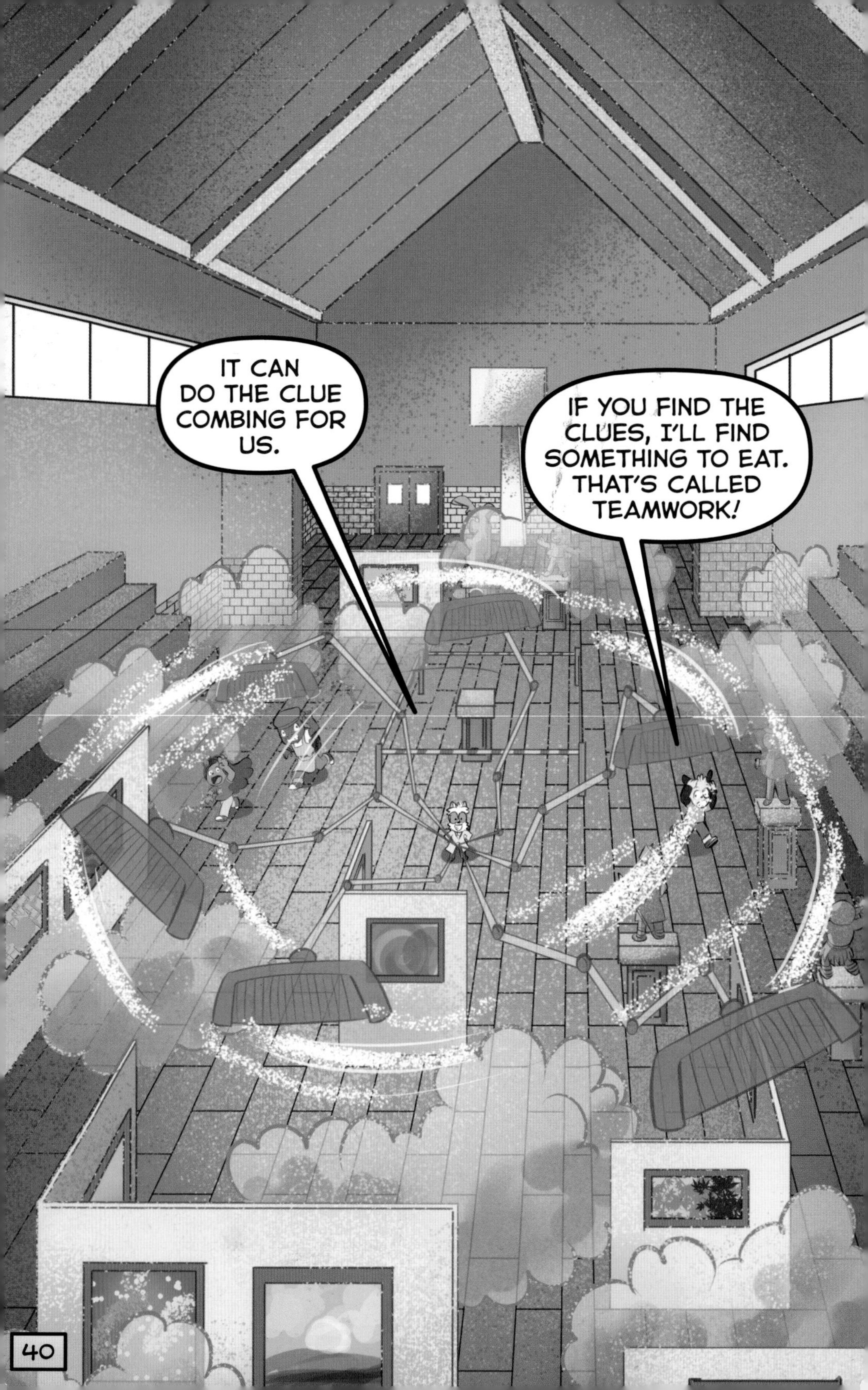
IT CAN DO THE CLUE COMBING FOR US.
IF YOU FIND THE CLUES, I'LL FIND SOMETHING TO EAT. THAT'S CALLED TEAMWORK!

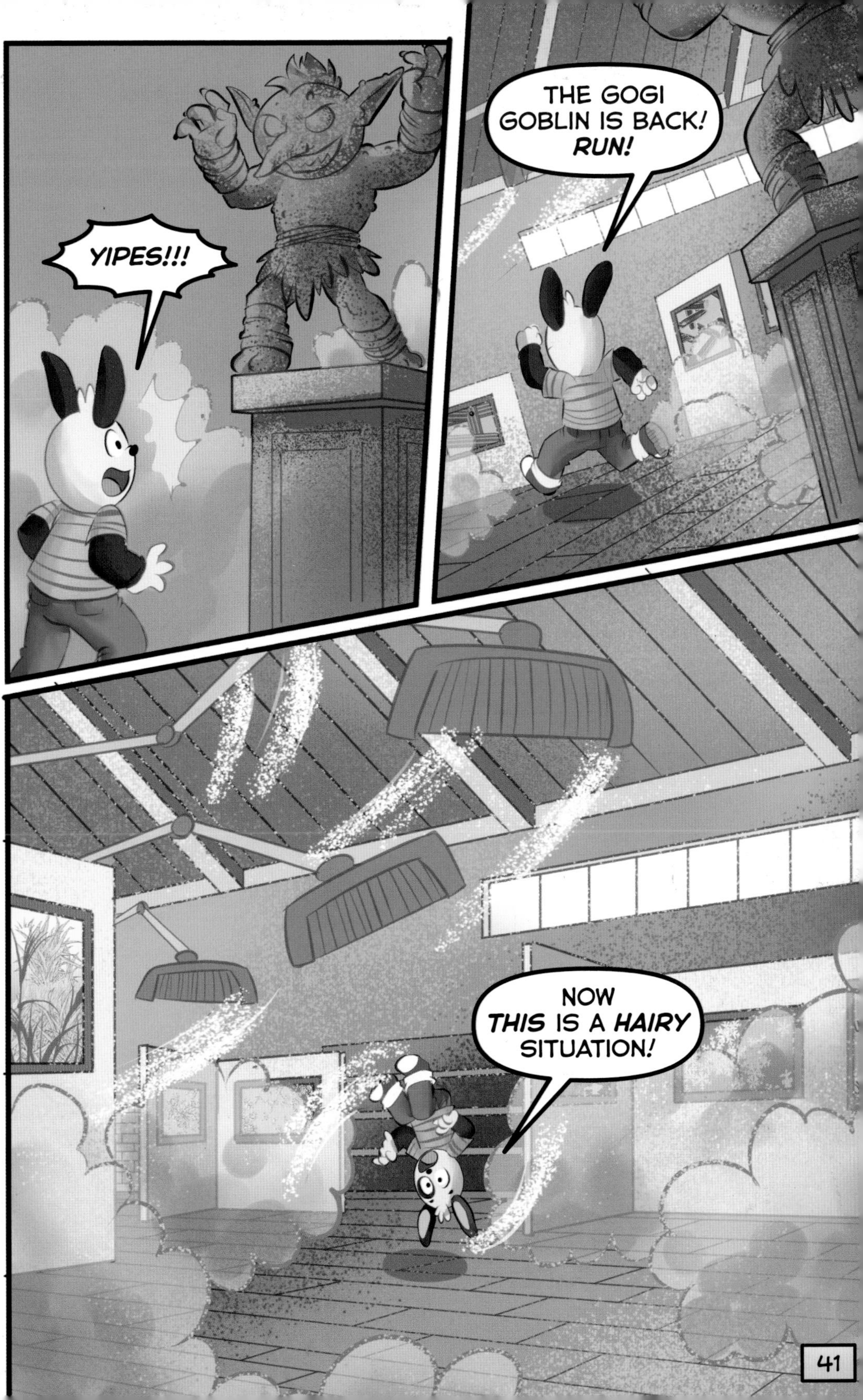
YIPES!!!
THE GOGI GOBLIN IS BACK! RUN!
NOW THIS IS A HAIRY SITUATION!

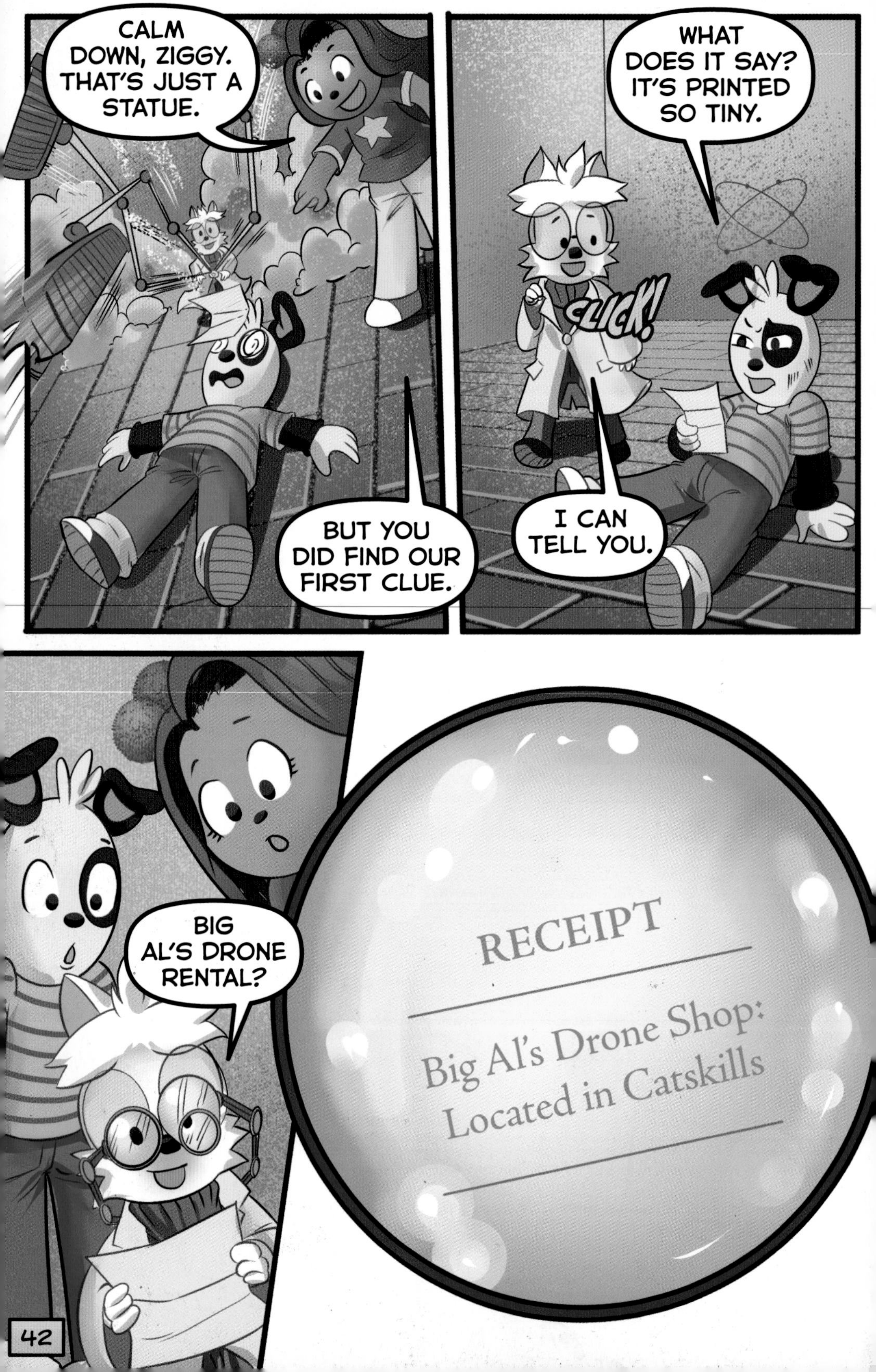
CALM DOWN, ZIGGY. THAT'S JUST A STATUE.
BUT YOU DID FIND OUR FIRST CLUE.
WHAT DOES IT SAY? IT'S PRINTED SO TINY.
CLICK!
I CAN TELL YOU.
BIG AL'S DRONE RENTAL?
RECEIPT
Big Al's Drone Shop:
Located in Catskills

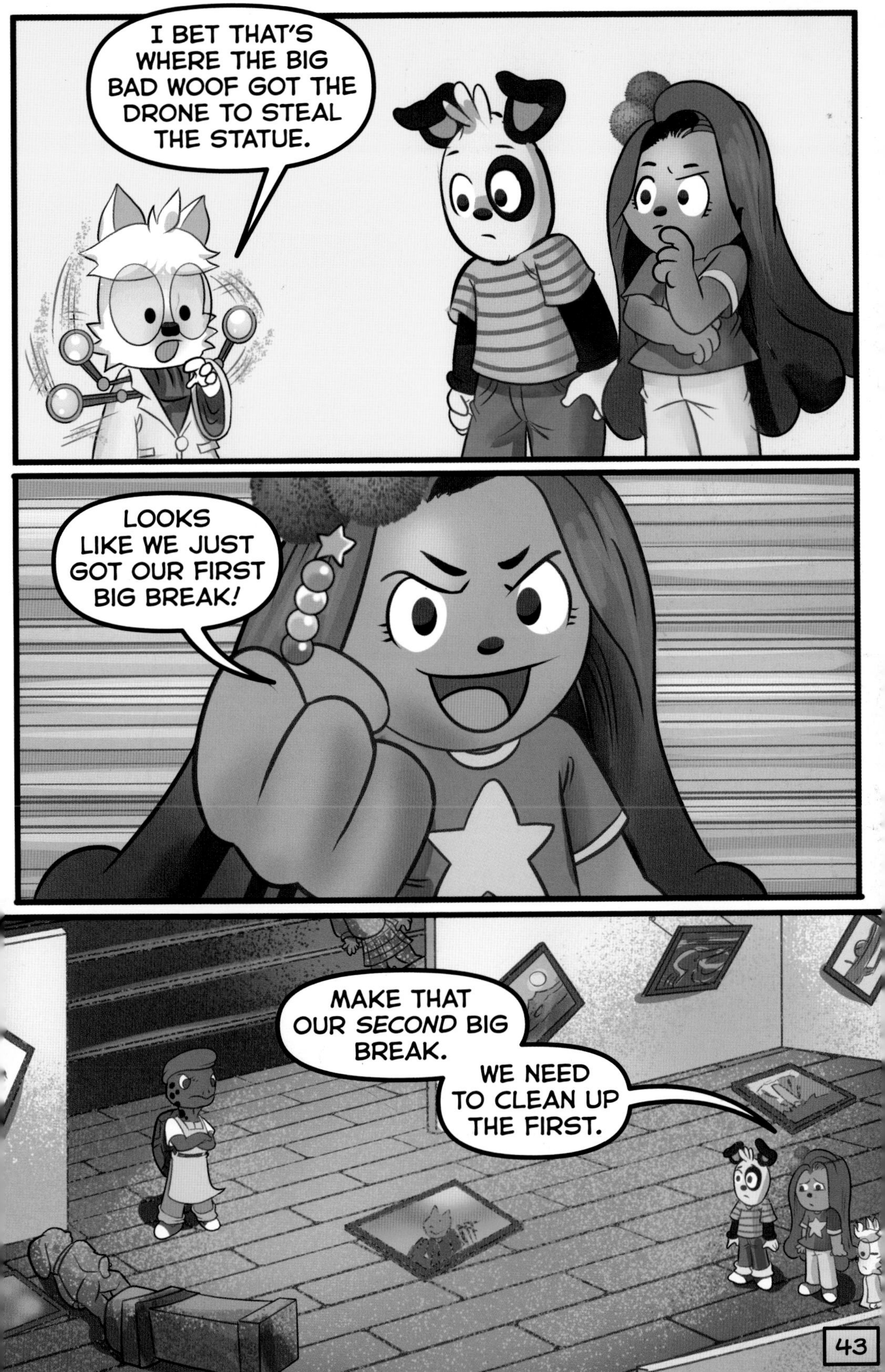
I BET THAT'S WHERE THE BIG BAD WOOF GOT THE DRONE TO STEAL THE STATUE.
LOOKS LIKE WE JUST GOT OUR FIRST BIG BREAK!
MAKE THAT OUR *SECOND* BIG BREAK.
WE NEED TO CLEAN UP THE FIRST.

CHAPTER 4

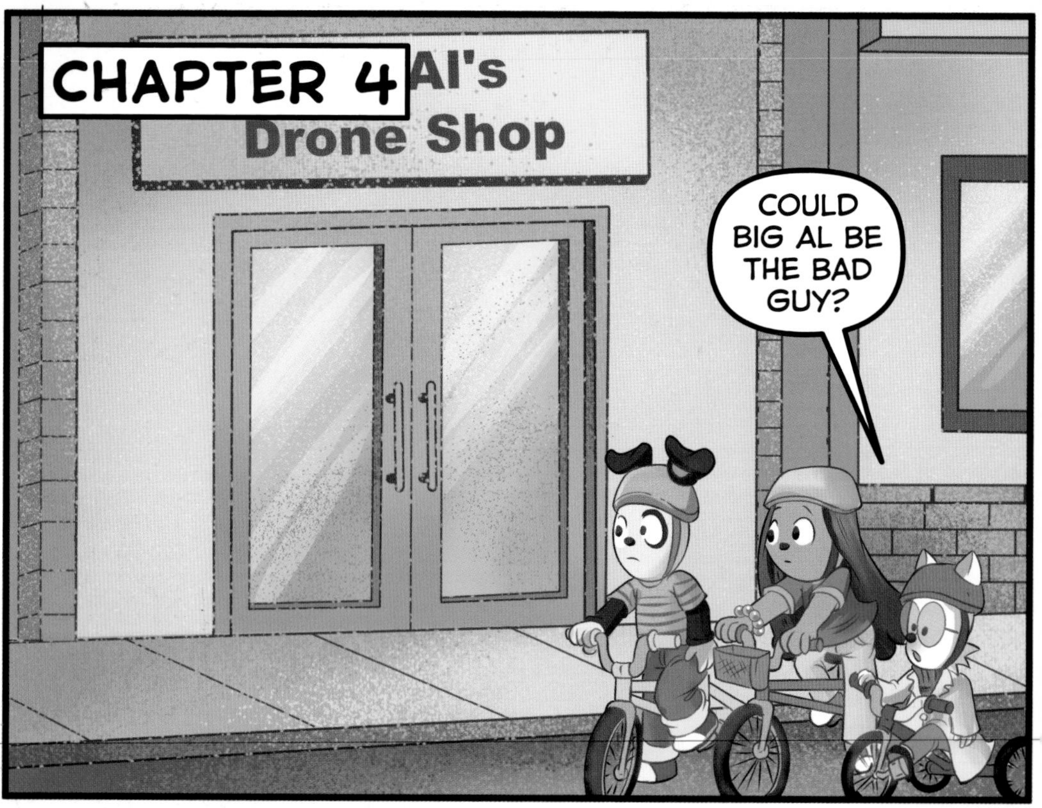
Al's
Drone Shop
COULD BIG AL BE THE BAD GUY?

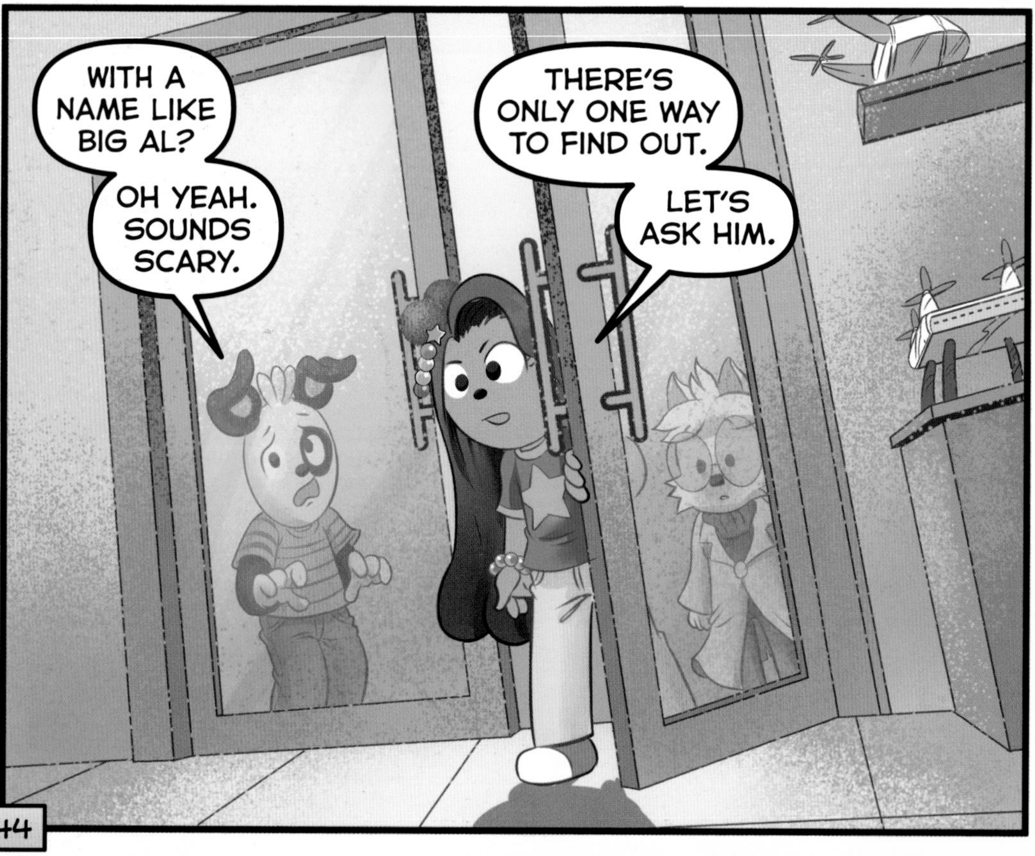
WITH A NAME LIKE BIG AL?
OH YEAH. SOUNDS SCARY.
THERE'S ONLY ONE WAY TO FIND OUT.
LET'S ASK HIM.

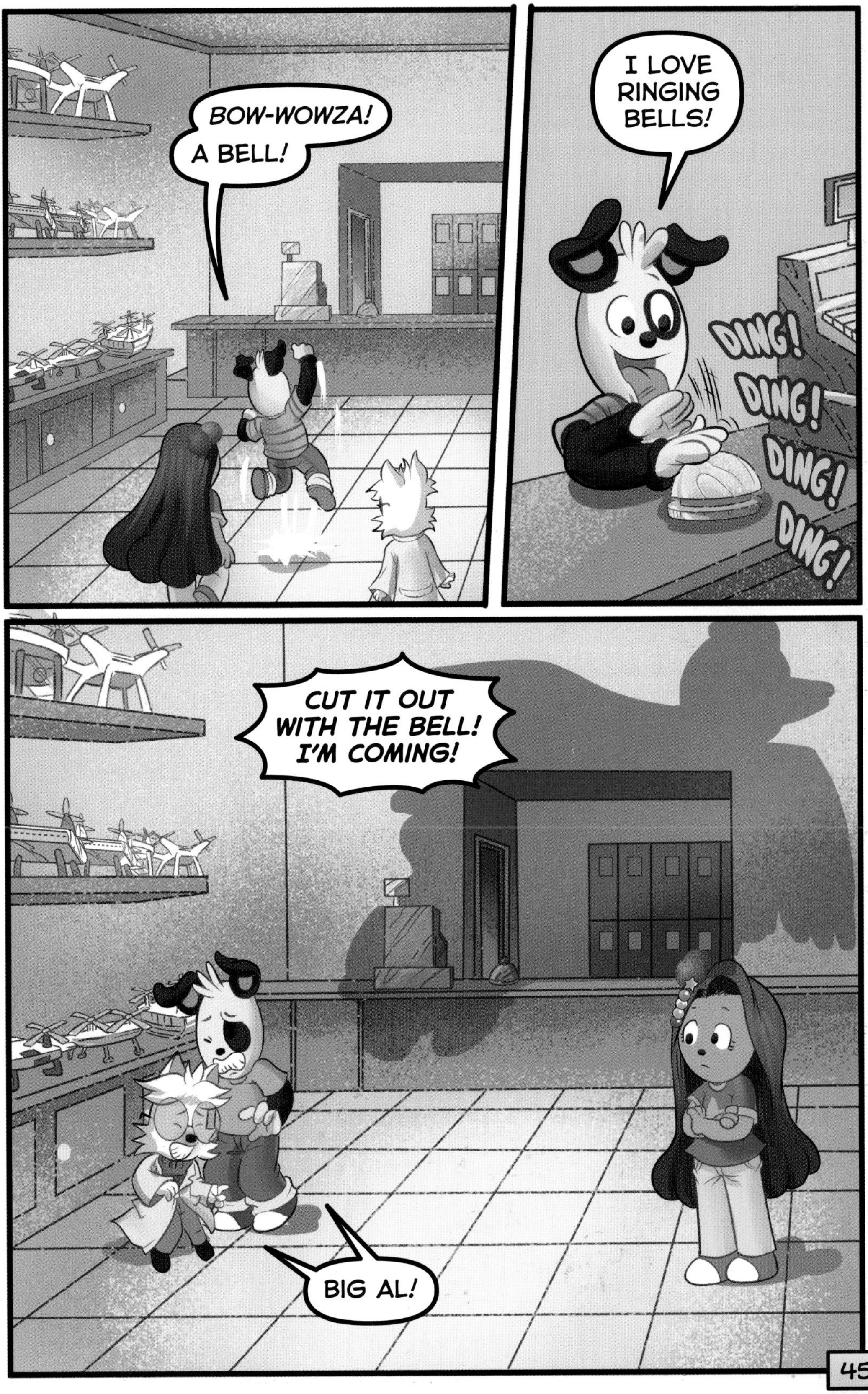
BOW-WOWZA!
A BELL!
I LOVE RINGING BELLS!
DING!
DING!
DING!
DING!
CUT IT OUT WITH THE BELL! I'M COMING!
BIG AL!

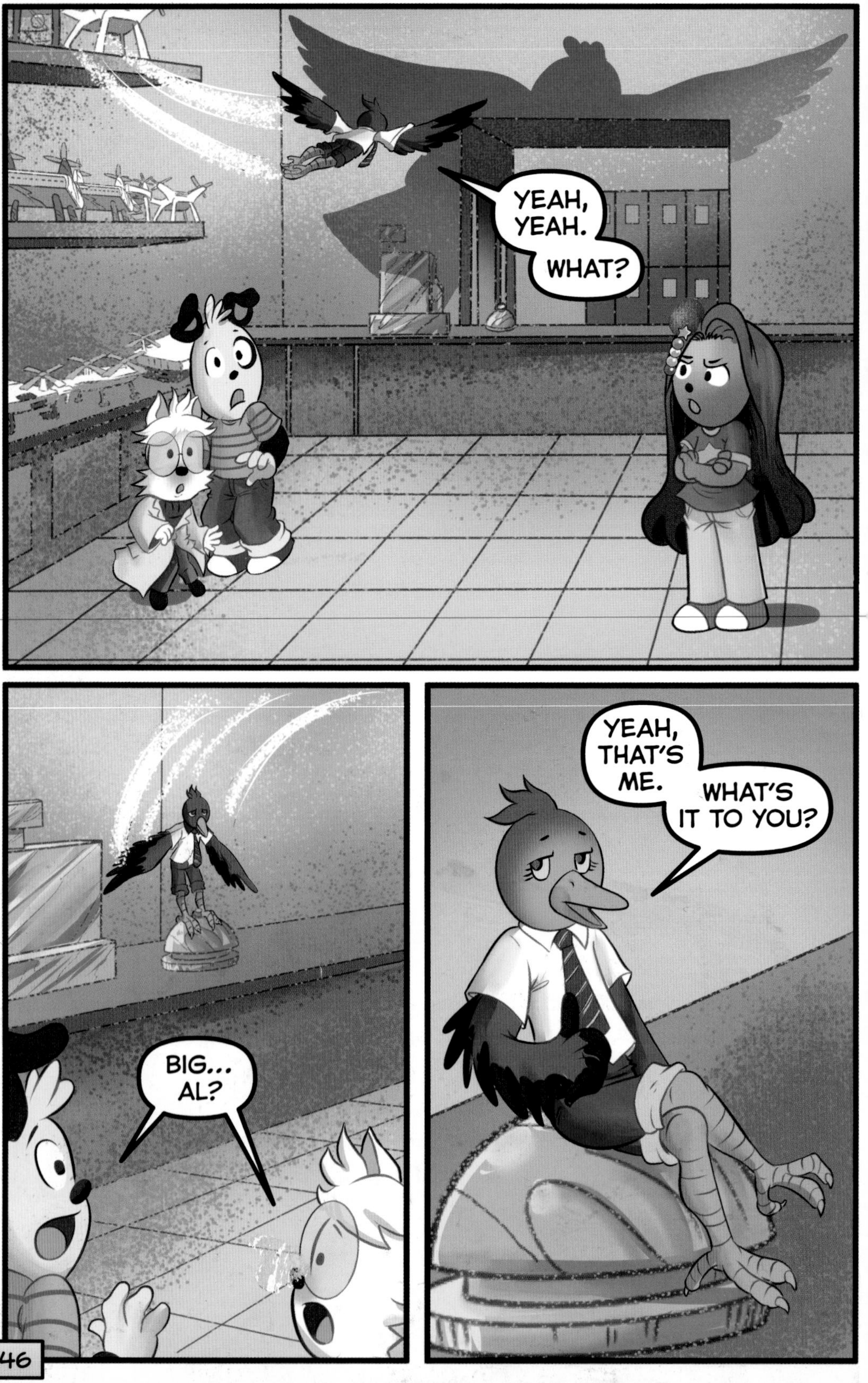
YEAH, YEAH.
WHAT?
BIG... AL?
YEAH, THAT'S ME.
WHAT'S IT TO YOU?

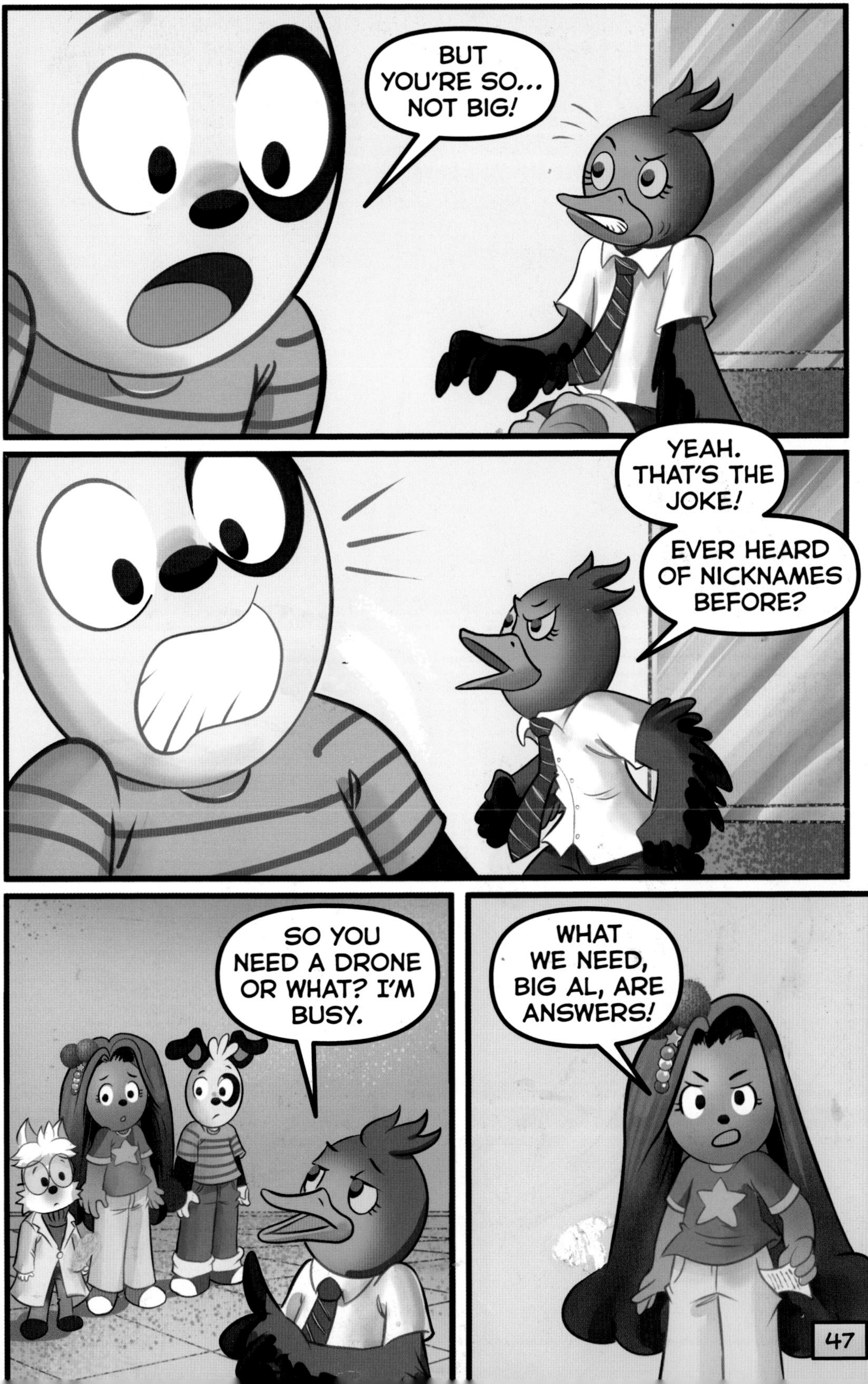
BUT YOU'RE SO... NOT BIG!
YEAH. THAT'S THE JOKE!
EVER HEARD OF NICKNAMES BEFORE?
SO YOU NEED A DRONE OR WHAT? I'M BUSY.
WHAT WE NEED, BIG AL, ARE ANSWERS!

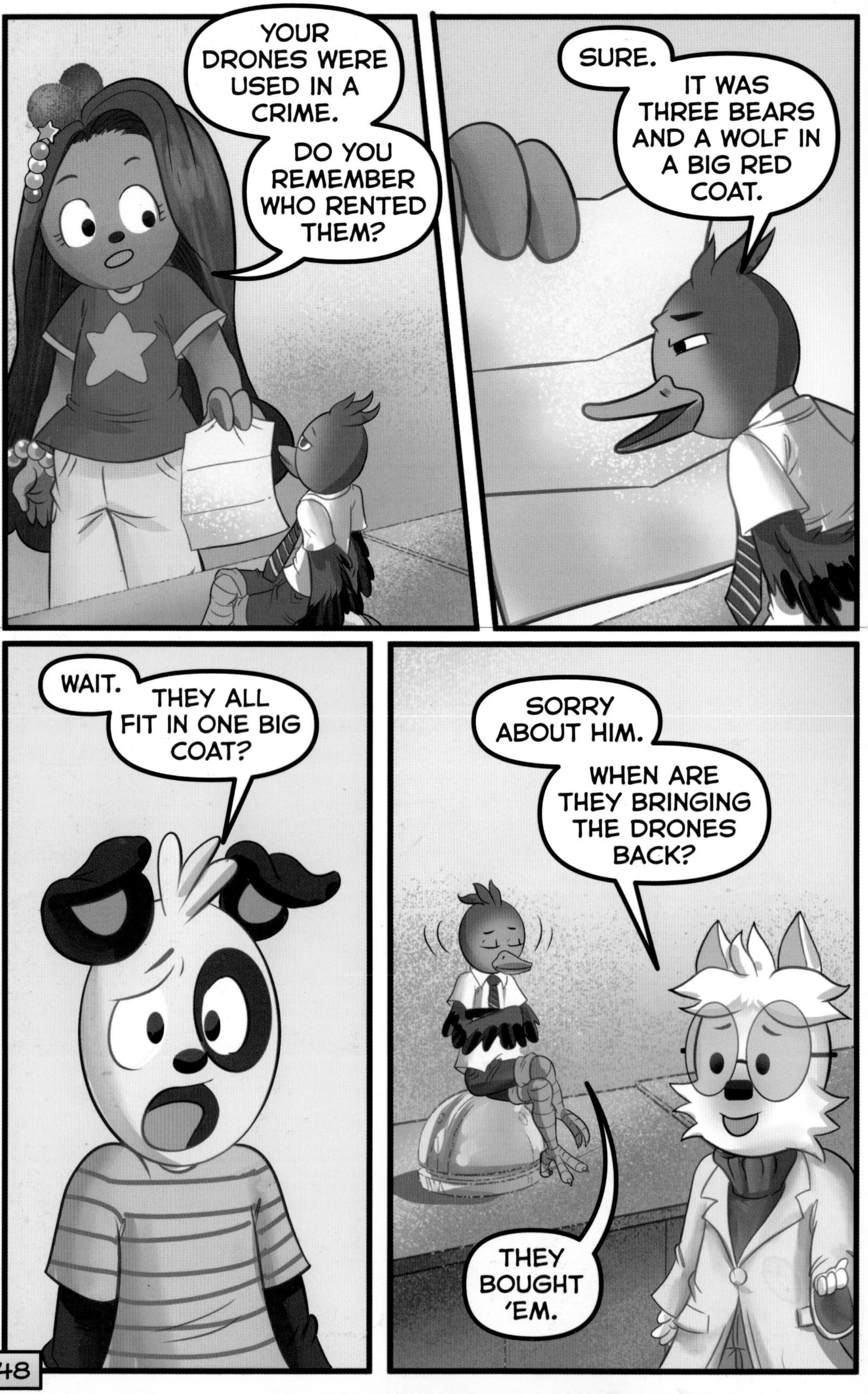
YOUR DRONES WERE USED IN A CRIME.
DO YOU REMEMBER WHO RENTED THEM?
SURE.
IT WAS THREE BEARS AND A WOLF IN A BIG RED COAT.
WAIT.
THEY ALL FIT IN ONE BIG COAT?
SORRY ABOUT HIM.
WHEN ARE THEY BRINGING THE DRONES BACK?
THEY BOUGHT 'EM.

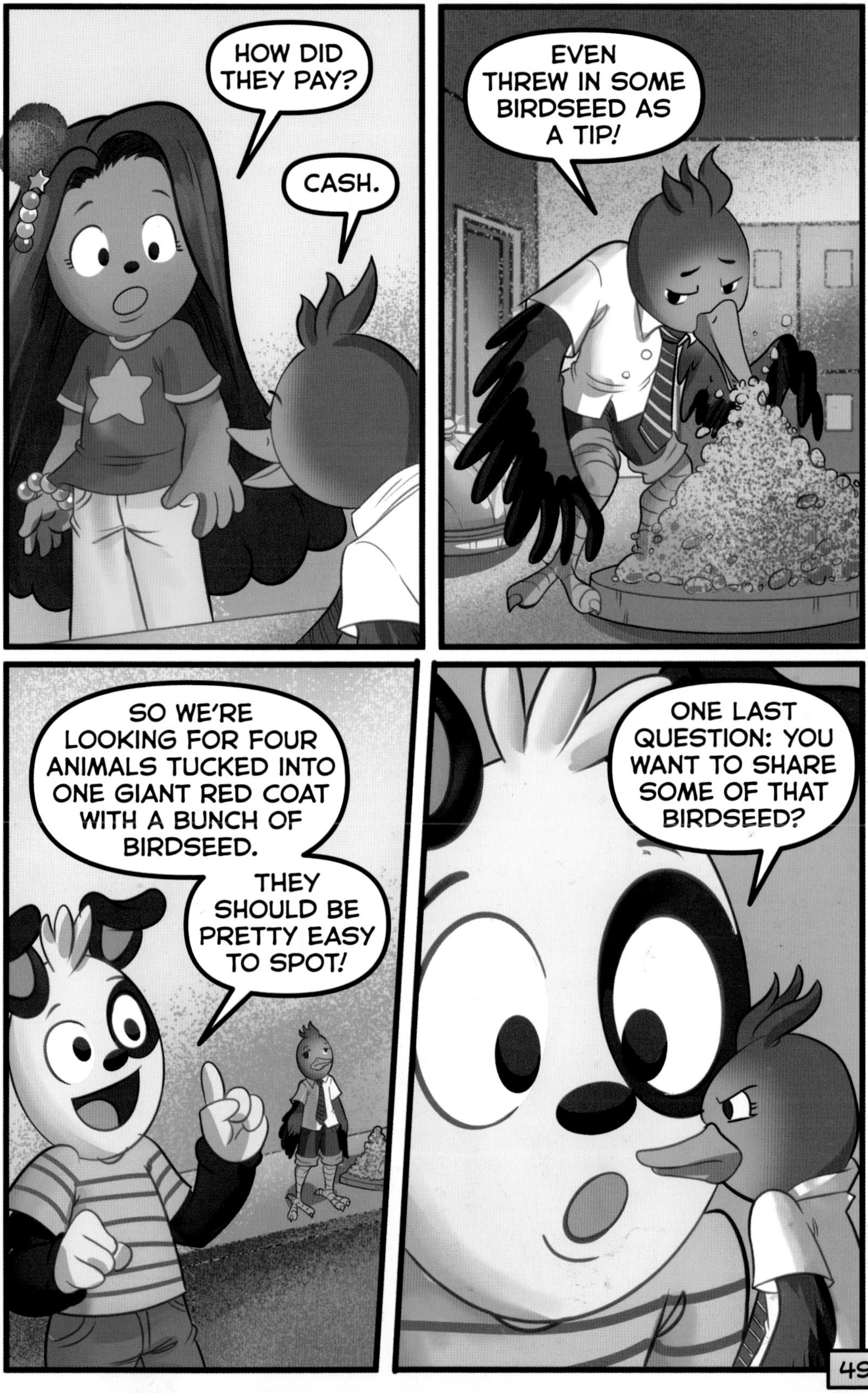
HOW DID THEY PAY?
CASH.
EVEN THREW IN SOME BIRDSEED AS A TIP!
SO WE'RE LOOKING FOR FOUR ANIMALS TUCKED INTO ONE GIANT RED COAT WITH A BUNCH OF BIRDSEED.
THEY SHOULD BE PRETTY EASY TO SPOT!
ONE LAST QUESTION: YOU WANT TO SHARE SOME OF THAT BIRDSEED?

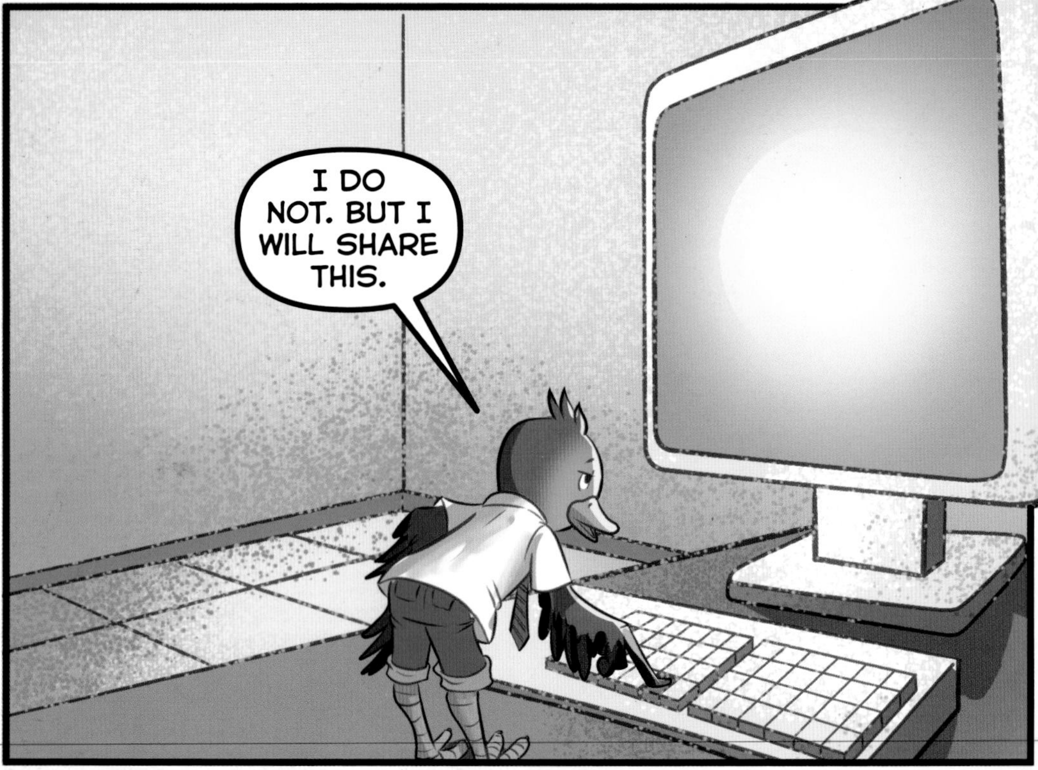
I DO NOT. BUT I WILL SHARE THIS.

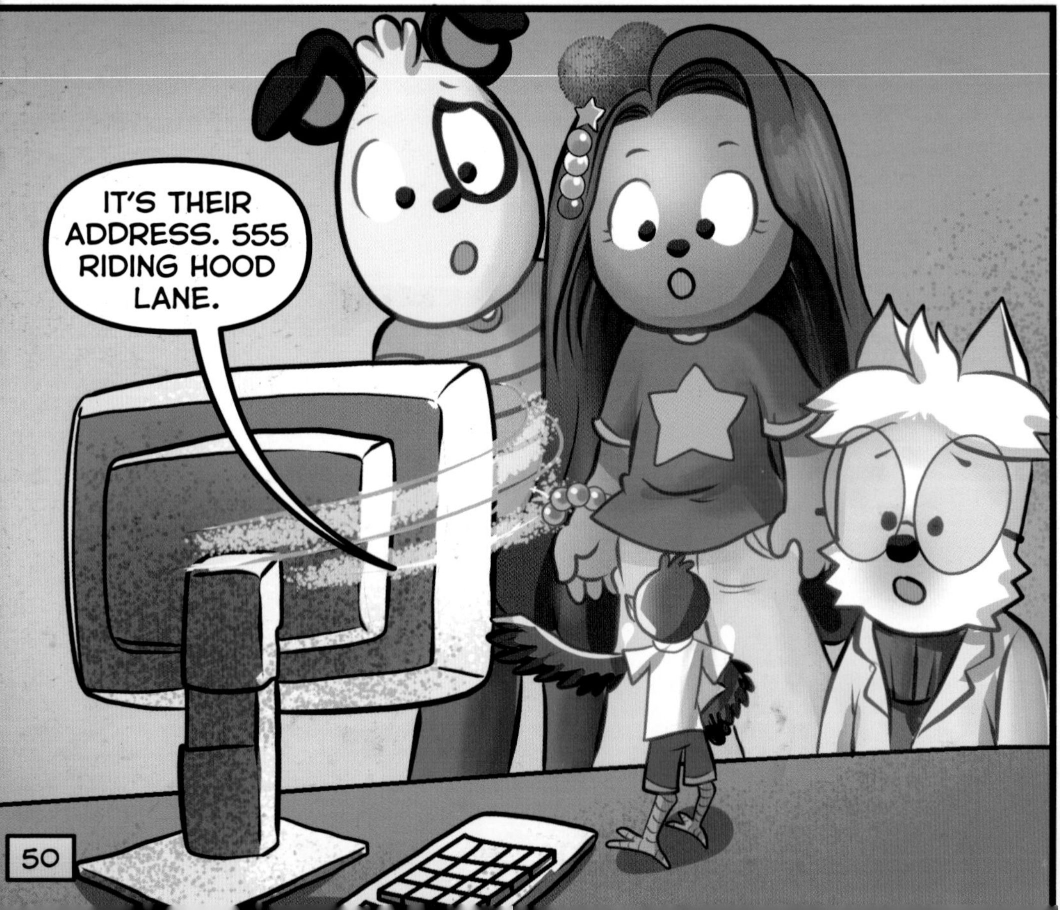
IT'S THEIR ADDRESS. 555 RIDING HOOD LANE.

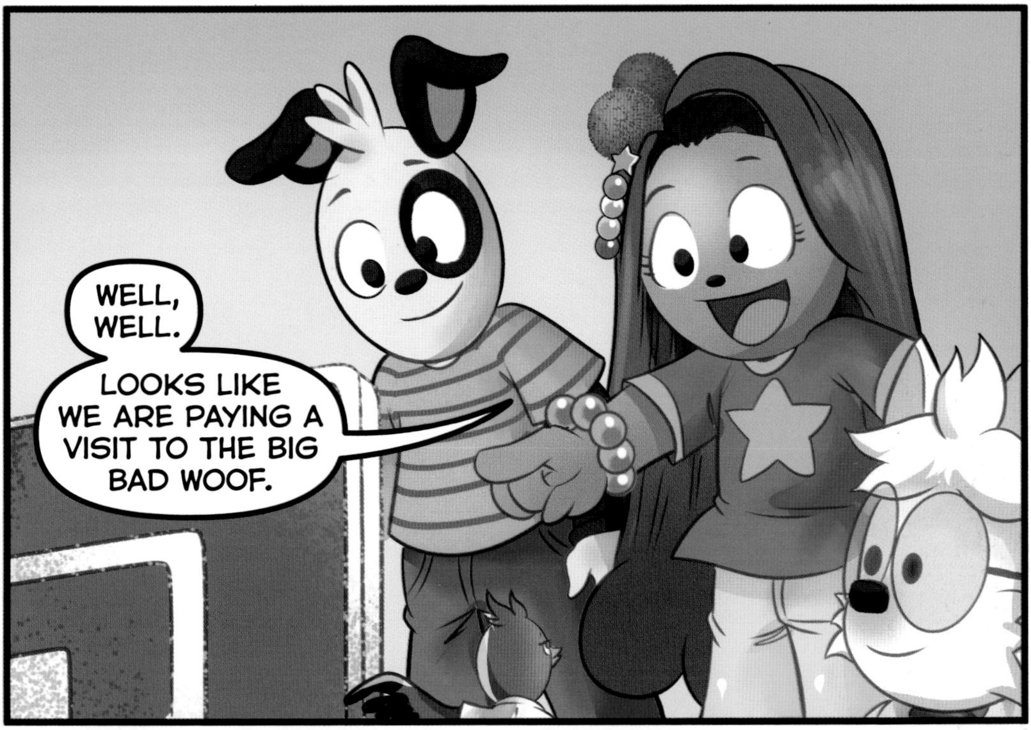
WELL, WELL.
LOOKS LIKE WE ARE PAYING A VISIT TO THE BIG BAD WOOF.

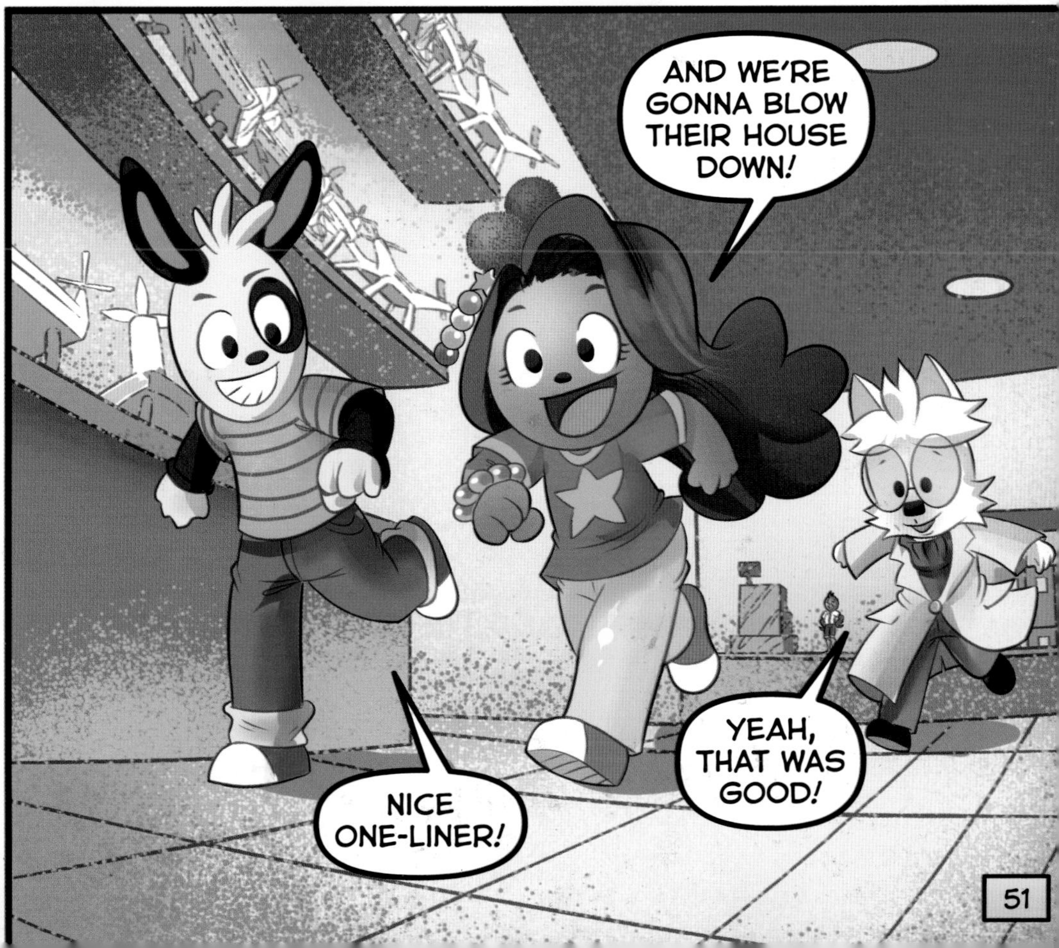
AND WE'RE GONNA BLOW THEIR HOUSE DOWN!
NICE ONE-LINER!
YEAH, THAT WAS GOOD!

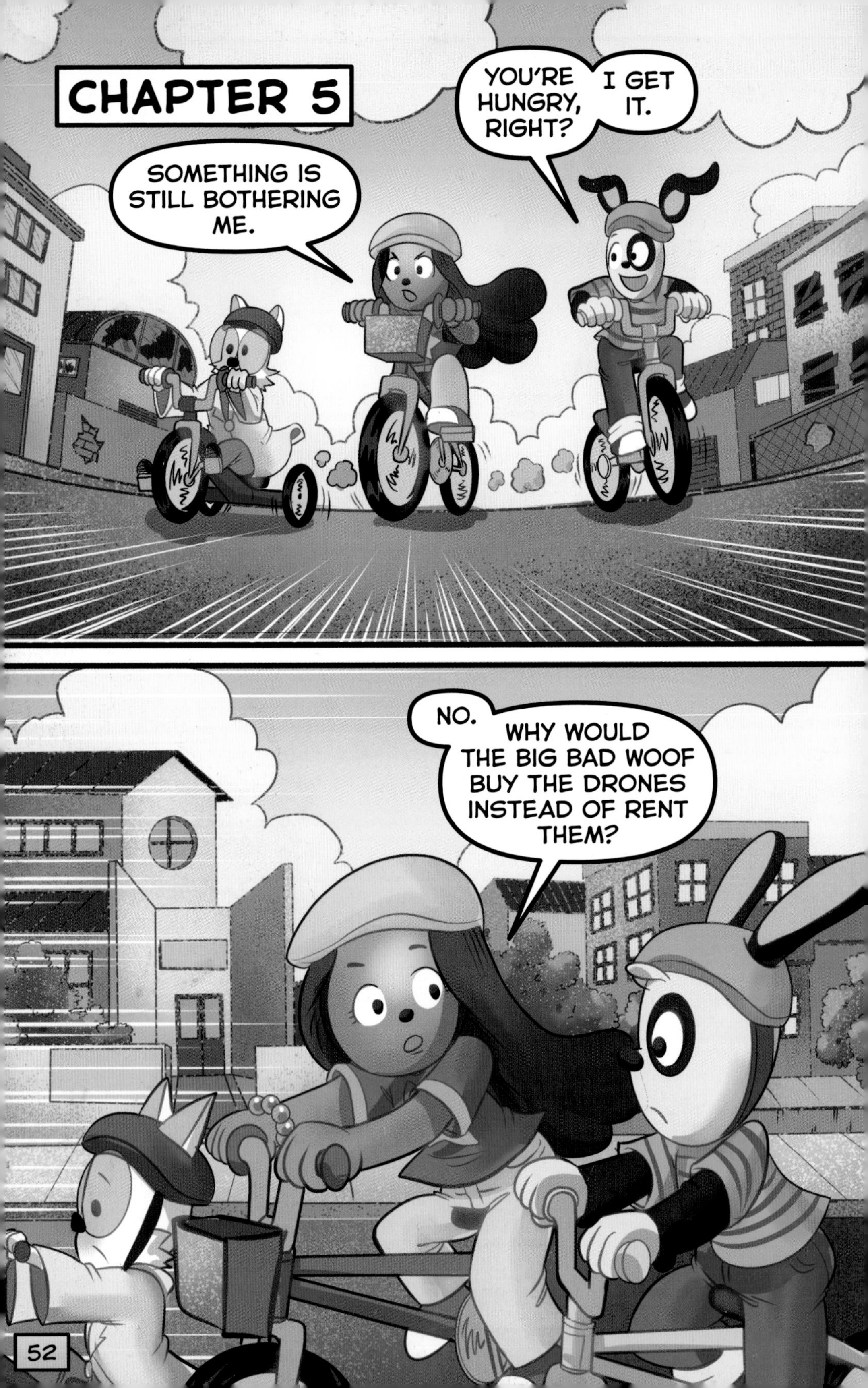
CHAPTER 5
SOMETHING IS STILL BOTHERING ME.
YOU'RE HUNGRY, RIGHT?
I GET IT.
NO.
WHY WOULD THE BIG BAD WOOF BUY THE DRONES INSTEAD OF RENT THEM?

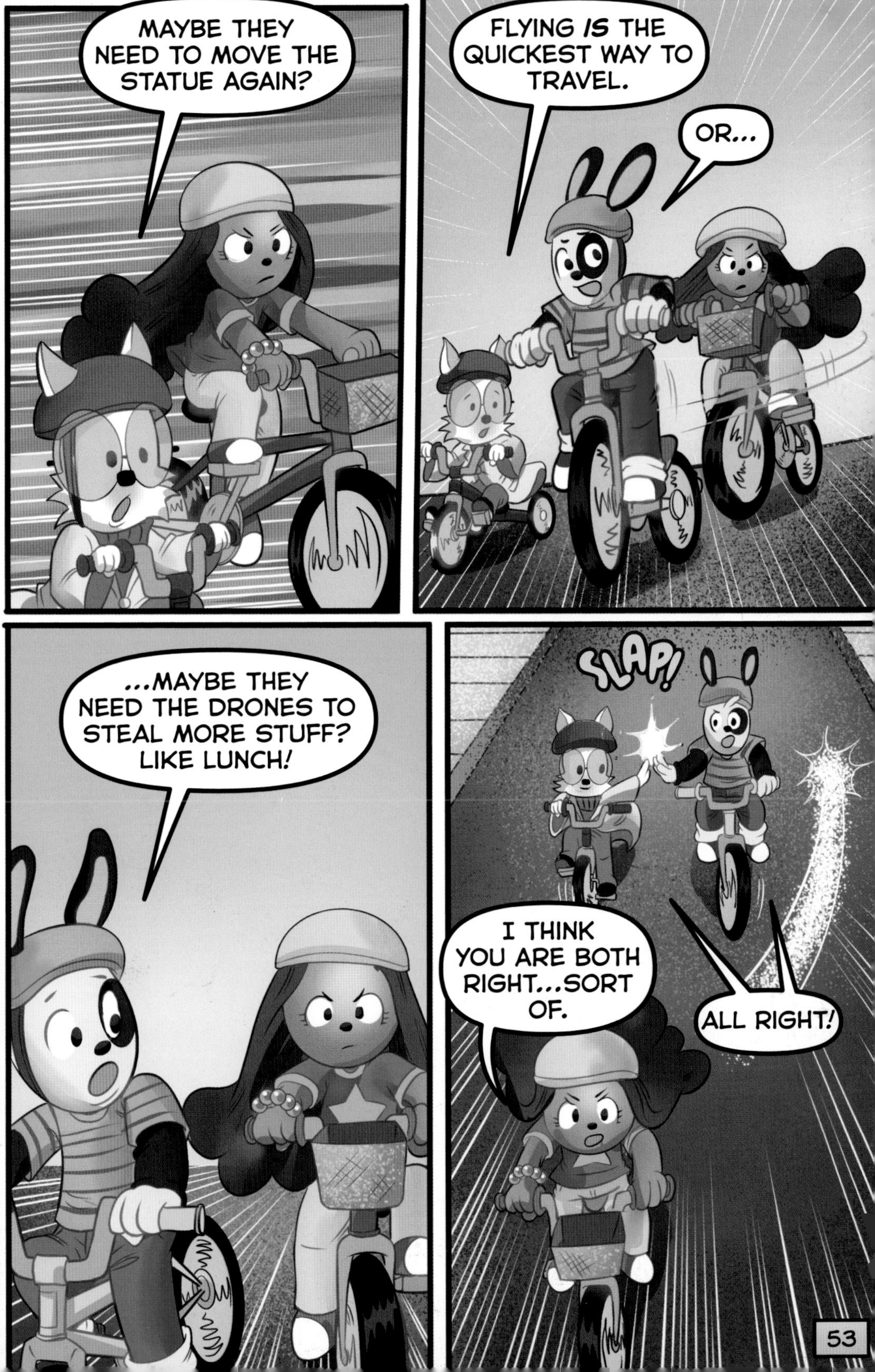
MAYBE THEY NEED TO MOVE THE STATUE AGAIN?
FLYING IS THE QUICKEST WAY TO TRAVEL.
OR...
...MAYBE THEY NEED THE DRONES TO STEAL MORE STUFF? LIKE LUNCH!
SLAP!
I THINK YOU ARE BOTH RIGHT...SORT OF.
ALL RIGHT!

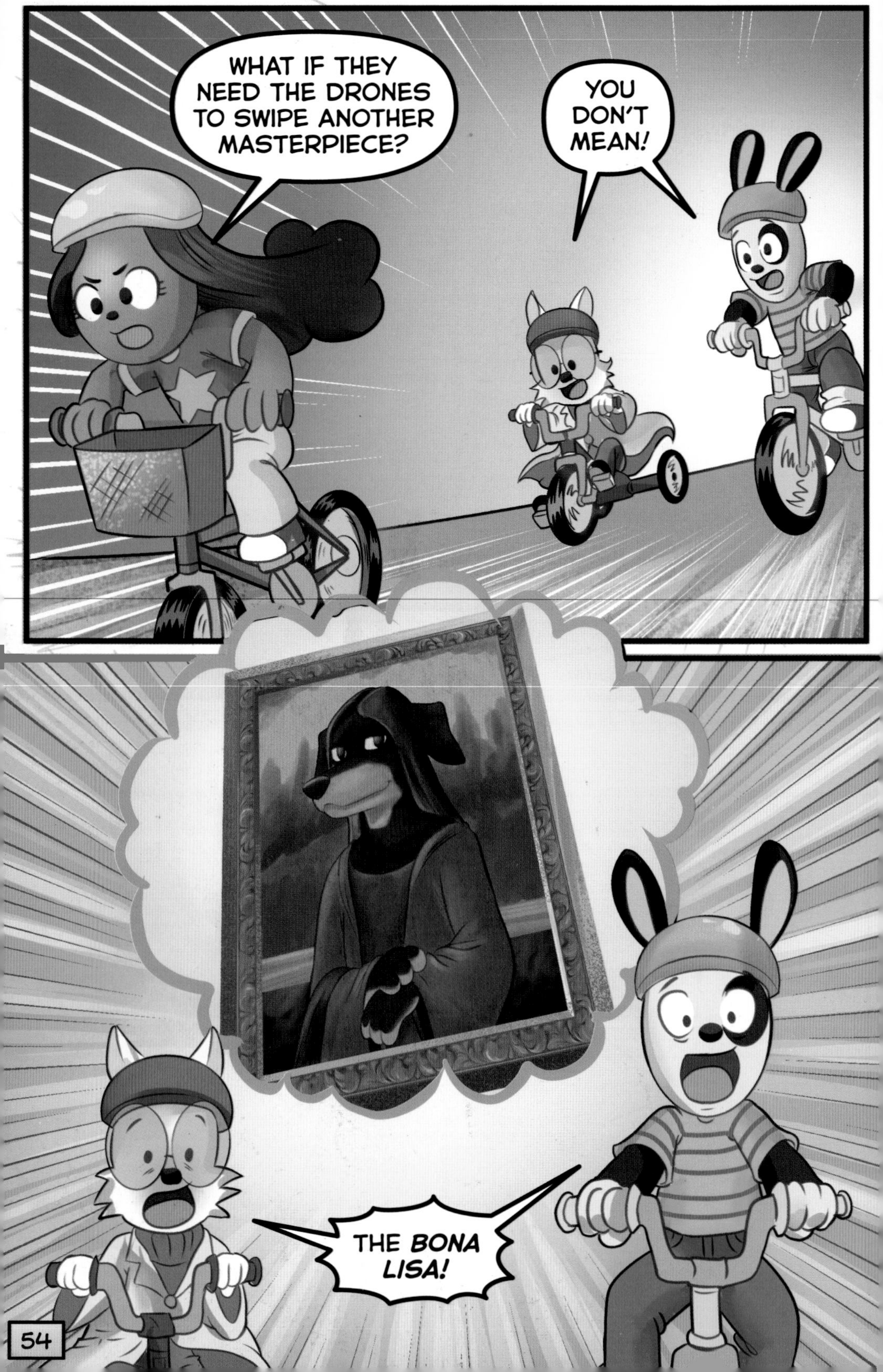
WHAT IF THEY NEED THE DRONES TO SWIPE ANOTHER MASTERPIECE?
YOU DON'T MEAN!
THE *BONA LISA!*

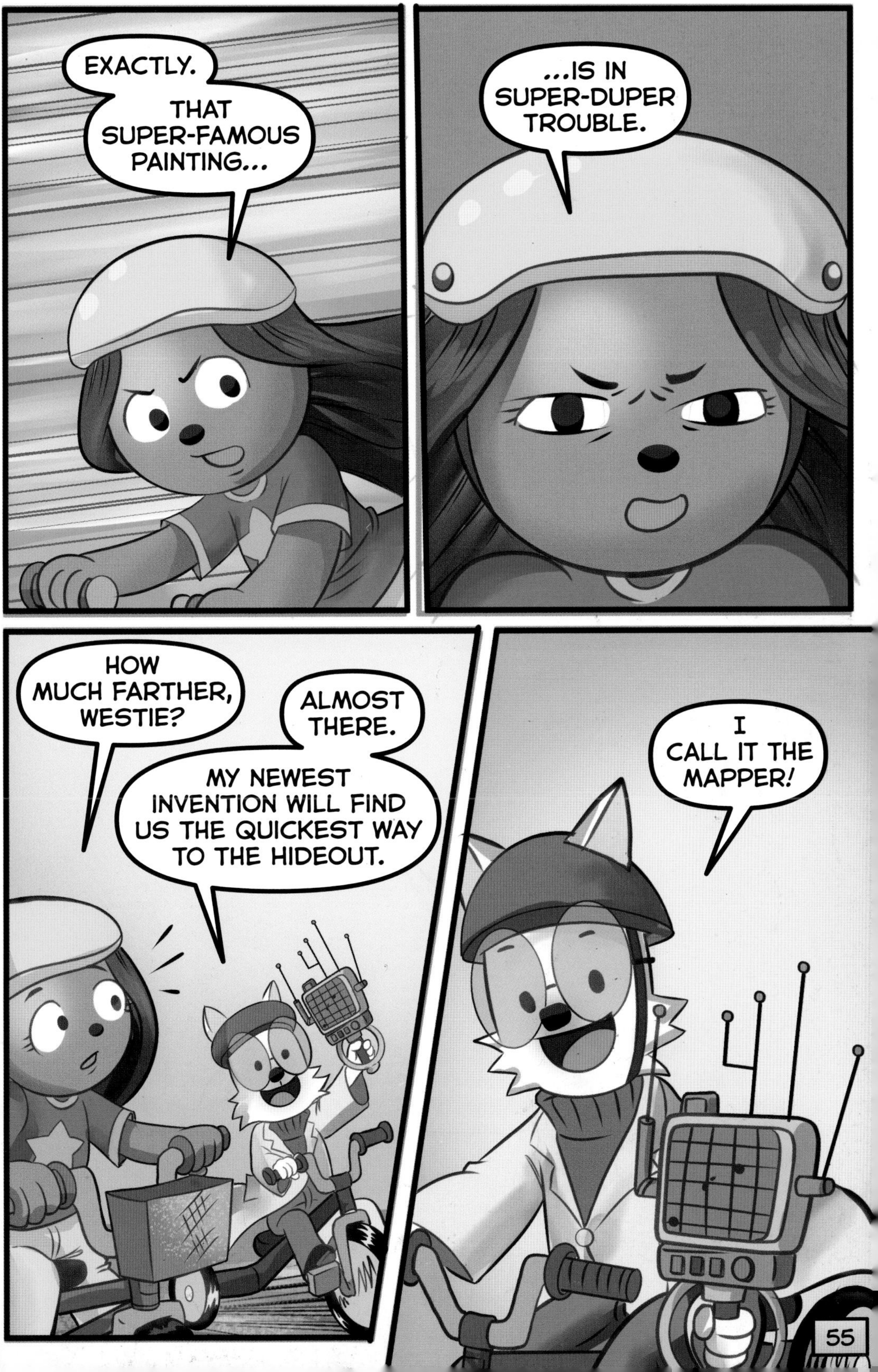
EXACTLY.
THAT SUPER-FAMOUS PAINTING...
...IS IN SUPER-DUPER TROUBLE.
HOW MUCH FARTHER, WESTIE?
ALMOST THERE.
MY NEWEST INVENTION WILL FIND US THE QUICKEST WAY TO THE HIDEOUT.
I CALL IT THE MAPPER!

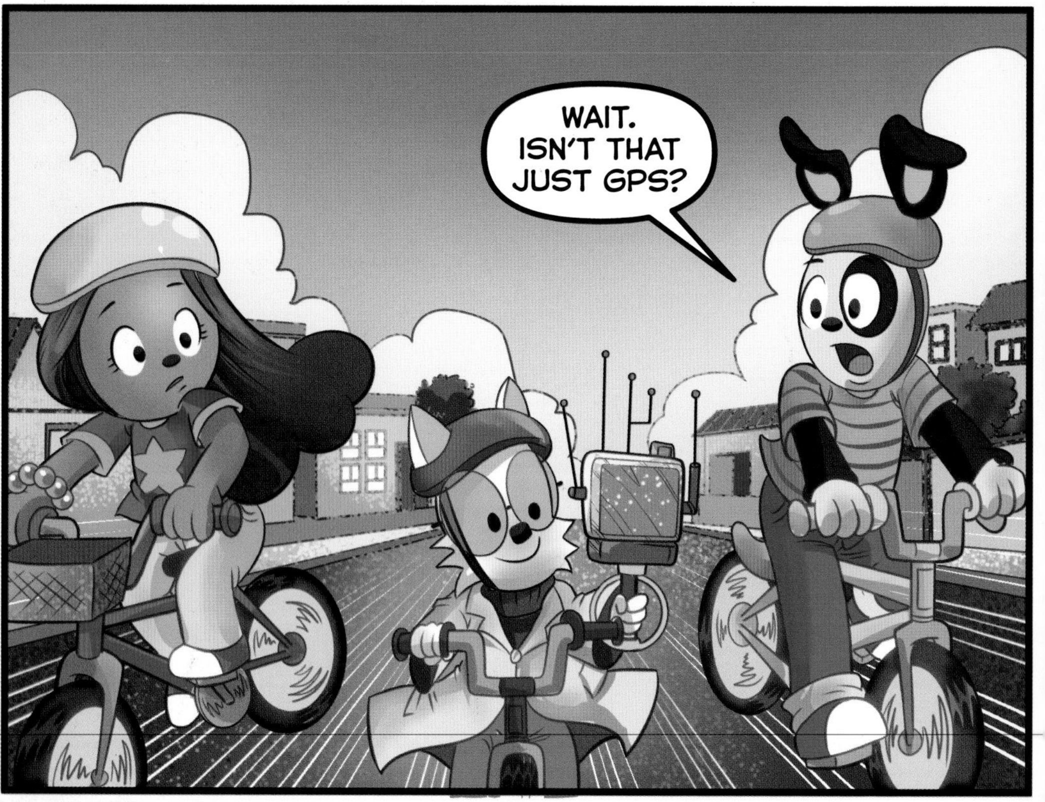
WAIT. ISN'T THAT JUST GPS?

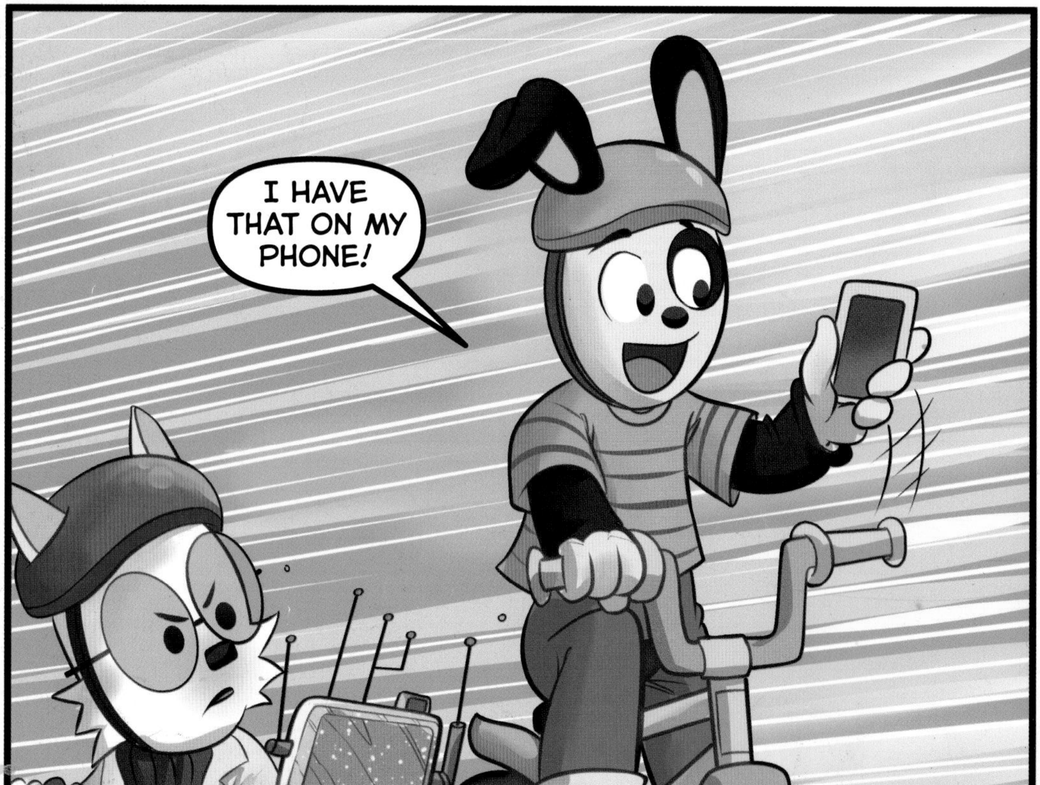
I HAVE THAT ON MY PHONE!

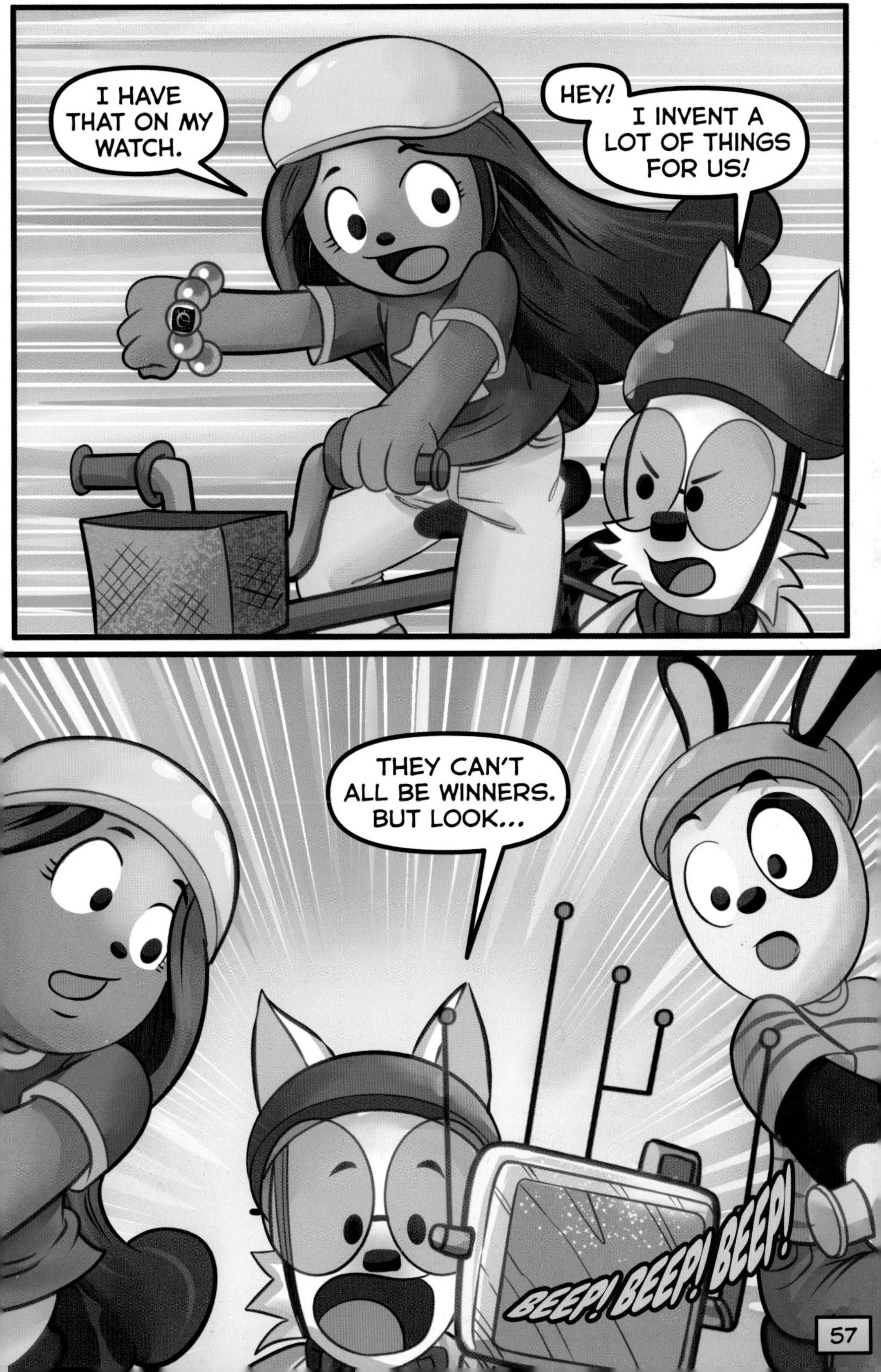
I HAVE THAT ON MY WATCH.
HEY!
I INVENT A LOT OF THINGS FOR US!
THEY CAN'T ALL BE WINNERS. BUT LOOK...
BEEP! BEEP! BEEP!

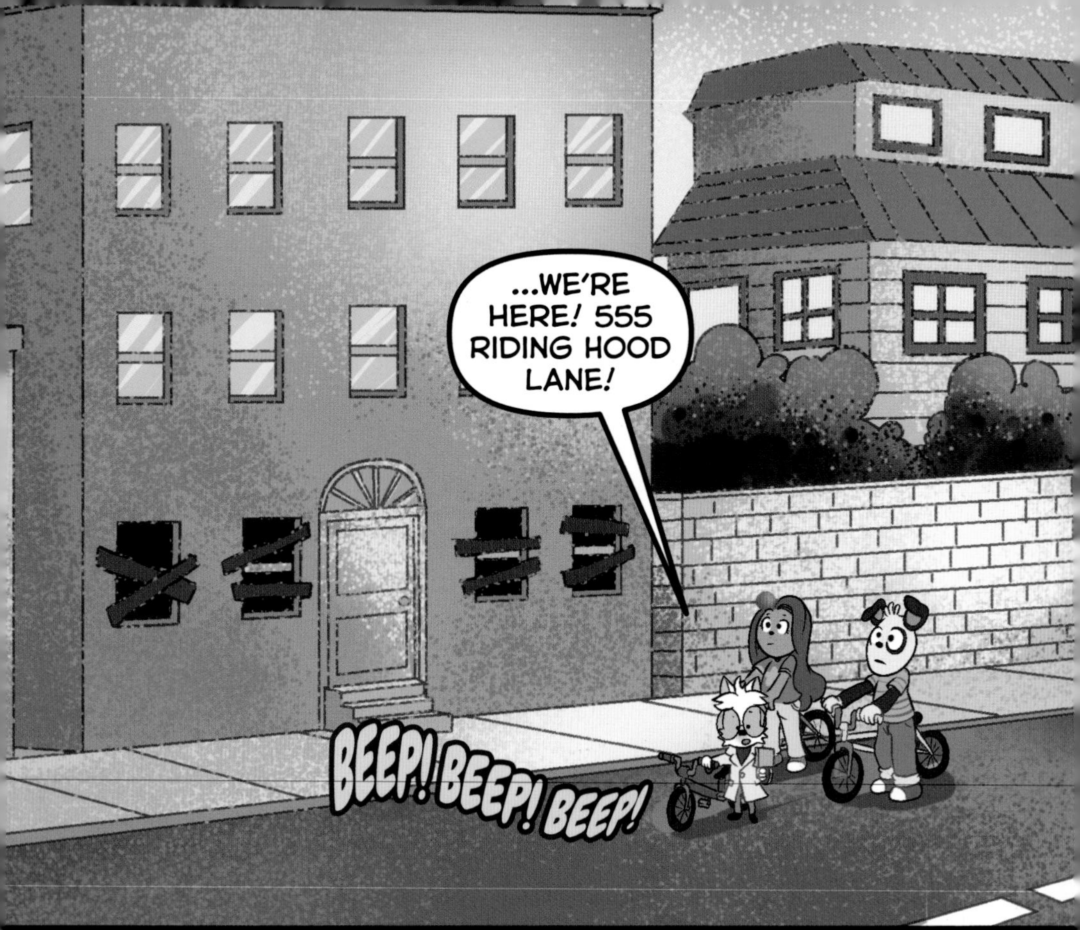
...WE'RE HERE! 555 RIDING HOOD LANE!
BEEP! BEEP! BEEP!

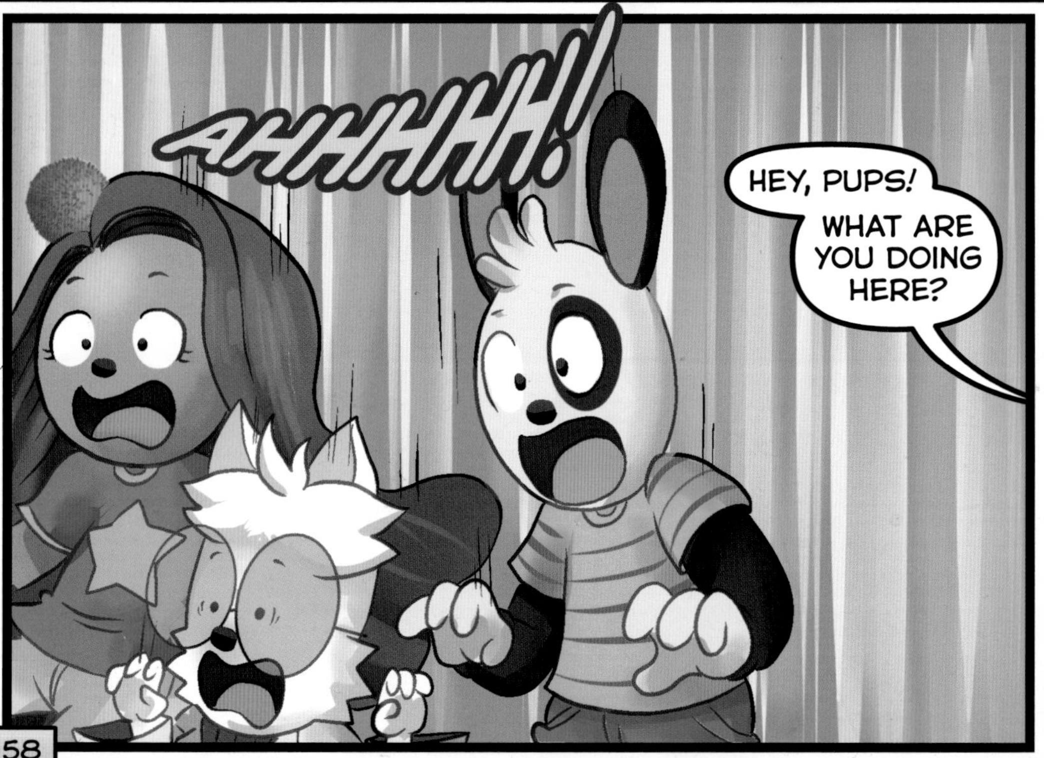
AHHHHH!
HEY, PUPS!
WHAT ARE YOU DOING HERE?

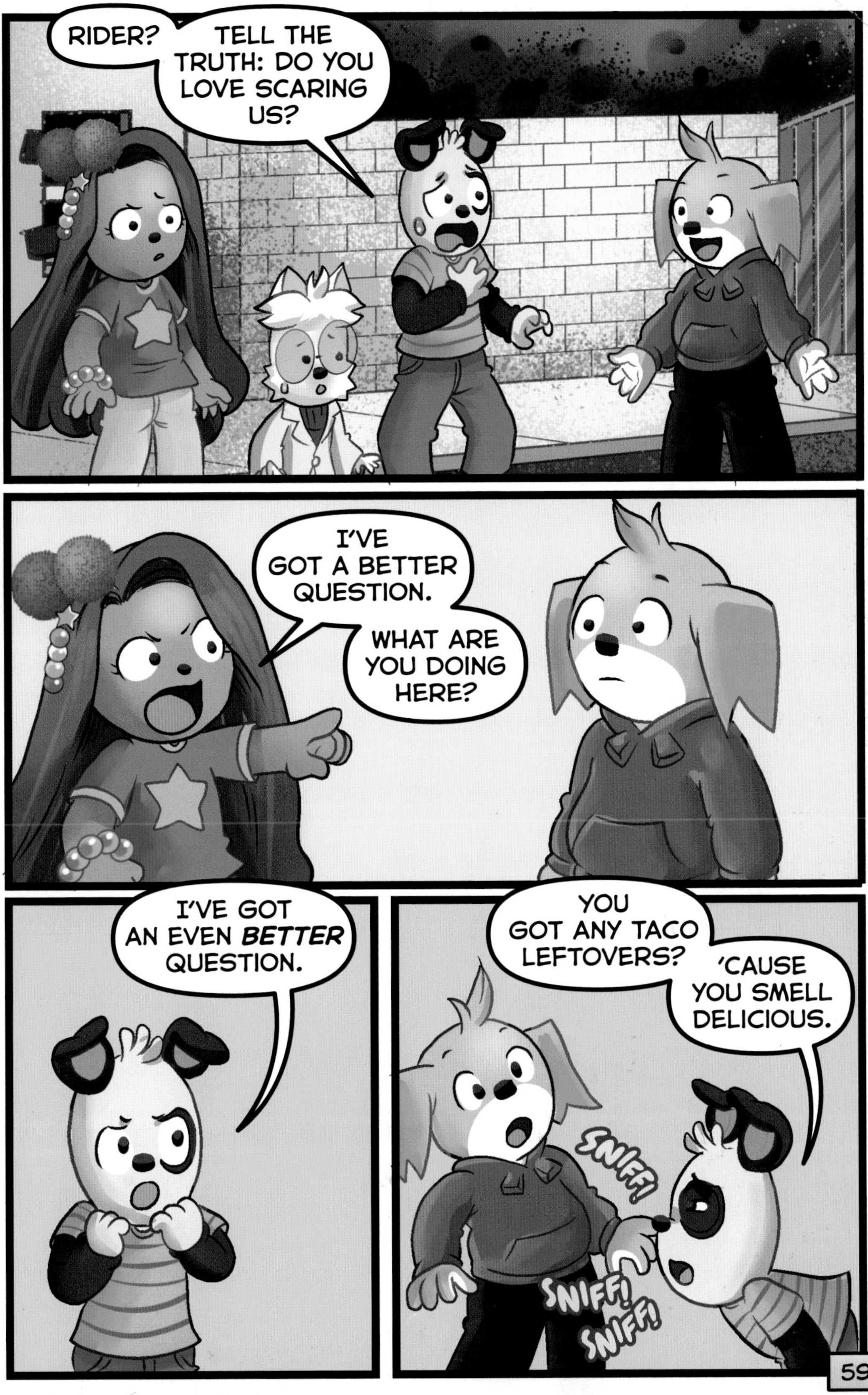
RIDER?
TELL THE TRUTH: DO YOU LOVE SCARING US?
I'VE GOT A BETTER QUESTION.
WHAT ARE YOU DOING HERE?
I'VE GOT AN EVEN *BETTER* QUESTION.
YOU GOT ANY TACO LEFTOVERS?
'CAUSE YOU SMELL DELICIOUS.
SNIFF!
SNIFF!
SNIFF!

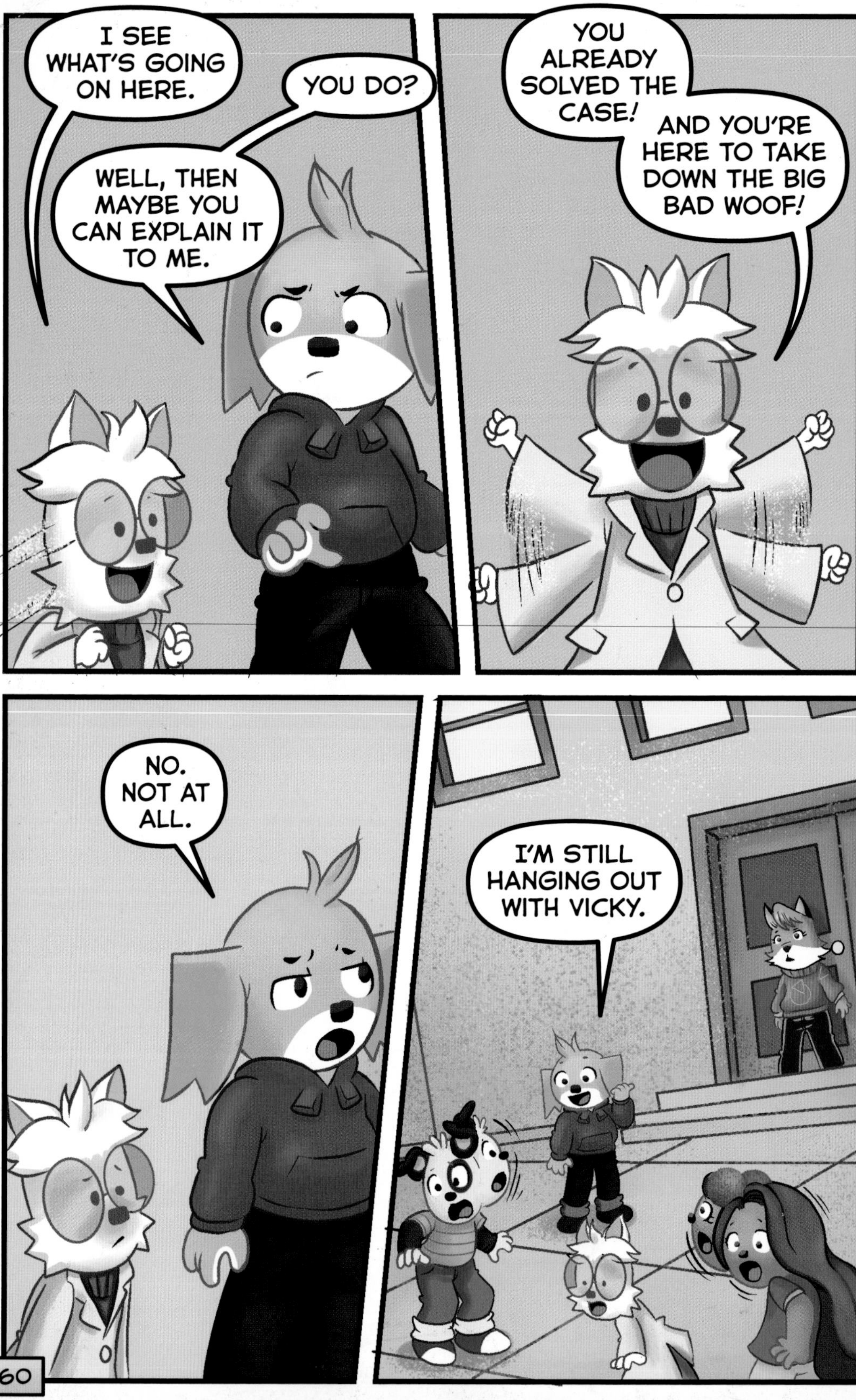
I SEE WHAT'S GOING ON HERE.
YOU DO?
WELL, THEN MAYBE YOU CAN EXPLAIN IT TO ME.
YOU ALREADY SOLVED THE CASE!
AND YOU'RE HERE TO TAKE DOWN THE BIG BAD WOOF!
NO. NOT AT ALL.
I'M STILL HANGING OUT WITH VICKY.

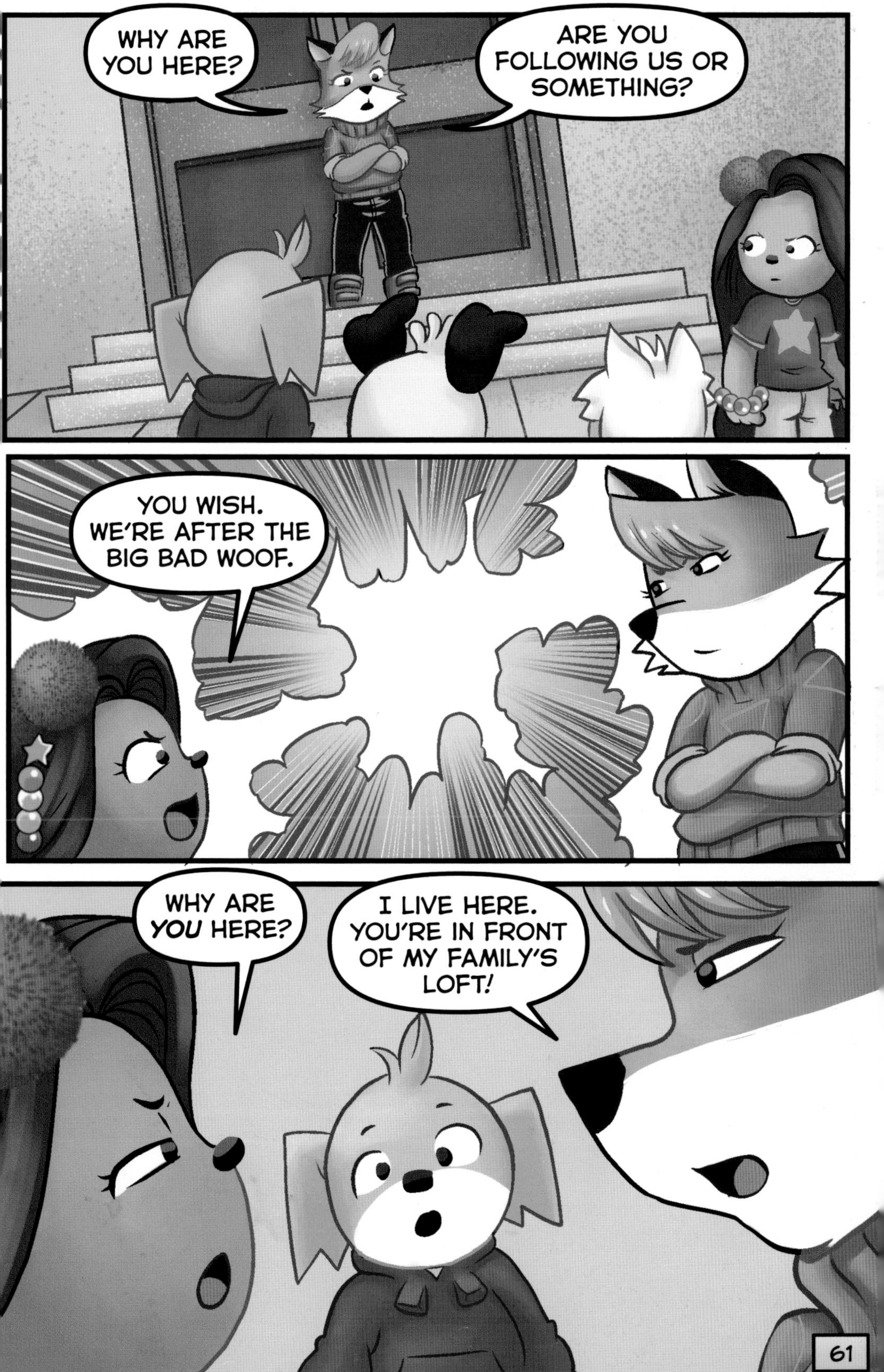
WHY ARE YOU HERE?
ARE YOU FOLLOWING US OR SOMETHING?
YOU WISH. WE'RE AFTER THE BIG BAD WOOF.
WHY ARE *YOU* HERE?
I LIVE HERE. YOU'RE IN FRONT OF MY FAMILY'S LOFT!

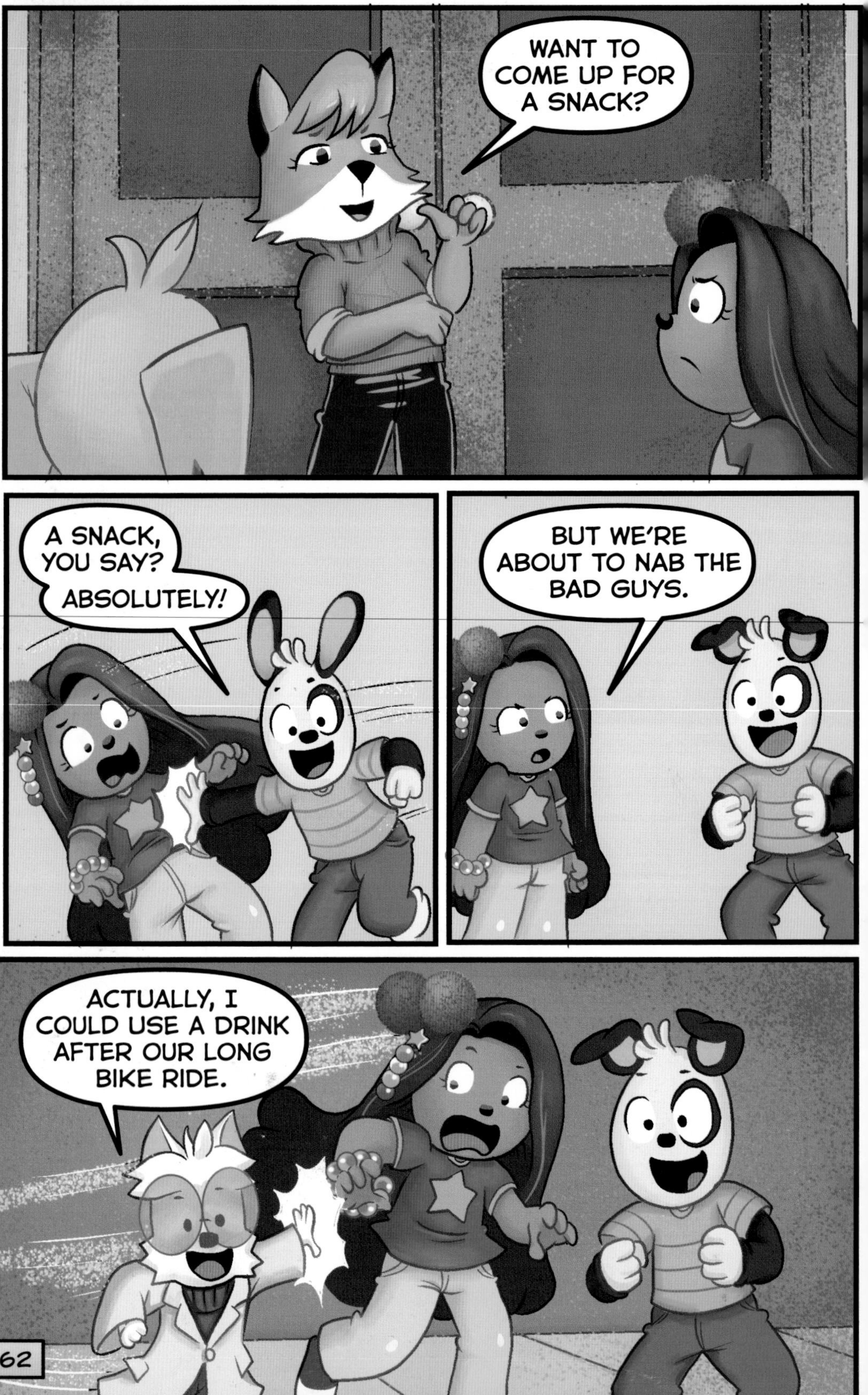
WANT TO COME UP FOR A SNACK?
A SNACK, YOU SAY? ABSOLUTELY!
BUT WE'RE ABOUT TO NAB THE BAD GUYS.
ACTUALLY, I COULD USE A DRINK AFTER OUR LONG BIKE RIDE.

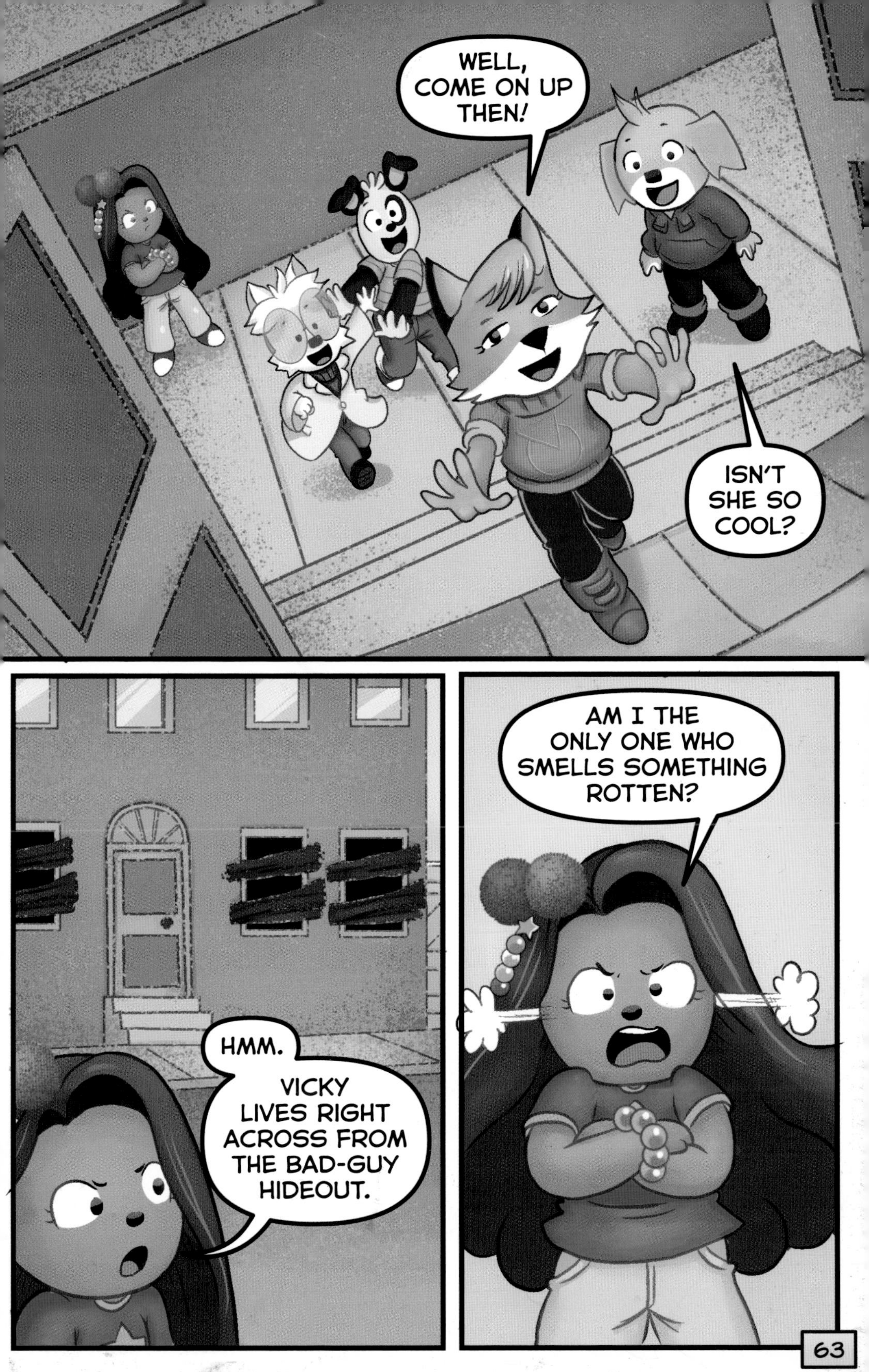
WELL, COME ON UP THEN!
ISN'T SHE SO COOL?
HMM.
VICKY LIVES RIGHT ACROSS FROM THE BAD-GUY HIDEOUT.
AM I THE ONLY ONE WHO SMELLS SOMETHING ROTTEN?

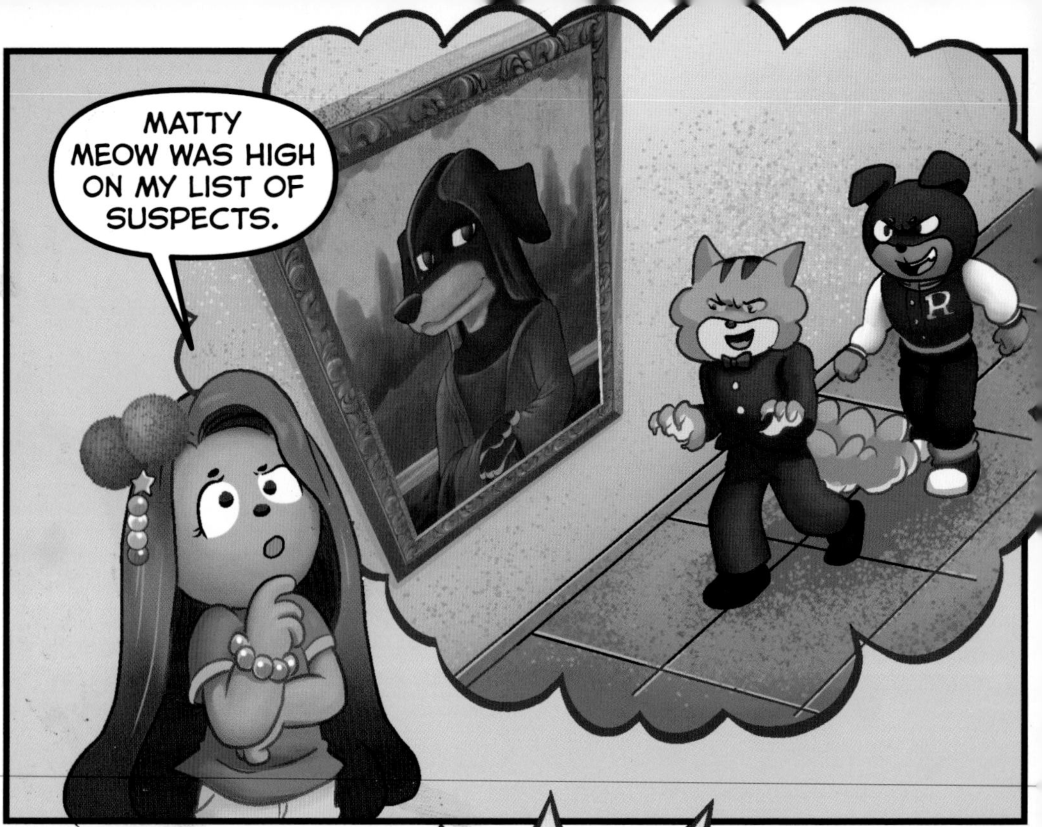
MATTY MEOW WAS HIGH ON MY LIST OF SUSPECTS.

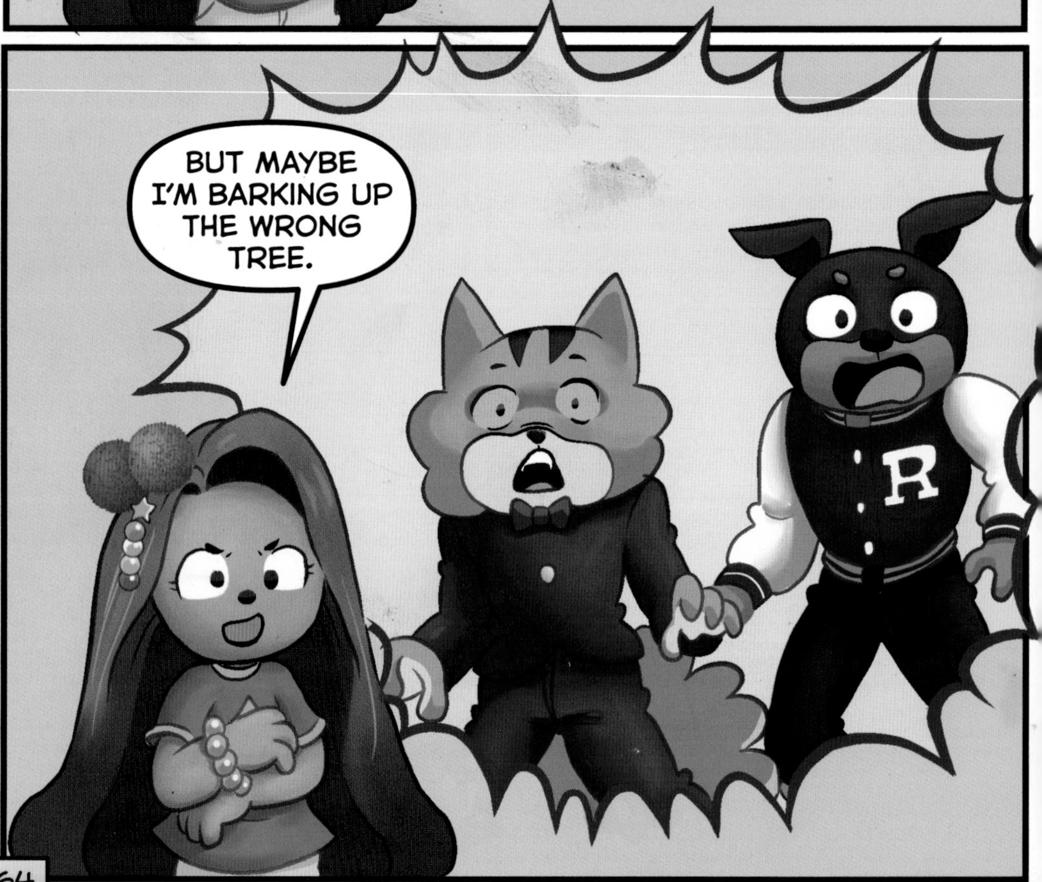
BUT MAYBE I'M BARKING UP THE WRONG TREE.

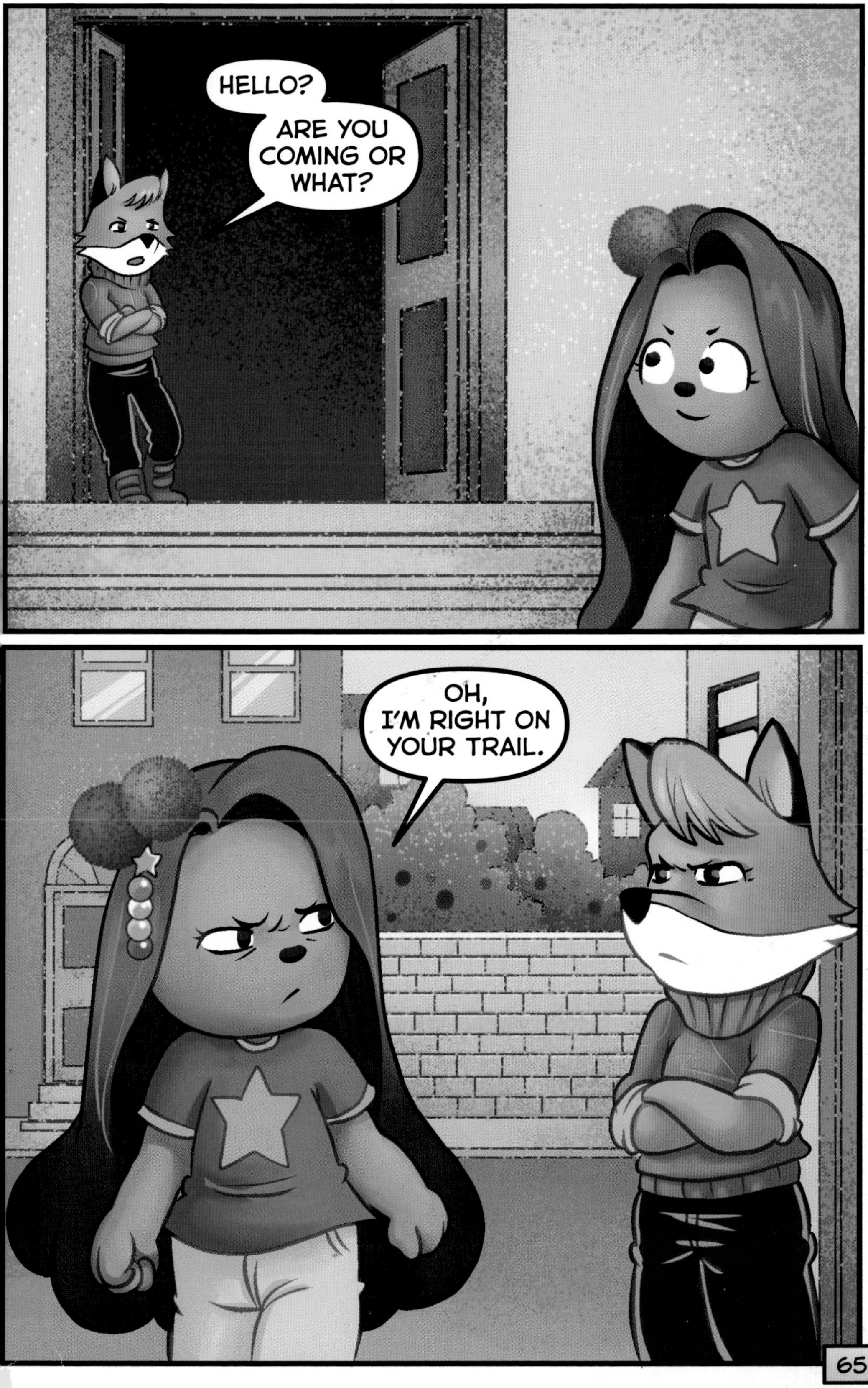
HELLO?
ARE YOU COMING OR WHAT?
OH, I'M RIGHT ON YOUR TRAIL.

CHAPTER 6

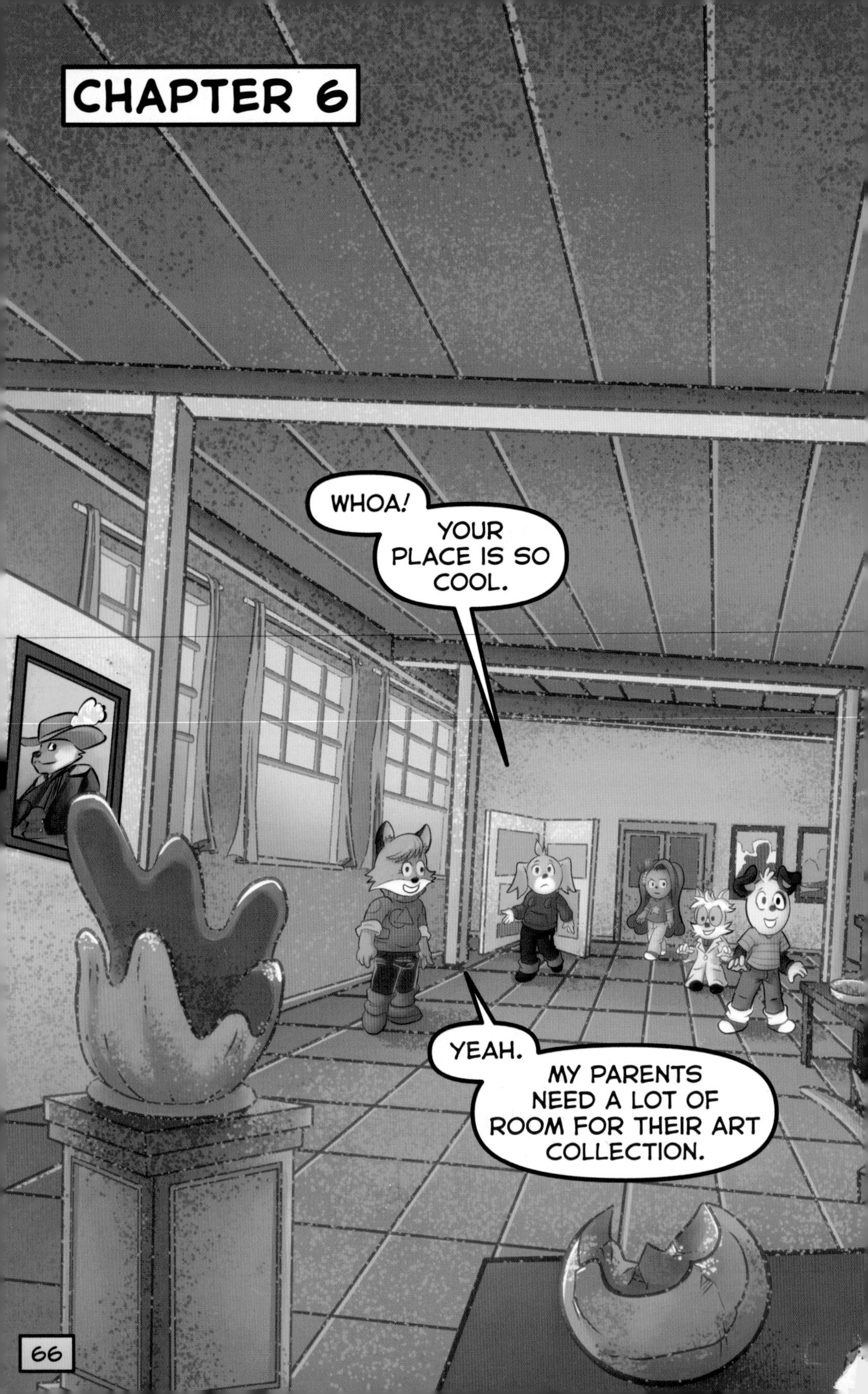
WHOA! YOUR PLACE IS SO COOL.
YEAH. MY PARENTS NEED A LOT OF ROOM FOR THEIR ART COLLECTION.

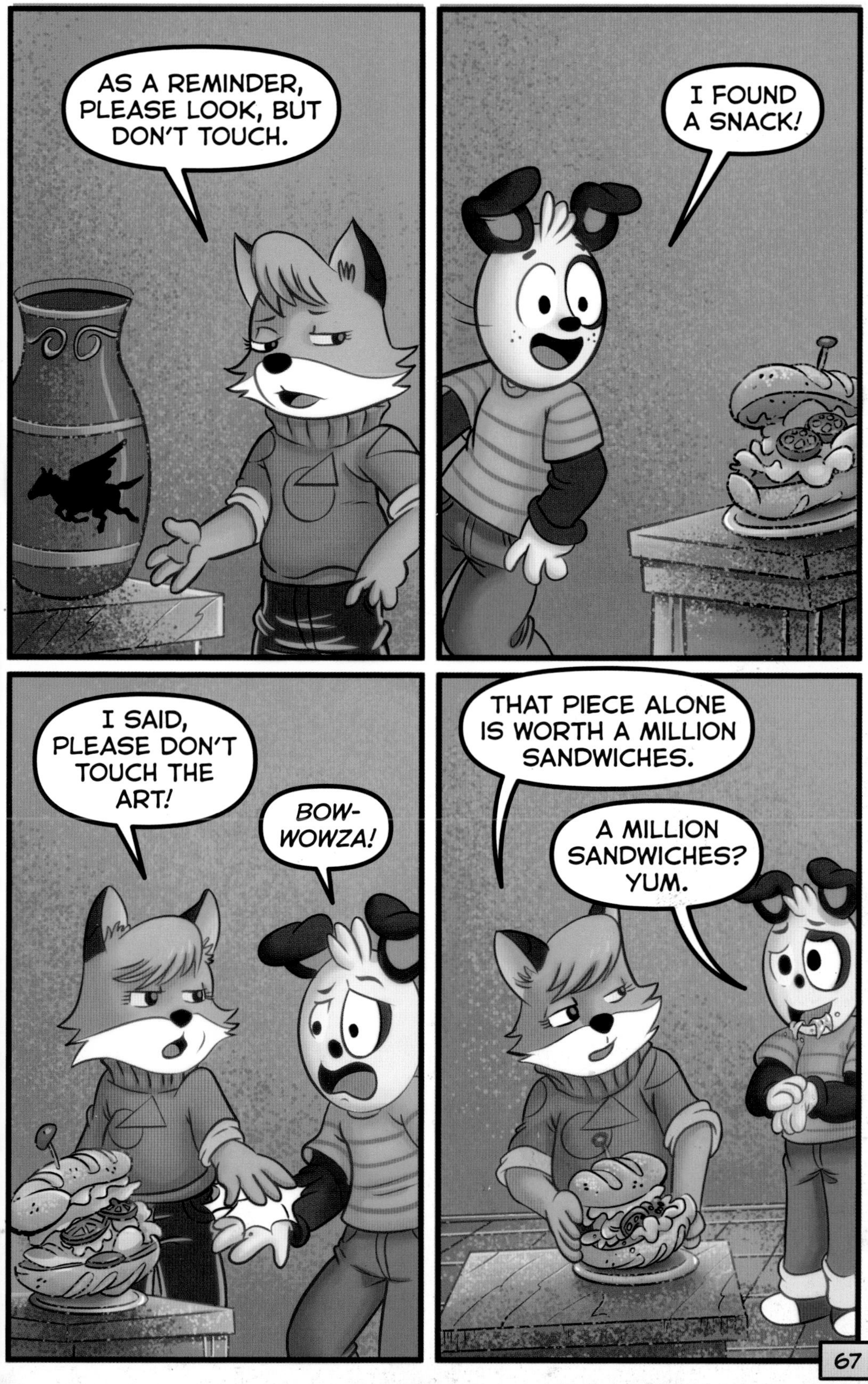
AS A REMINDER, PLEASE LOOK, BUT DON'T TOUCH.
I FOUND A SNACK!
I SAID, PLEASE DON'T TOUCH THE ART!
BOW-WOWZA!
THAT PIECE ALONE IS WORTH A MILLION SANDWICHES.
A MILLION SANDWICHES? YUM.

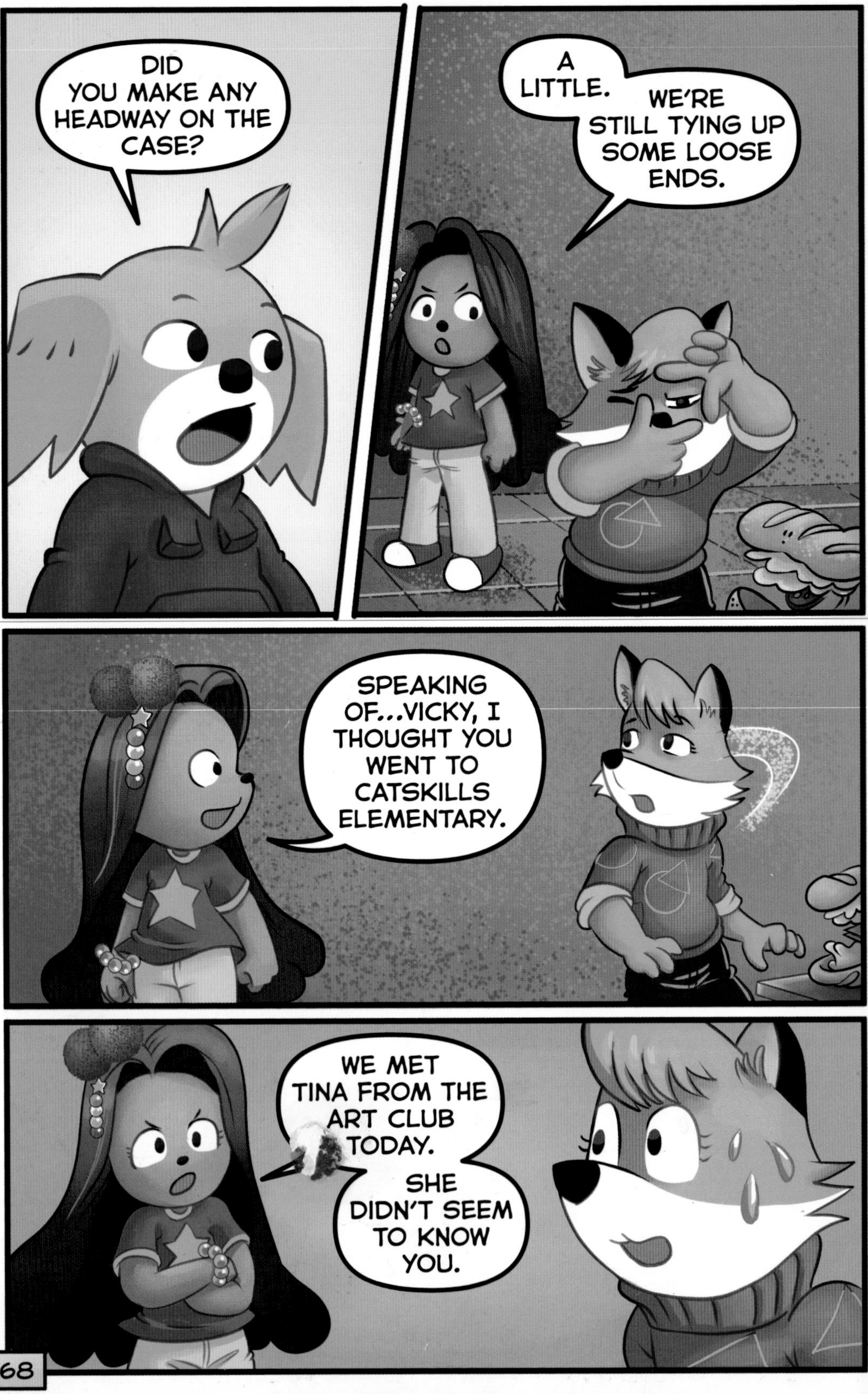

DID YOU MAKE ANY HEADWAY ON THE CASE?
A LITTLE.
WE'RE STILL TYING UP SOME LOOSE ENDS.
SPEAKING OF...VICKY, I THOUGHT YOU WENT TO CATSKILLS ELEMENTARY.
WE MET TINA FROM THE ART CLUB TODAY.
SHE DIDN'T SEEM TO KNOW YOU.

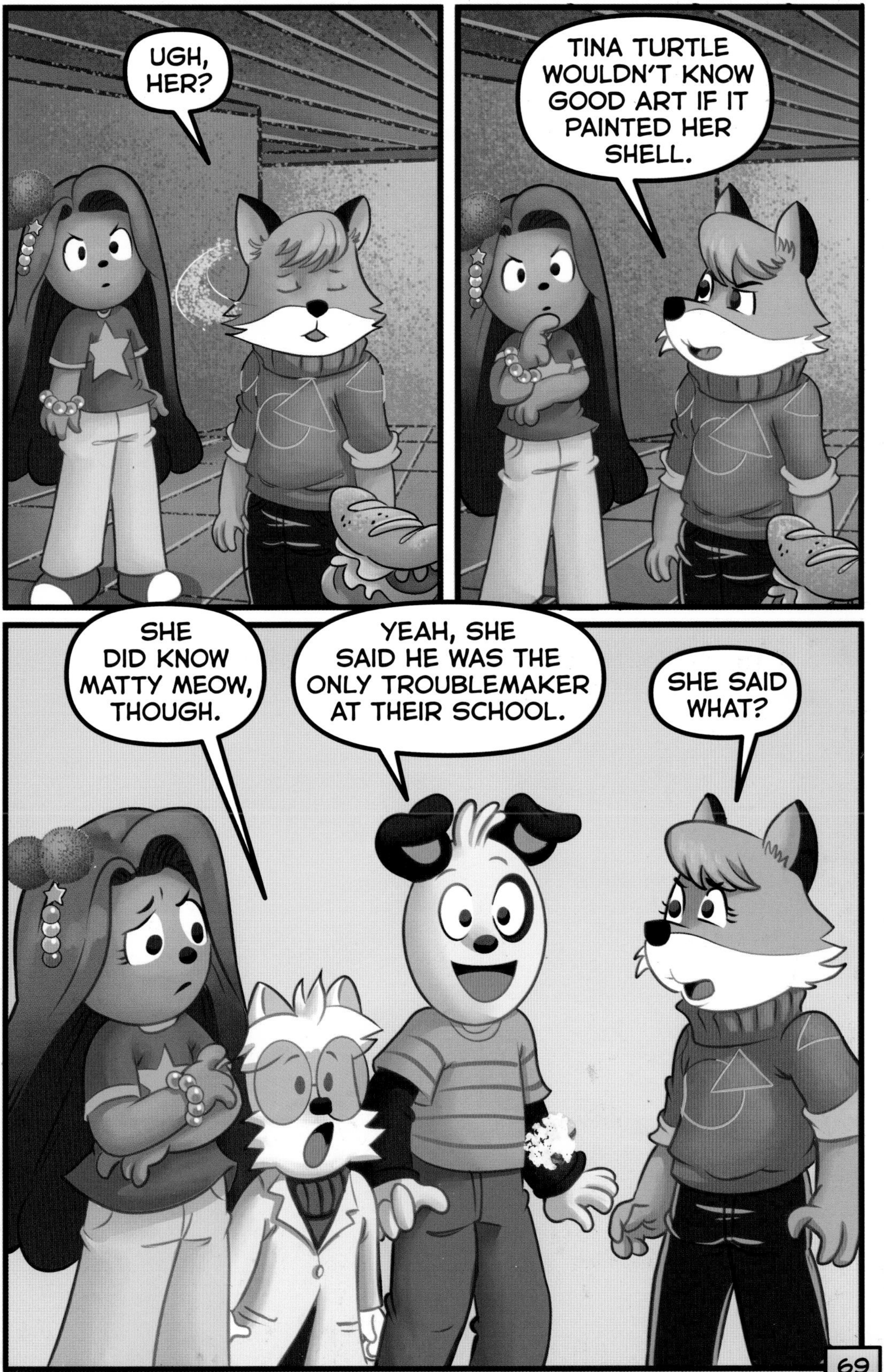

UGH, HER?
TINA TURTLE WOULDN'T KNOW GOOD ART IF IT PAINTED HER SHELL.
SHE DID KNOW MATTY MEOW, THOUGH.
YEAH, SHE SAID HE WAS THE ONLY TROUBLEMAKER AT THEIR SCHOOL.
SHE SAID WHAT?

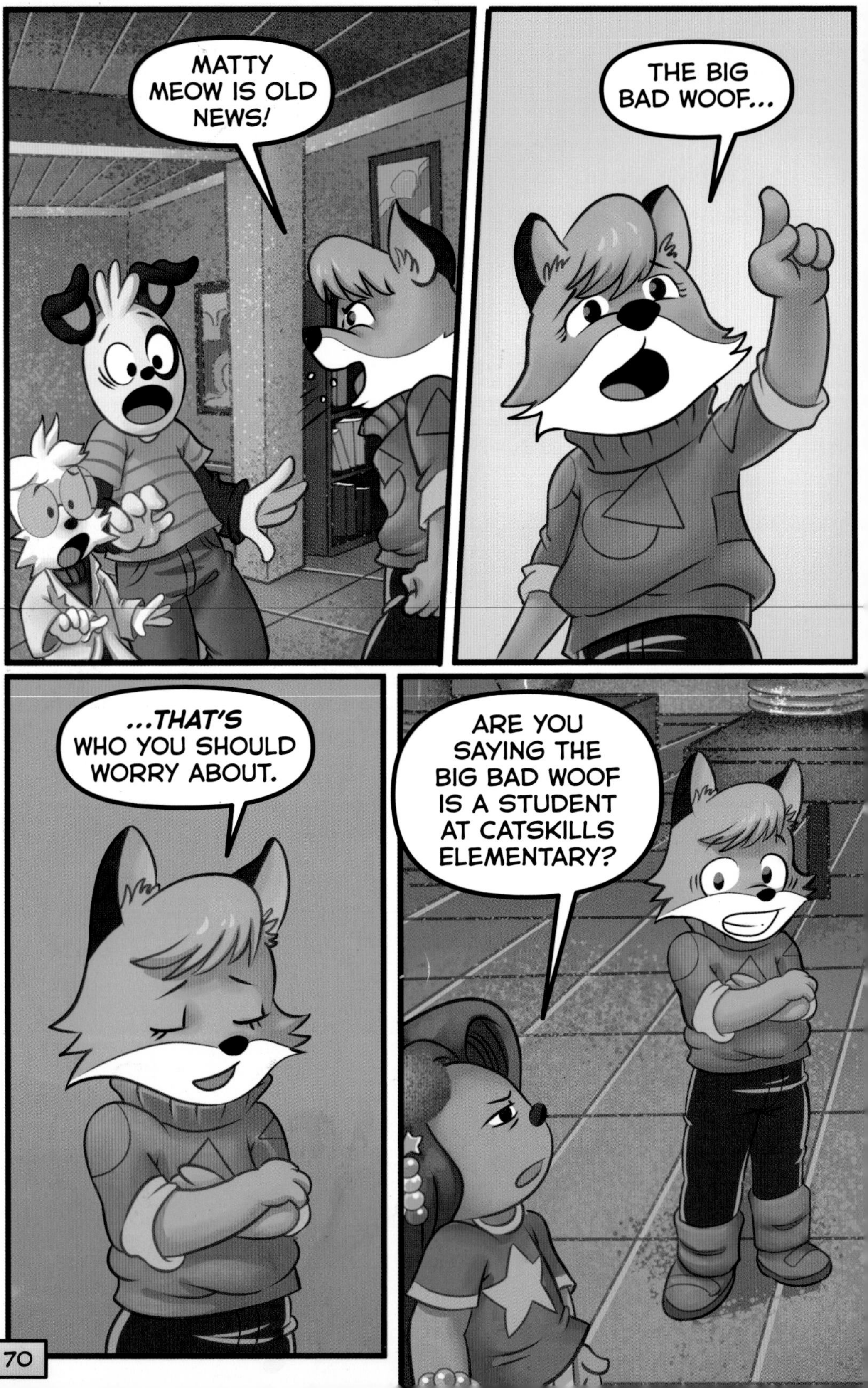
MATTY MEOW IS OLD NEWS!
THE BIG BAD WOOF...
...THAT'S WHO YOU SHOULD WORRY ABOUT.
ARE YOU SAYING THE BIG BAD WOOF IS A STUDENT AT CATSKILLS ELEMENTARY?

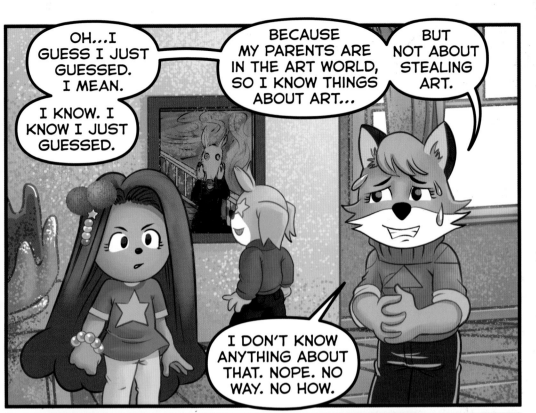

OH...I GUESS I JUST GUESSED. I MEAN.

I KNOW. I KNOW I JUST GUESSED.

BECAUSE MY PARENTS ARE IN THE ART WORLD, SO I KNOW THINGS ABOUT ART...

BUT NOT ABOUT STEALING ART.

I DON'T KNOW ANYTHING ABOUT THAT. NOPE. NO WAY. NO HOW.

RIDER, ARE YOU LISTENING TO THIS?

WHOA.

AN ORIGINAL AARDVARK MUNCH PAINTING?

71

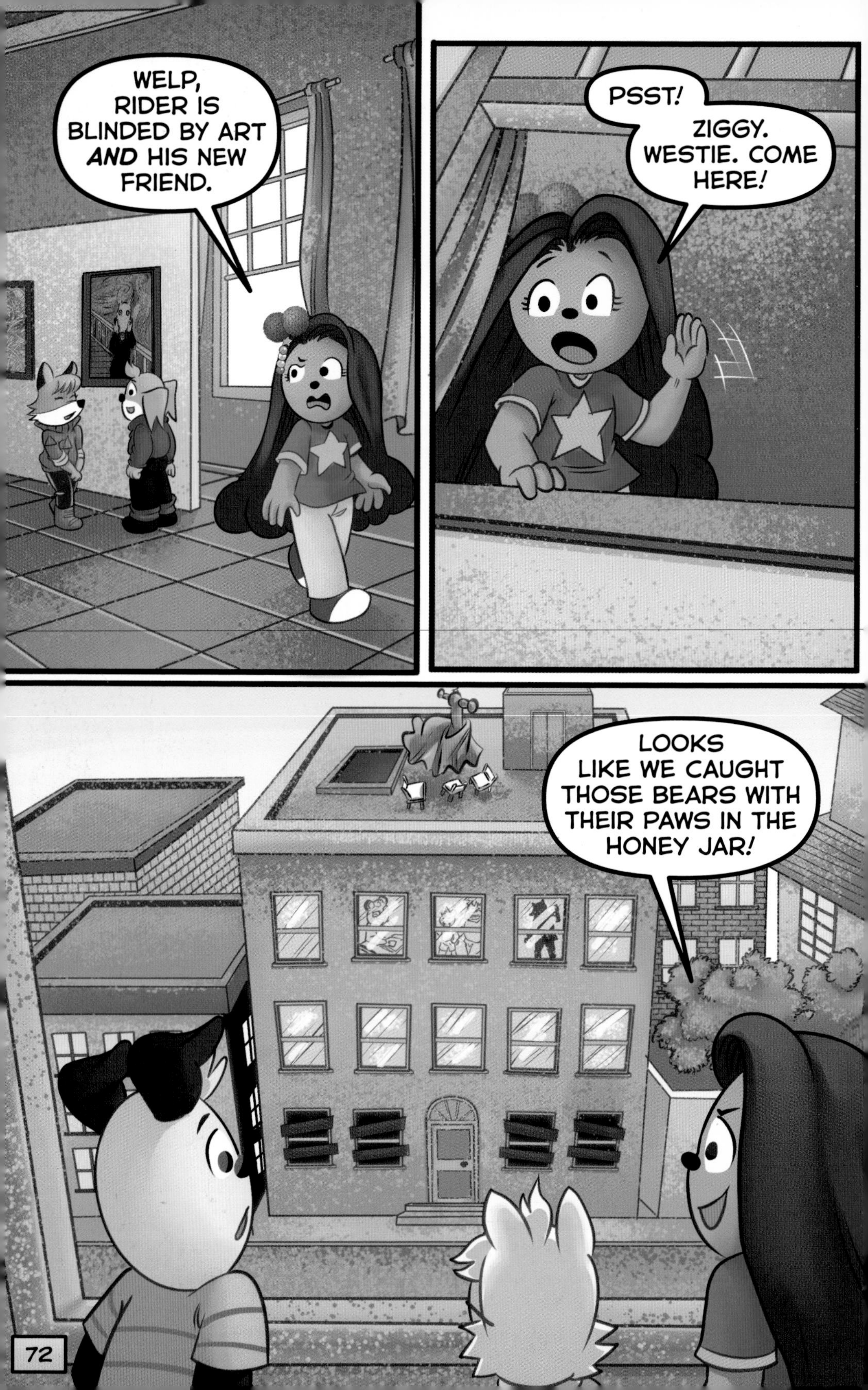
WELP, RIDER IS BLINDED BY ART *AND* HIS NEW FRIEND.
PSST!
ZIGGY. WESTIE. COME HERE!
LOOKS LIKE WE CAUGHT THOSE BEARS WITH THEIR PAWS IN THE HONEY JAR!

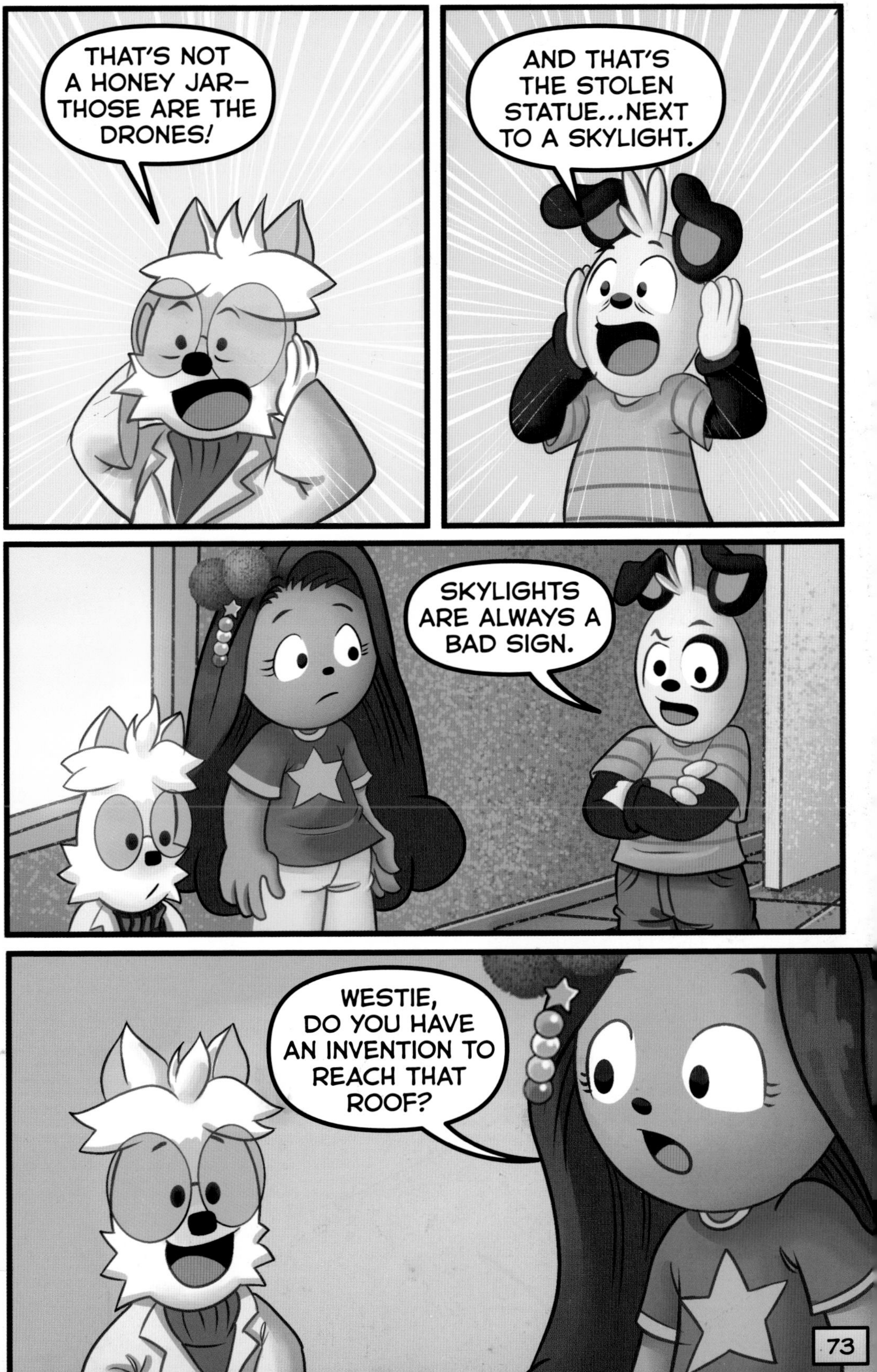
THAT'S NOT A HONEY JAR—THOSE ARE THE DRONES!
AND THAT'S THE STOLEN STATUE...NEXT TO A SKYLIGHT.
SKYLIGHTS ARE ALWAYS A BAD SIGN.
WESTIE, DO YOU HAVE AN INVENTION TO REACH THAT ROOF?

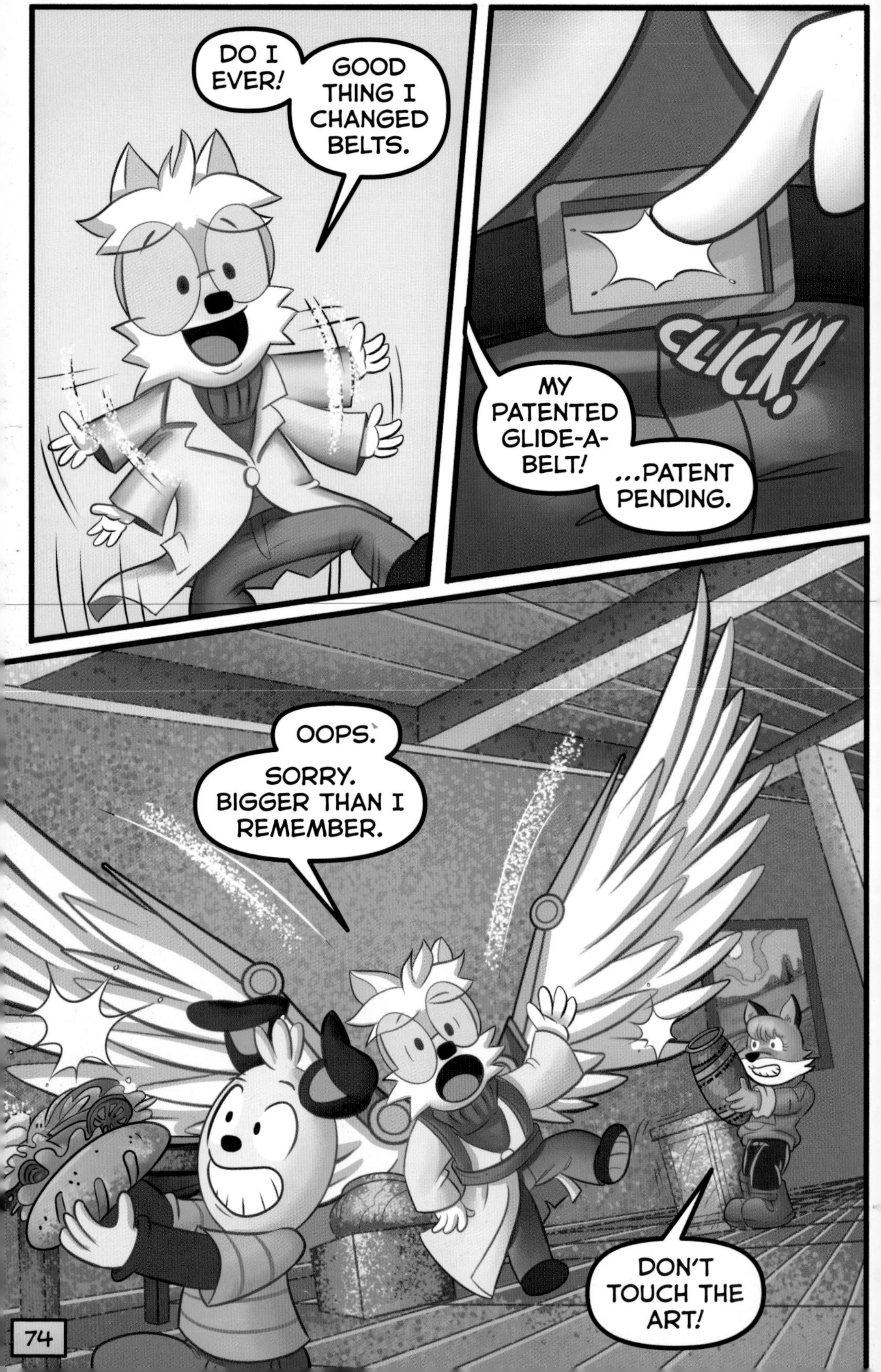
DO I EVER!
GOOD THING I CHANGED BELTS.
CLICK!
MY PATENTED GLIDE-A-BELT!
...PATENT PENDING.
OOPS.
SORRY. BIGGER THAN I REMEMBER.
DON'T TOUCH THE ART!

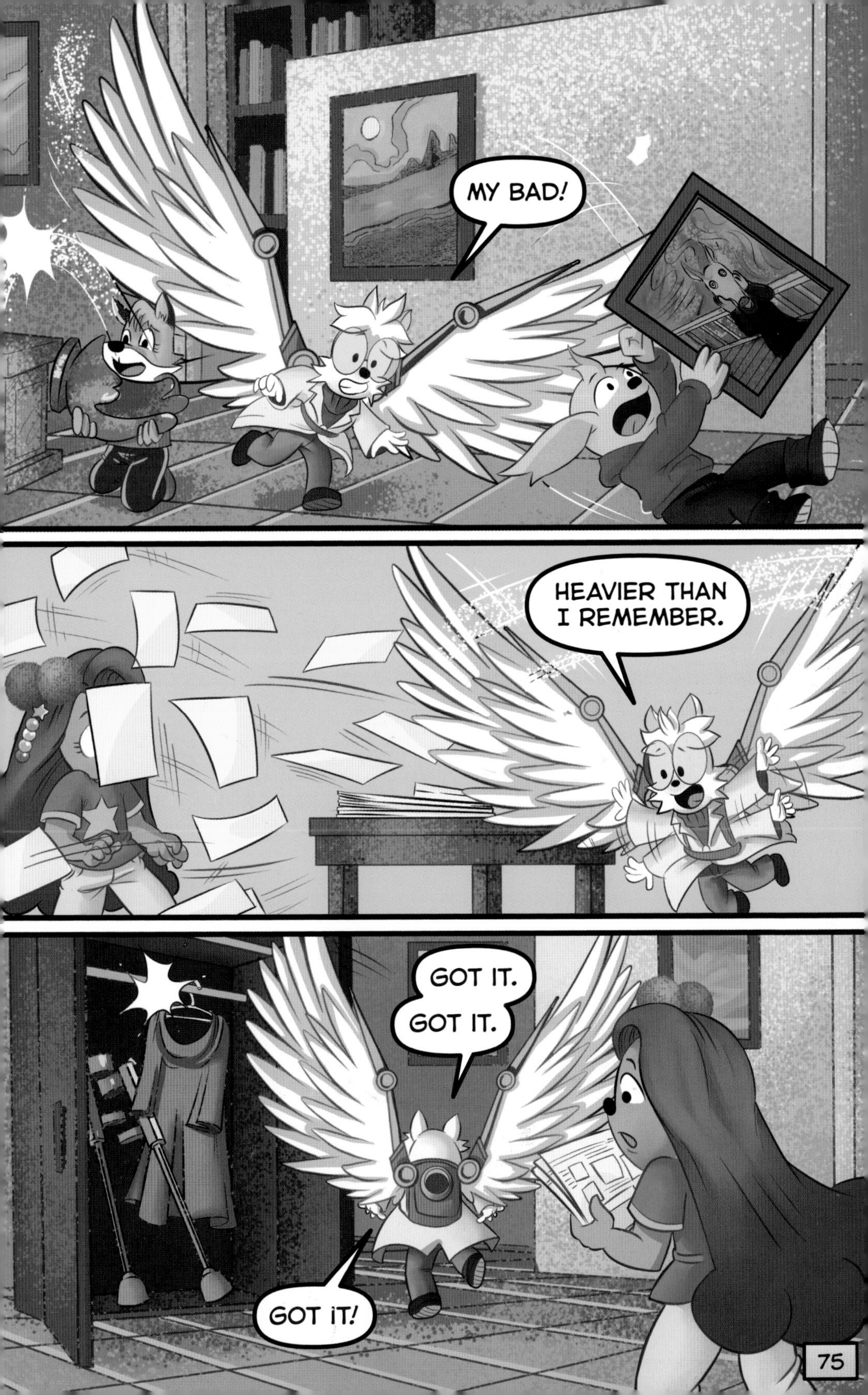
MY BAD!
HEAVIER THAN I REMEMBER.
GOT IT.
GOT IT.
GOT IT!

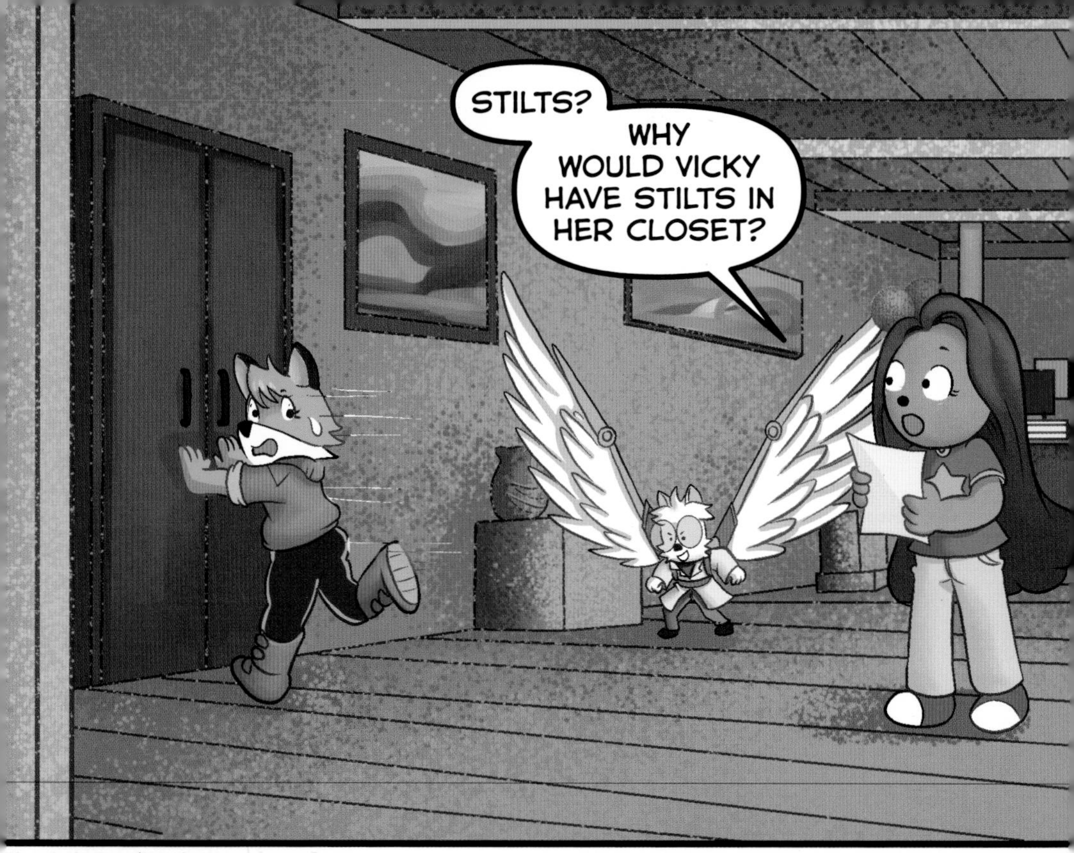
STILTS?
WHY WOULD VICKY HAVE STILTS IN HER CLOSET?

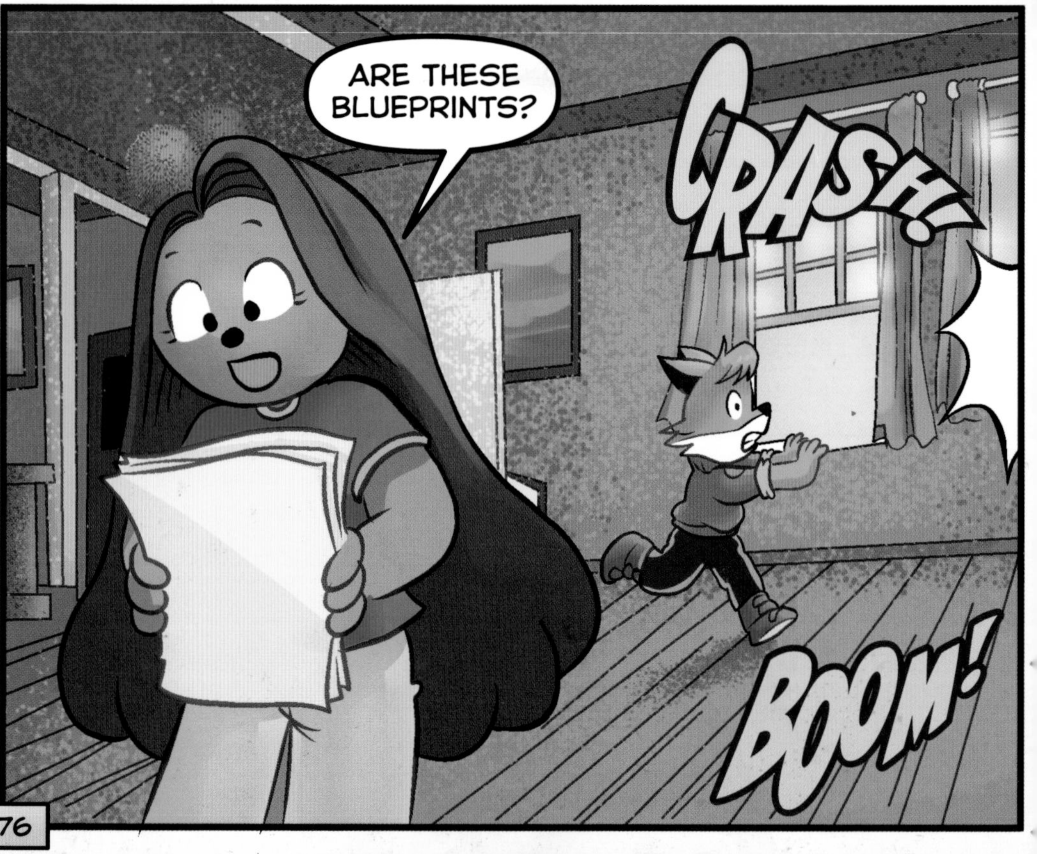
ARE THESE BLUEPRINTS?
CRASH!
BOOM!

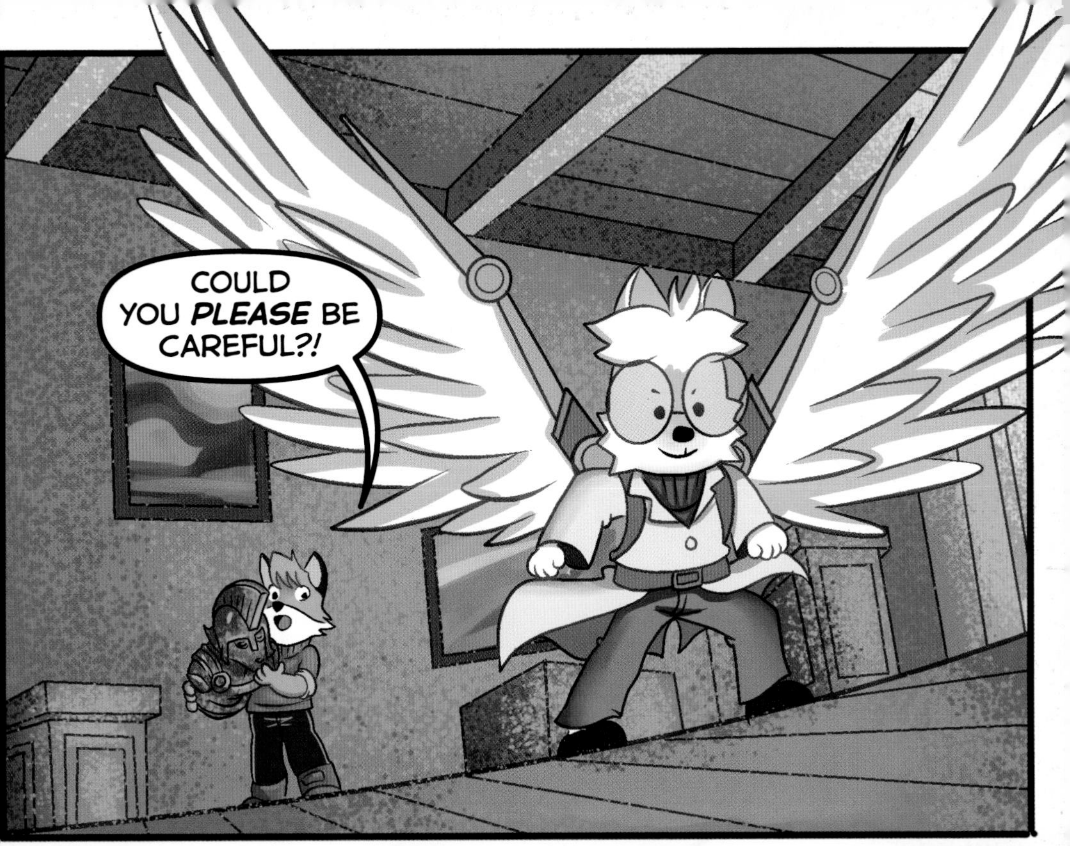
COULD YOU *PLEASE* BE CAREFUL?!

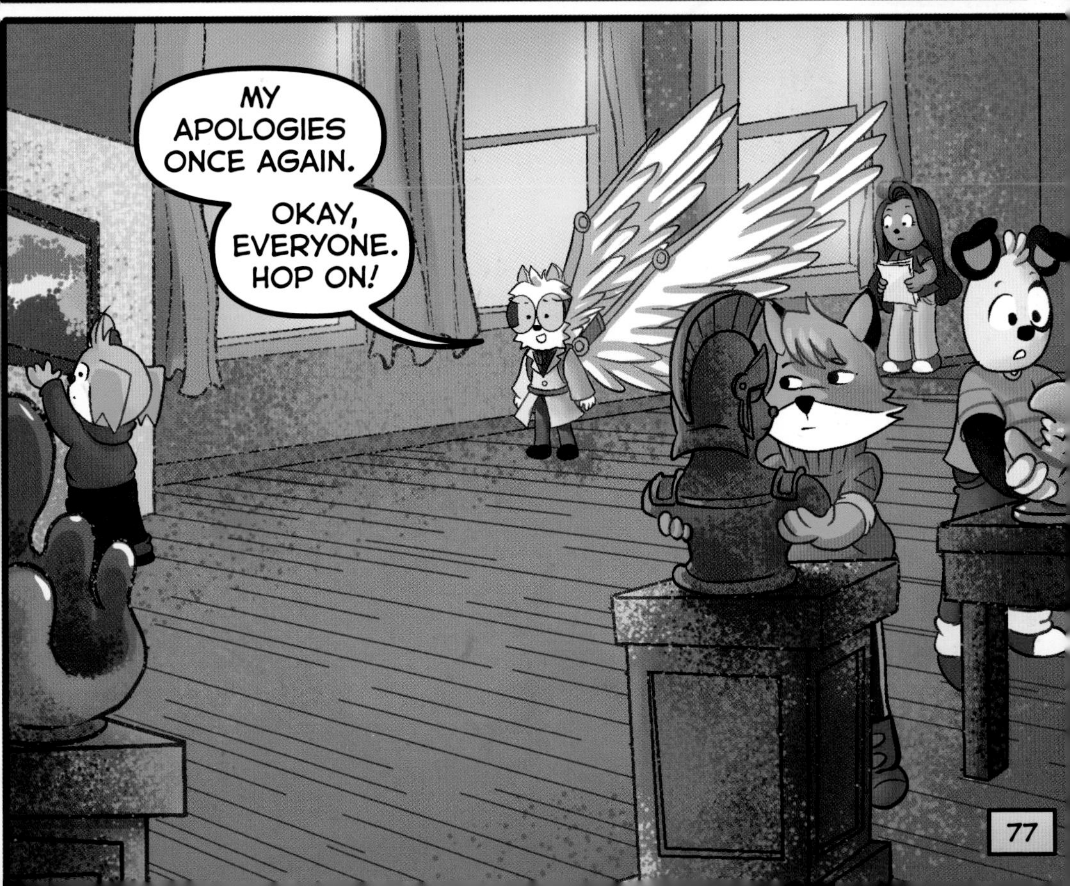
MY APOLOGIES ONCE AGAIN.
OKAY, EVERYONE. HOP ON!

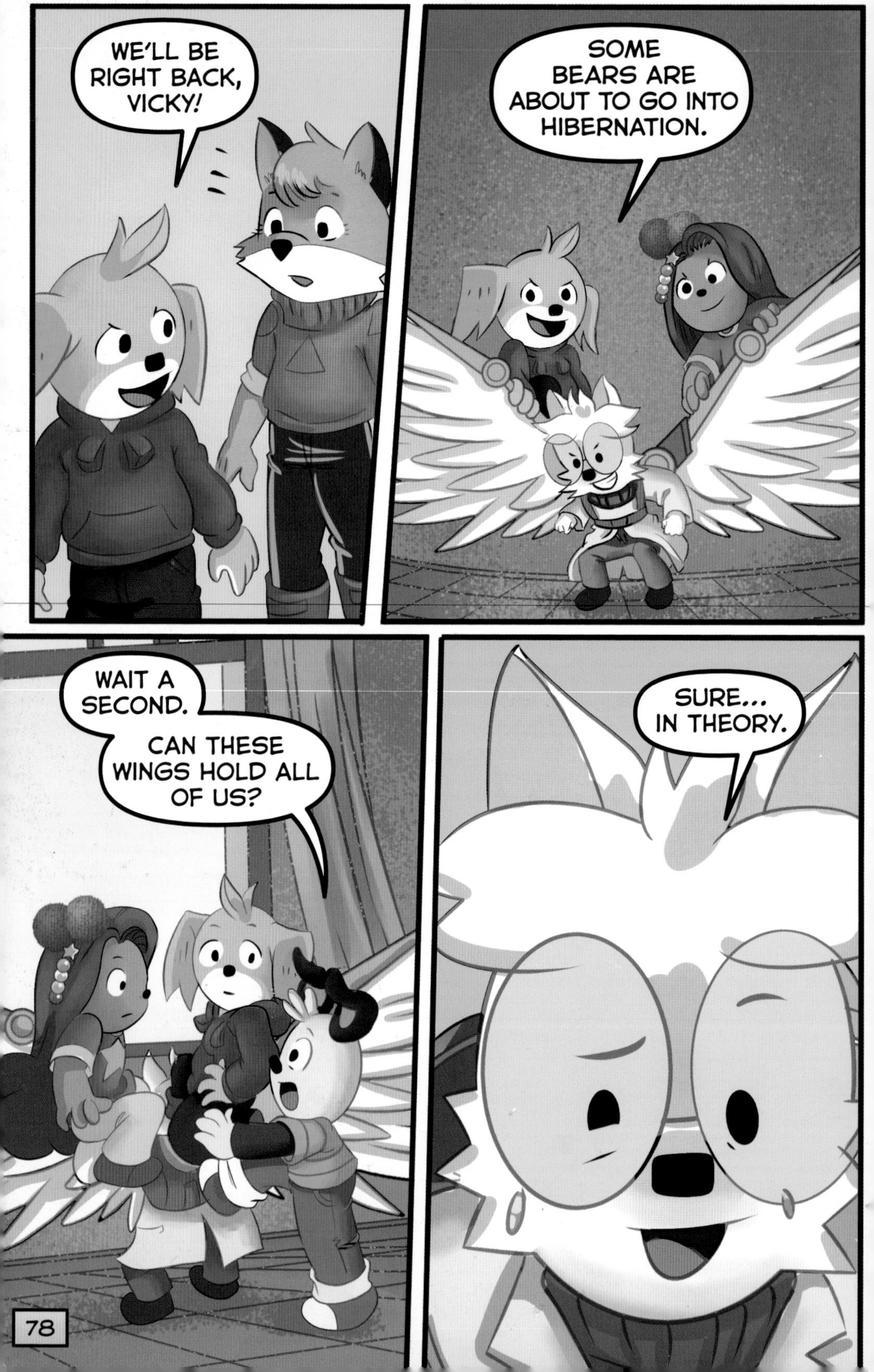
WE'LL BE RIGHT BACK, VICKY!
SOME BEARS ARE ABOUT TO GO INTO HIBERNATION.
WAIT A SECOND.
CAN THESE WINGS HOLD ALL OF US?
SURE... IN THEORY.

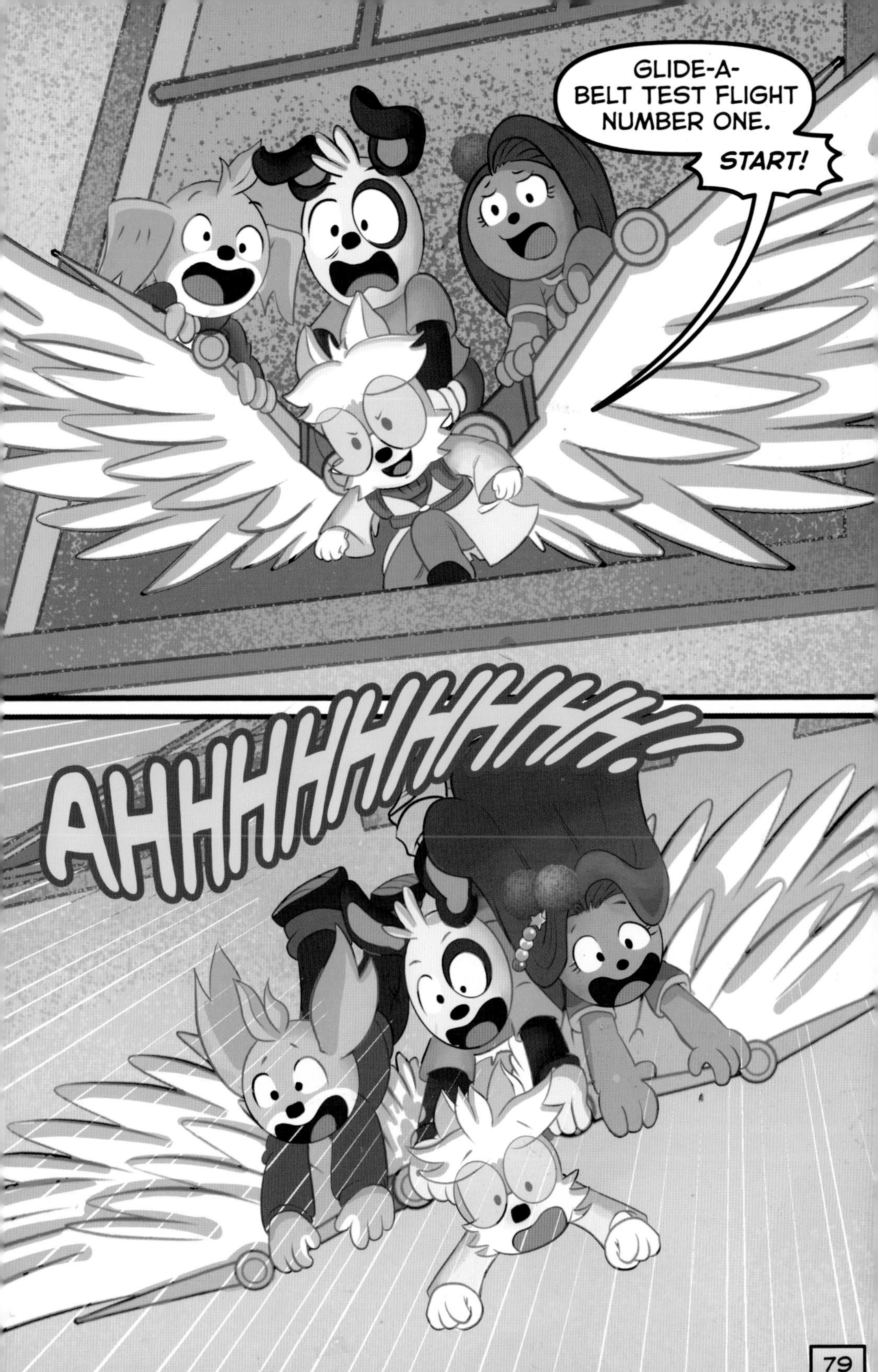
GLIDE-A-BELT TEST FLIGHT NUMBER ONE.
START!
AHHHHHHHHHH!

CHAPTER 7

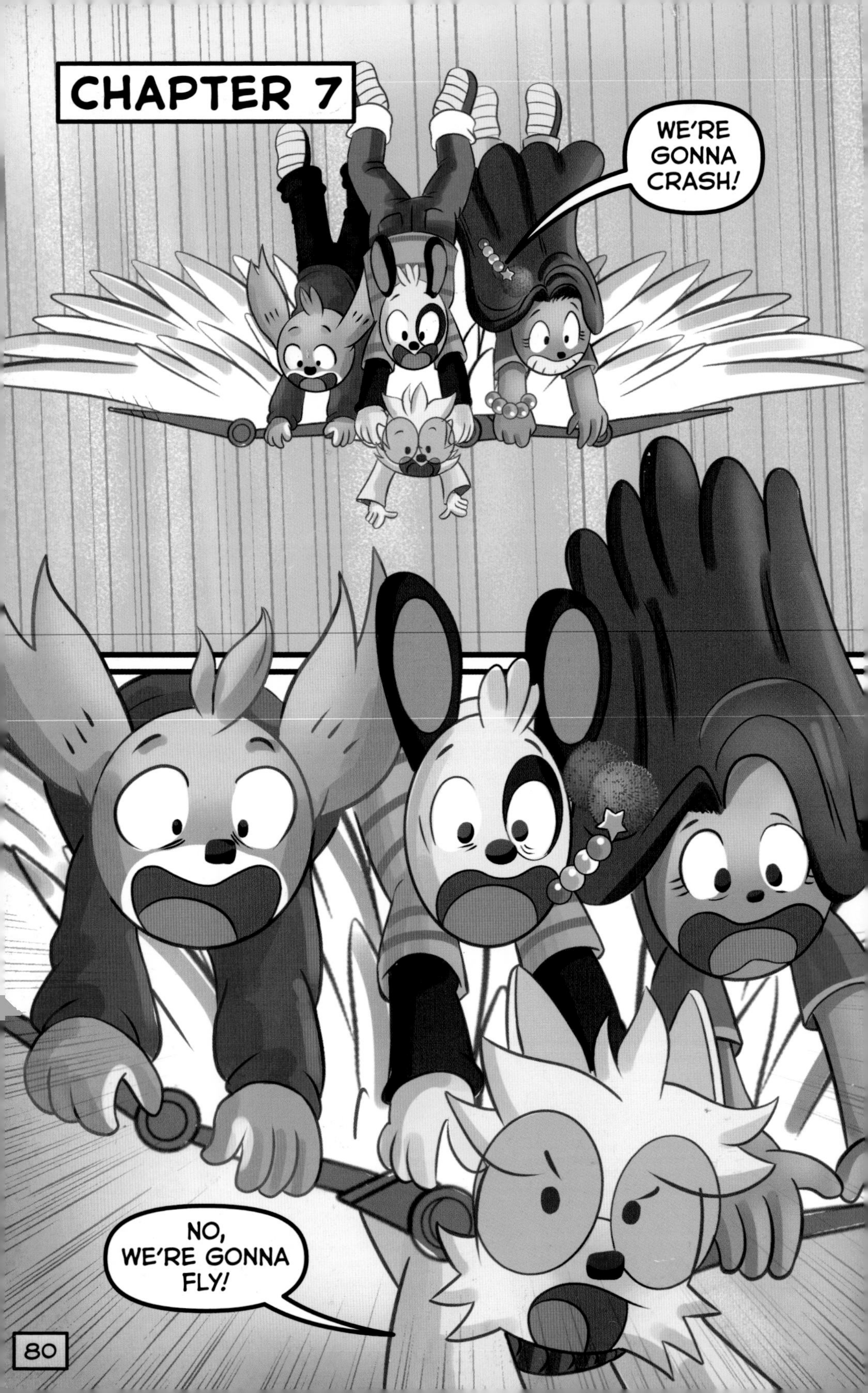
WE'RE GONNA CRASH!
NO, WE'RE GONNA FLY!

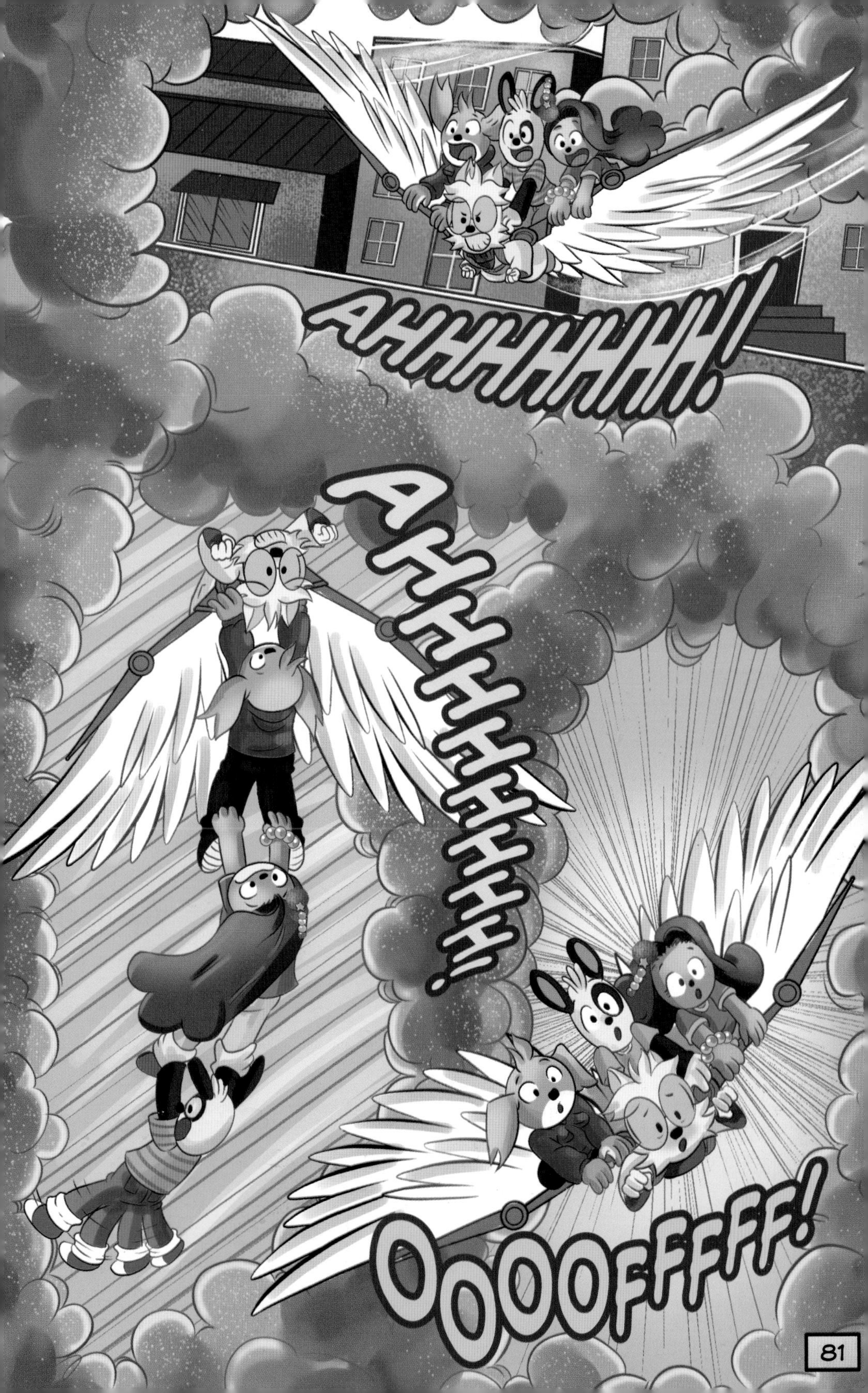
AHHHHHHH!
AHHHHHHHHHH!!
OOOOFFFF!

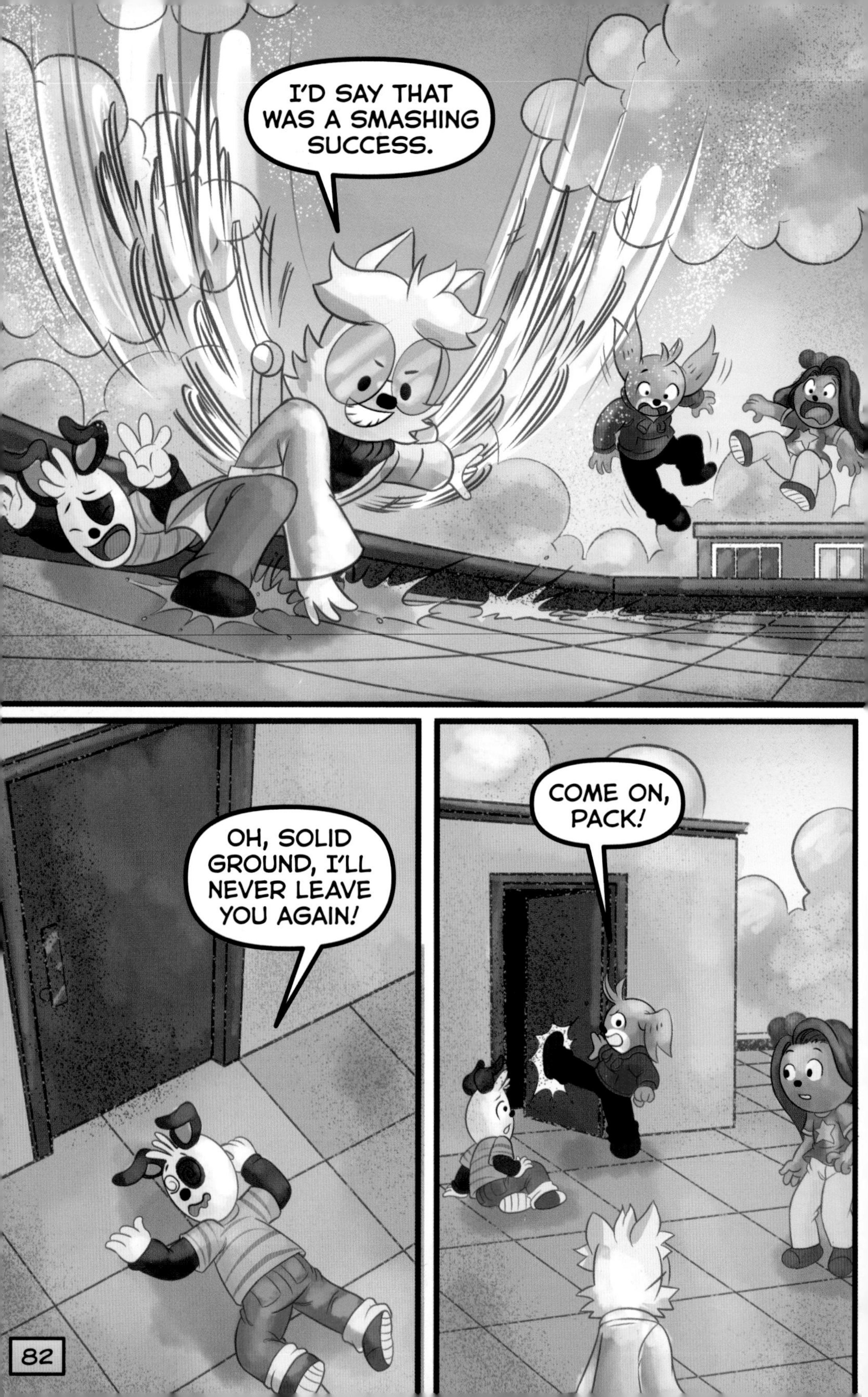
I'D SAY THAT WAS A SMASHING SUCCESS.
OH, SOLID GROUND, I'LL NEVER LEAVE YOU AGAIN!
COME ON, PACK!

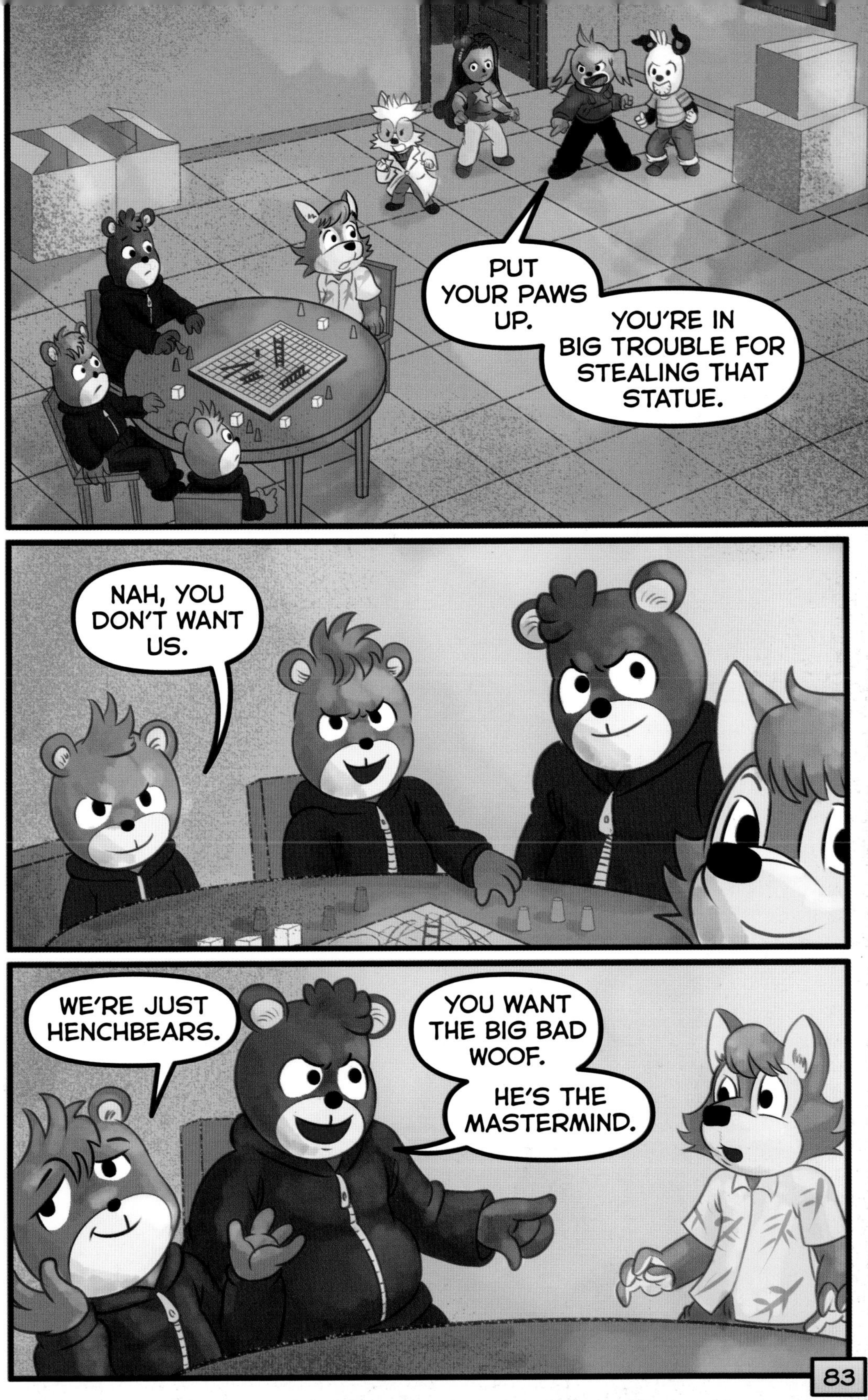
PUT YOUR PAWS UP.
YOU'RE IN BIG TROUBLE FOR STEALING THAT STATUE.
NAH, YOU DON'T WANT US.
WE'RE JUST HENCHBEARS.
YOU WANT THE BIG BAD WOOF.
HE'S THE MASTERMIND.

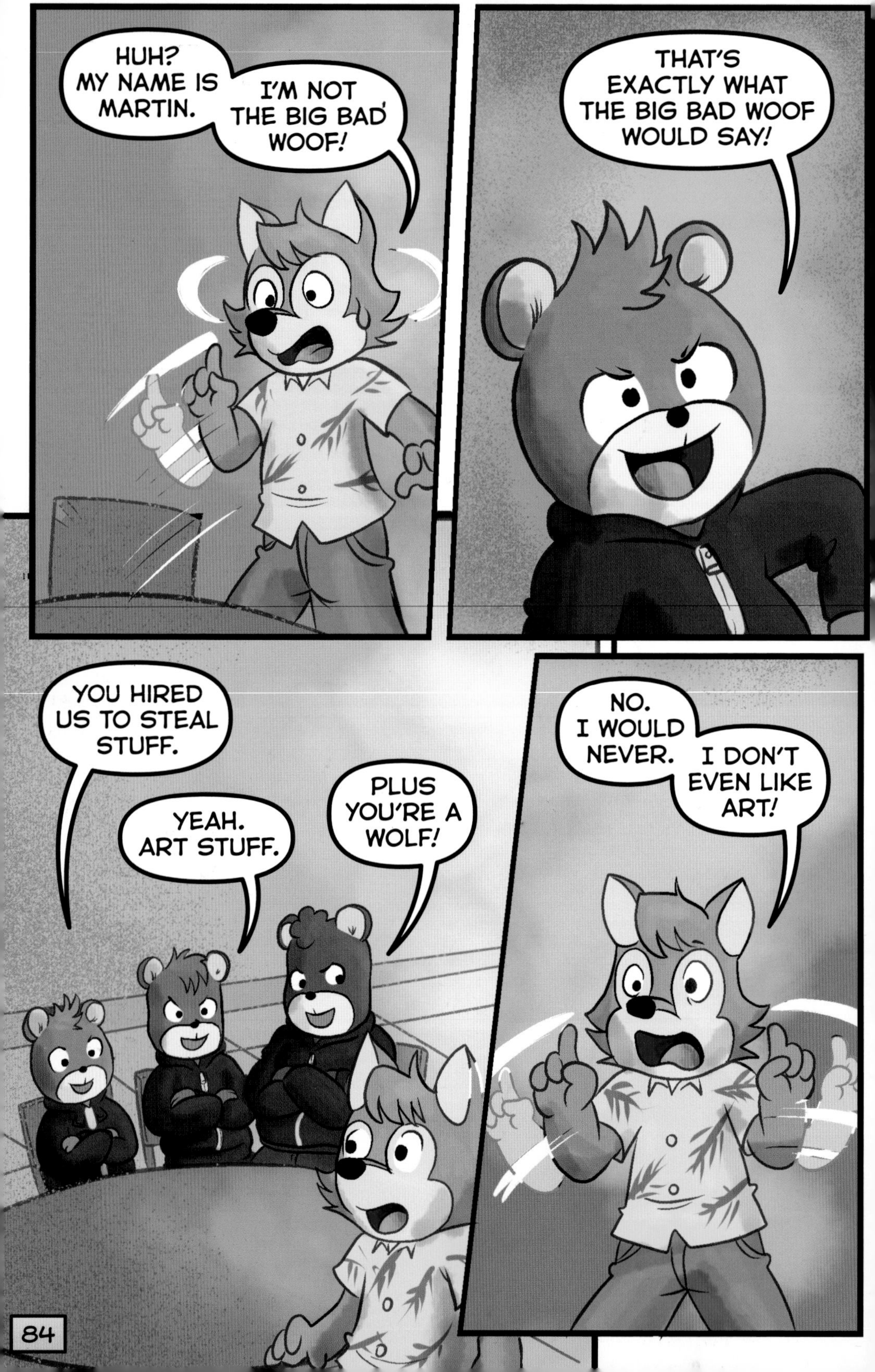
HUH? MY NAME IS MARTIN.
I'M NOT THE BIG BAD WOOF!
THAT'S EXACTLY WHAT THE BIG BAD WOOF WOULD SAY!
YOU HIRED US TO STEAL STUFF.
YEAH. ART STUFF.
PLUS YOU'RE A WOLF!
NO. I WOULD NEVER.
I DON'T EVEN LIKE ART!

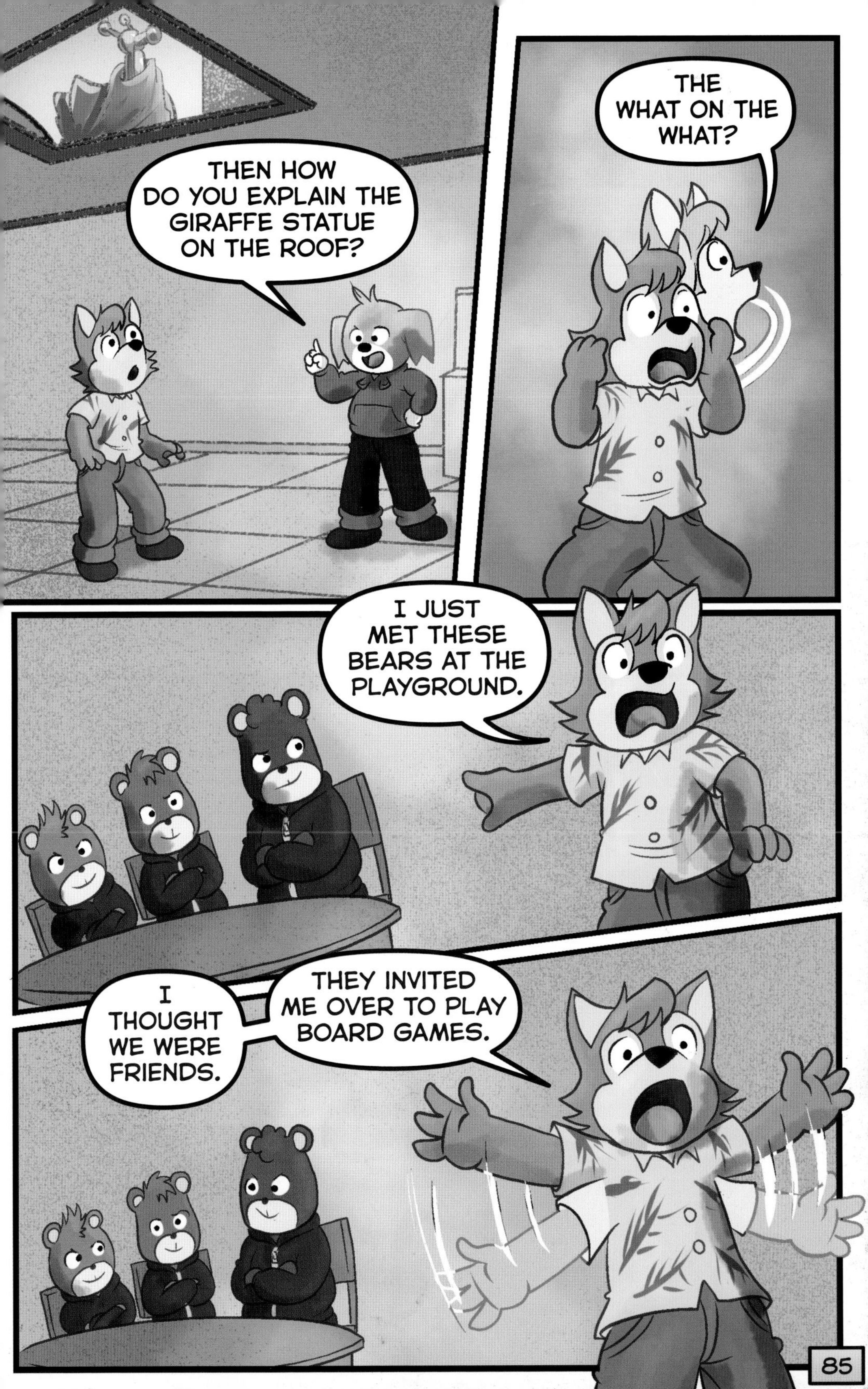
THEN HOW DO YOU EXPLAIN THE GIRAFFE STATUE ON THE ROOF?
THE WHAT ON THE WHAT?
I JUST MET THESE BEARS AT THE PLAYGROUND.
THEY INVITED ME OVER TO PLAY BOARD GAMES.
I THOUGHT WE WERE FRIENDS.

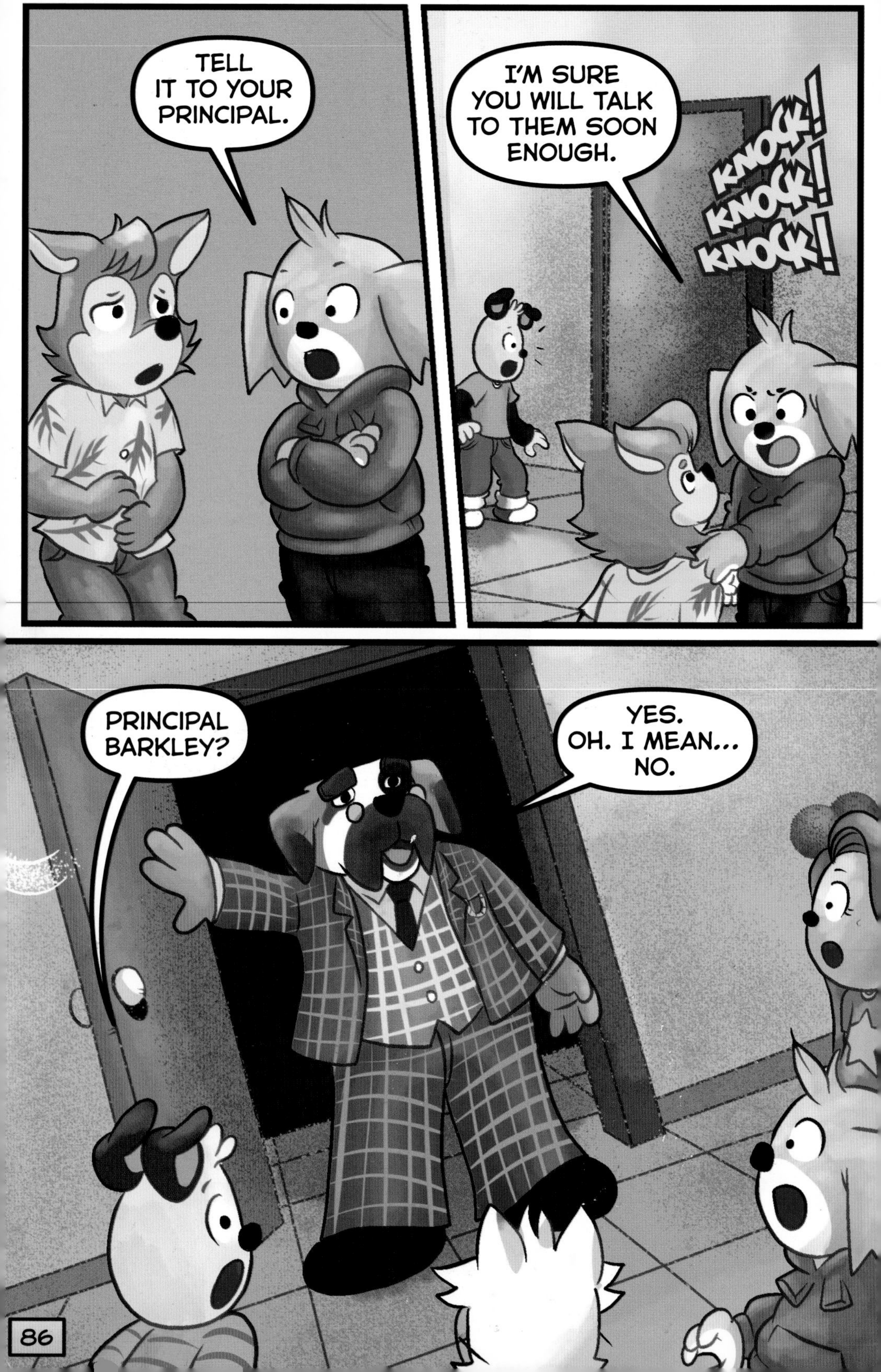
TELL IT TO YOUR PRINCIPAL.
I'M SURE YOU WILL TALK TO THEM SOON ENOUGH.
KNOCK! KNOCK! KNOCK!
PRINCIPAL BARKLEY?
YES. OH. I MEAN... NO.

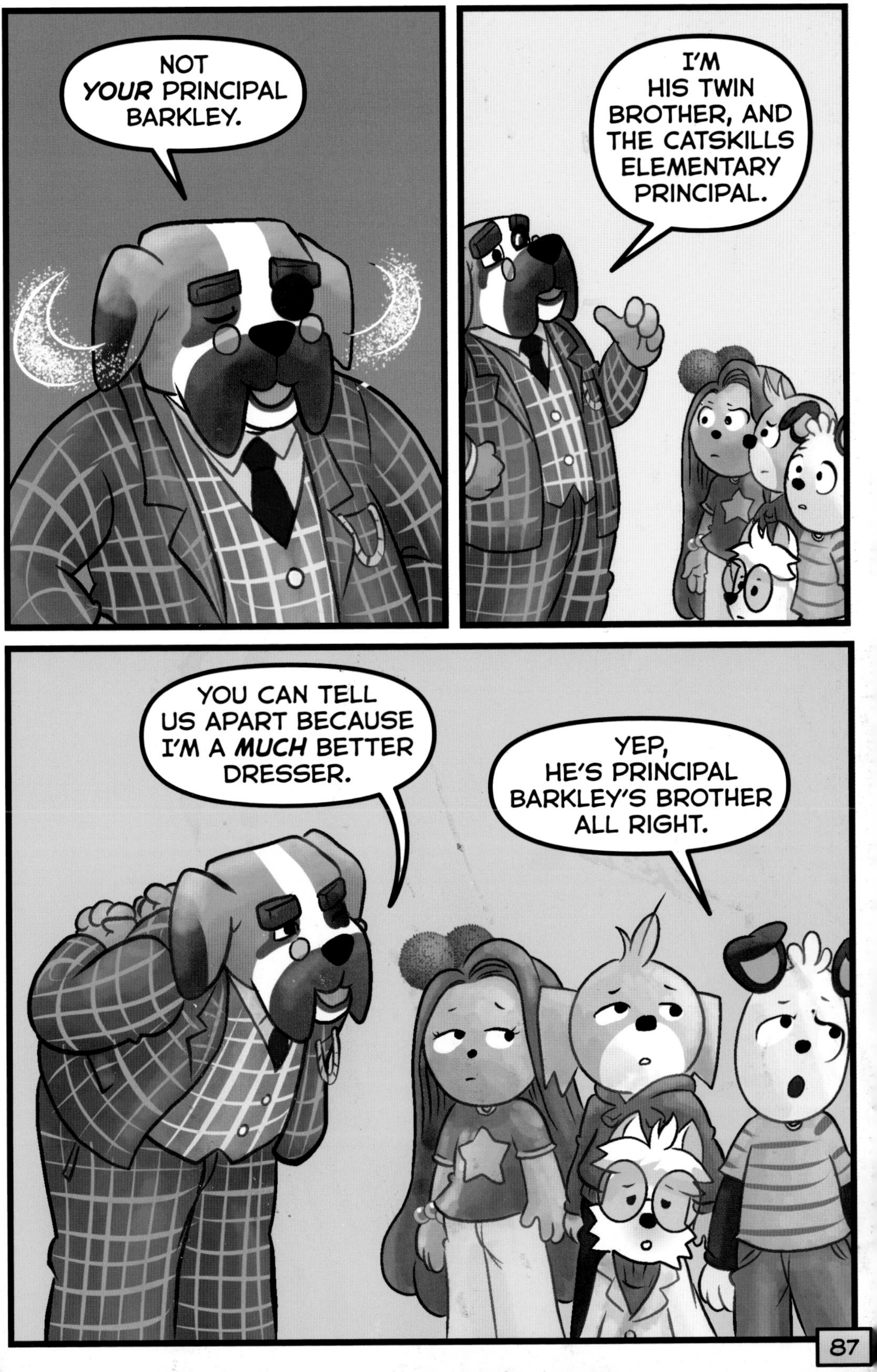
NOT *YOUR* PRINCIPAL BARKLEY.
I'M HIS TWIN BROTHER, AND THE CATSKILLS ELEMENTARY PRINCIPAL.
YOU CAN TELL US APART BECAUSE I'M A *MUCH* BETTER DRESSER.
YEP, HE'S PRINCIPAL BARKLEY'S BROTHER ALL RIGHT.

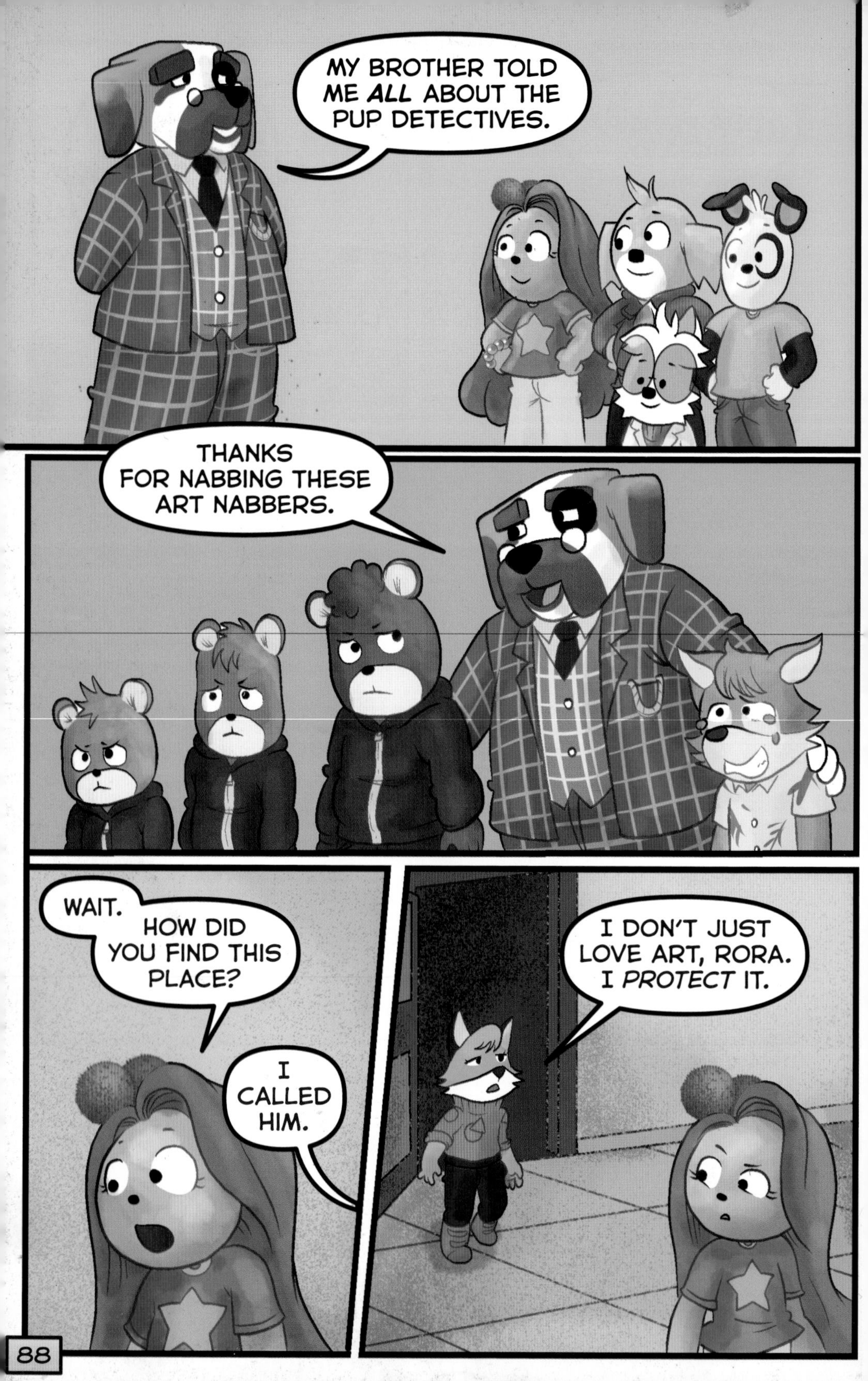
MY BROTHER TOLD ME ALL ABOUT THE PUP DETECTIVES.
THANKS FOR NABBING THESE ART NABBERS.
WAIT.
HOW DID YOU FIND THIS PLACE?
I CALLED HIM.
I DON'T JUST LOVE ART, RORA. I PROTECT IT.

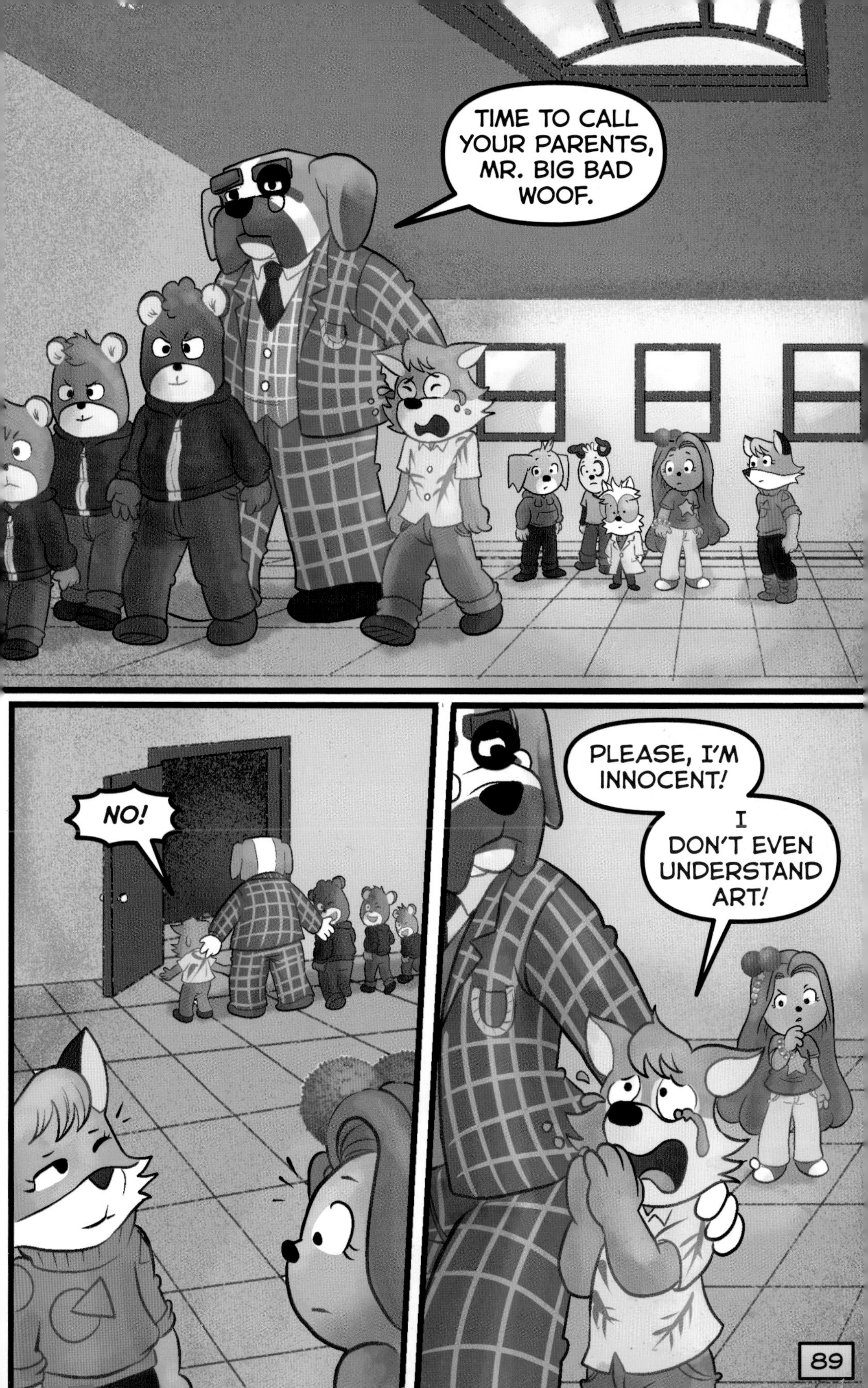
TIME TO CALL YOUR PARENTS, MR. BIG BAD WOOF.
NO!
PLEASE, I'M INNOCENT!
I DON'T EVEN UNDERSTAND ART!

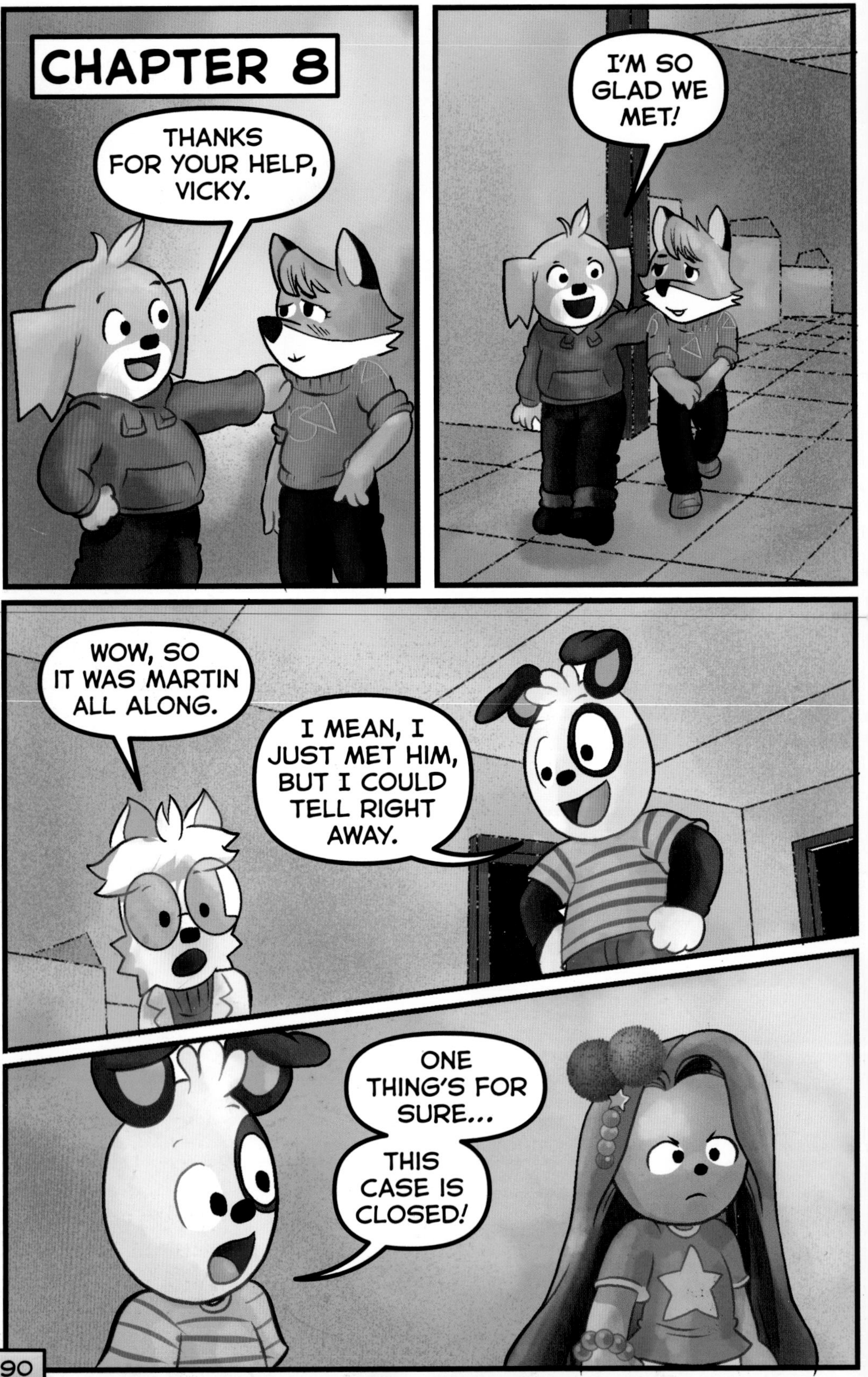
CHAPTER 8
THANKS FOR YOUR HELP, VICKY.
I'M SO GLAD WE MET!
WOW, SO IT WAS MARTIN ALL ALONG.
I MEAN, I JUST MET HIM, BUT I COULD TELL RIGHT AWAY.
ONE THING'S FOR SURE...
THIS CASE IS CLOSED!

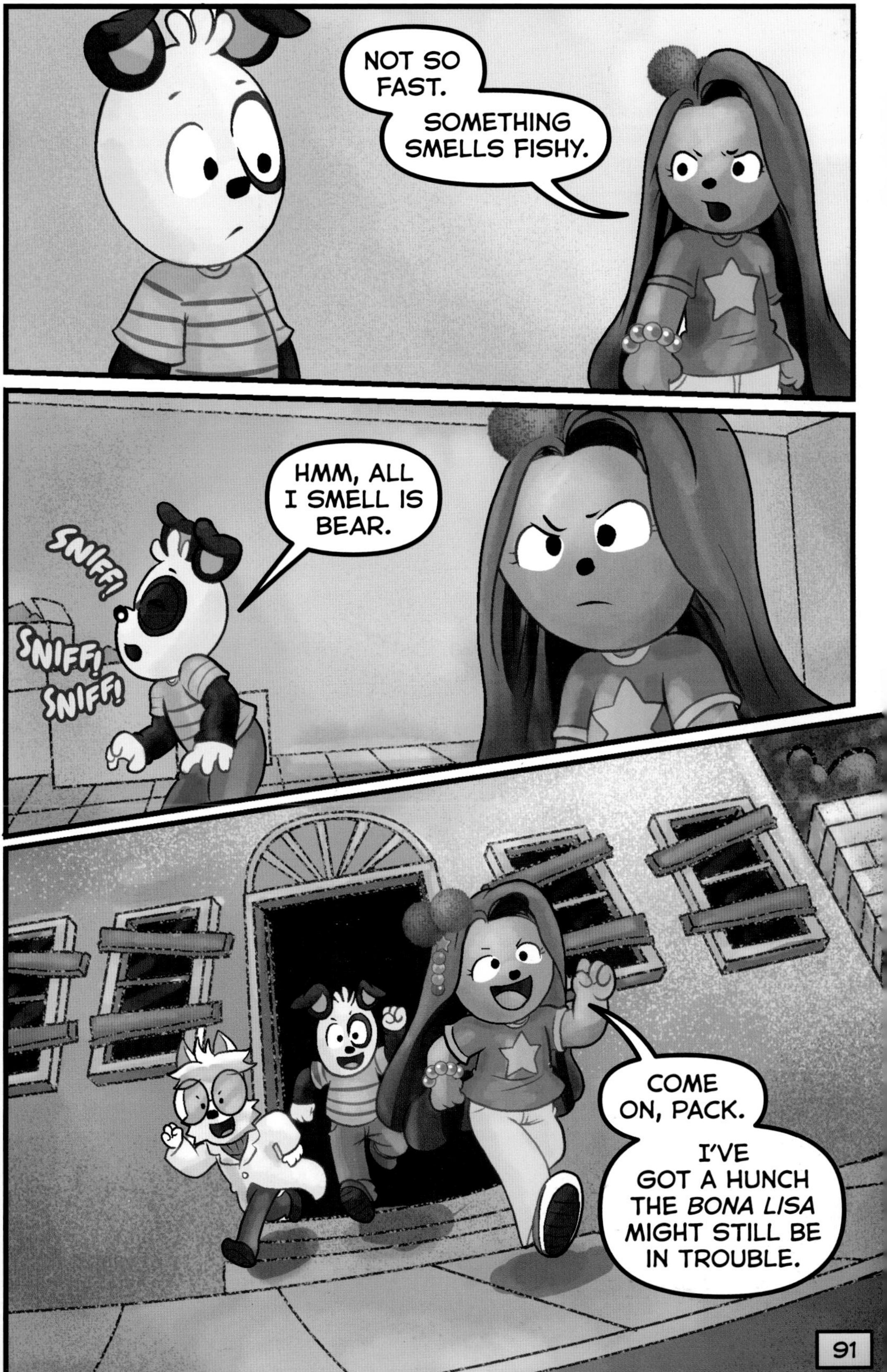
NOT SO FAST.
SOMETHING SMELLS FISHY.
SNIFF!
SNIFF!
SNIFF!
HMM, ALL I SMELL IS BEAR.
COME ON, PACK.
I'VE GOT A HUNCH THE *BONA LISA* MIGHT STILL BE IN TROUBLE.

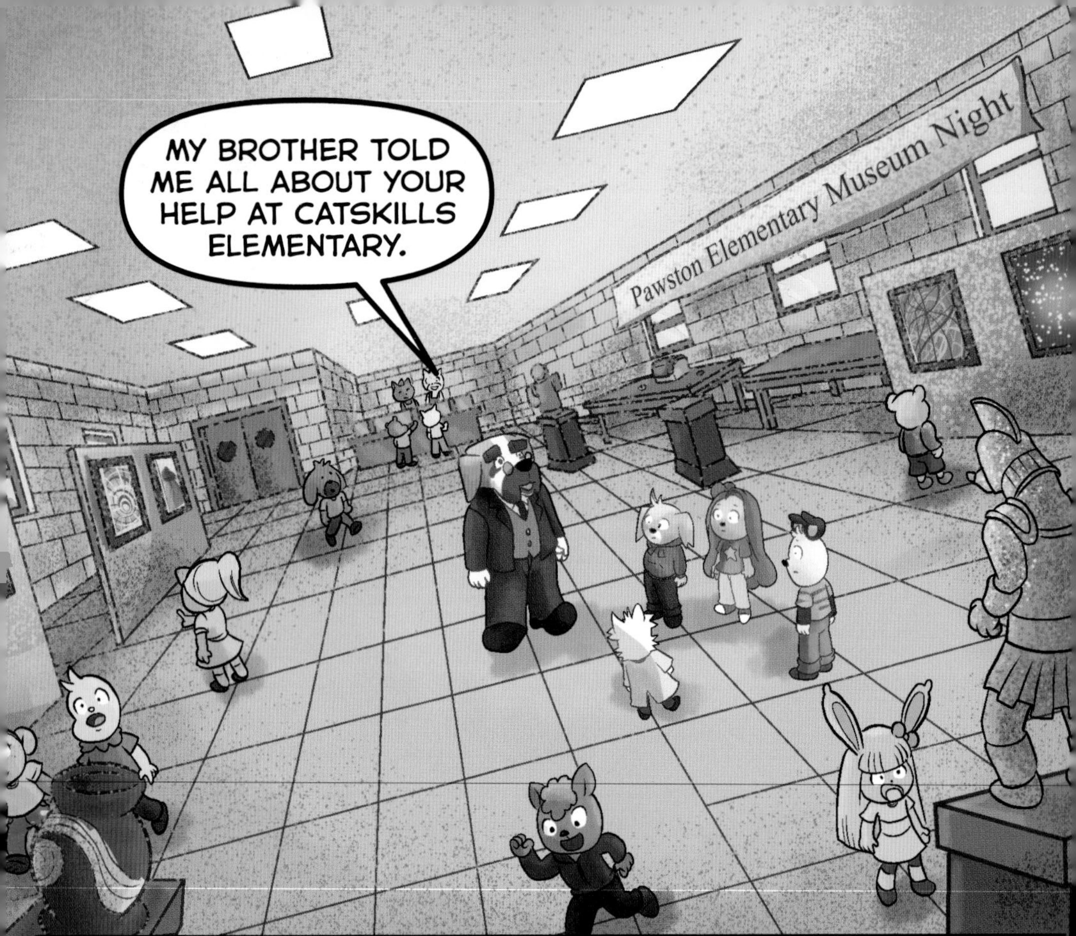
Pawston Elementary Museum Night
MY BROTHER TOLD ME ALL ABOUT YOUR HELP AT CATSKILLS ELEMENTARY.

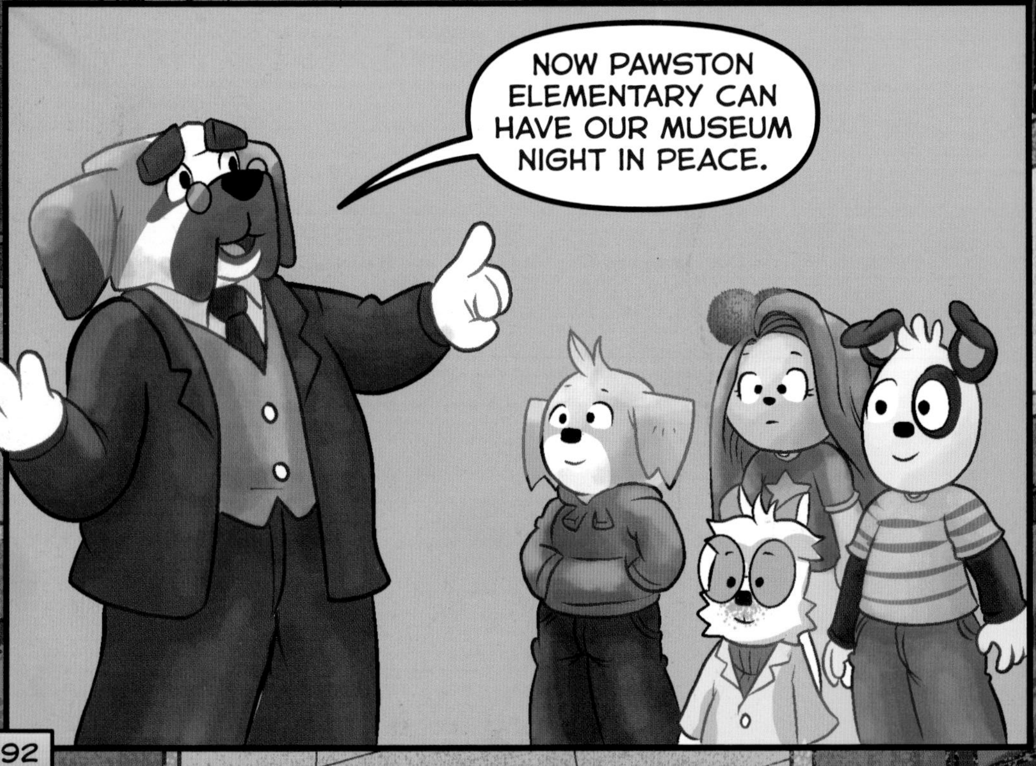
NOW PAWSTON ELEMENTARY CAN HAVE OUR MUSEUM NIGHT IN PEACE.

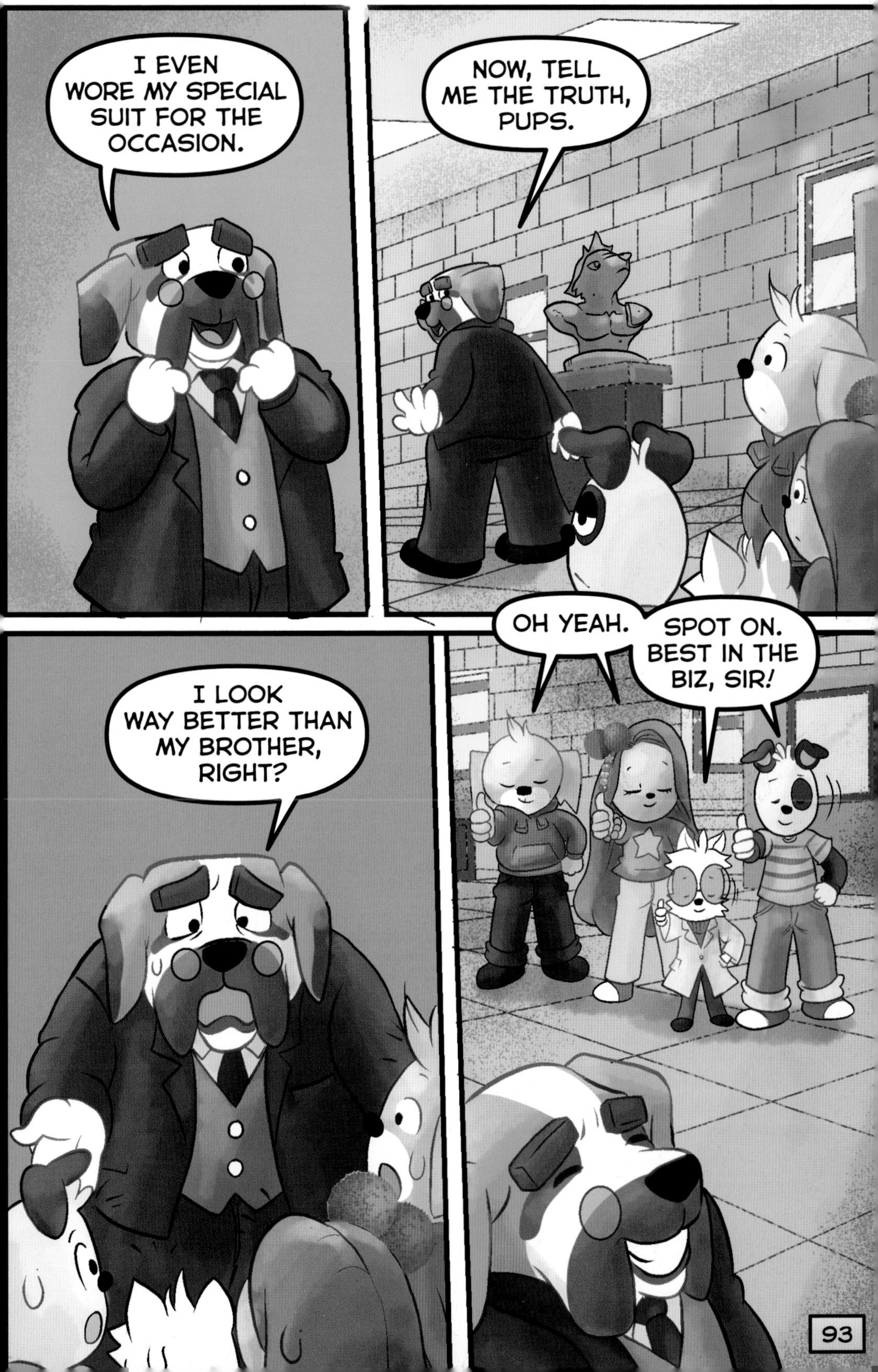
I EVEN WORE MY SPECIAL SUIT FOR THE OCCASION.
NOW, TELL ME THE TRUTH, PUPS.
I LOOK WAY BETTER THAN MY BROTHER, RIGHT?
OH YEAH.
SPOT ON. BEST IN THE BIZ, SIR!

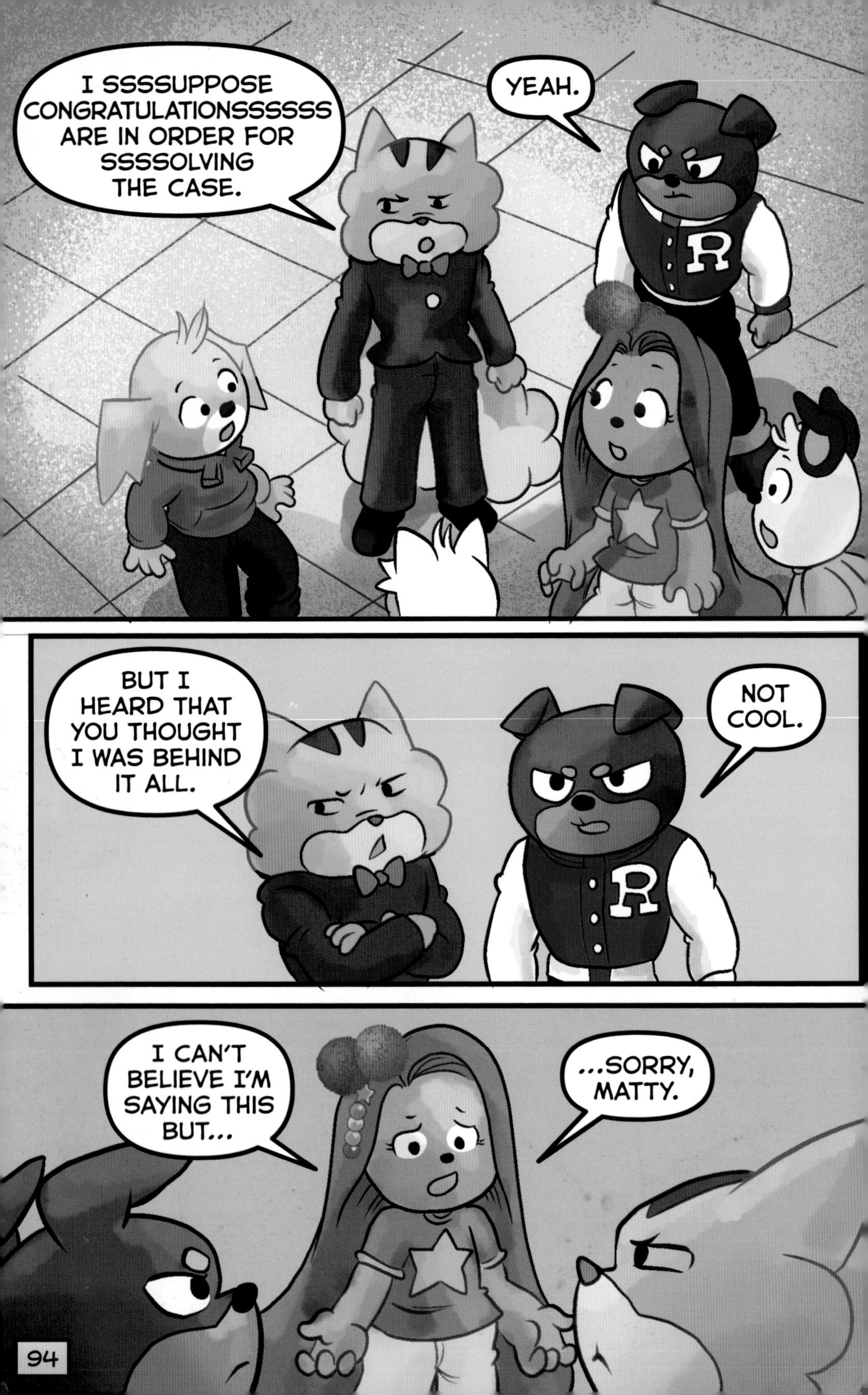
I SSSSUPPOSE CONGRATULATIONSSSSSS ARE IN ORDER FOR SSSSOLVING THE CASE.
YEAH.
BUT I HEARD THAT YOU THOUGHT I WAS BEHIND IT ALL.
NOT COOL.
I CAN'T BELIEVE I'M SAYING THIS BUT...
...SORRY, MATTY.

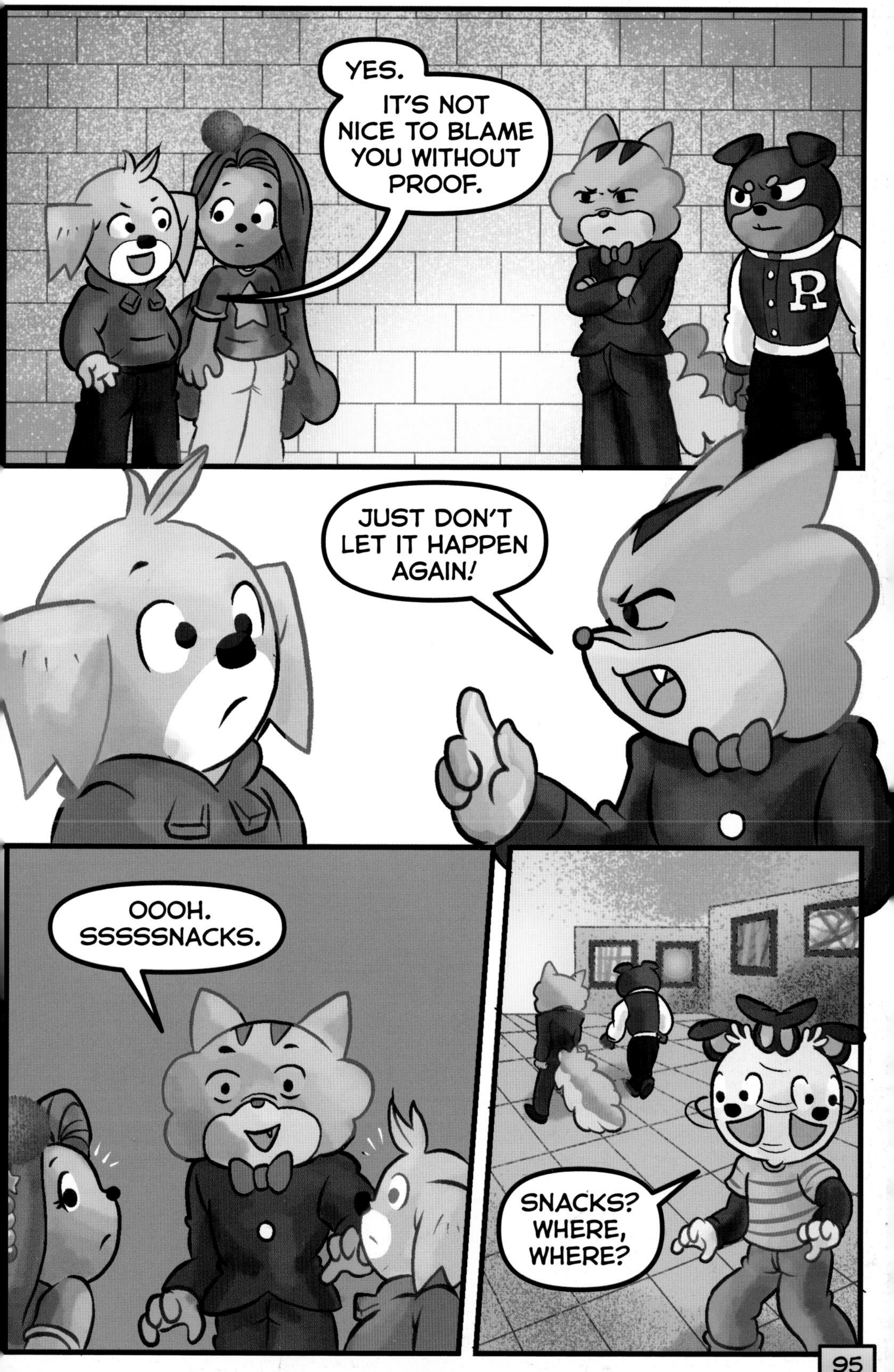
YES.
IT'S NOT NICE TO BLAME YOU WITHOUT PROOF.
JUST DON'T LET IT HAPPEN AGAIN!
OOOH. SSSSSNACKS.
SNACKS? WHERE, WHERE?

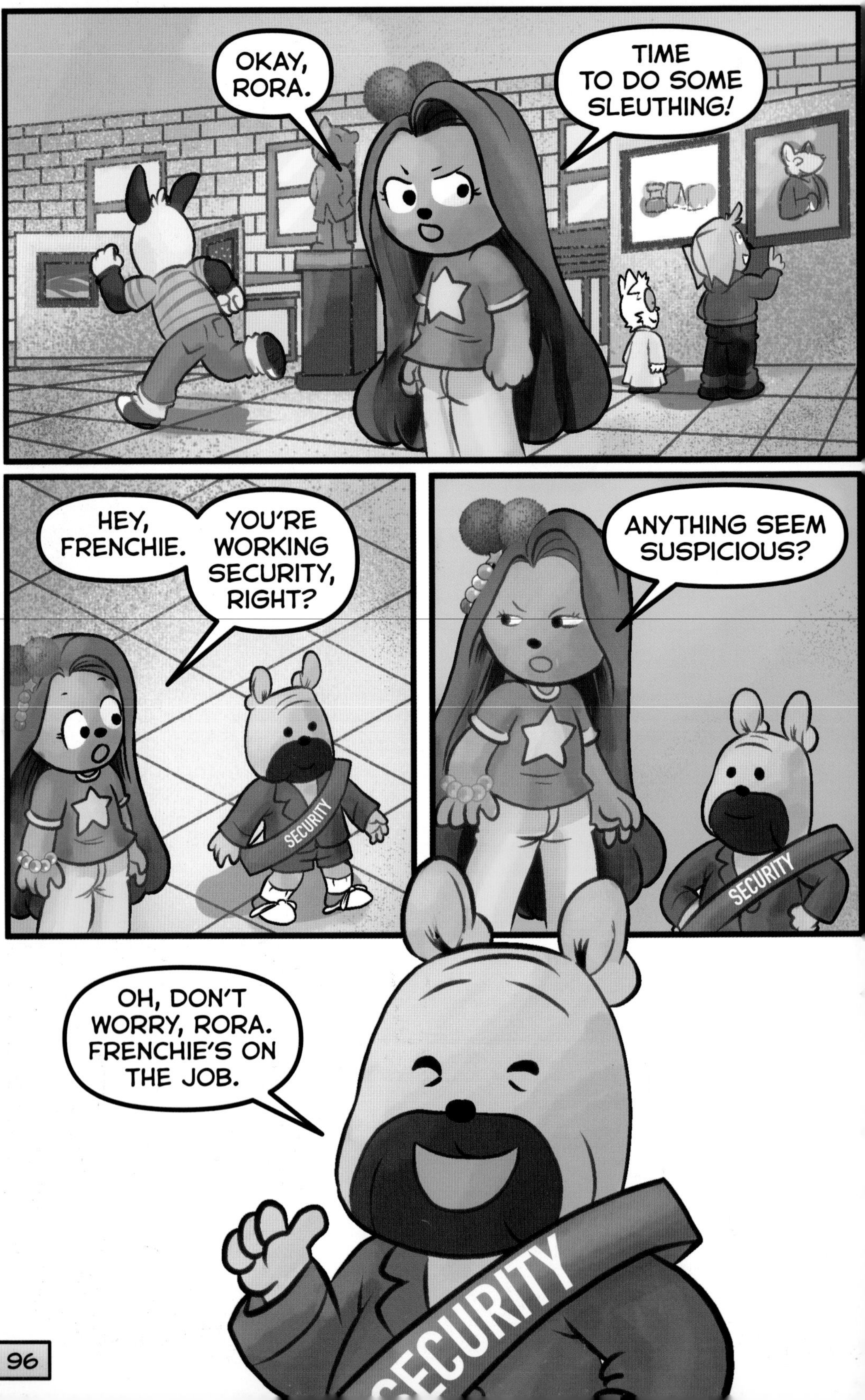
OKAY, RORA.
TIME TO DO SOME SLEUTHING!
HEY, FRENCHIE.
YOU'RE WORKING SECURITY, RIGHT?
SECURITY
ANYTHING SEEM SUSPICIOUS?
SECURITY
OH, DON'T WORRY, RORA. FRENCHIE'S ON THE JOB.
SECURITY

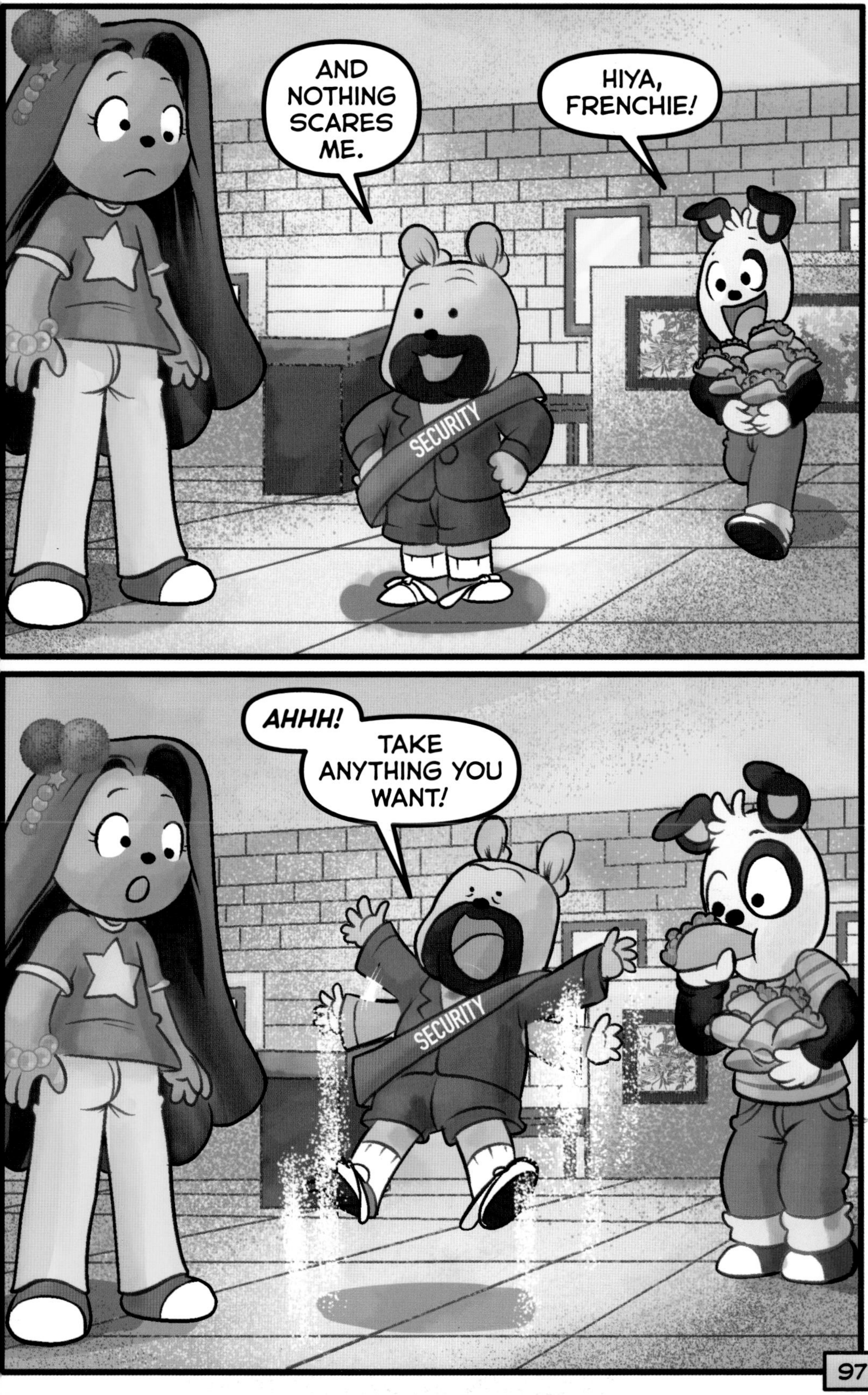
AND NOTHING SCARES ME.
HIYA, FRENCHIE!
SECURITY
AHHH!
TAKE ANYTHING YOU WANT!
SECURITY

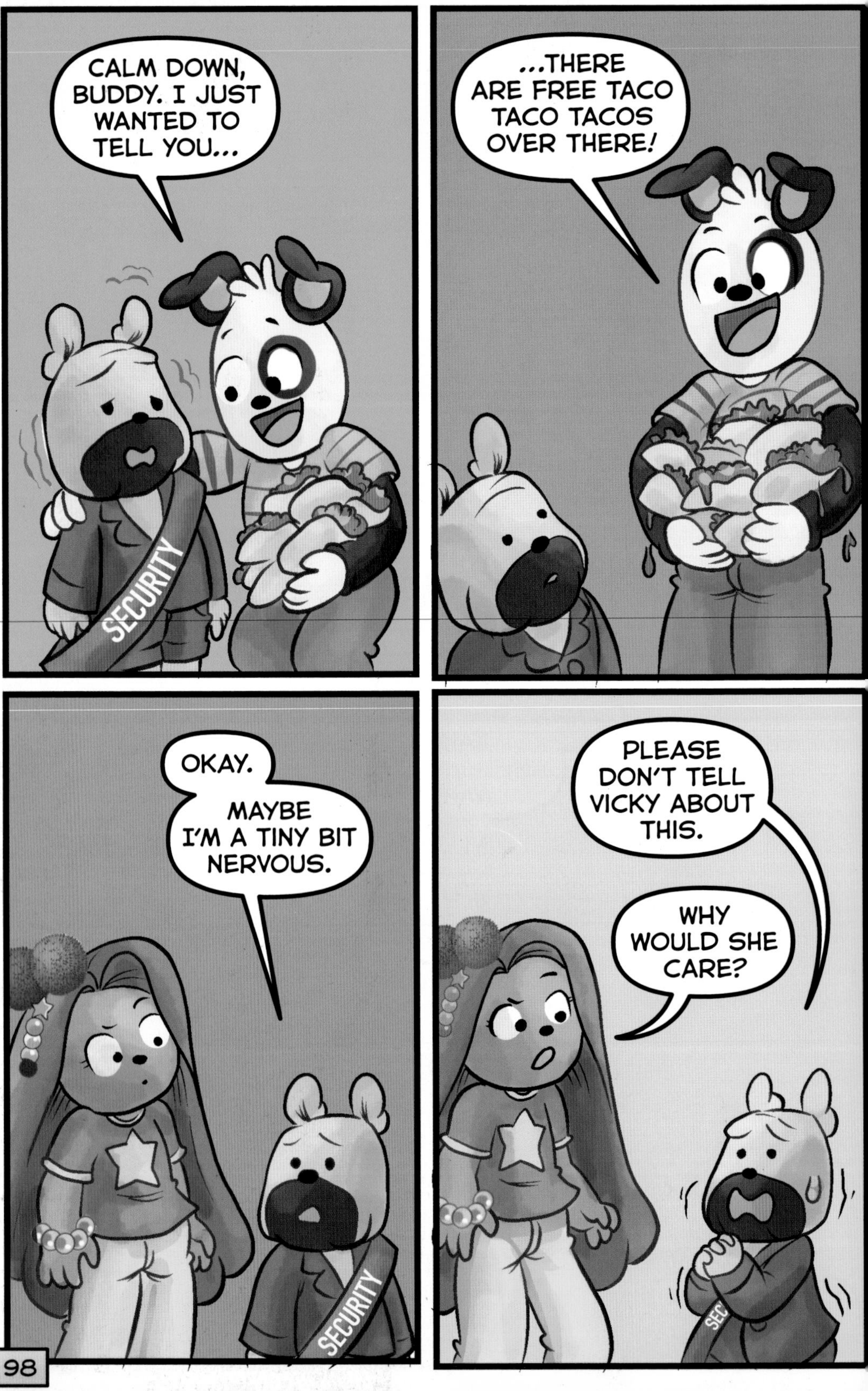
CALM DOWN, BUDDY. I JUST WANTED TO TELL YOU...
SECURITY
...THERE ARE FREE TACO TACO TACOS OVER THERE!
OKAY.
MAYBE I'M A TINY BIT NERVOUS.
SECURITY
PLEASE DON'T TELL VICKY ABOUT THIS.
WHY WOULD SHE CARE?
SEC

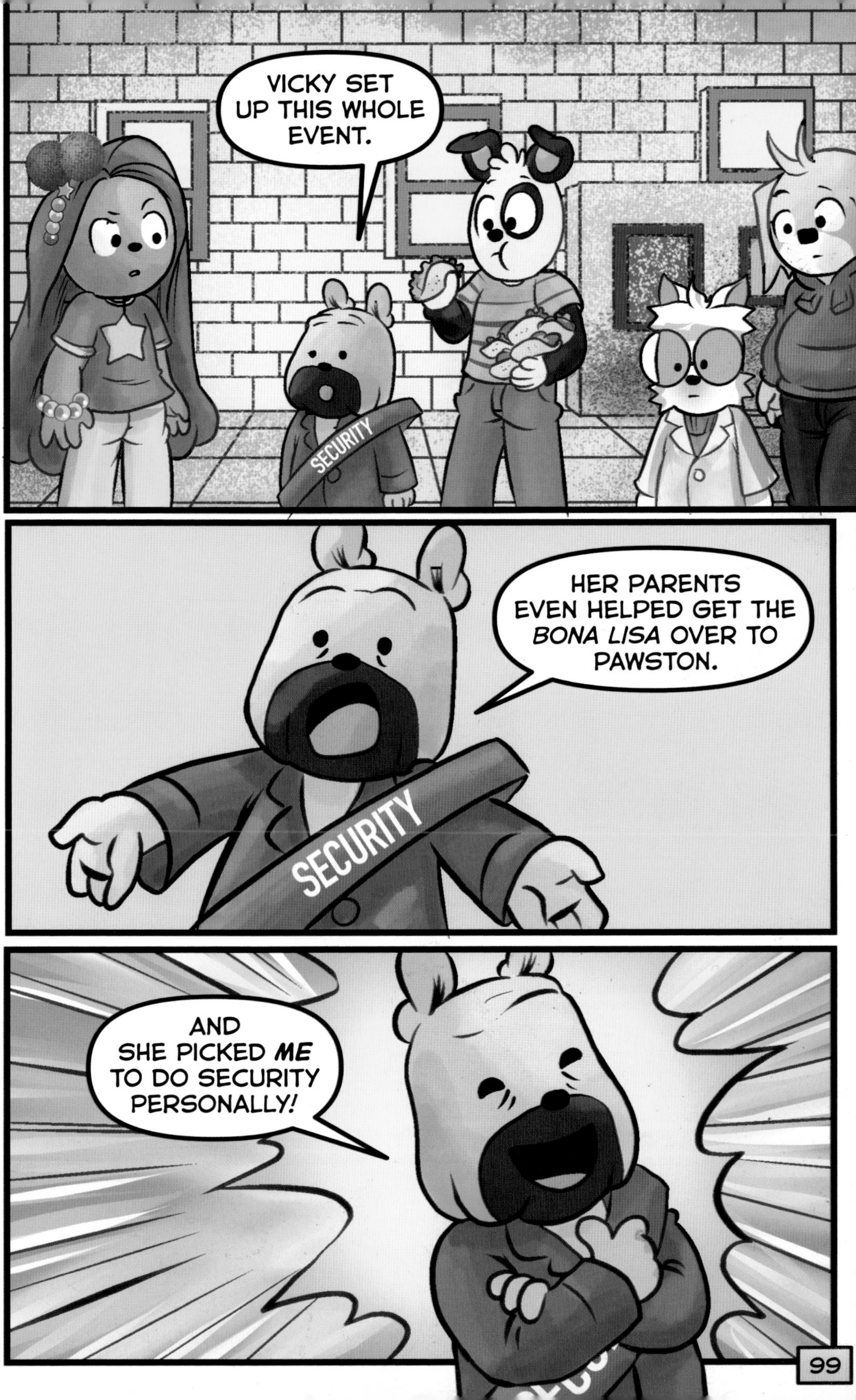
VICKY SET UP THIS WHOLE EVENT.
SECURITY
HER PARENTS EVEN HELPED GET THE *BONA LISA* OVER TO PAWSTON.
SECURITY
AND SHE PICKED *ME* TO DO SECURITY PERSONALLY!

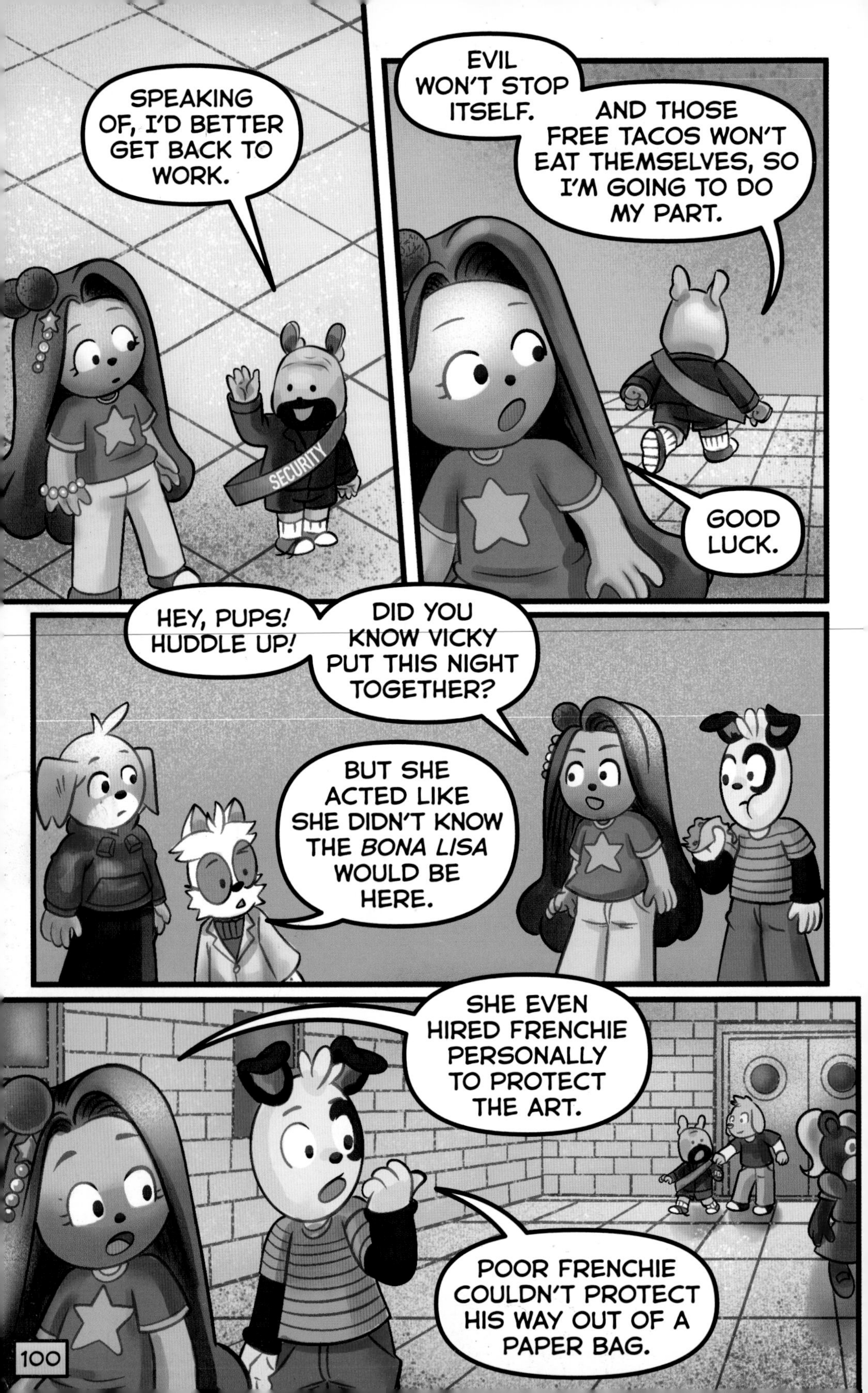
SPEAKING OF, I'D BETTER GET BACK TO WORK.
SECURITY
EVIL WON'T STOP ITSELF.
AND THOSE FREE TACOS WON'T EAT THEMSELVES, SO I'M GOING TO DO MY PART.
GOOD LUCK.
HEY, PUPS! HUDDLE UP!
DID YOU KNOW VICKY PUT THIS NIGHT TOGETHER?
BUT SHE ACTED LIKE SHE DIDN'T KNOW THE *BONA LISA* WOULD BE HERE.
SHE EVEN HIRED FRENCHIE PERSONALLY TO PROTECT THE ART.
POOR FRENCHIE COULDN'T PROTECT HIS WAY OUT OF A PAPER BAG.

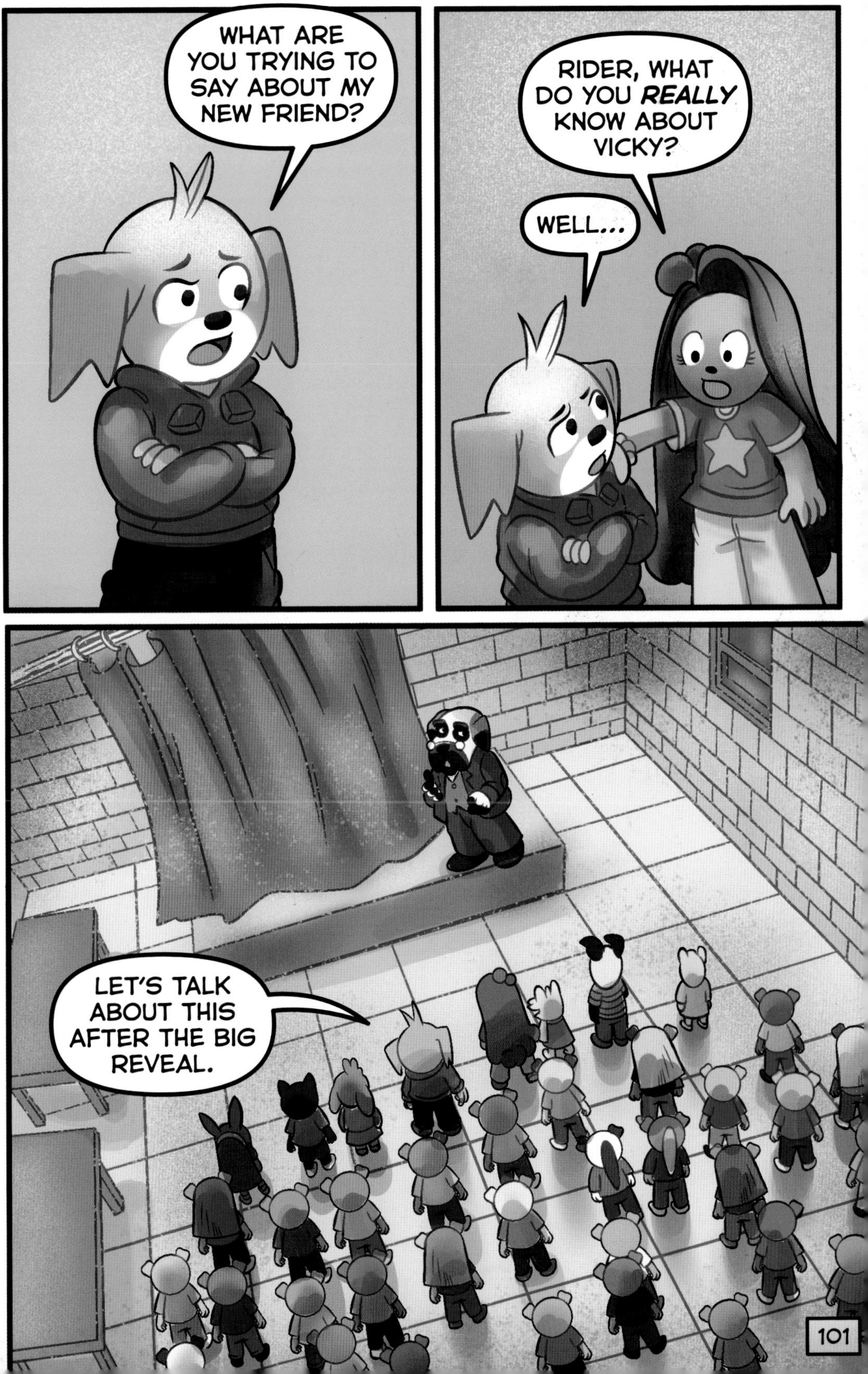
WHAT ARE YOU TRYING TO SAY ABOUT MY NEW FRIEND?
RIDER, WHAT DO YOU *REALLY* KNOW ABOUT VICKY?
WELL...
LET'S TALK ABOUT THIS AFTER THE BIG REVEAL.

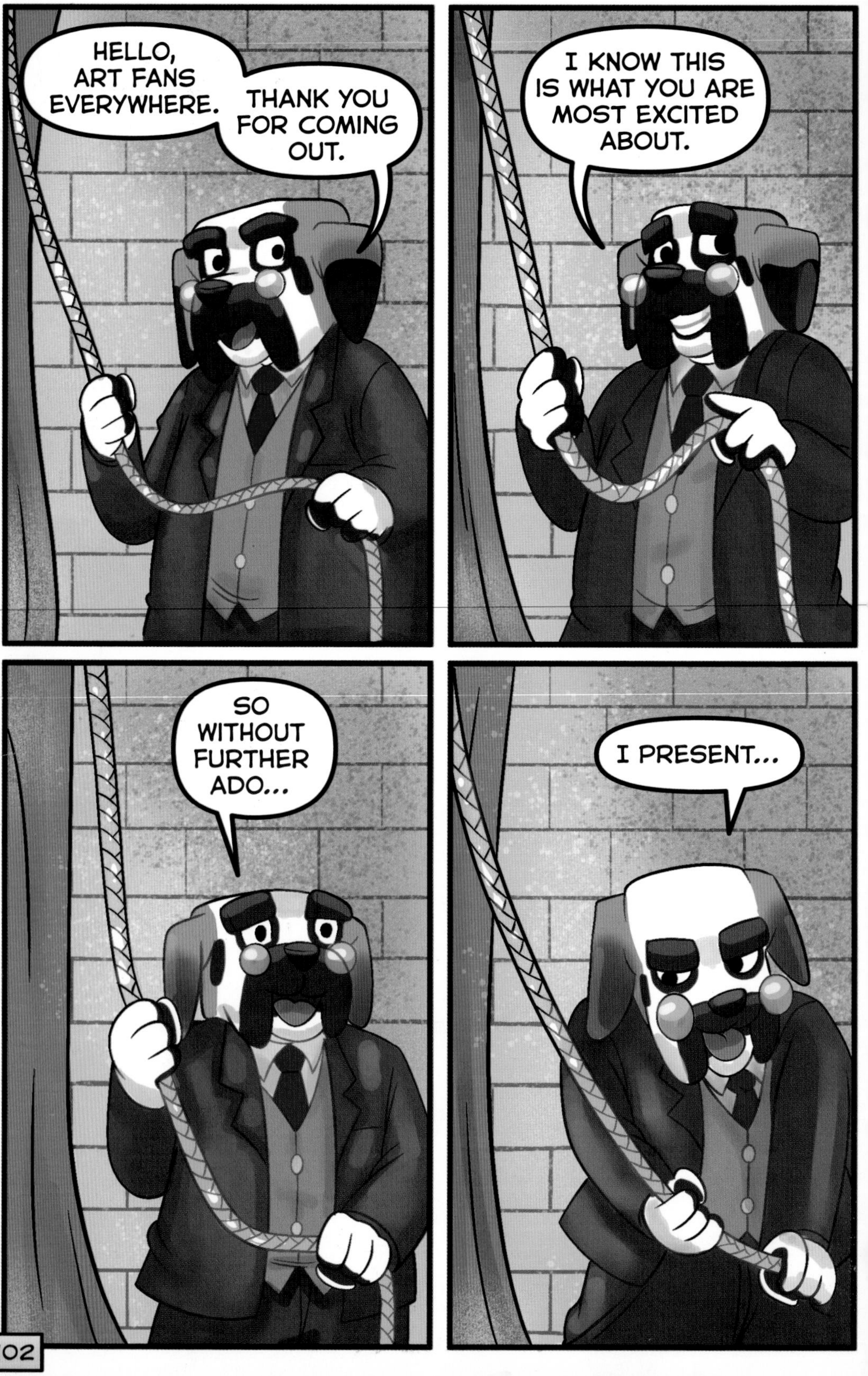
HELLO, ART FANS EVERYWHERE.
THANK YOU FOR COMING OUT.
I KNOW THIS IS WHAT YOU ARE MOST EXCITED ABOUT.
SO WITHOUT FURTHER ADO...
I PRESENT...

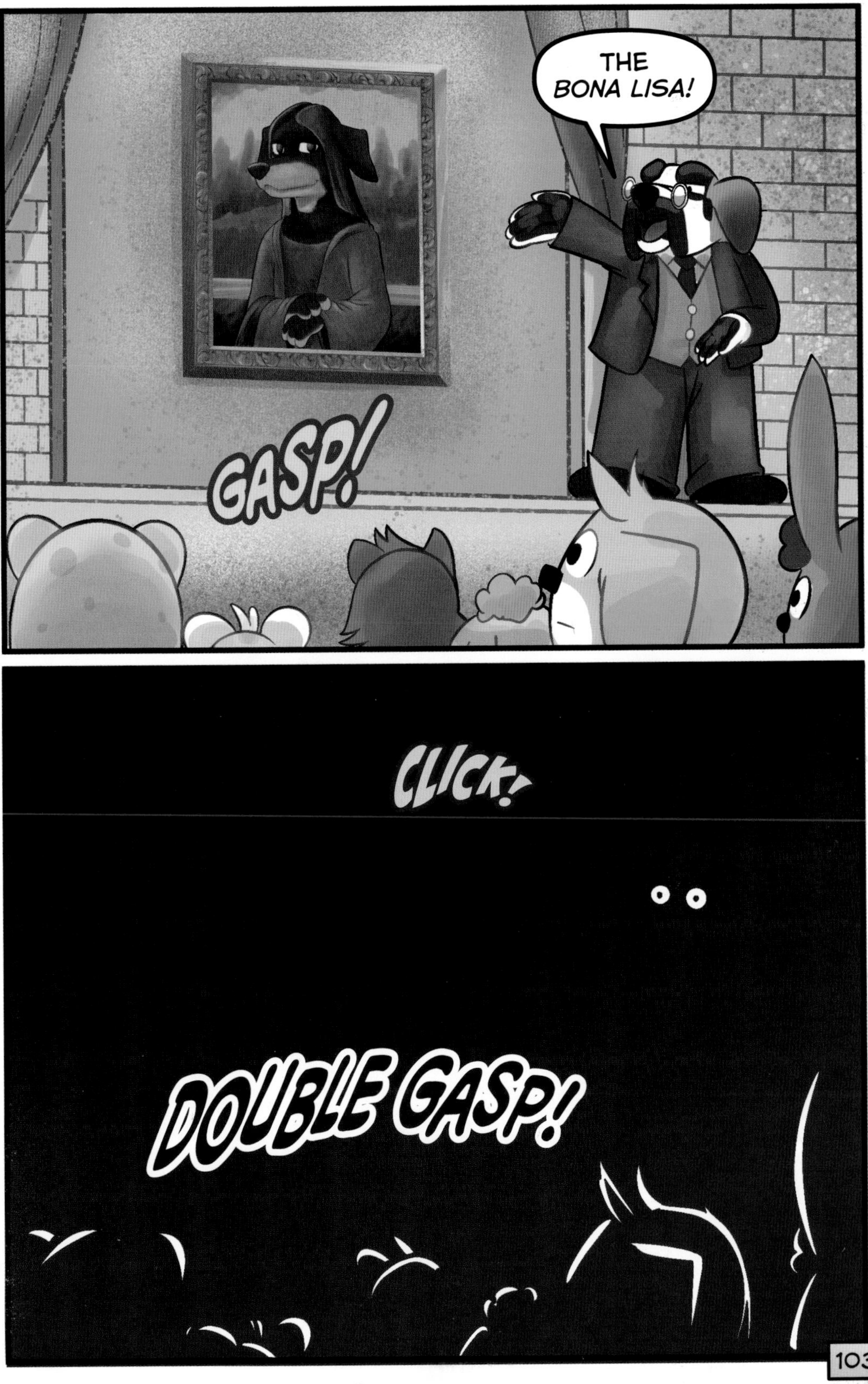
THE BONA LISA!
GASP!
CLICK!
DOUBLE GASP!

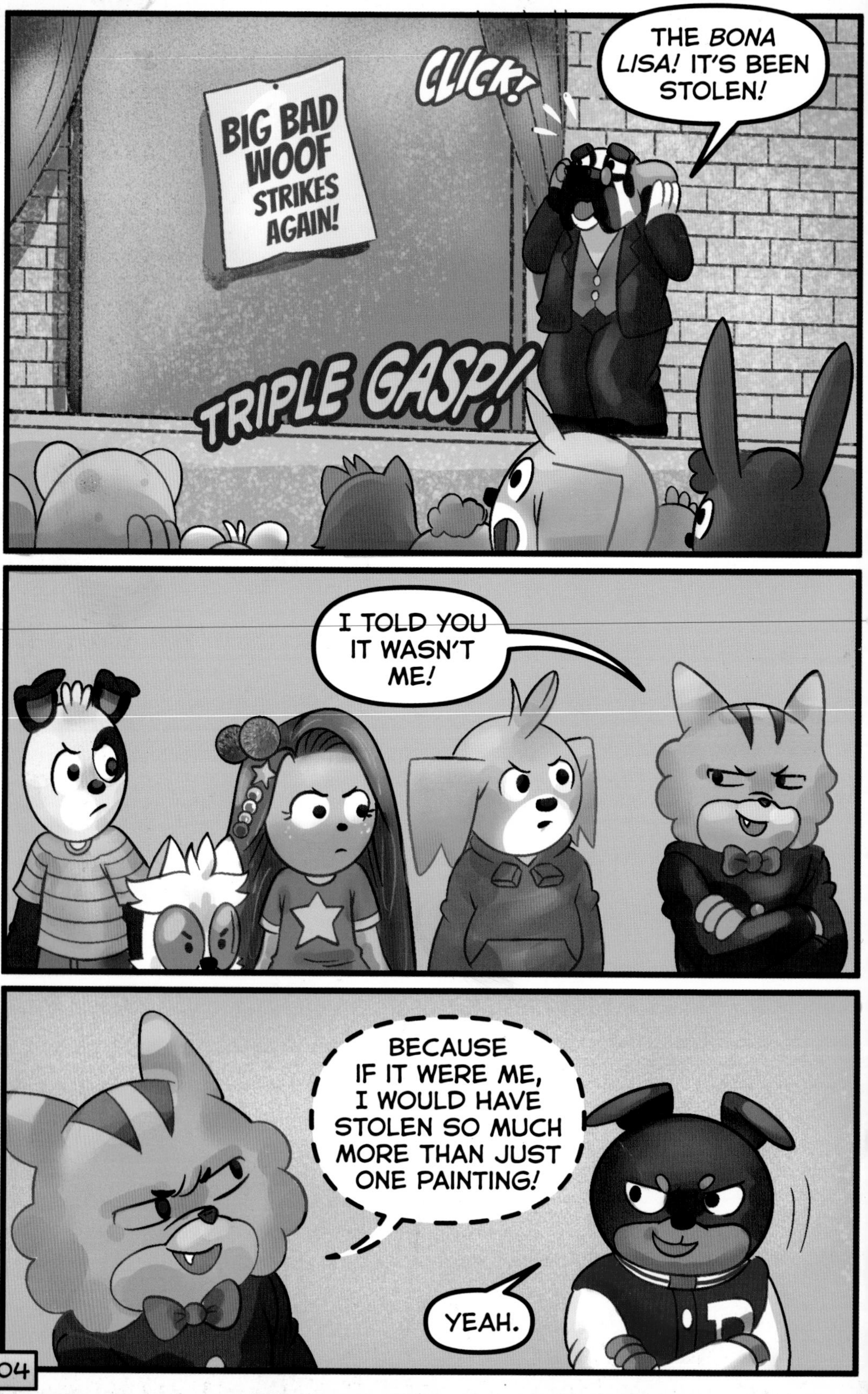
BIG BAD WOOF STRIKES AGAIN!
CLICK!
THE *BONA LISA!* IT'S BEEN STOLEN!
TRIPLE GASP!
I TOLD YOU IT WASN'T ME!
BECAUSE IF IT WERE ME, I WOULD HAVE STOLEN SO MUCH MORE THAN JUST ONE PAINTING!
YEAH.

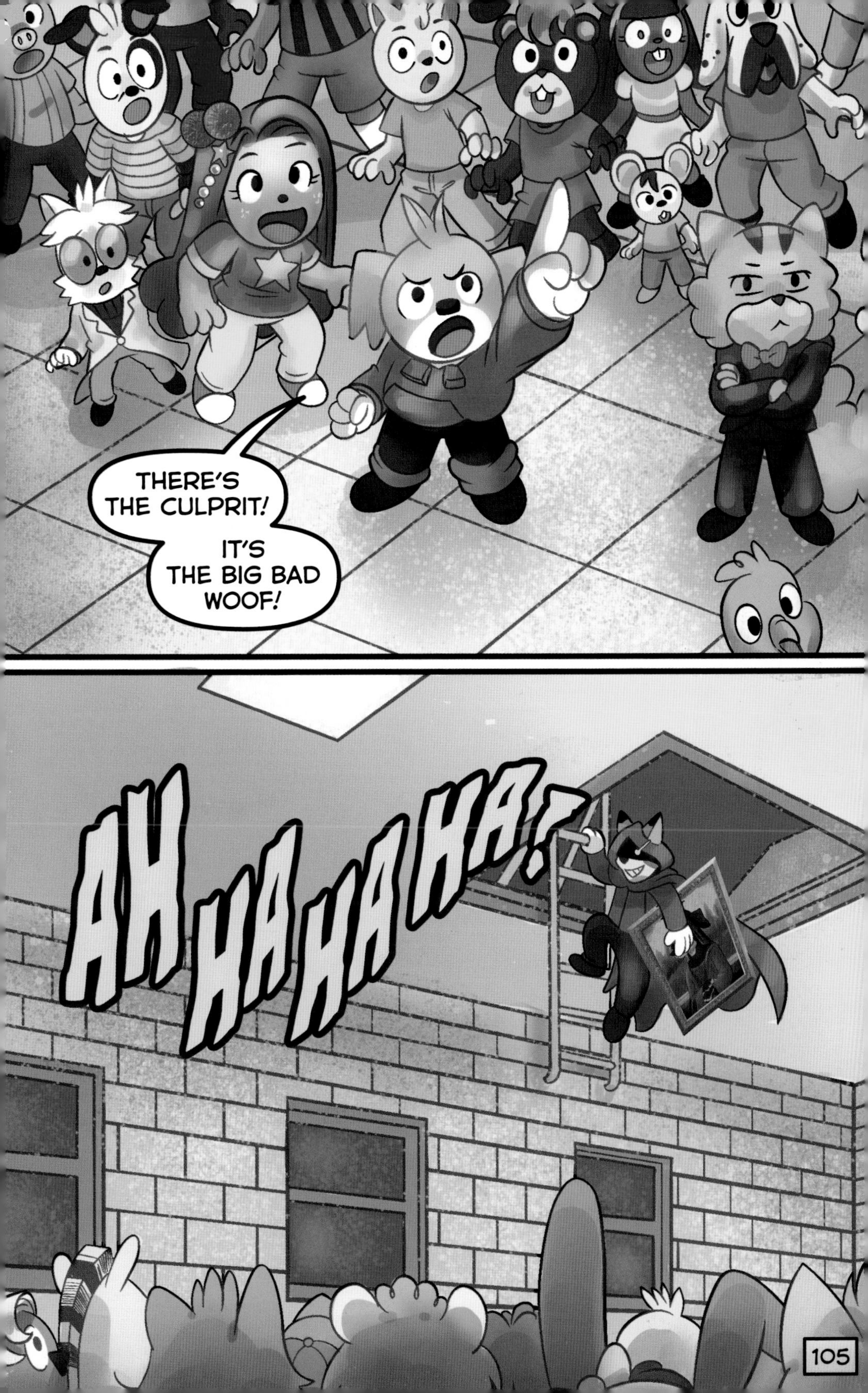
THERE'S THE CULPRIT!
IT'S THE BIG BAD WOOF!
AH HA HA HA HA!

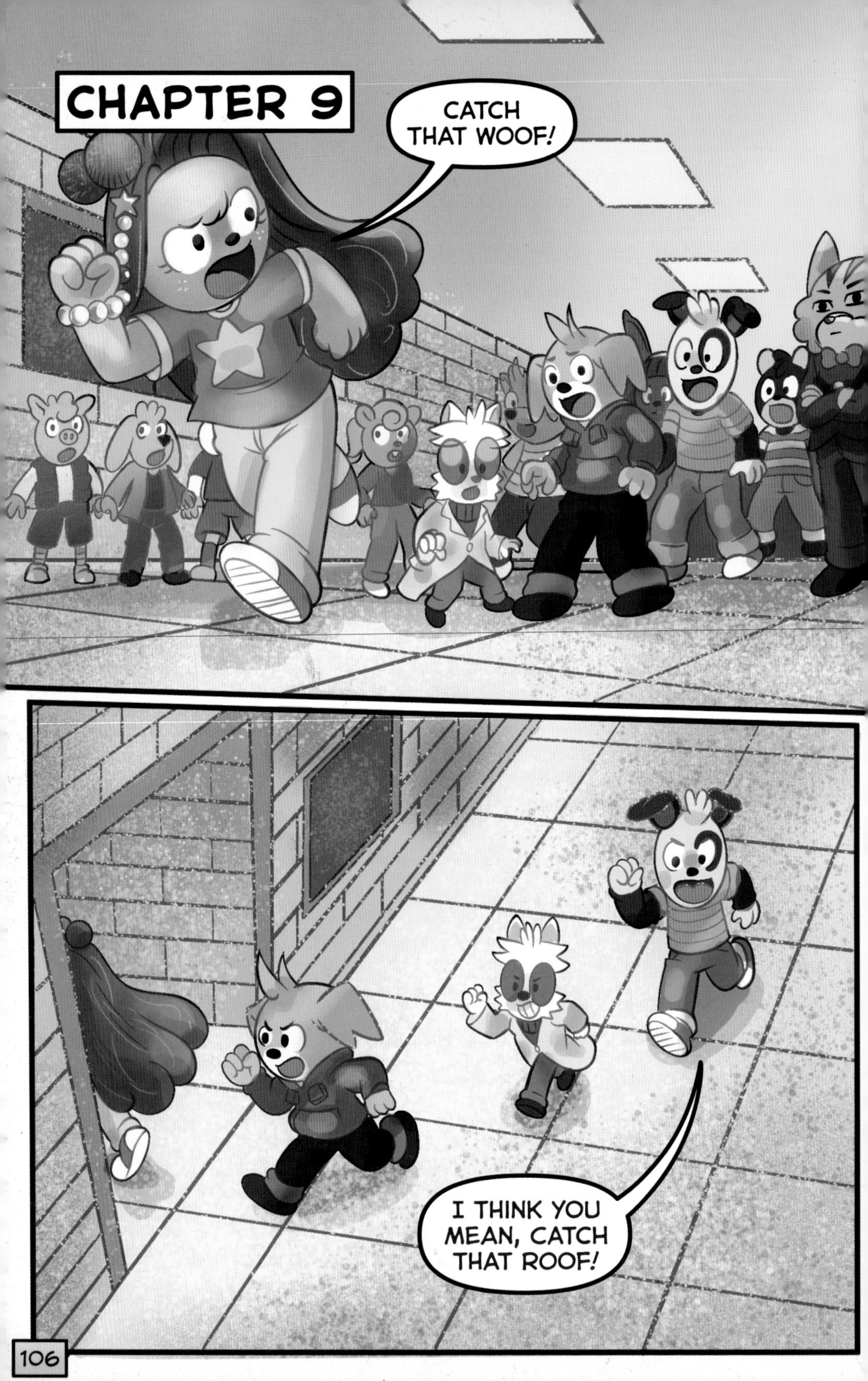
CHAPTER 9
CATCH THAT WOOF!
I THINK YOU MEAN, CATCH THAT ROOF!

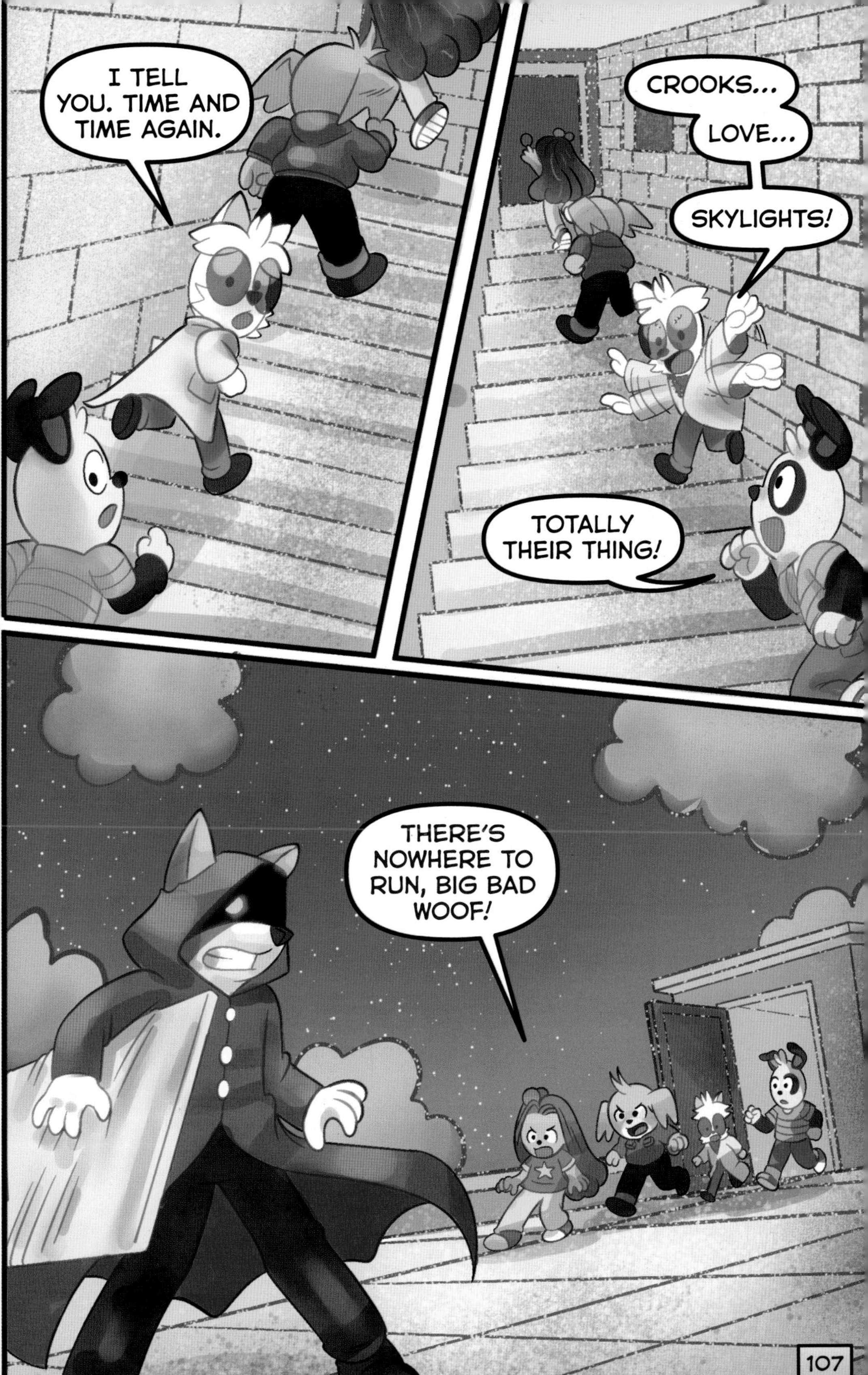
I TELL YOU. TIME AND TIME AGAIN.
CROOKS...
LOVE...
SKYLIGHTS!
TOTALLY THEIR THING!
THERE'S NOWHERE TO RUN, BIG BAD WOOF!

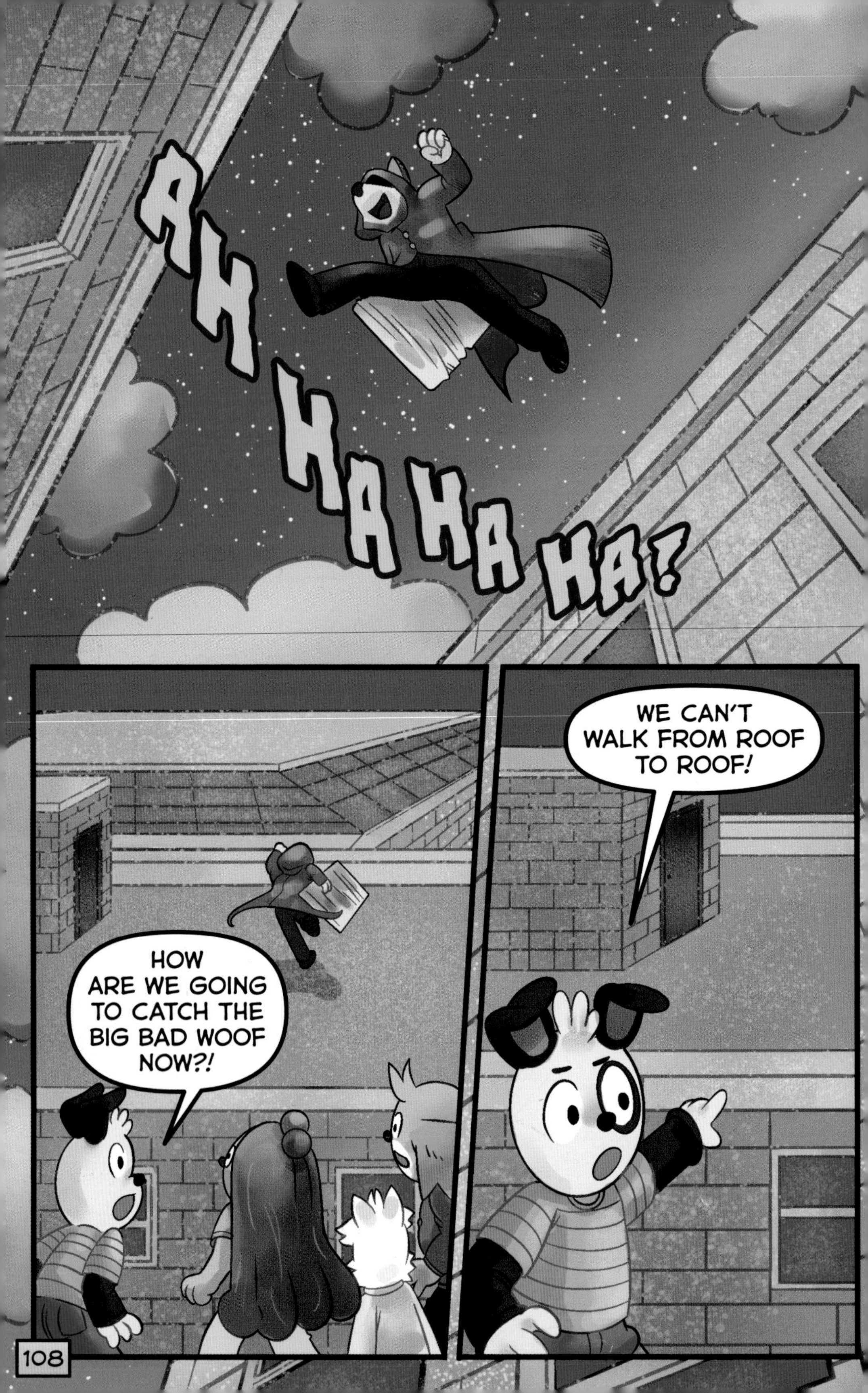
AH HA HA HA HA!
HOW ARE WE GOING TO CATCH THE BIG BAD WOOF NOW?!
WE CAN'T WALK FROM ROOF TO ROOF!

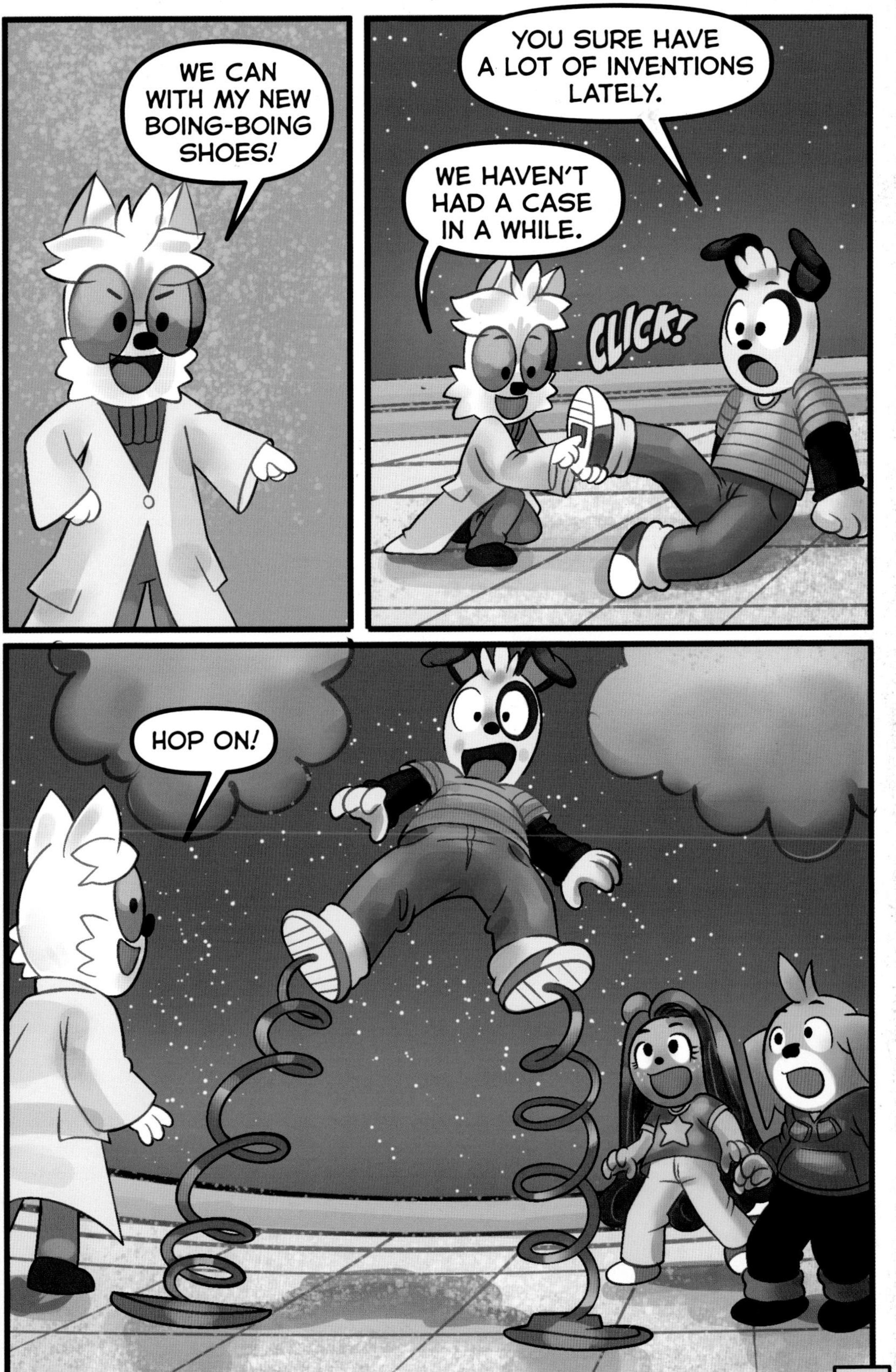
WE CAN WITH MY NEW BOING-BOING SHOES!
YOU SURE HAVE A LOT OF INVENTIONS LATELY.
WE HAVEN'T HAD A CASE IN A WHILE.
CLICK!
HOP ON!

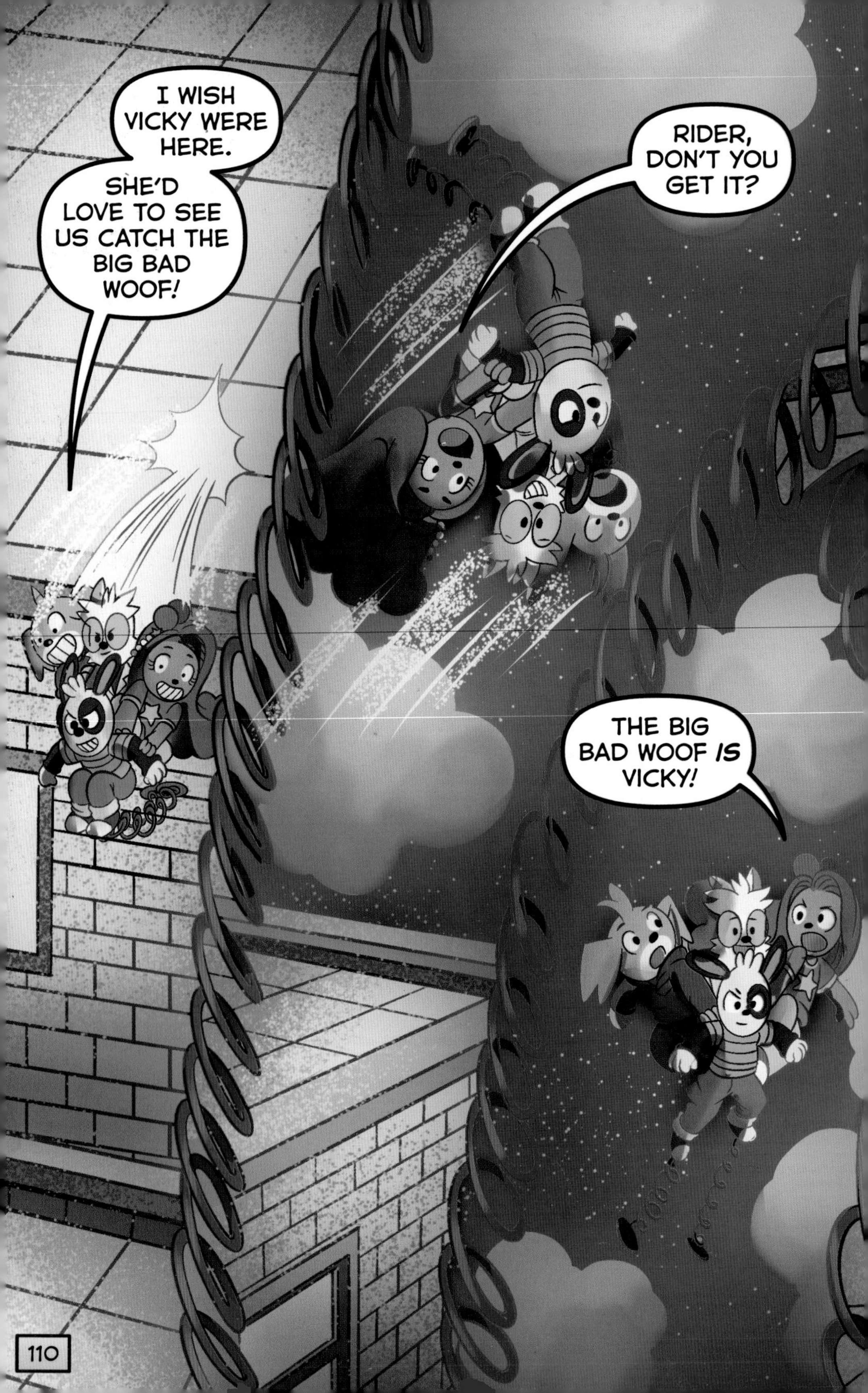
I WISH VICKY WERE HERE.
SHE'D LOVE TO SEE US CATCH THE BIG BAD WOOF!
RIDER, DON'T YOU GET IT?
THE BIG BAD WOOF *IS* VICKY!

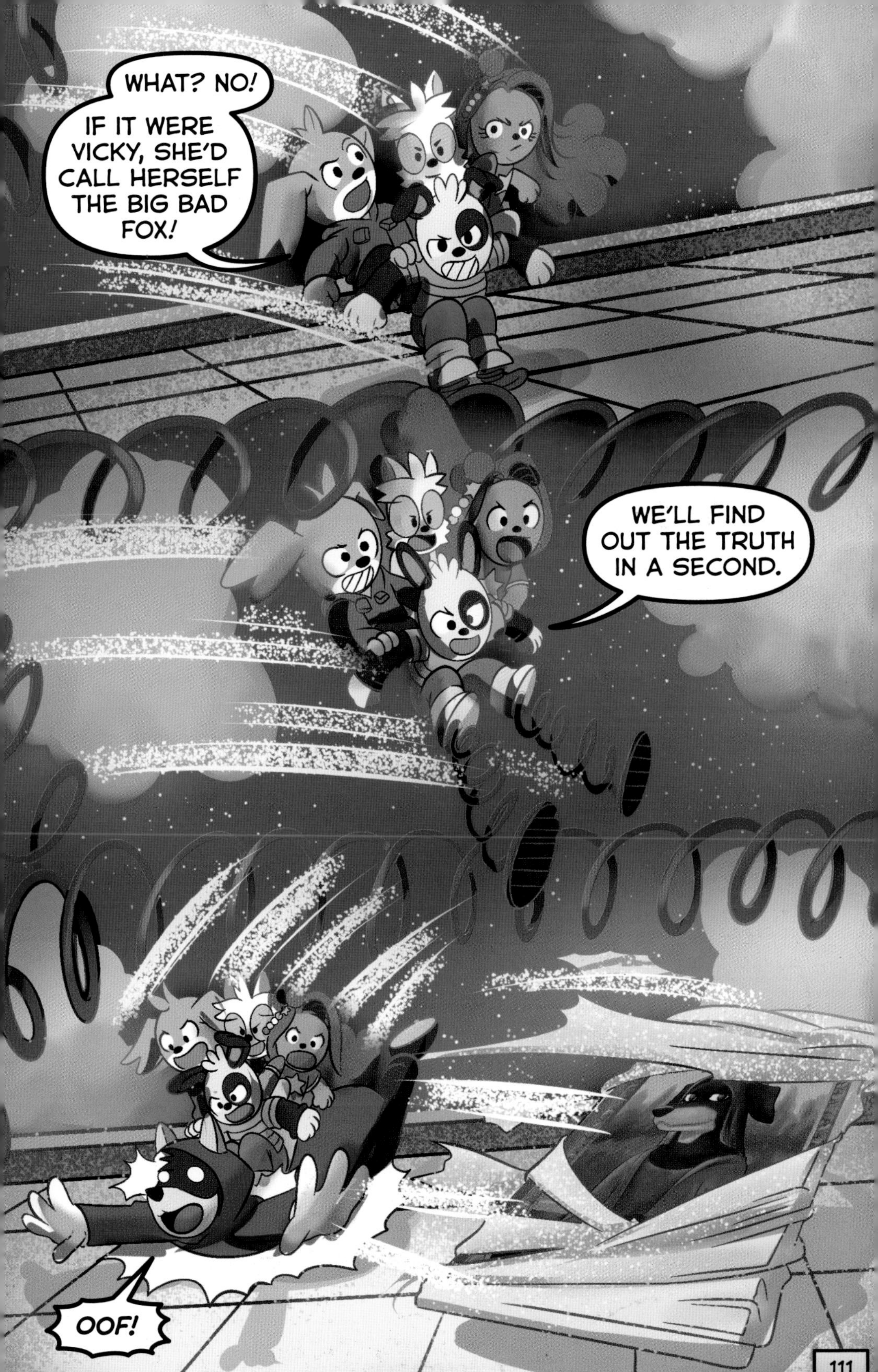
WHAT? NO!
IF IT WERE VICKY, SHE'D CALL HERSELF THE BIG BAD FOX!
WE'LL FIND OUT THE TRUTH IN A SECOND.
OOF!

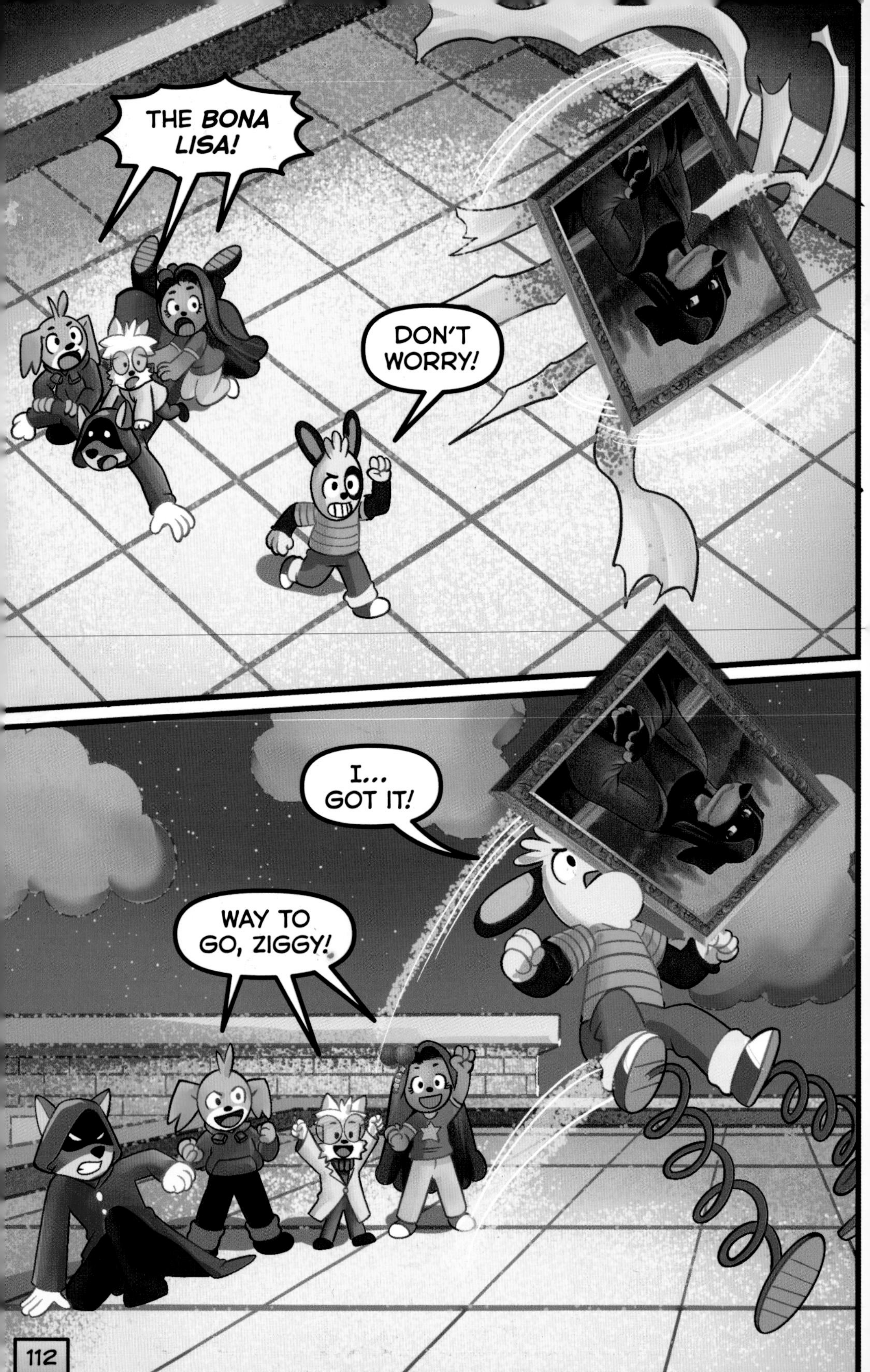
THE BONA LISA!
DON'T WORRY!
I... GOT IT!
WAY TO GO, ZIGGY!

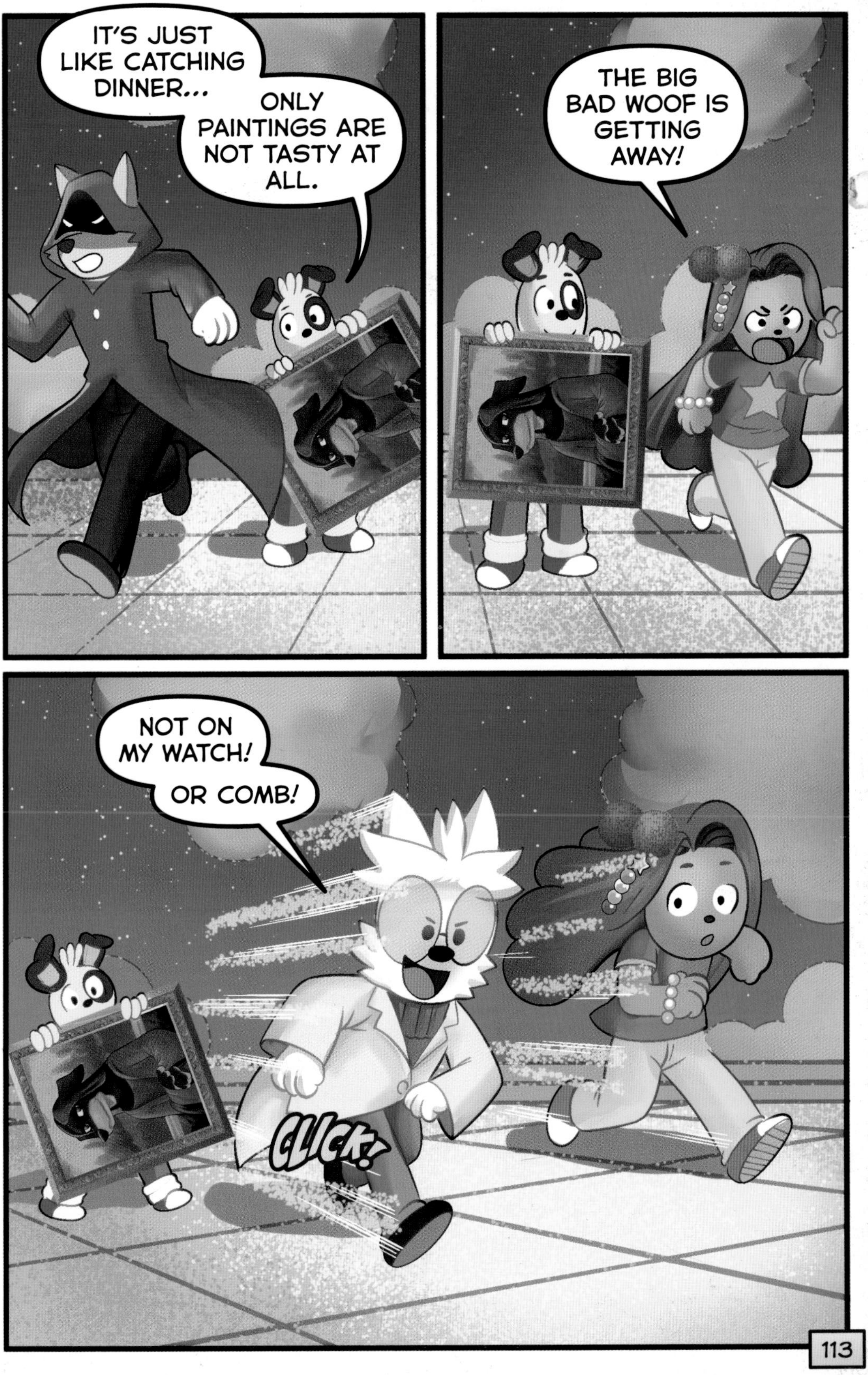
IT'S JUST LIKE CATCHING DINNER...
ONLY PAINTINGS ARE NOT TASTY AT ALL.
THE BIG BAD WOOF IS GETTING AWAY!
NOT ON MY WATCH!
OR COMB!
CLICK!

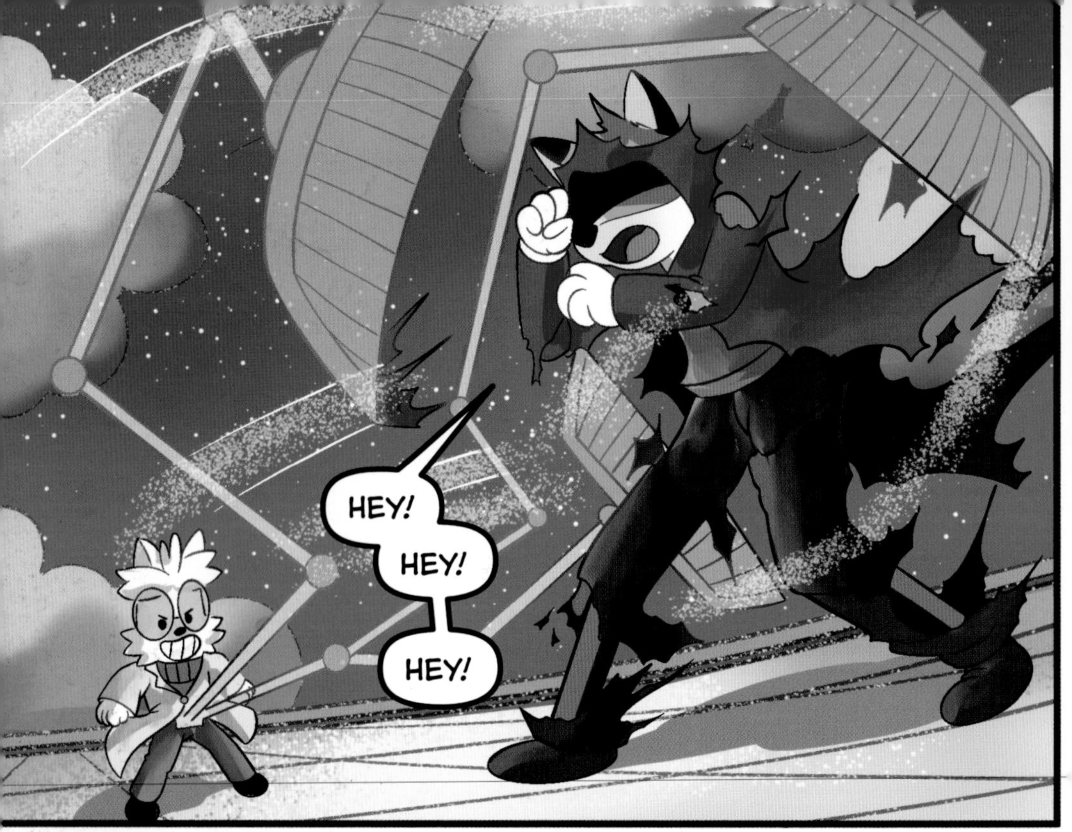
HEY!
HEY!
HEY!

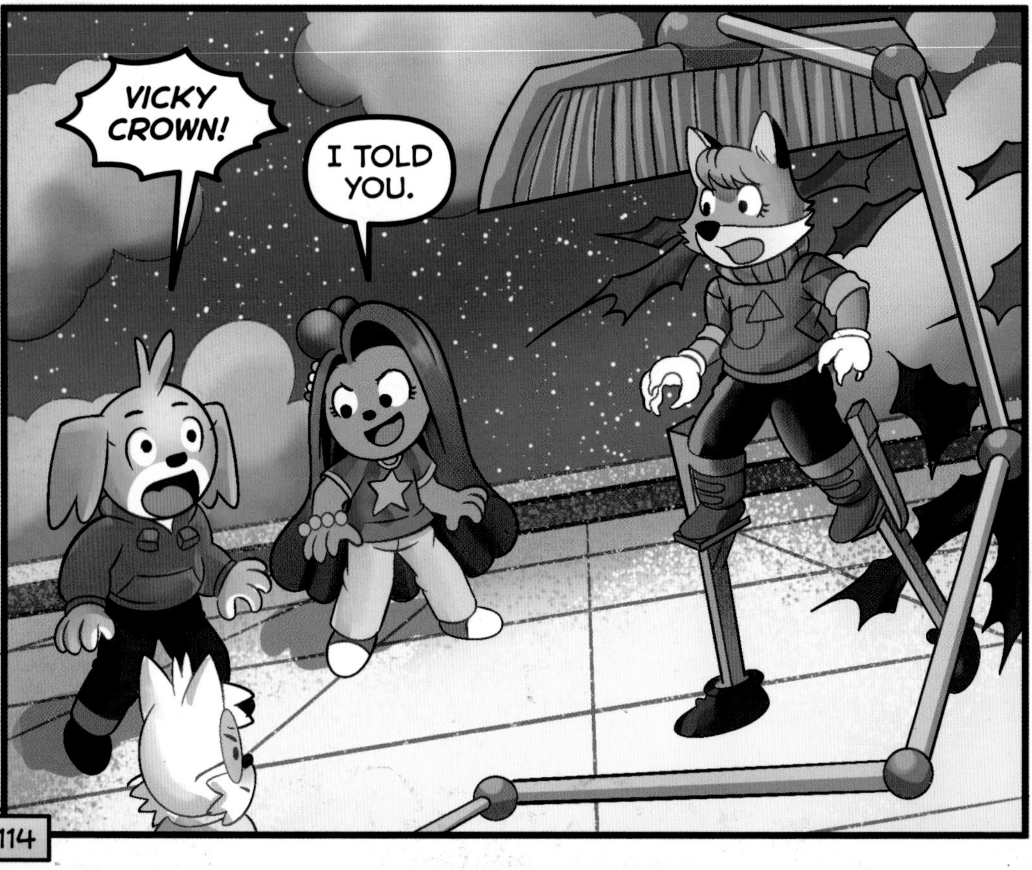
VICKY CROWN!
I TOLD YOU.

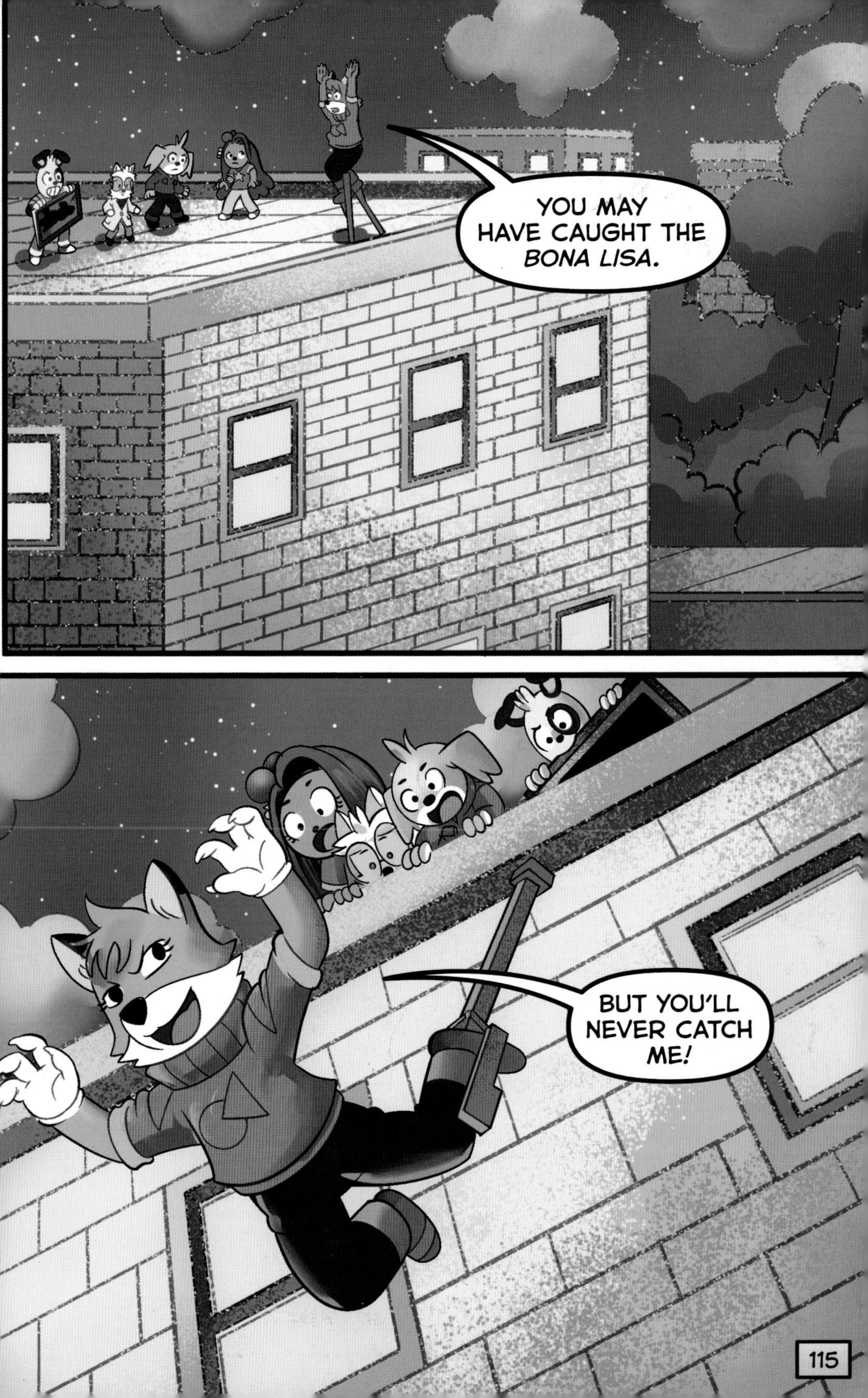
YOU MAY HAVE CAUGHT THE *BONA LISA*.
BUT YOU'LL NEVER CATCH ME!

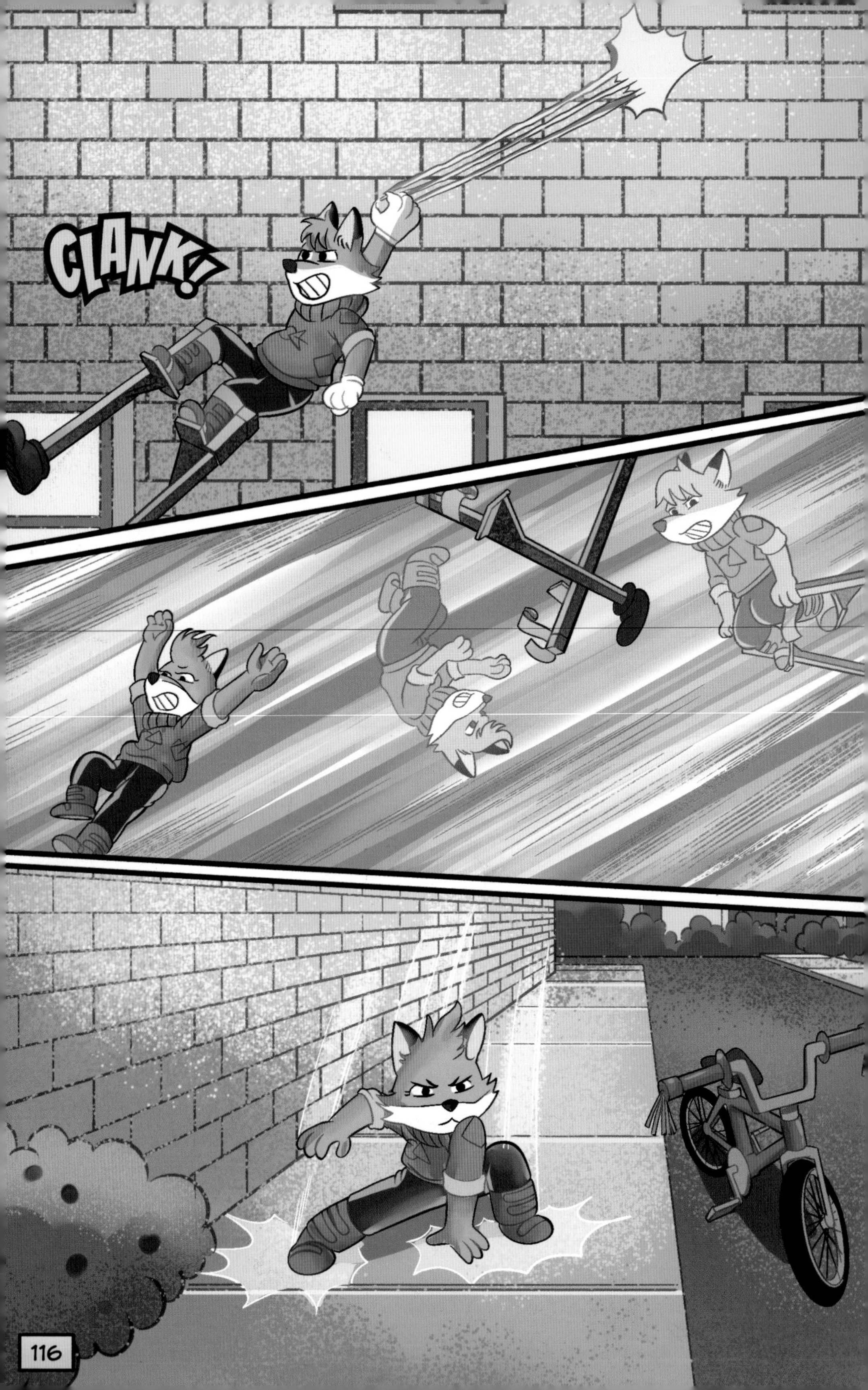
CLANK!

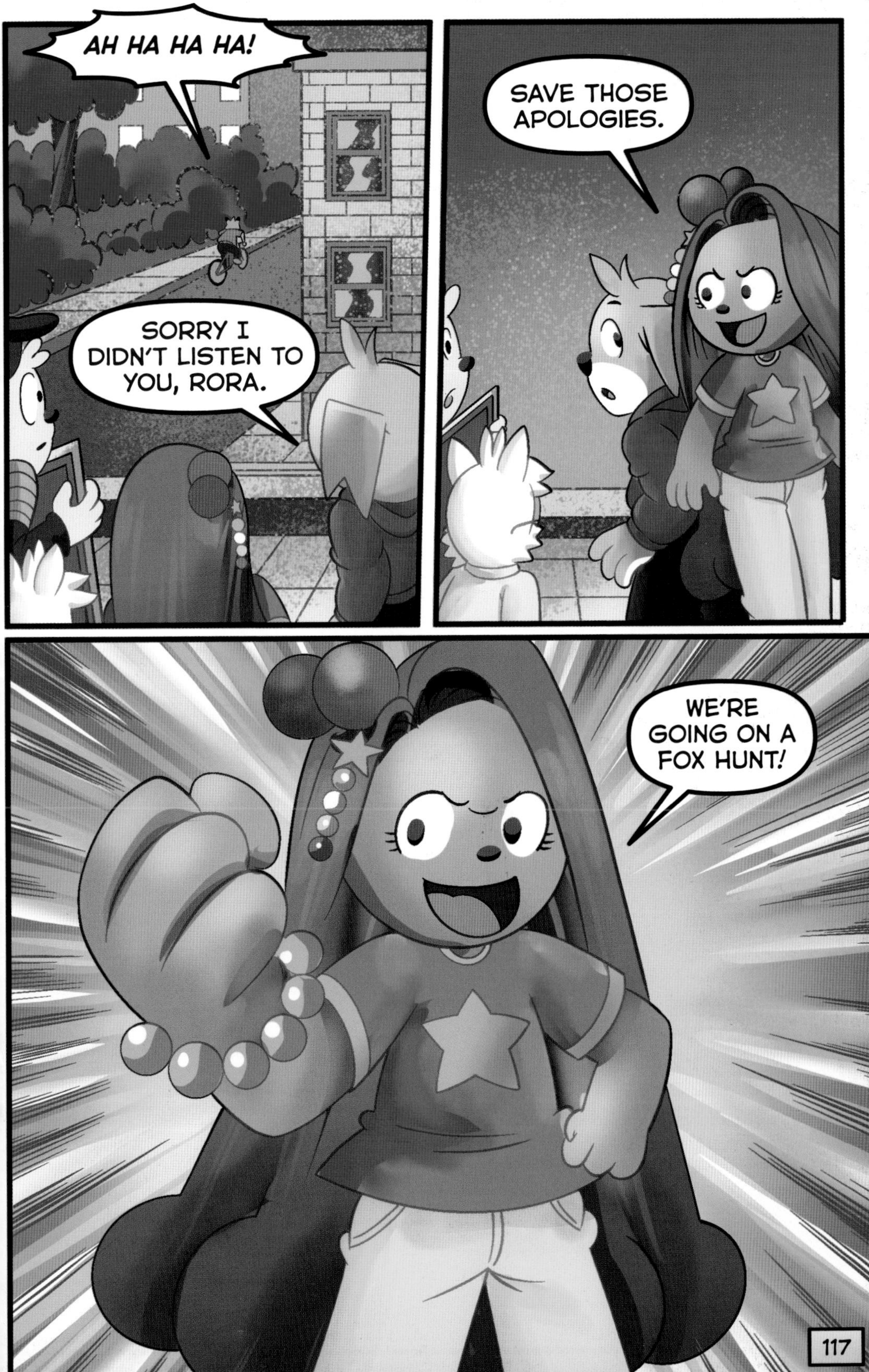
AH HA HA HA!
SORRY I DIDN'T LISTEN TO YOU, RORA.
SAVE THOSE APOLOGIES.
WE'RE GOING ON A FOX HUNT!

CHAPTER 10

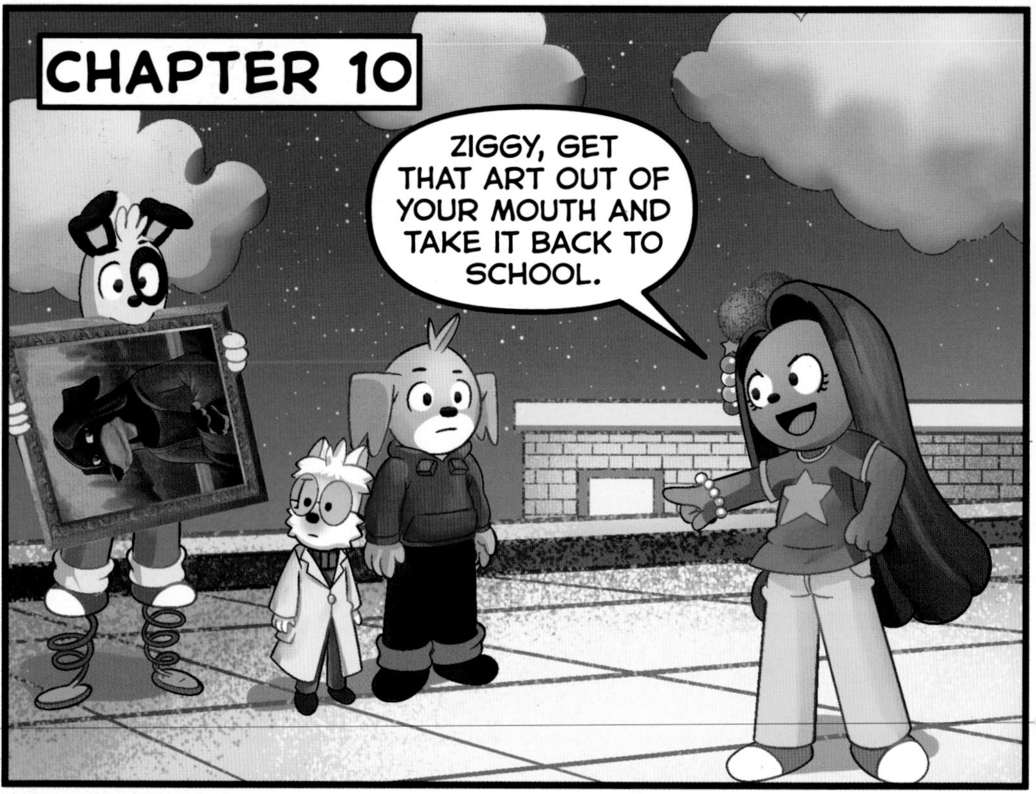
ZIGGY, GET THAT ART OUT OF YOUR MOUTH AND TAKE IT BACK TO SCHOOL.

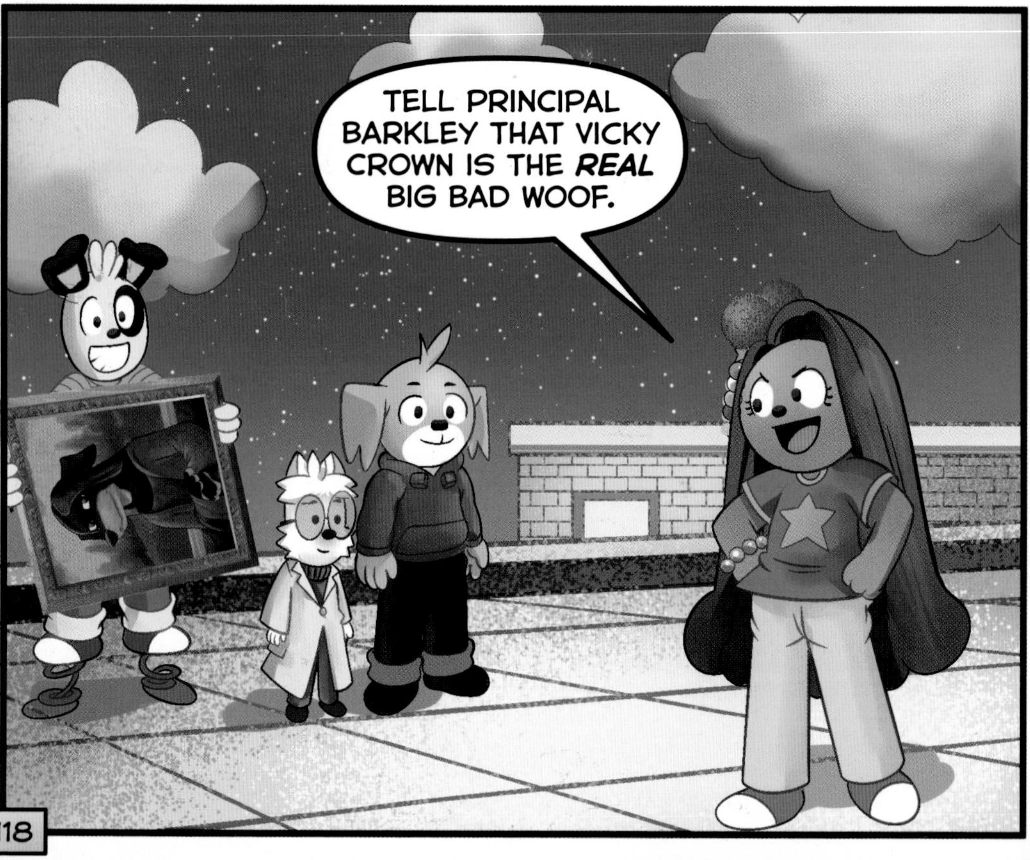
TELL PRINCIPAL BARKLEY THAT VICKY CROWN IS THE *REAL* BIG BAD WOOF.

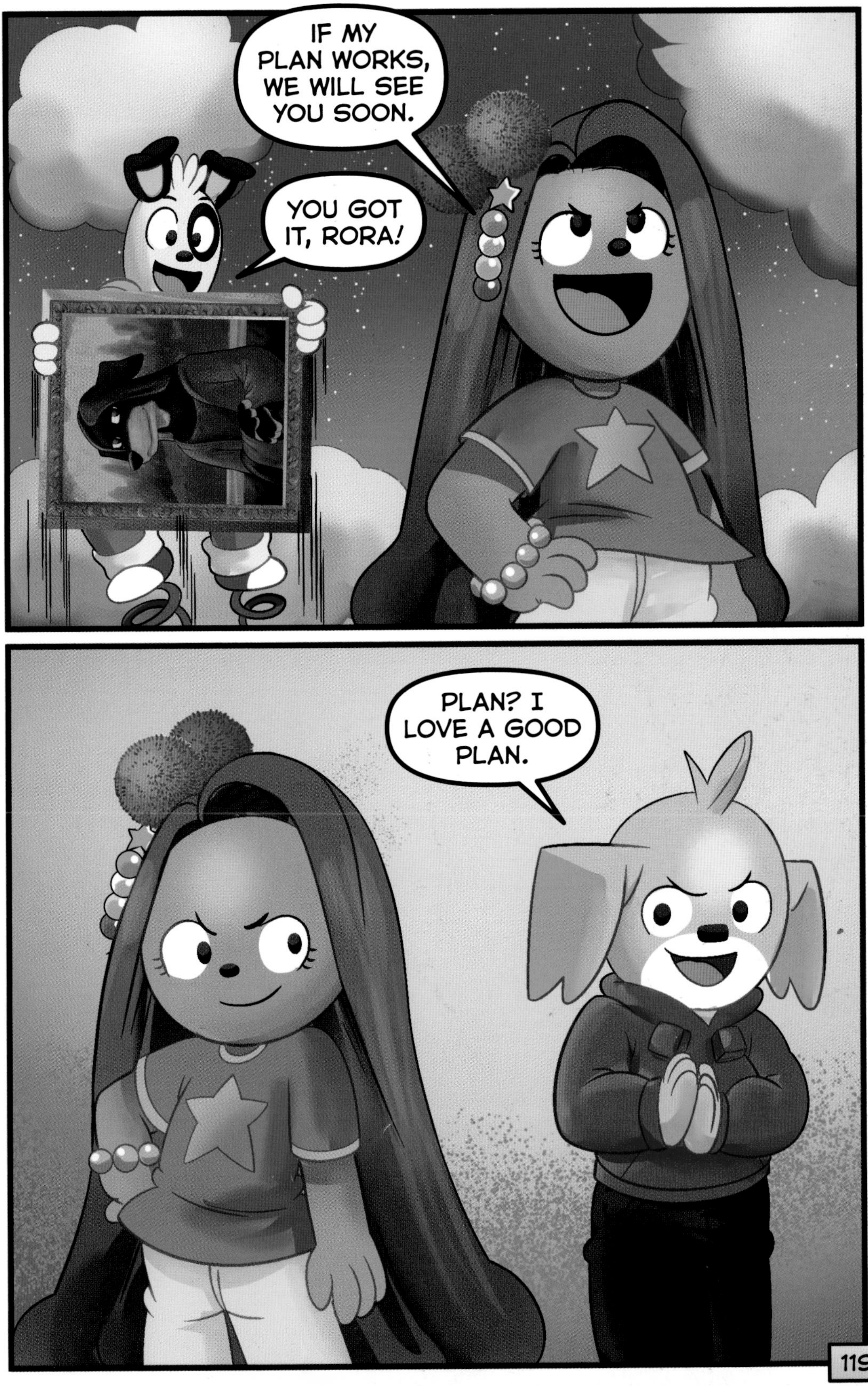
IF MY PLAN WORKS, WE WILL SEE YOU SOON.
YOU GOT IT, RORA!
PLAN? I LOVE A GOOD PLAN.

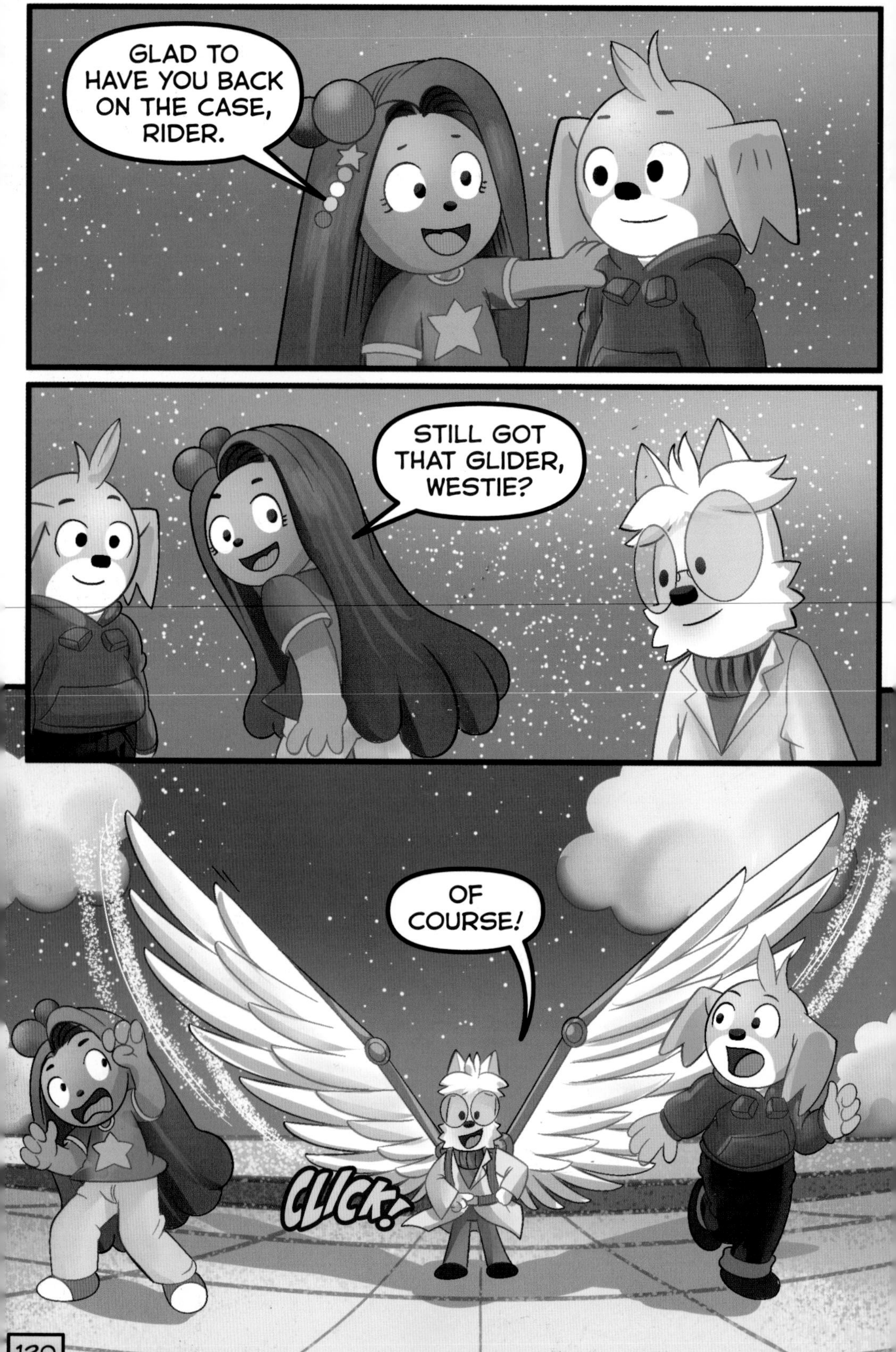
GLAD TO HAVE YOU BACK ON THE CASE, RIDER.
STILL GOT THAT GLIDER, WESTIE?
OF COURSE!
CLICK!

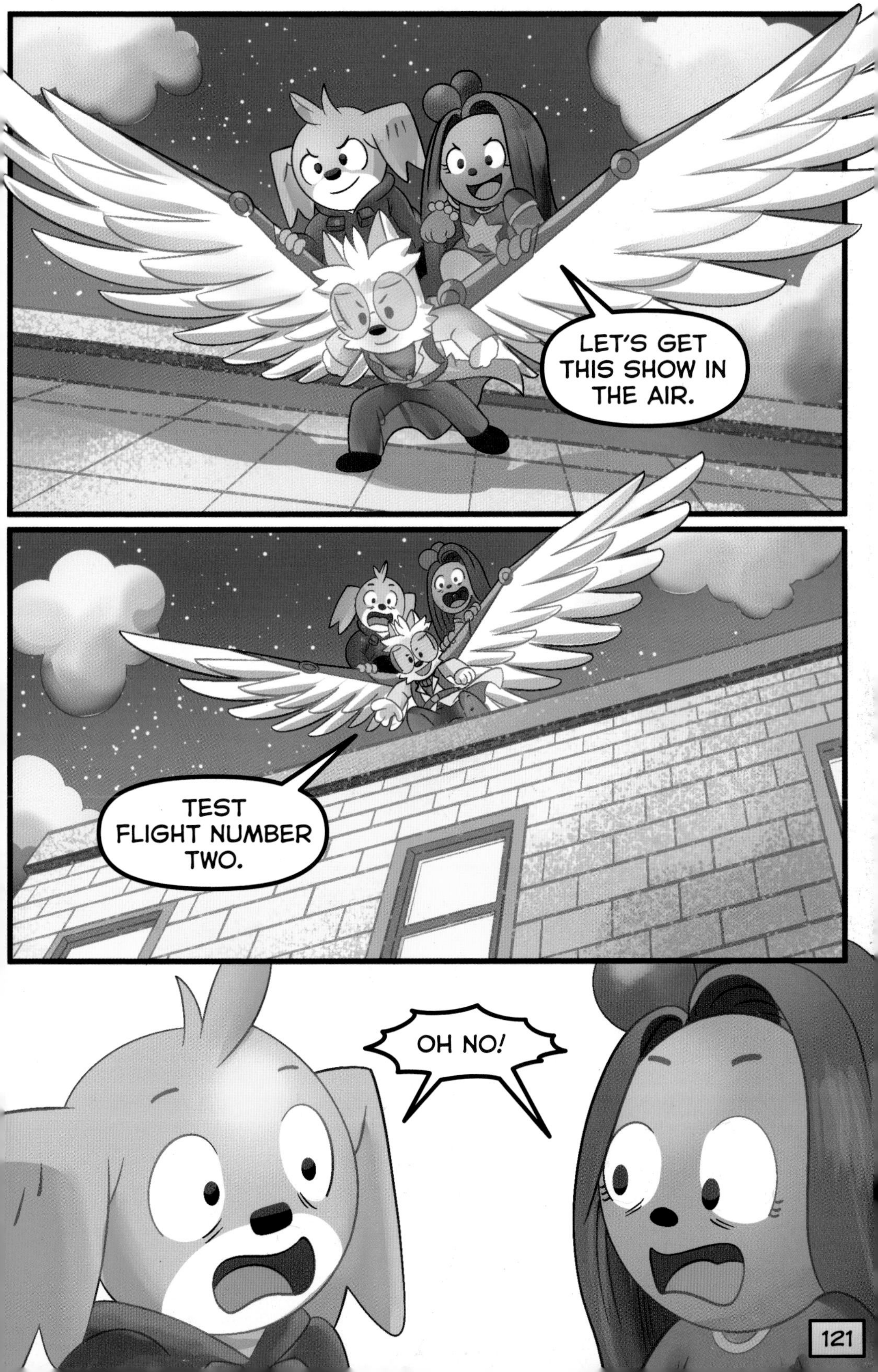
LET'S GET THIS SHOW IN THE AIR.
TEST FLIGHT NUMBER TWO.
OH NO!

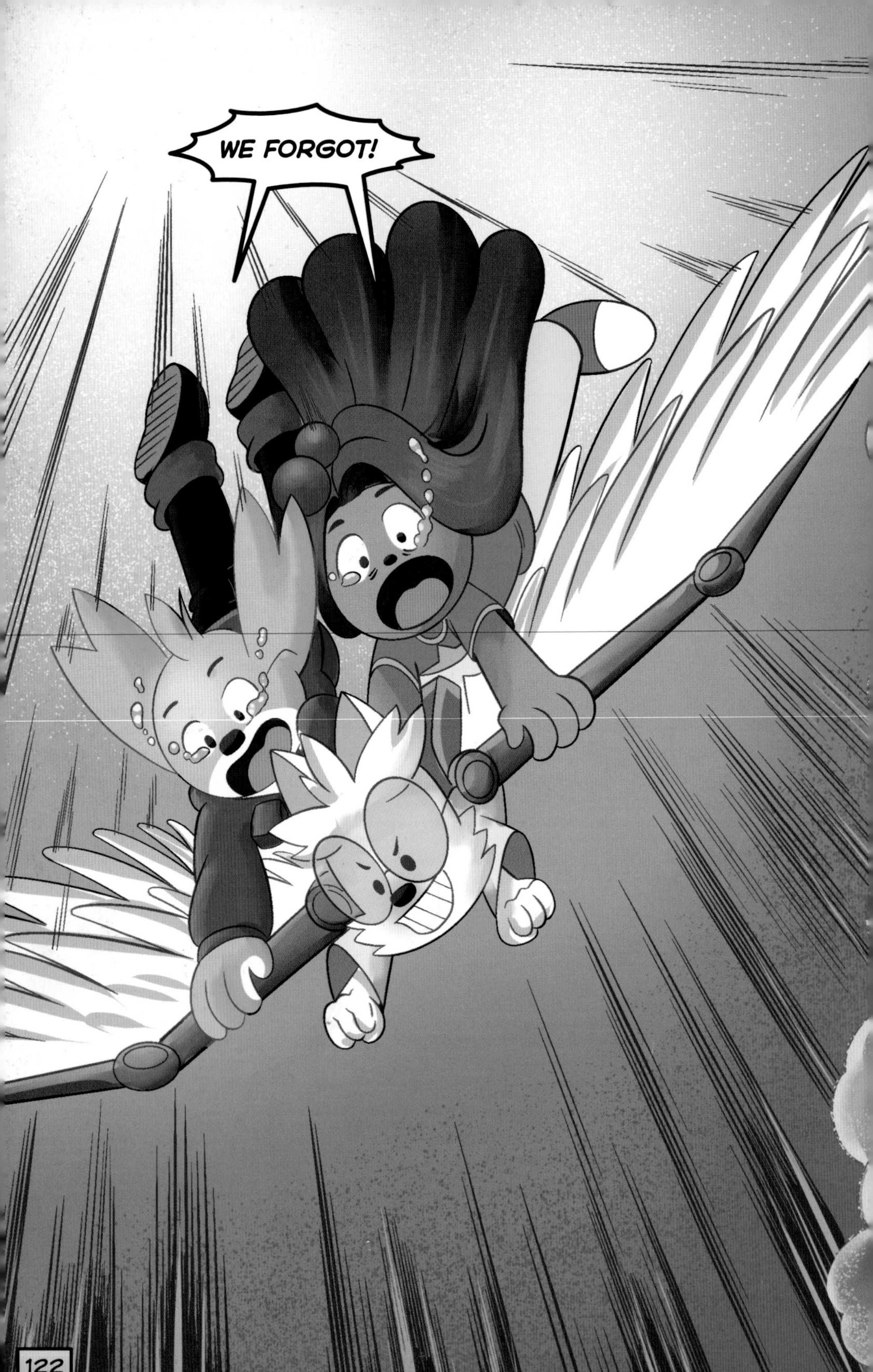
WE FORGOT!

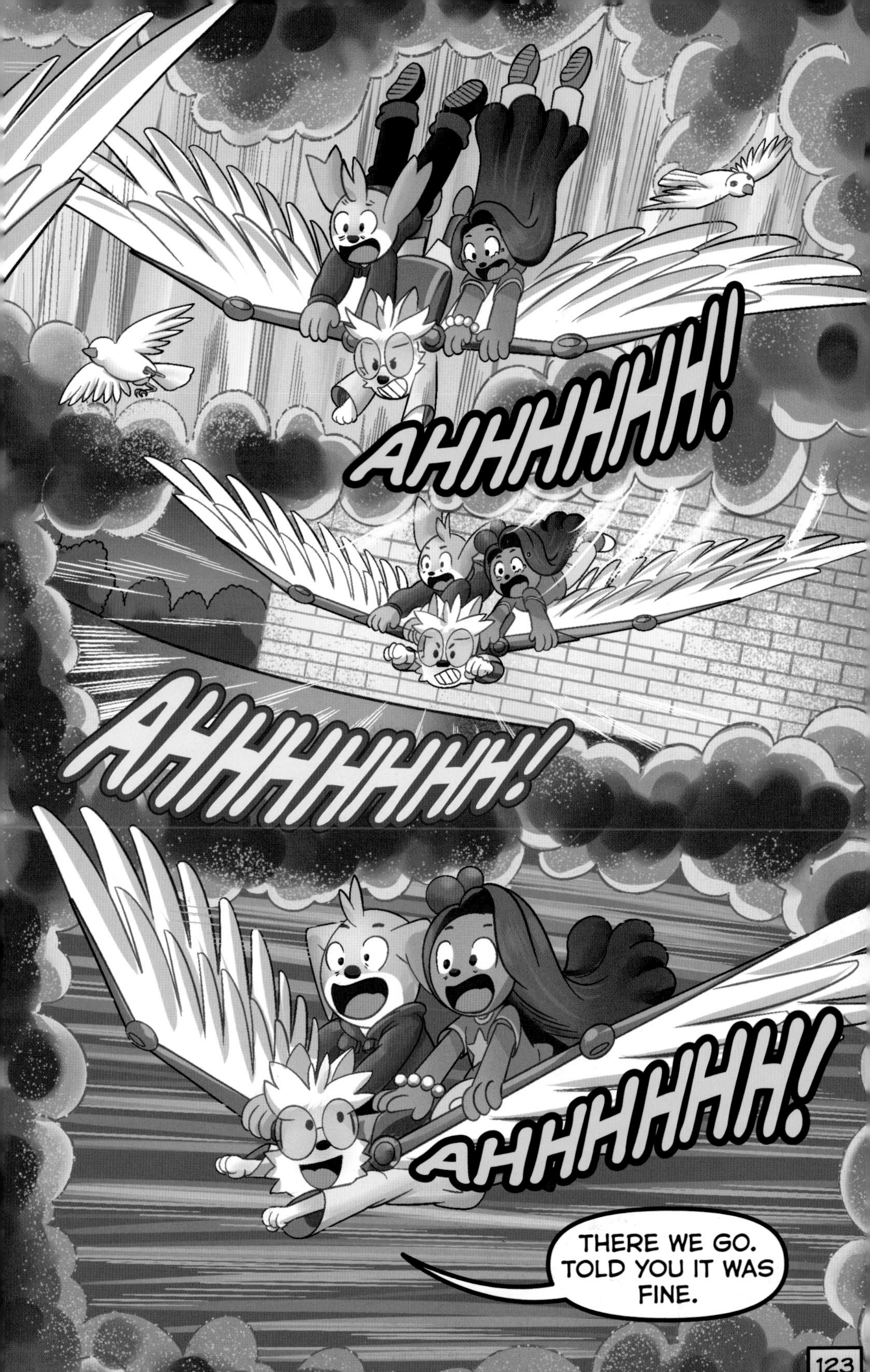
AHHHHHH!
AHHHHHHH!
AHHHHHH!
THERE WE GO. TOLD YOU IT WAS FINE.

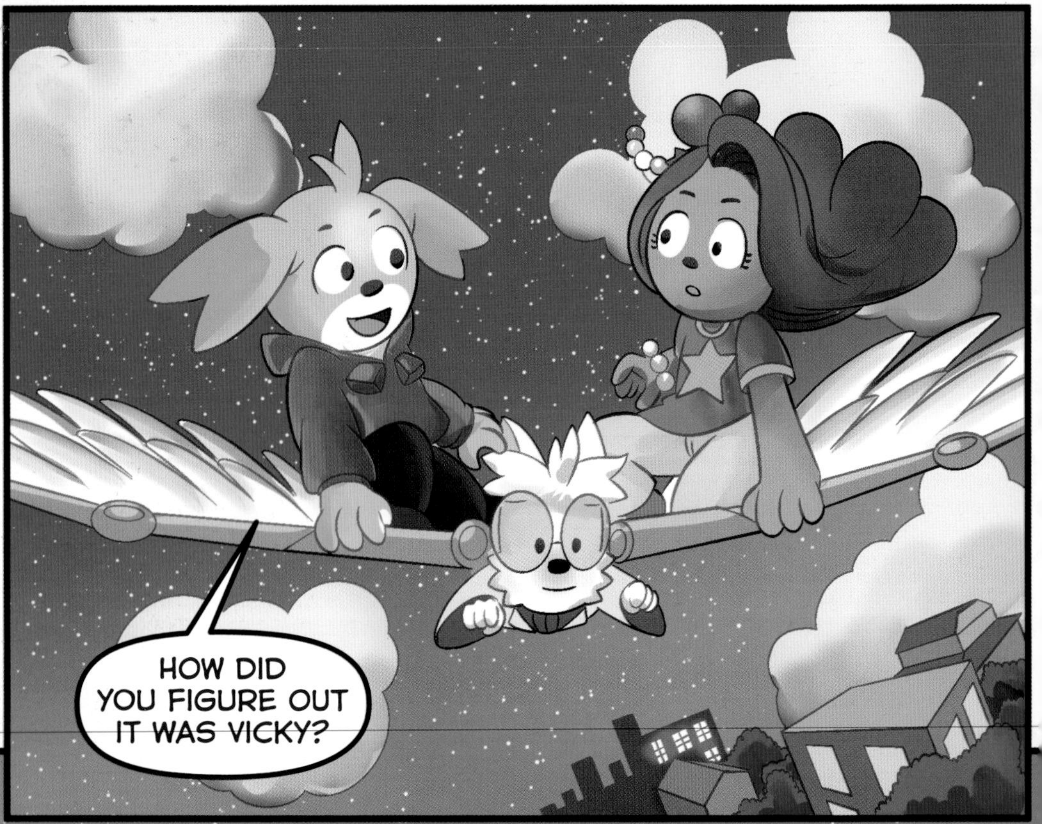
HOW DID YOU FIGURE OUT IT WAS VICKY?

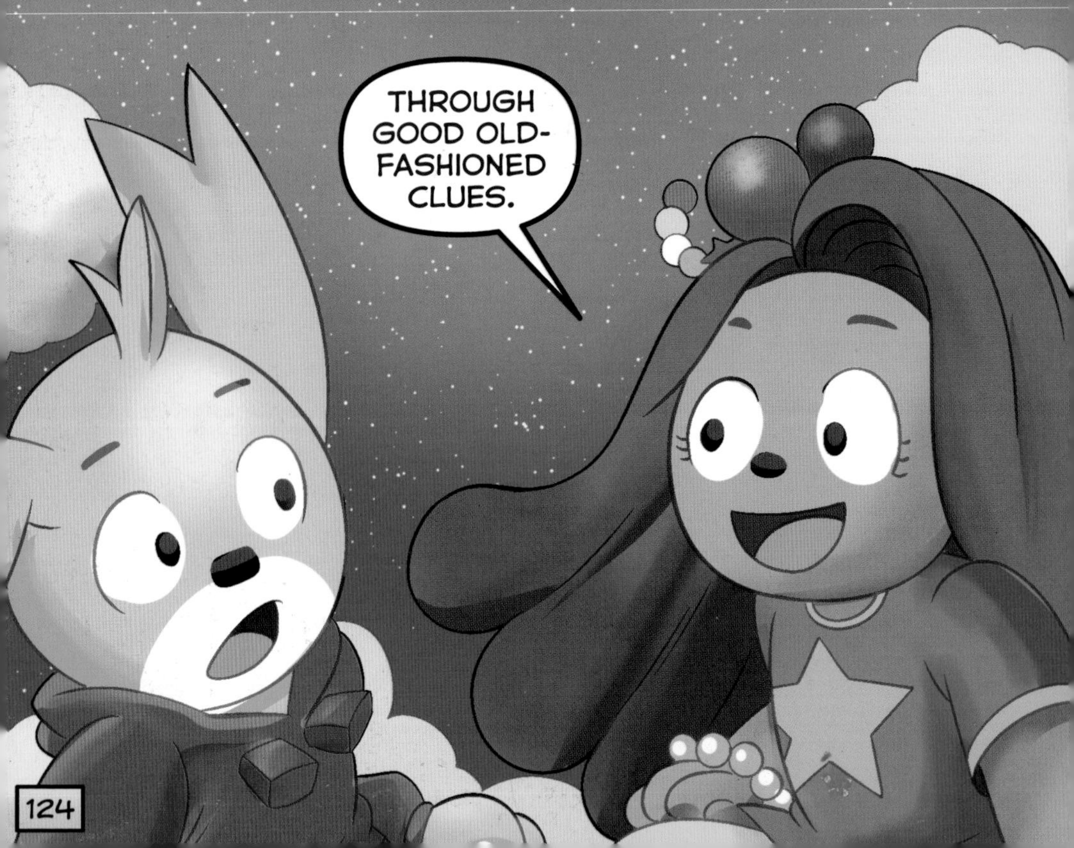
THROUGH GOOD OLD-FASHIONED CLUES.

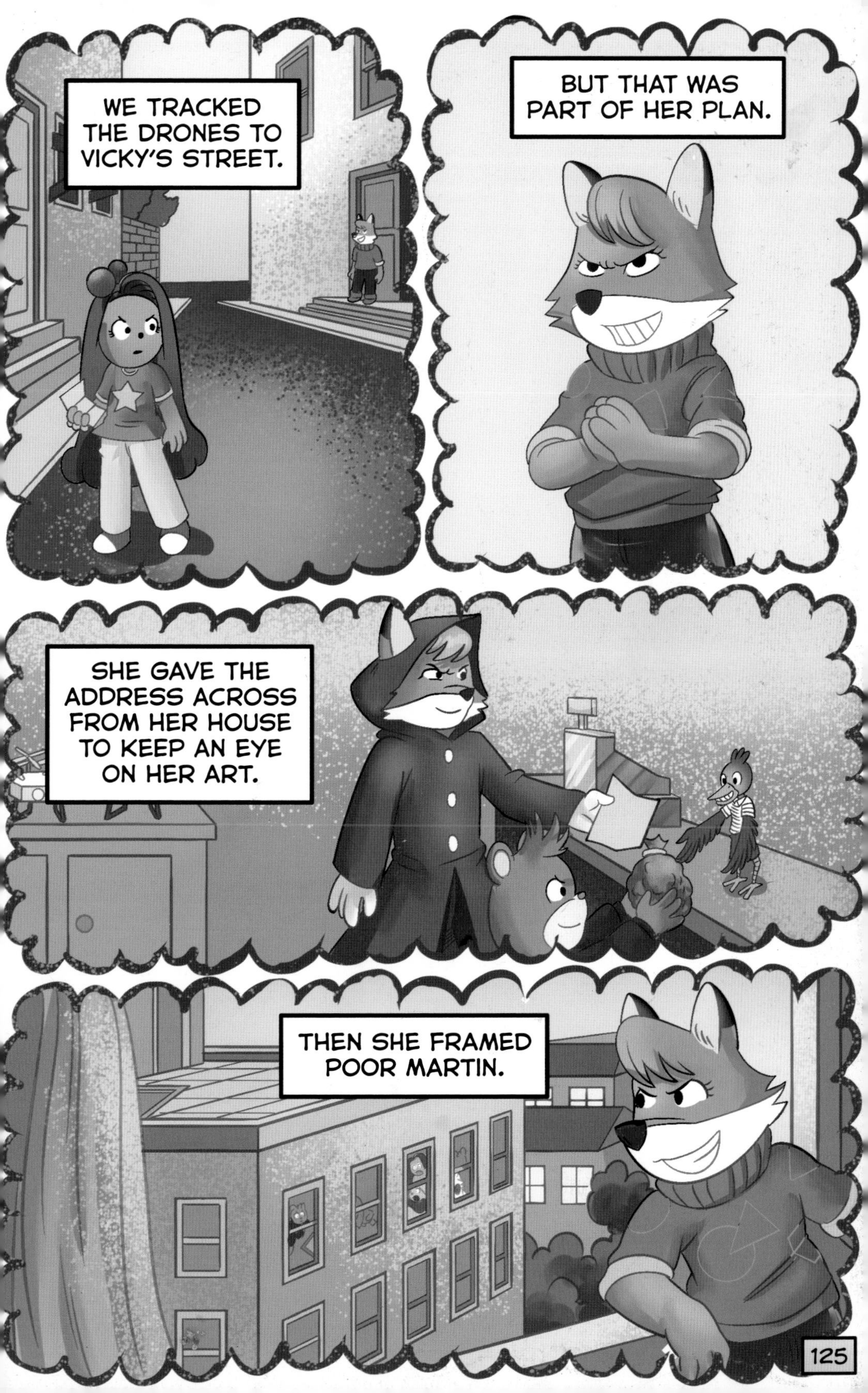
WE TRACKED THE DRONES TO VICKY'S STREET.
BUT THAT WAS PART OF HER PLAN.
SHE GAVE THE ADDRESS ACROSS FROM HER HOUSE TO KEEP AN EYE ON HER ART.
THEN SHE FRAMED POOR MARTIN.

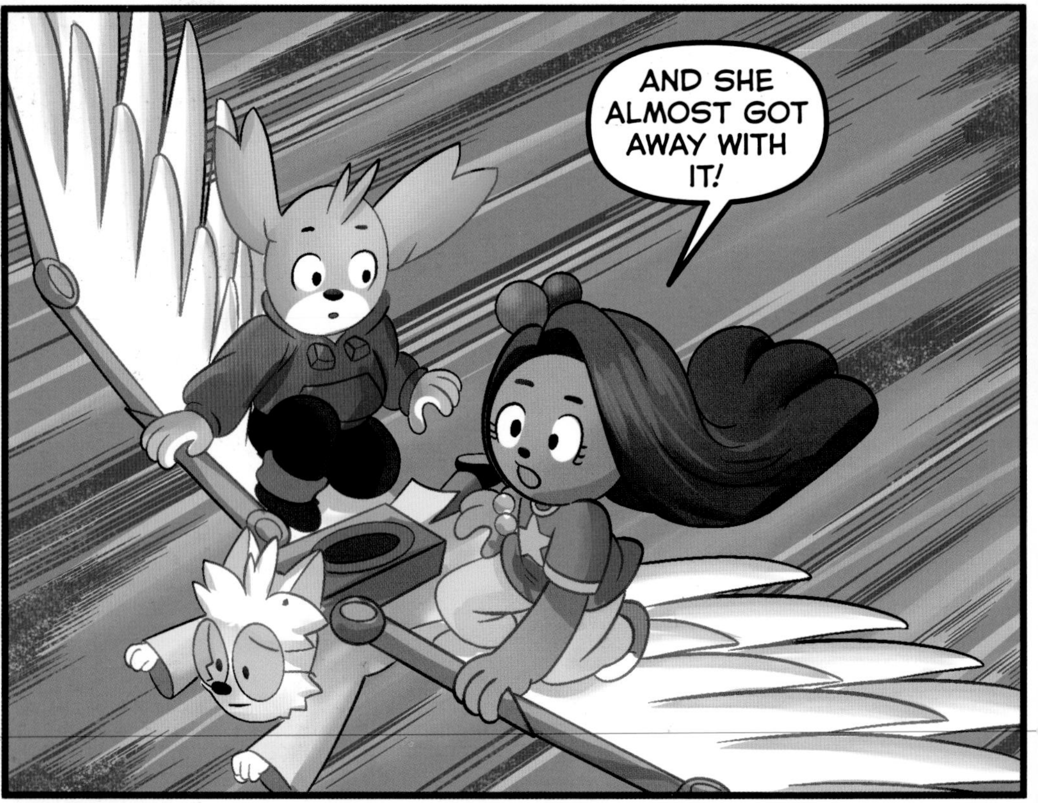
AND SHE ALMOST GOT AWAY WITH IT!

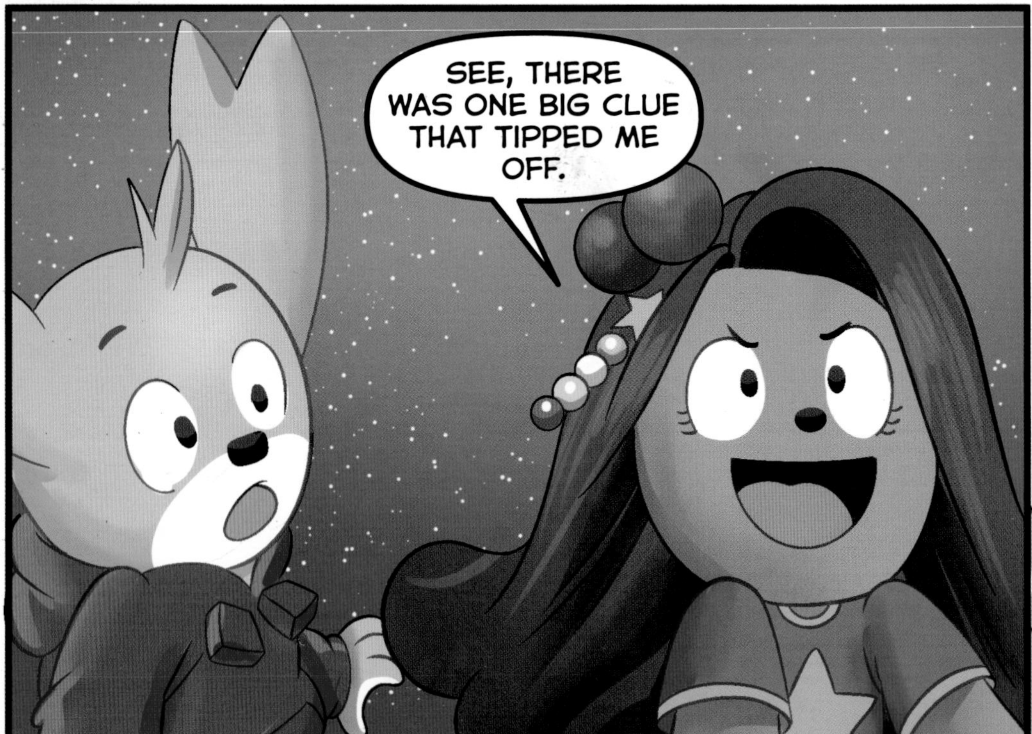
SEE, THERE WAS ONE BIG CLUE THAT TIPPED ME OFF.

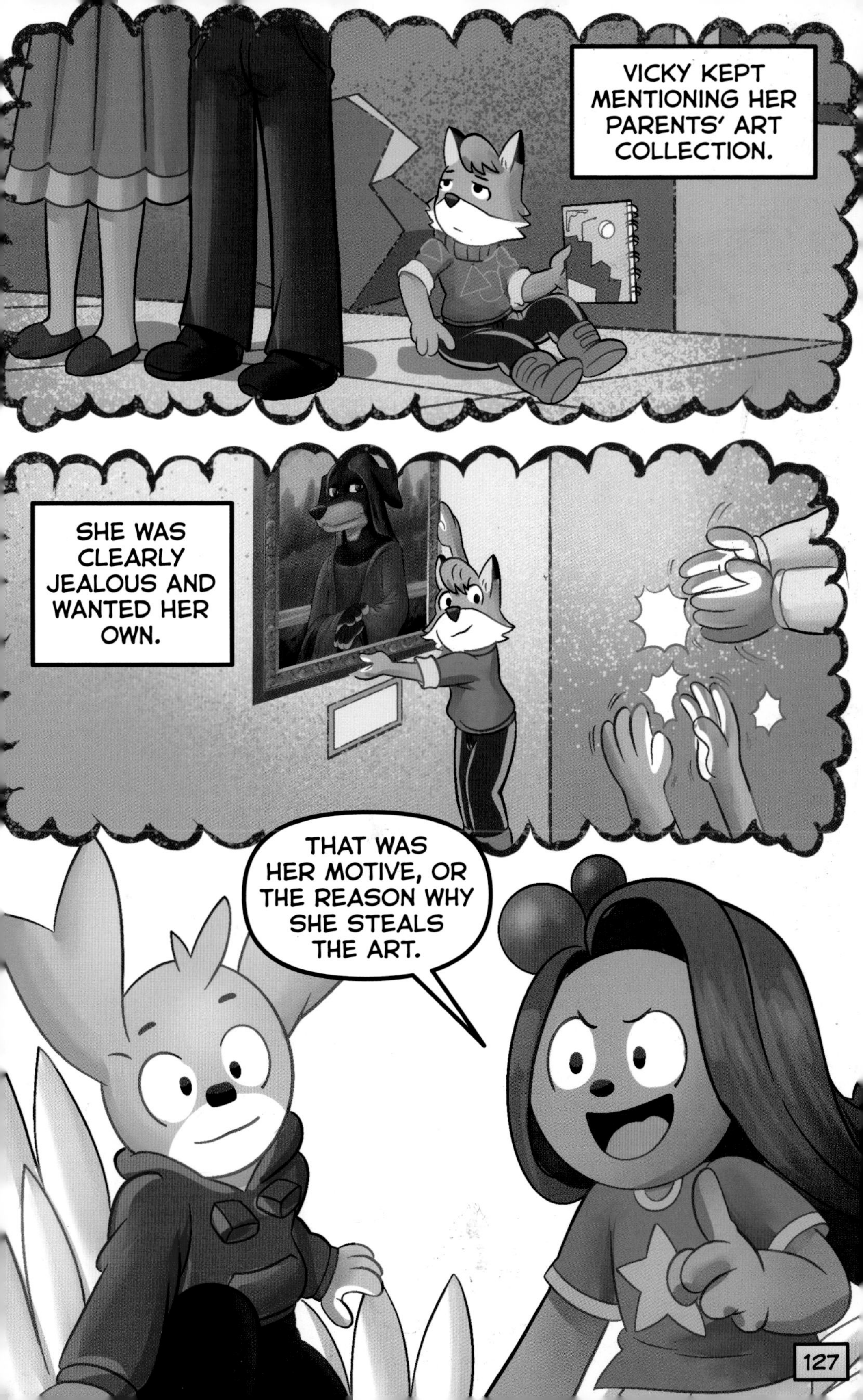
VICKY KEPT MENTIONING HER PARENTS' ART COLLECTION.
SHE WAS CLEARLY JEALOUS AND WANTED HER OWN.
THAT WAS HER MOTIVE, OR THE REASON WHY SHE STEALS THE ART.

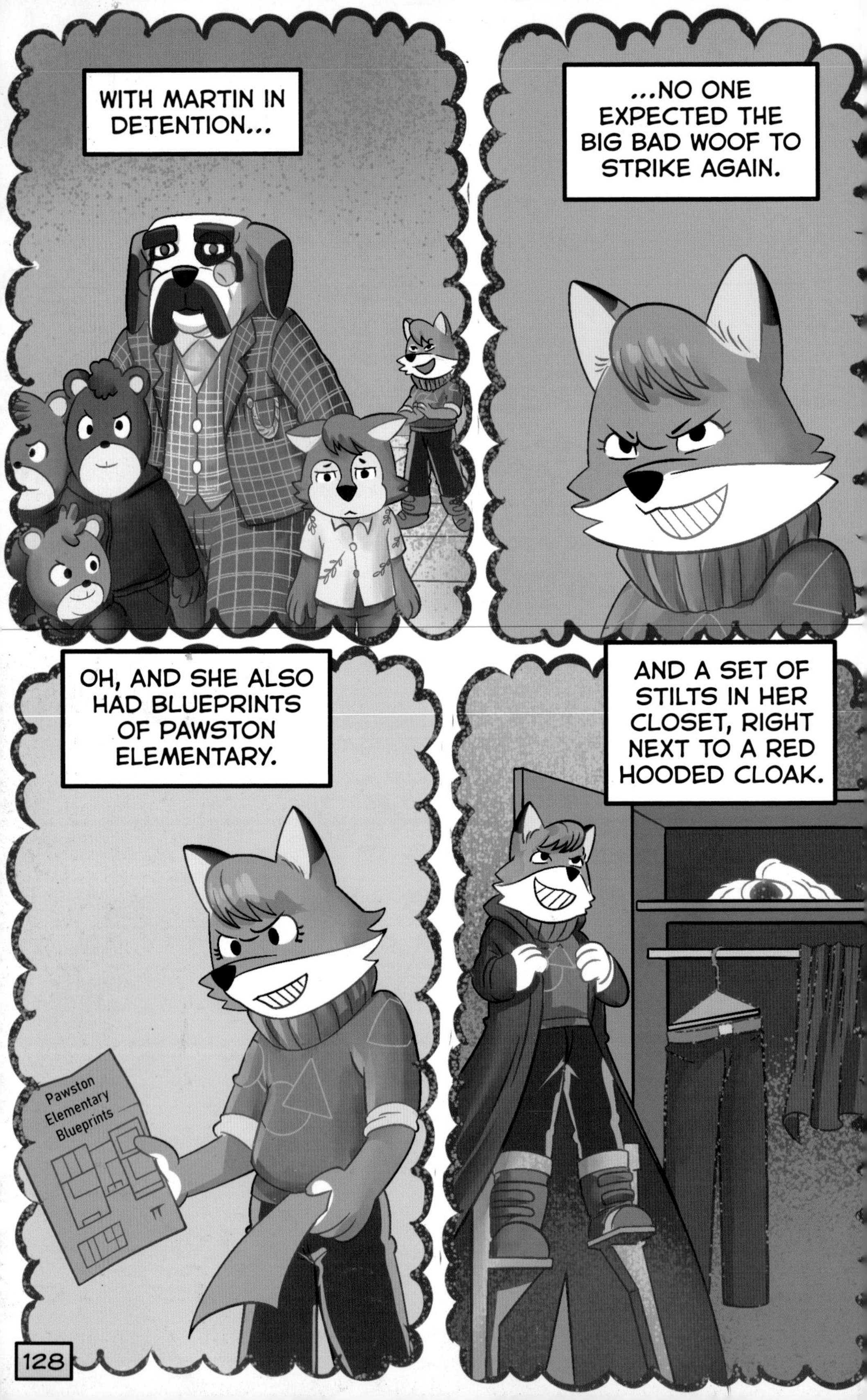
WITH MARTIN IN DETENTION...
...NO ONE EXPECTED THE BIG BAD WOOF TO STRIKE AGAIN.
OH, AND SHE ALSO HAD BLUEPRINTS OF PAWSTON ELEMENTARY.
Pawston Elementary Blueprints
AND A SET OF STILTS IN HER CLOSET, RIGHT NEXT TO A RED HOODED CLOAK.

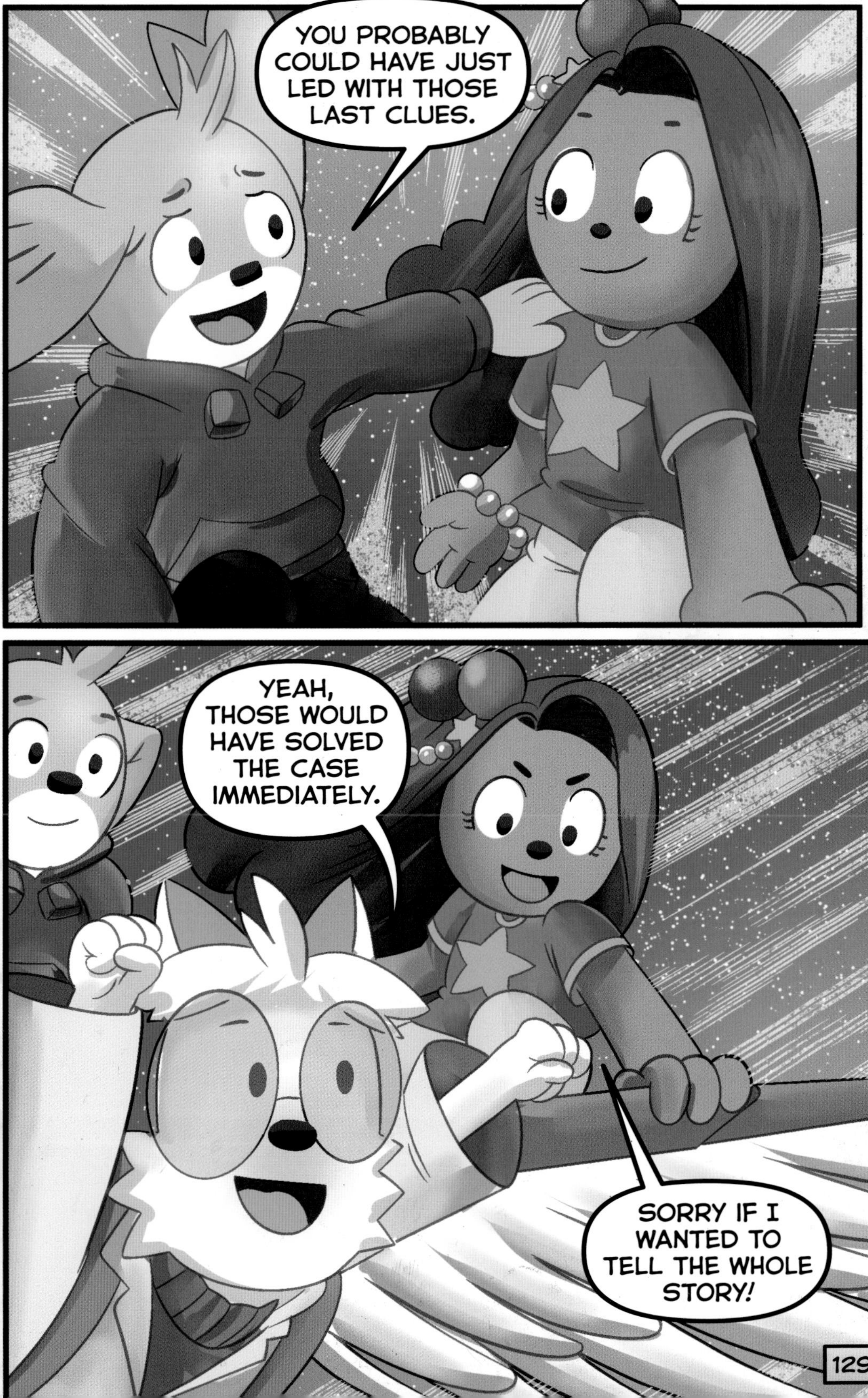
YOU PROBABLY COULD HAVE JUST LED WITH THOSE LAST CLUES.
YEAH, THOSE WOULD HAVE SOLVED THE CASE IMMEDIATELY.
SORRY IF I WANTED TO TELL THE WHOLE STORY!

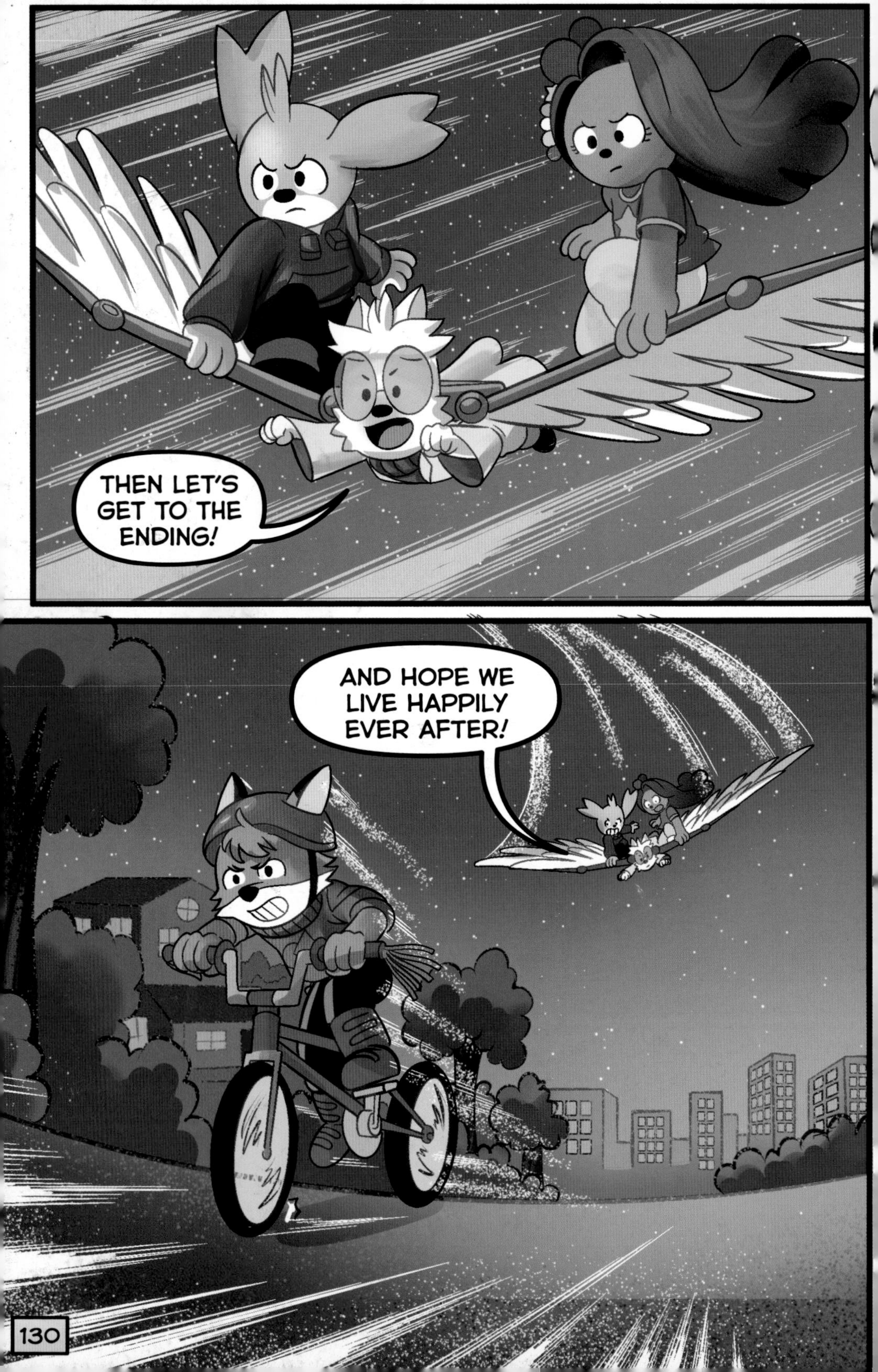
THEN LET'S GET TO THE ENDING!
AND HOPE WE LIVE HAPPILY EVER AFTER!

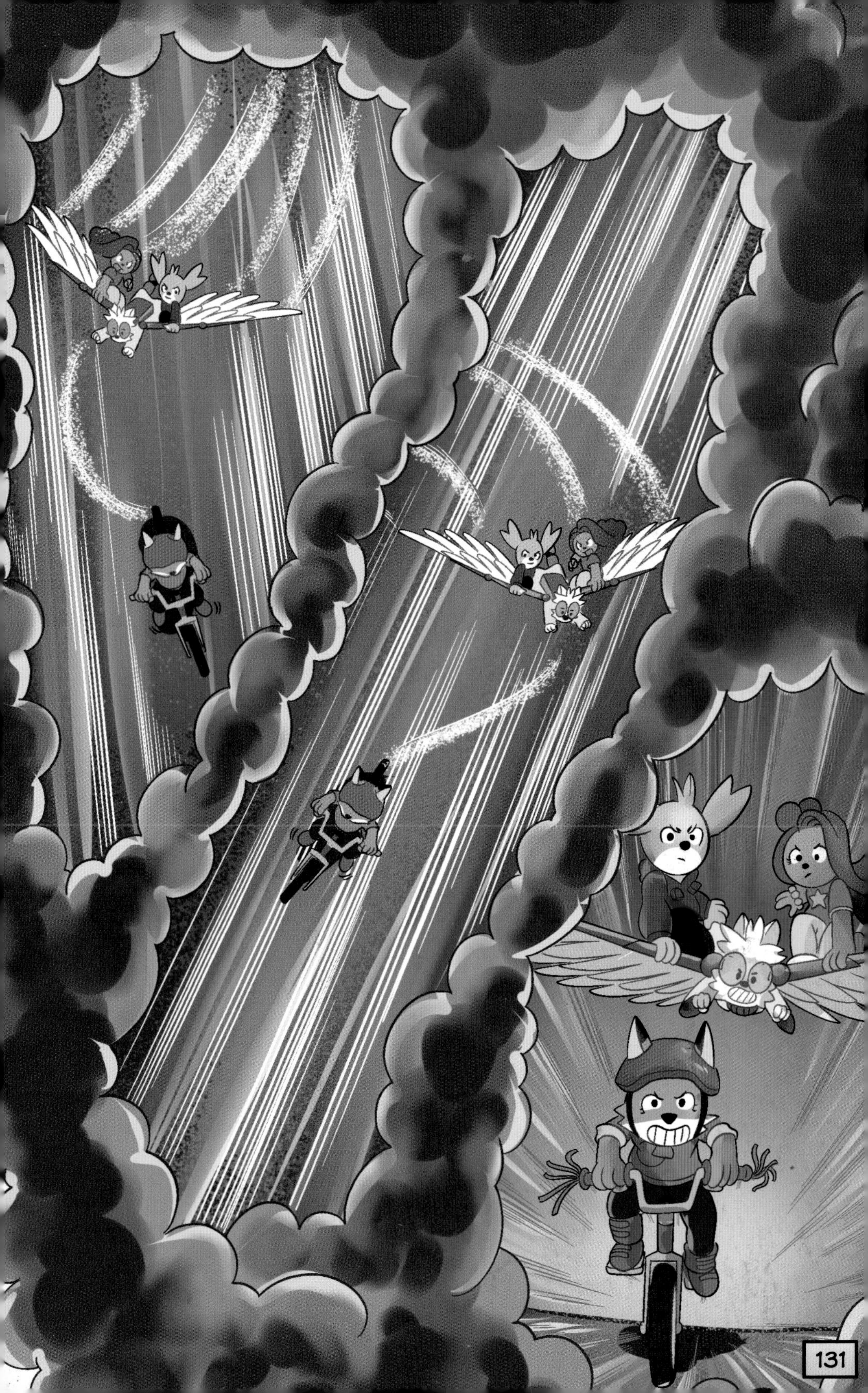

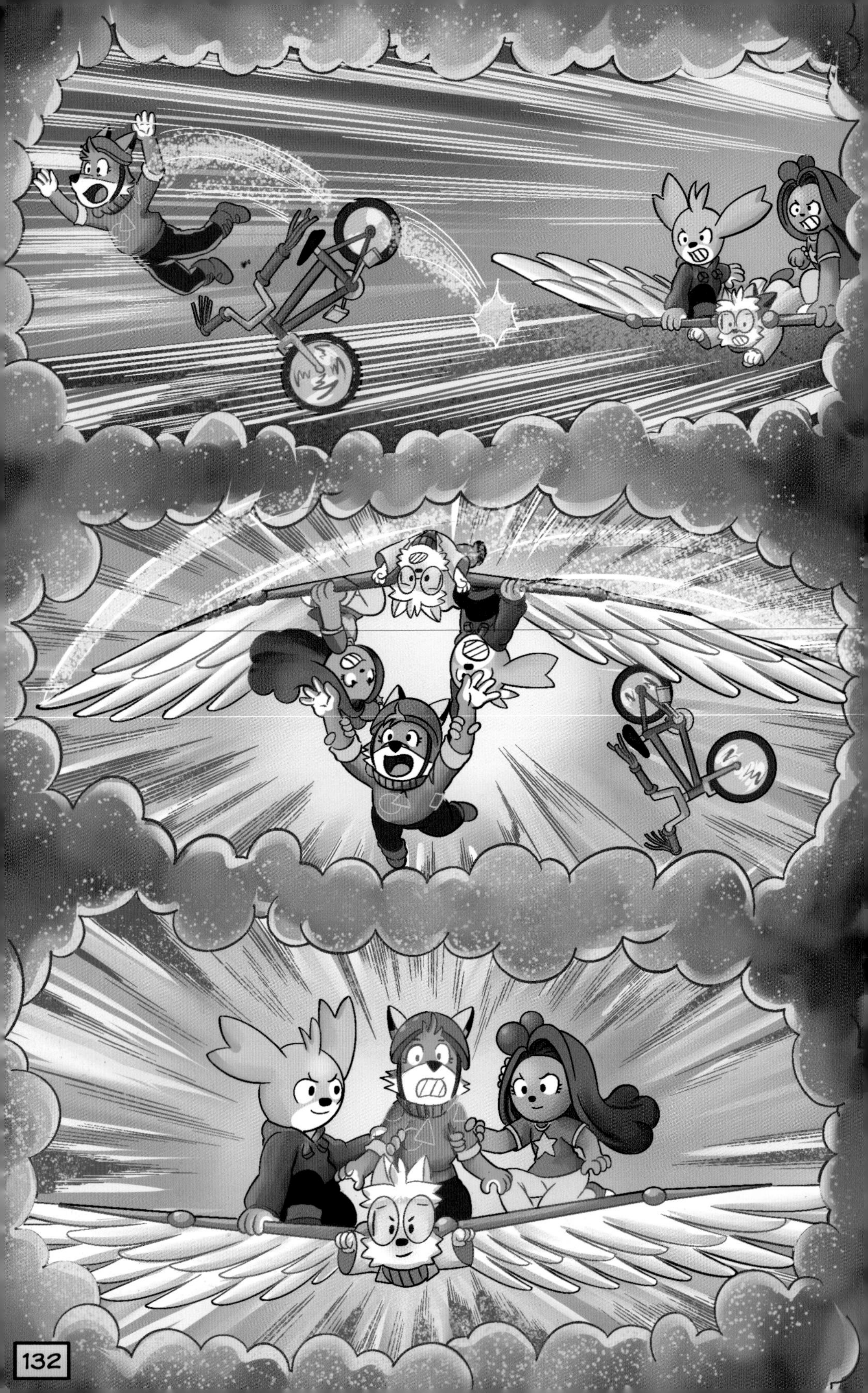

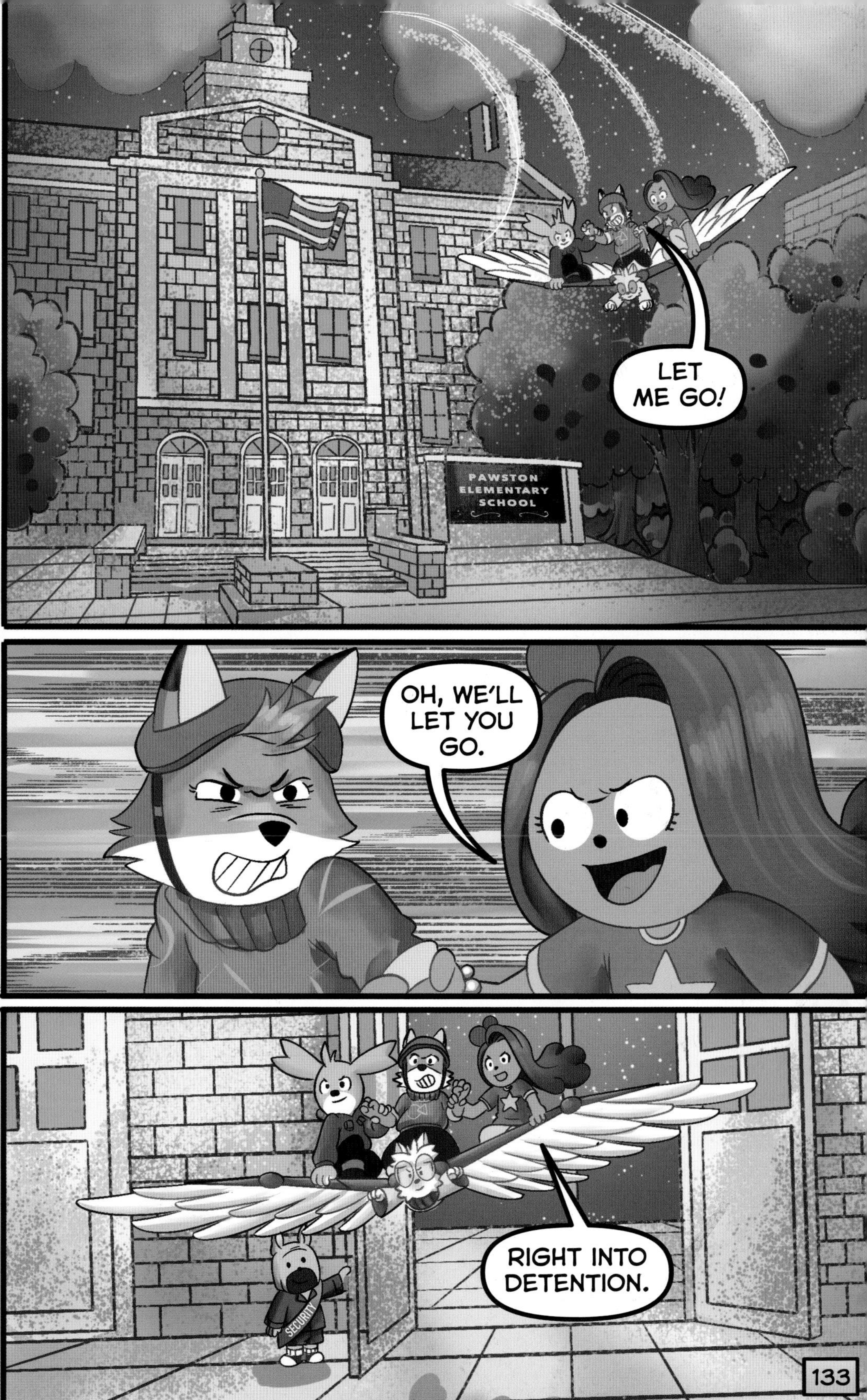
LET ME GO!
PAWSTON ELEMENTARY SCHOOL
OH, WE'LL LET YOU GO.
RIGHT INTO DETENTION.
SECURITY

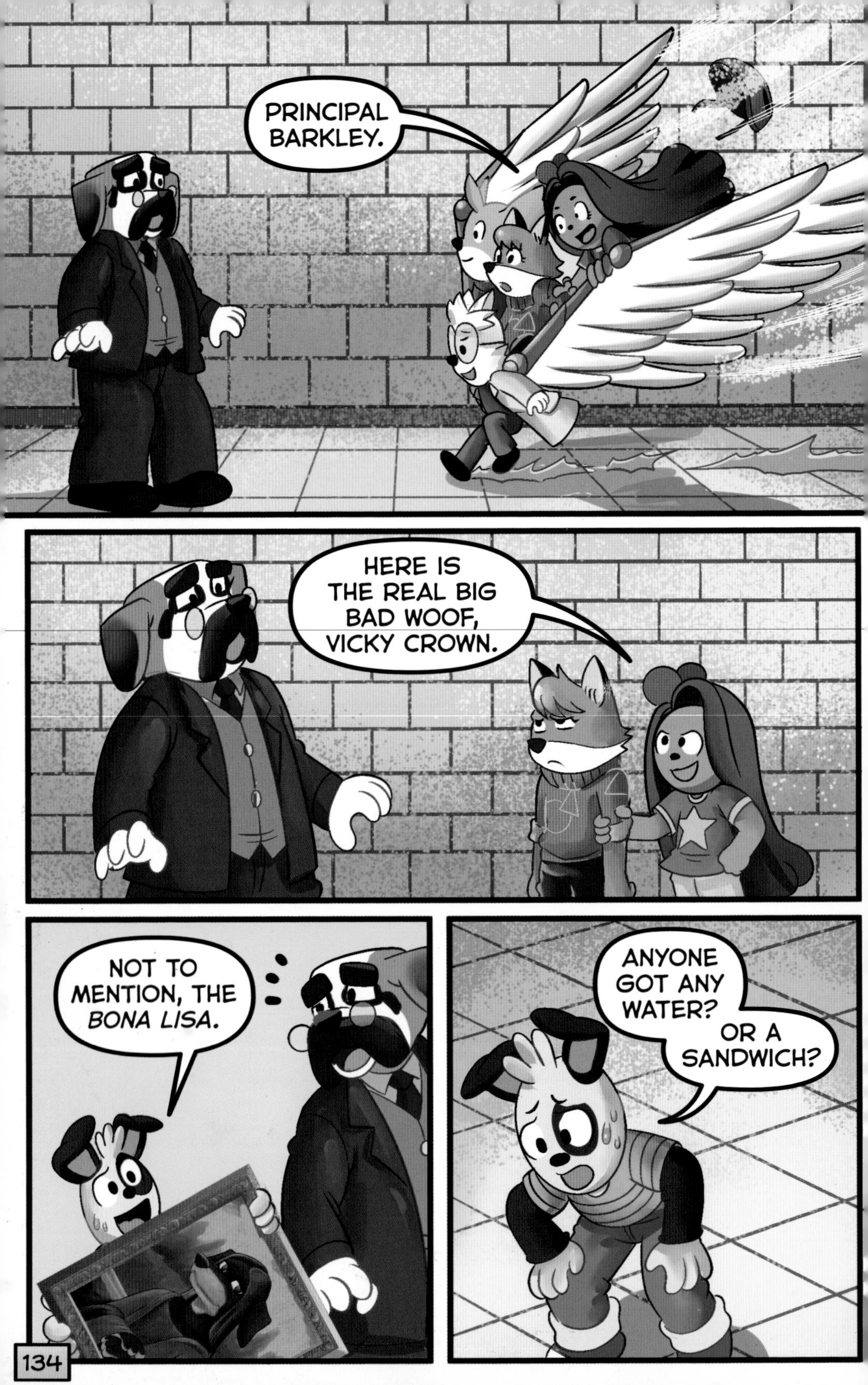
PRINCIPAL BARKLEY.
HERE IS THE REAL BIG BAD WOOF, VICKY CROWN.
NOT TO MENTION, THE *BONA LISA*.
ANYONE GOT ANY WATER?
OR A SANDWICH?

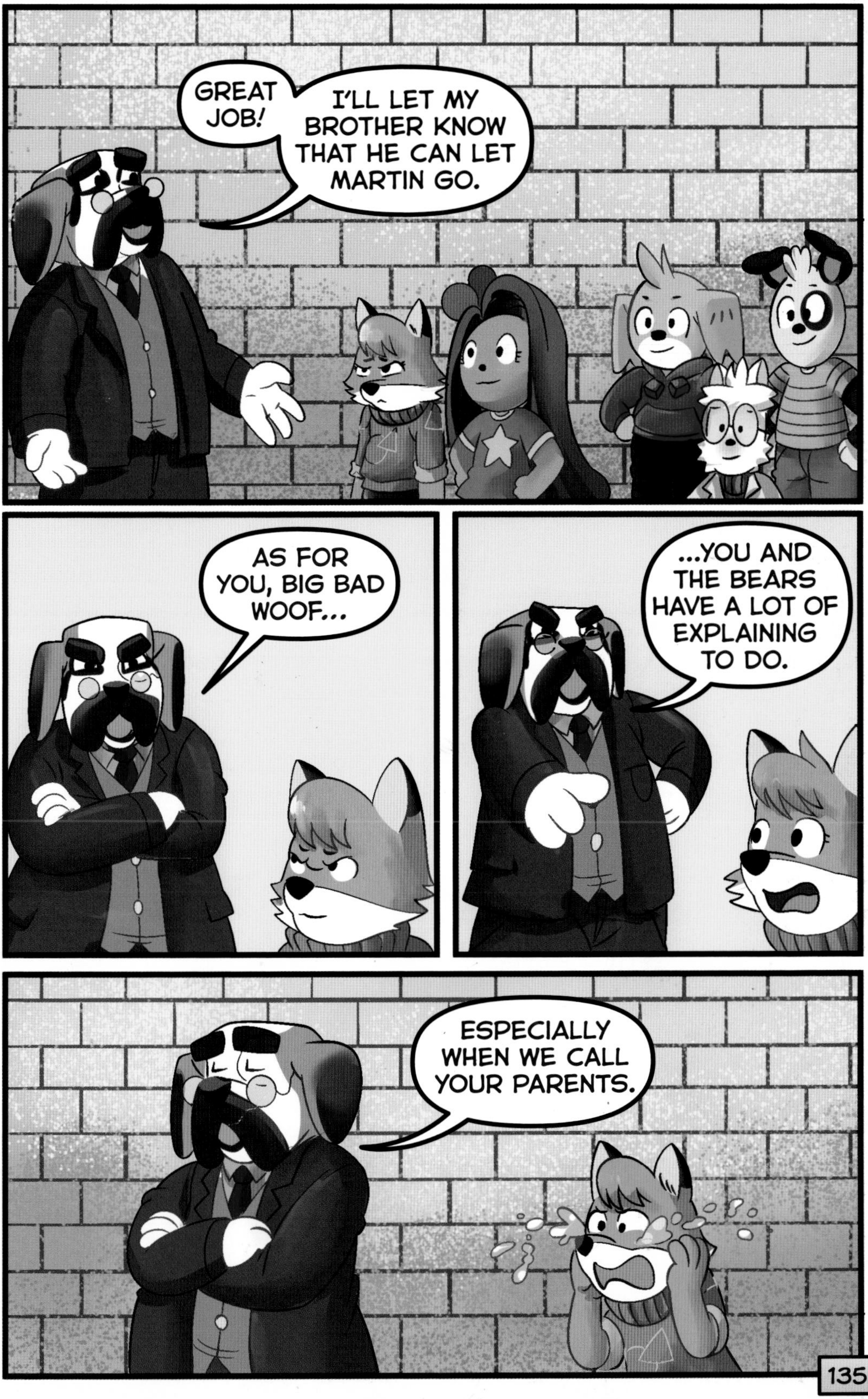
GREAT JOB!
I'LL LET MY BROTHER KNOW THAT HE CAN LET MARTIN GO.
AS FOR YOU, BIG BAD WOOF...
...YOU AND THE BEARS HAVE A LOT OF EXPLAINING TO DO.
ESPECIALLY WHEN WE CALL YOUR PARENTS.

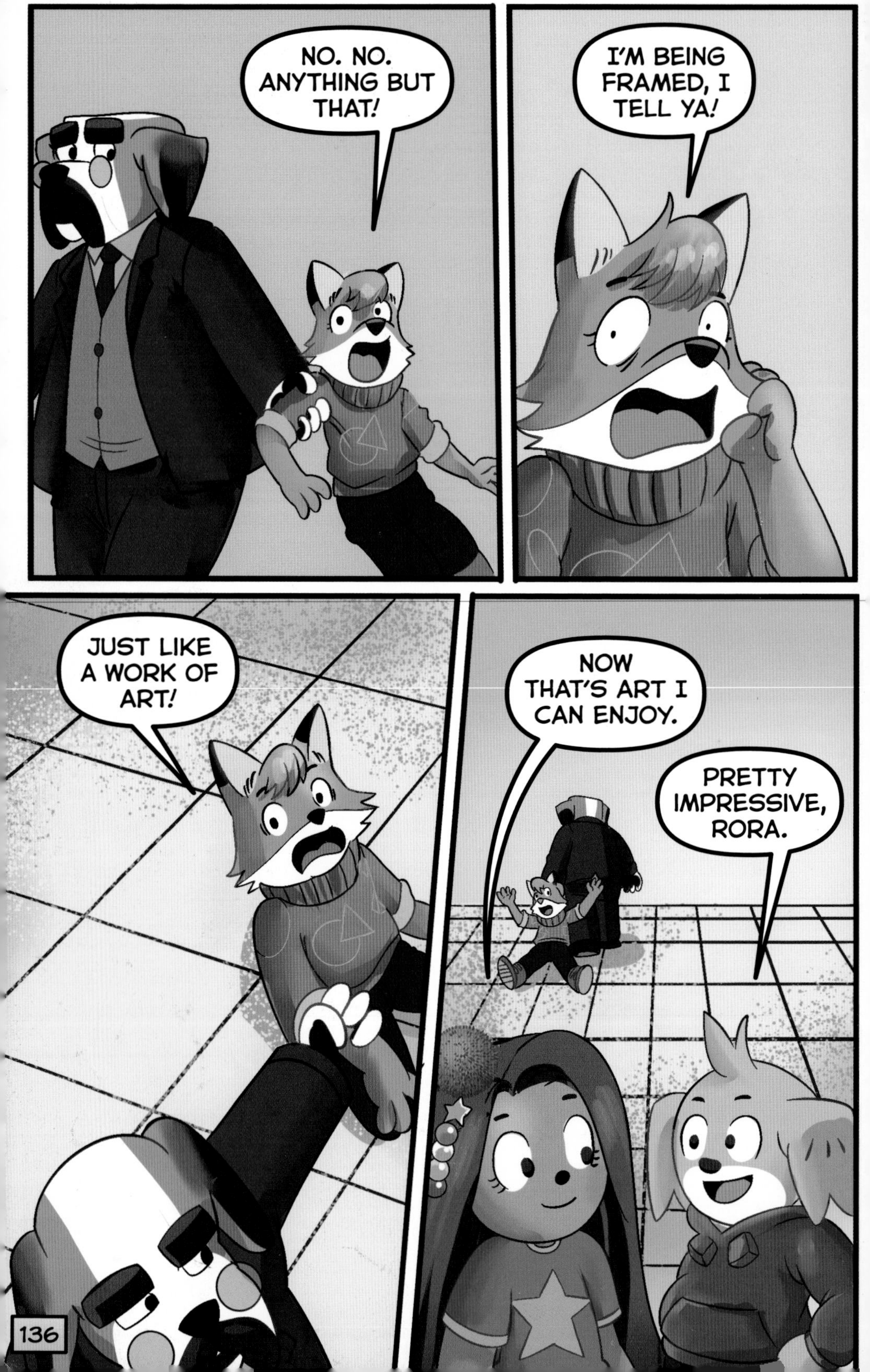
NO. NO. ANYTHING BUT THAT!
I'M BEING FRAMED, I TELL YA!
JUST LIKE A WORK OF ART!
NOW THAT'S ART I CAN ENJOY.
PRETTY IMPRESSIVE, RORA.

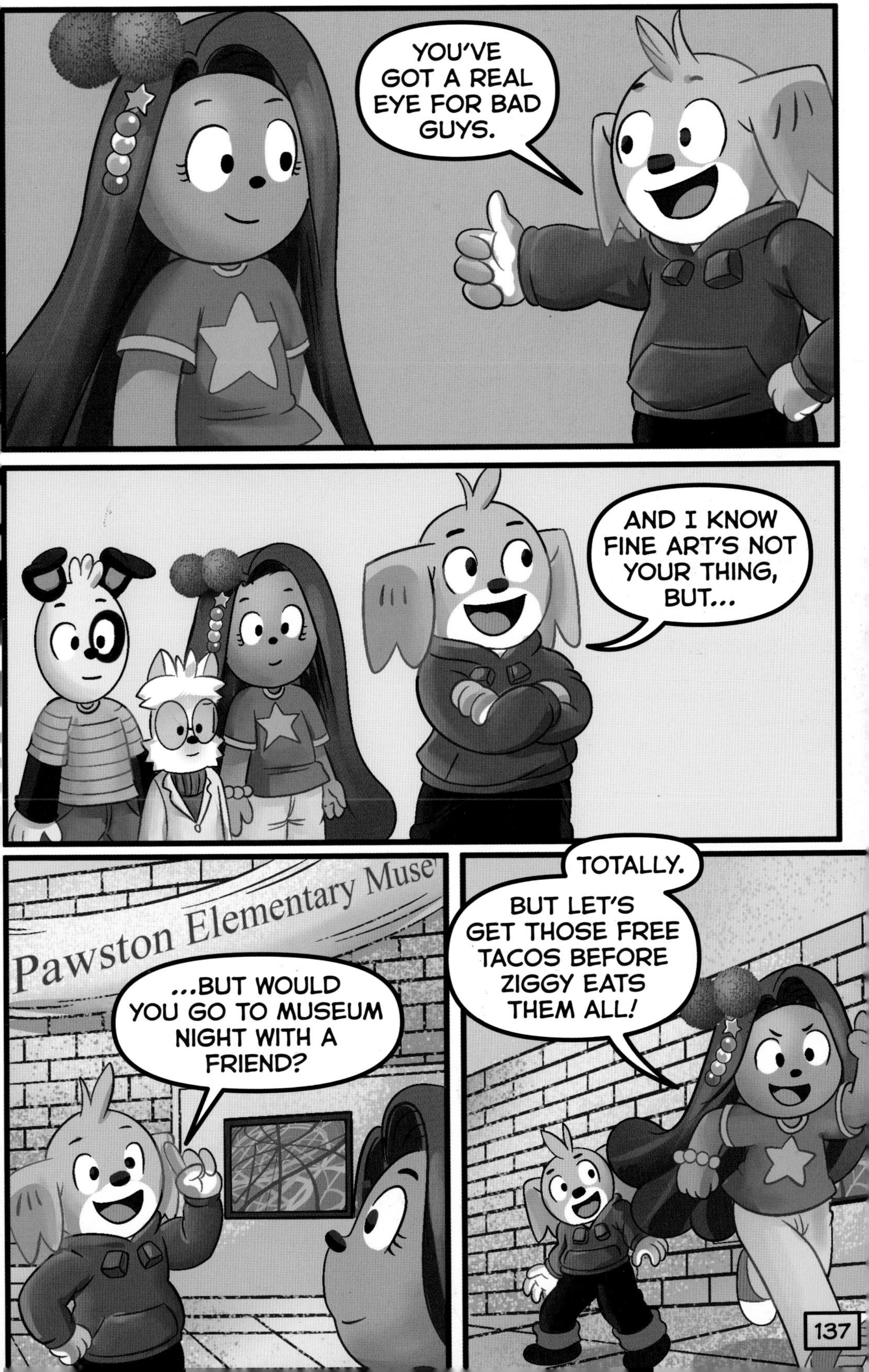
YOU'VE GOT A REAL EYE FOR BAD GUYS.
AND I KNOW FINE ART'S NOT YOUR THING, BUT...
Pawston Elementary Muse
...BUT WOULD YOU GO TO MUSEUM NIGHT WITH A FRIEND?
TOTALLY.
BUT LET'S GET THOSE FREE TACOS BEFORE ZIGGY EATS THEM ALL!

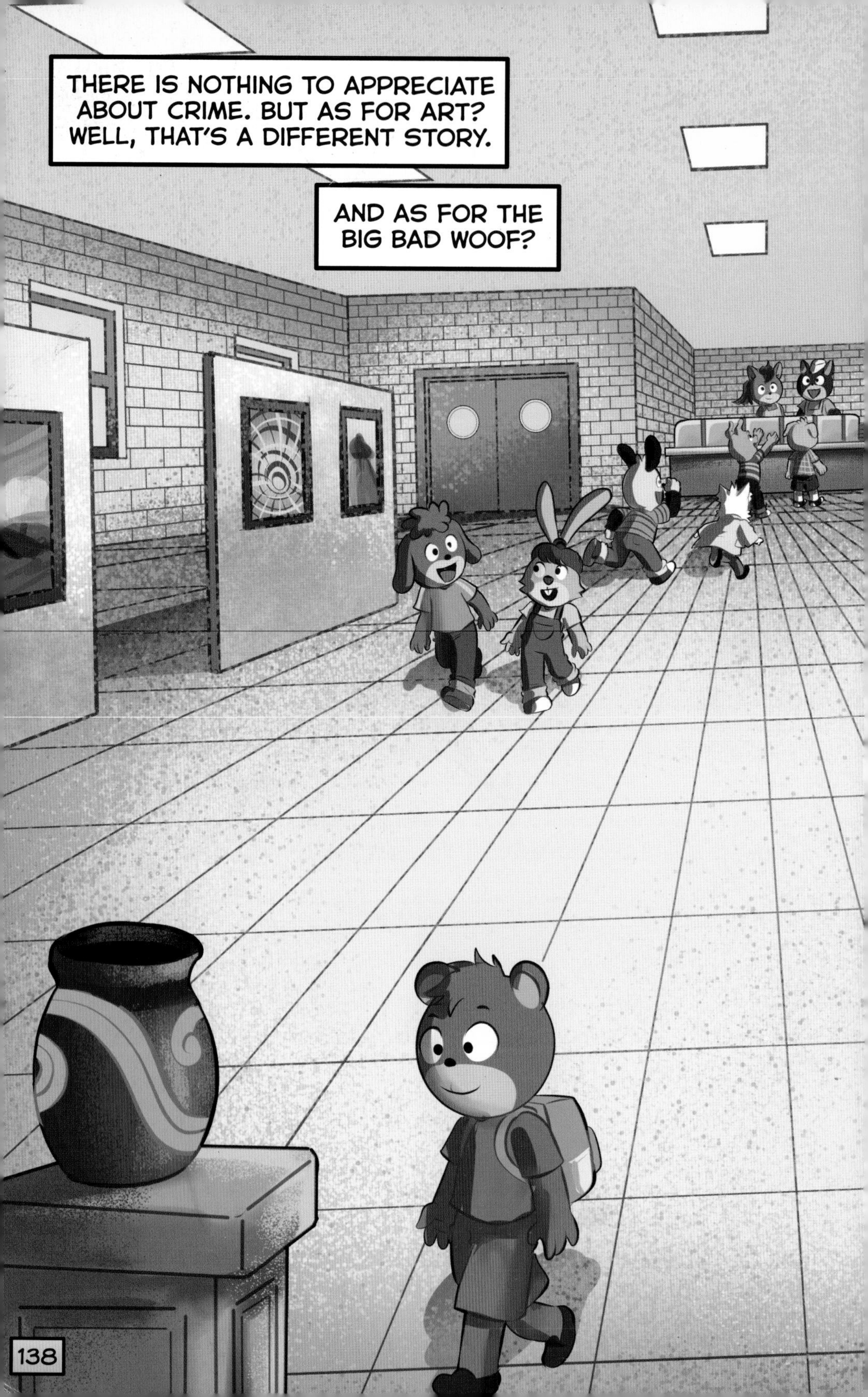
THERE IS NOTHING TO APPRECIATE ABOUT CRIME. BUT AS FOR ART? WELL, THAT'S A DIFFERENT STORY.
AND AS FOR THE BIG BAD WOOF?

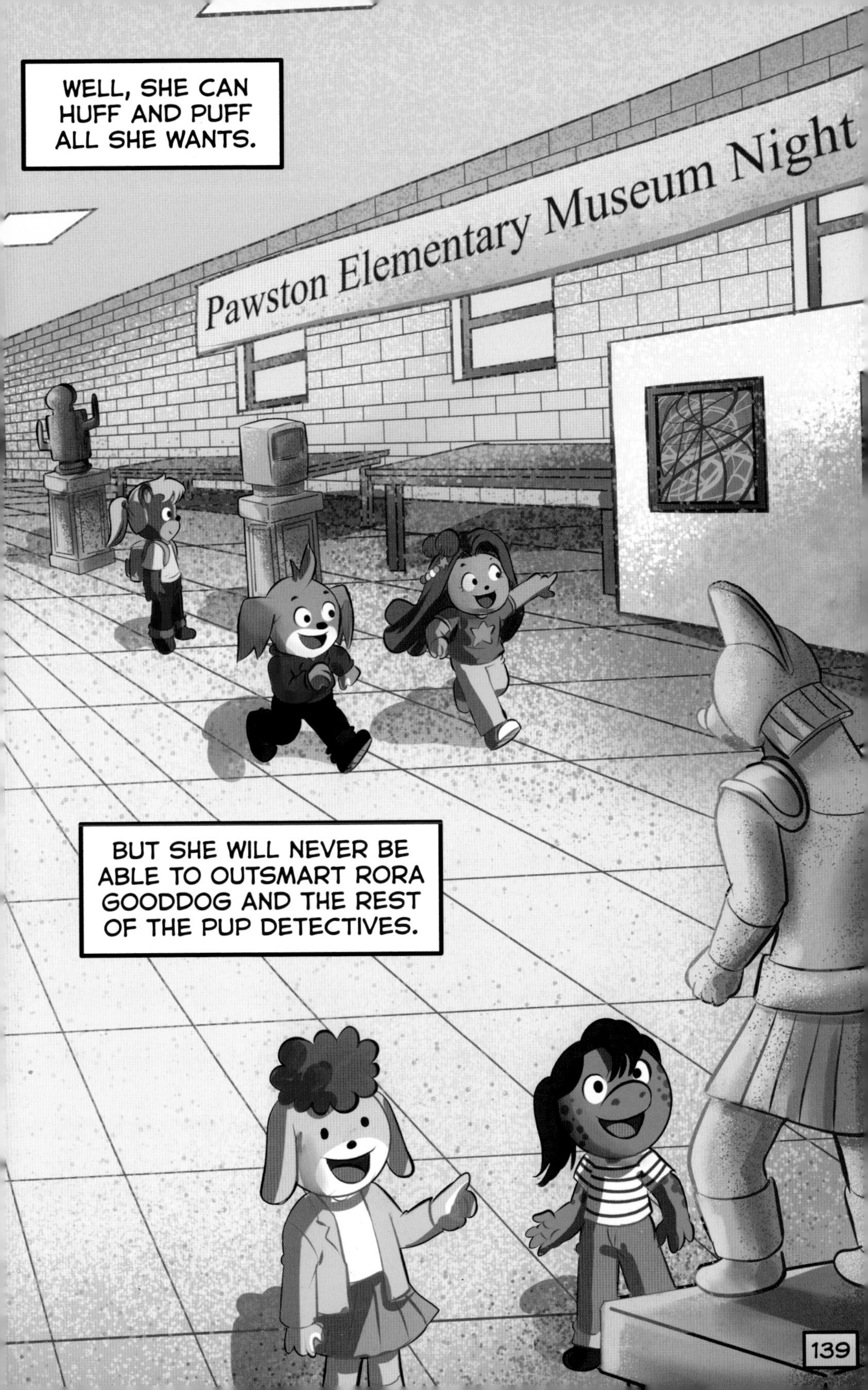
WELL, SHE CAN HUFF AND PUFF ALL SHE WANTS.
Pawston Elementary Museum Night
BUT SHE WILL NEVER BE ABLE TO OUTSMART RORA GOODDOG AND THE REST OF THE PUP DETECTIVES.

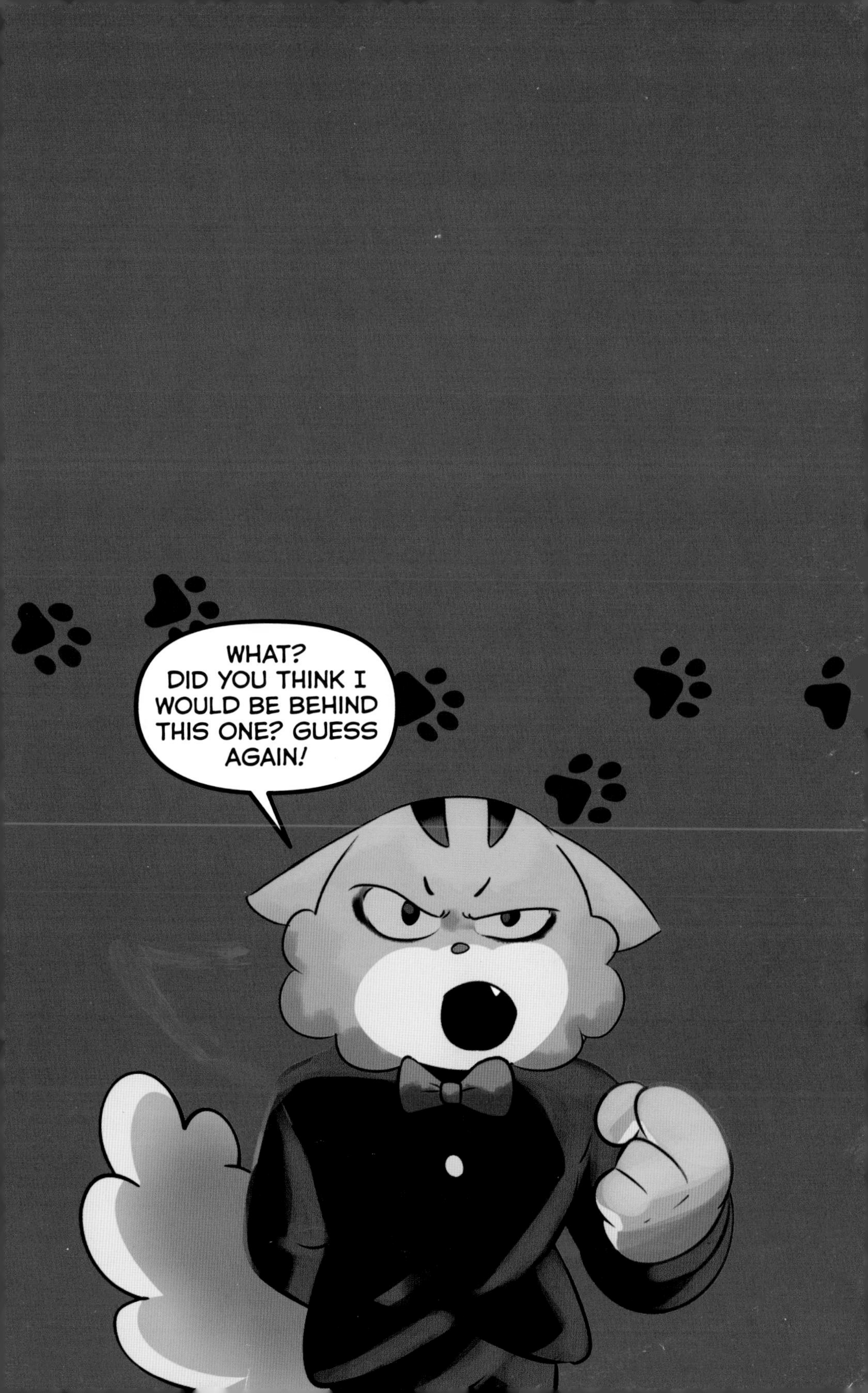
WHAT? DID YOU THINK I WOULD BE BEHIND THIS ONE? GUESS AGAIN!

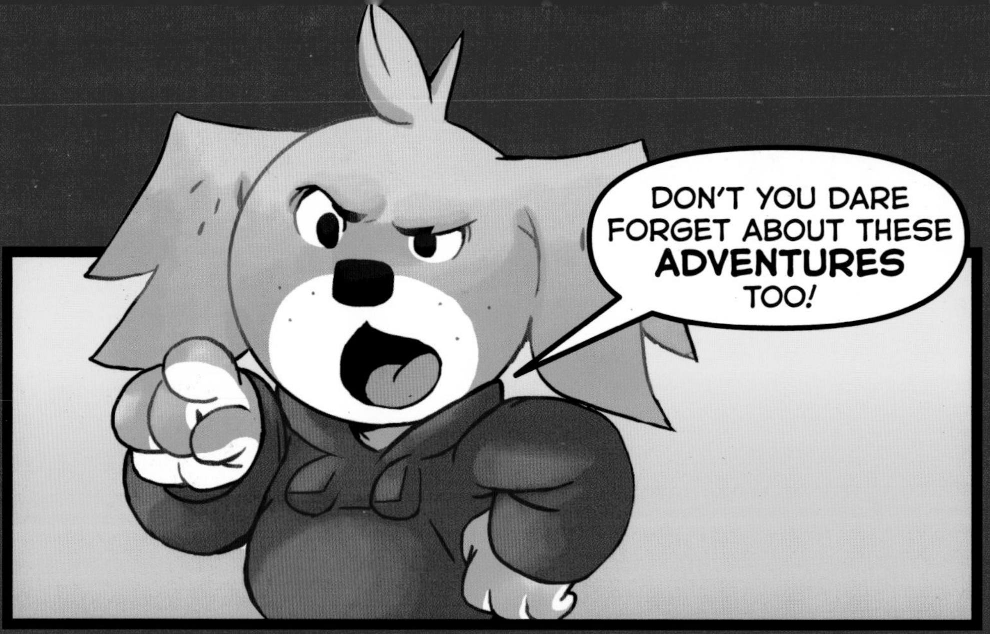
DON'T YOU DARE FORGET ABOUT THESE ADVENTURES TOO!

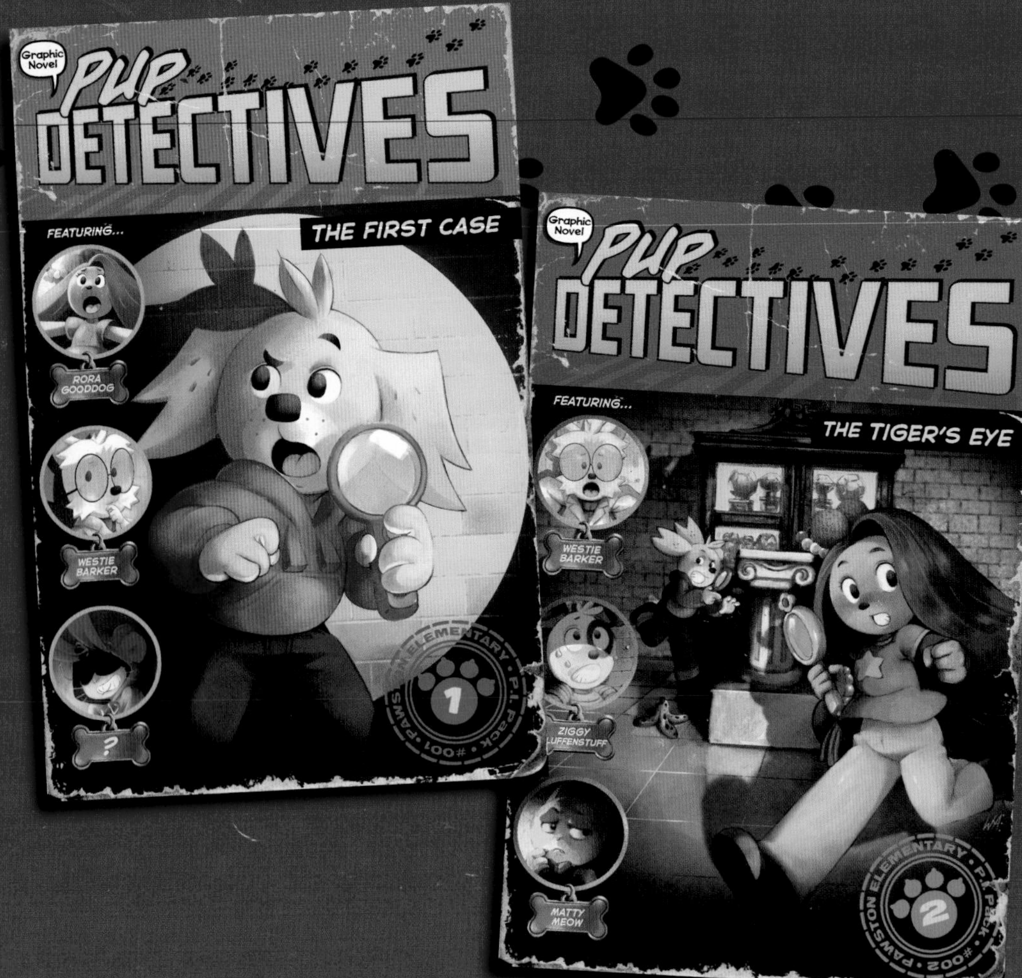
Graphic Novel
PUP DETECTIVES
FEATURING...
THE FIRST CASE
RORA GOODDOG
WESTIE BARKER
?
PAWS ELEMENTARY P.I. PACK #001
1
Graphic Novel
PUP DETECTIVES
FEATURING...
THE TIGER'S EYE
WESTIE BARKER
ZIGGY LUFFENSTUFF
MATTY MEOW
PAWSTON ELEMENTARY P.I. PACK #002
2

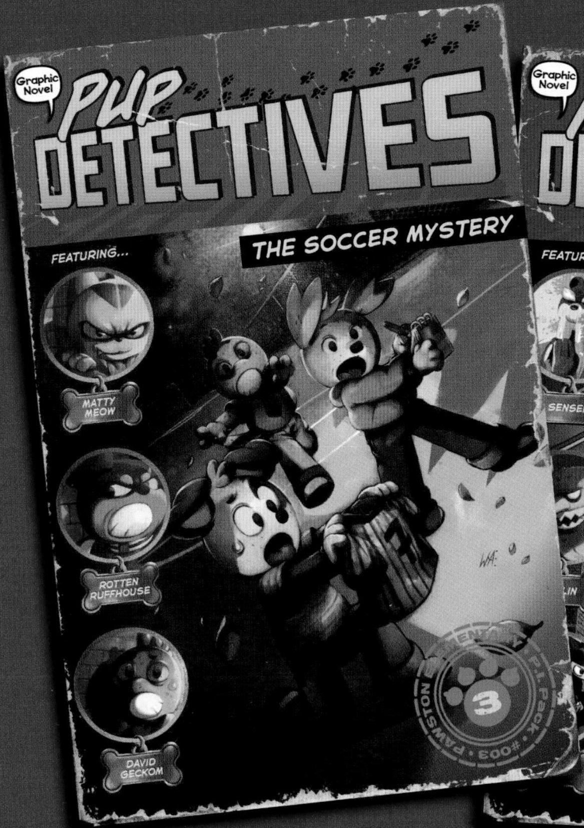
Graphic Novel
PUP DETECTIVES
FEATURING...
THE SOCCER MYSTERY
MATTY MEOW
ROTTEN RUFFHOUSE
DAVID GECKOM
PAWSTON ELEMENTARY P.I. Pack #003
3

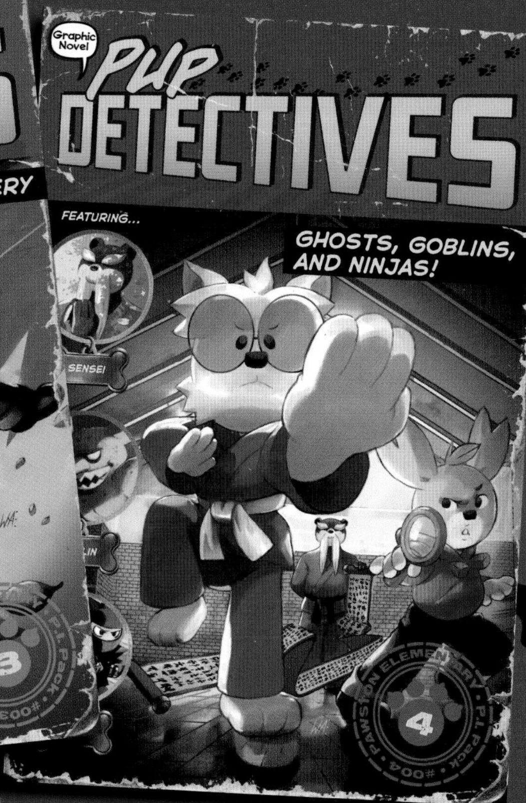
Graphic Novel
PUP DETECTIVES
FEATURING...
GHOSTS, GOBLINS, AND NINJAS!
SENSEI
PAWSTON ELEMENTARY P.I. Pack #004
4

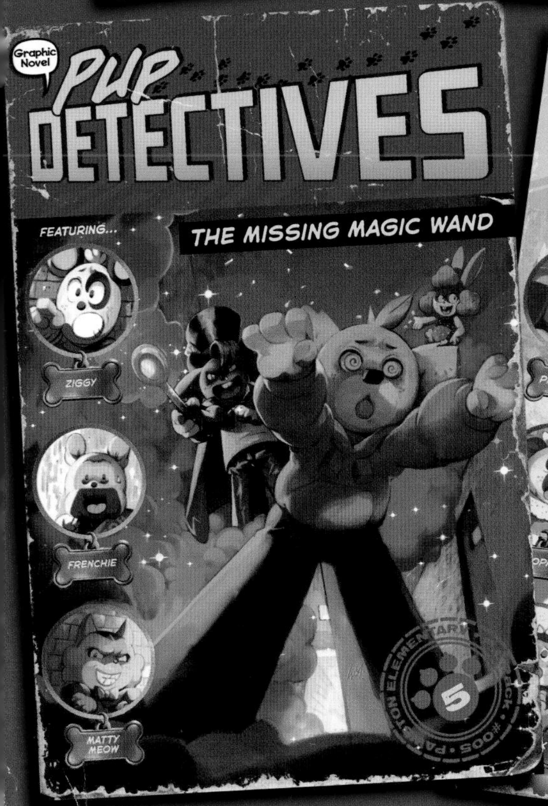
Graphic Novel
PUP DETECTIVES
FEATURING...
THE MISSING MAGIC WAND
ZIGGY
FRENCHIE
MATTY MEOW
PAWSTON ELEMENTARY P.I. Pack #005
5

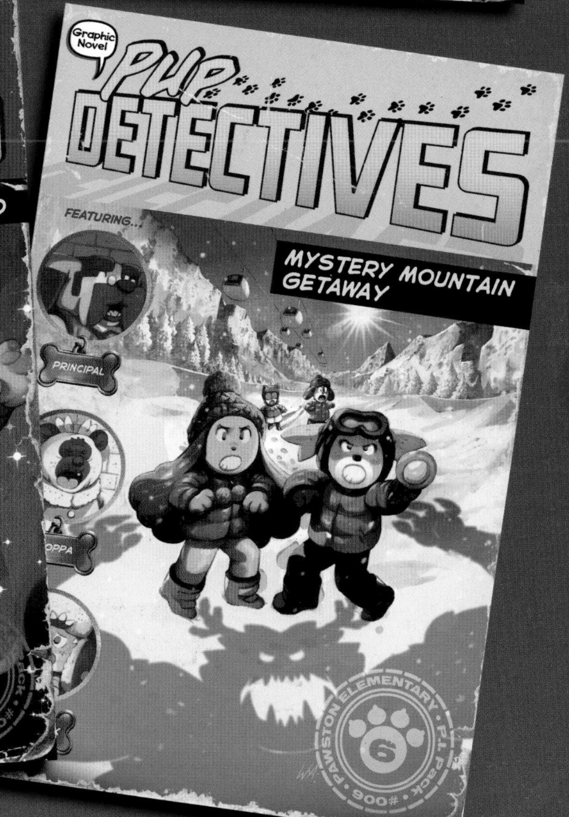
Graphic Novel
PUP DETECTIVES
FEATURING...
MYSTERY MOUNTAIN GETAWAY
PRINCIPAL
PAWSTON ELEMENTARY P.I. Pack #006
6

3 1901 10015 3594